PRAISE FOR

Bone Sw

"C. S. E. Cooney is one o
beautiful voices to come ou
with a wink in her eye and
—**Catherynne M. Valente**
  of the *Fairyland* novels

"Cooney's brilliantly execut
stew of science fiction, horror, and fantasy, marked by unforgettable
characters who plumb the depths of pathos and triumph . . .
Cooney's magical prose elicits laughter even as gruesome scenes
induce shudders, and her expert pacing breathlessly buoys the
reader to each story's conclusion. All of these stories could easily
serve as the foundation for novels while also working beautifully at
their current length. These well-crafted narratives defiantly refuse
to fade from memory long after the last word has been read."
—*Publishers Weekly*, **starred review**

"Writing without ostentation and featuring characters who may be
flippant, terse, or even tongue-tied, Cooney produces memorable
prose propelled by extraordinary ideas . . . Faced with such twisted
genius, I'll say no more!"
—*Locus*

"These stories are a pure joy. C. S. E. Cooney's imagination is
wild and varied, her stories bawdy, horrific, comic, and moving—
frequently all at the same time. Her characters are wickedly
appealing, and her language—O! her language. Lush, playful,
poetic, but never obscure or stilted, it makes her magic more
magic, her comedy more comic, and her tragic moments almost
unbearable."
—**Delia Sherman**, **author of** *Young Woman in a Garden: Stories*

"Like one of her characters, C. S. E. Cooney is a master piper, playing
songs within songs. Her stories are wild, theatrical, full of music
and murder and magic."
—**James Enge**, **author of** *Blood of Ambrose*

Bone Swans

Books by C. S. E. Cooney

Jack o' the Hills

How to Flirt in Faerieland and Other Wild Rhymes

The Witch in the Almond Tree

The Dark Breakers Trilogy
The Breaker Queen
The Two Paupers
Desdemona in the Deep (forthcoming)

More from Mythic Delirium Books

Clockwork Phoenix:
Tales of Beauty and Strangeness

Clockwork Phoenix 2:
More Tales of Beauty and Strangeness

Clockwork Phoenix 3:
New Tales of Beauty and Strangeness

Clockwork Phoenix 4

Mythic Delirium:
An International Anthology of Prose and Verse

Bone Swans

stories by
C. S. E. Cooney

introduction by
Gene Wolfe

Mythic Delirium
BOOKS

mythicdelirium.com

Bone Swans: Stories

Cover art by Kay Nielsen, illustration in *East of the Sun, West of the Moon: Old Tales from the North*, 1914.

Cover design © 2015 by Mike Allen

ISBN-10: 0-9889124-4-9

ISBN-13: 978-0-9889124-4-1

Published by Mythic Delirium Books
mythicdelirium.com

Our gratitude goes out to the following who because of their generosity are from now on designated as supporters of Mythic Delirium Books: Saira Ali, Cora Anderson, Anonymous, Patricia M. Cryan, Steve Dempsey, Oz Drummond, Patrick Dugan, Matthew Farrer, C. R. Fowler, Mary J. Lewis, Paul T. Muse, Jr., Shyam Nunley, Finny Pendragon, Kenneth Schneyer, and Delia Sherman.

This collection is dedicated to
John O'Neill and Tina Jens.

Contents

Introducing
C. S. E. Cooney

Gene Wolfe

Picture me sitting in a small used-book shop with a banana cream pie on my lap. The young man reading at the lectern has given us a short-short story that is certainly publishable and has now launched upon one that that is not. We have had the poetry that suggests a poor article in *Reader's Digest* cut up into uneven lengths, and the heart-wrenching personal memoir of the sister of a soldier killed overseas. And others. You know.

The readers are kept in order by Claire Cooney, a startling young blonde with a smile capable of lighting up a good-sized theater. At last she reads herself, a poem that rhymes and scans and grabs you from the opening line. The hero is a disfigured corpse floating down a city sewer, and it is funny when it is not horrible. (And sometimes when it is.) She chants it, and her voice is clear and musical. I couldn't be prouder of her if I were her father.

I met Claire when my friend Rory Cooney brought her around to see me. His daughter wrote, he explained, and he felt she had talent. Would I be willing to coach her a bit? I read some short pieces she had written and promised to do it. She was eighteen at the time.

Most writers begin by imitating some favorite writer, H. P. Lovecraft imitating Lord Dunsany, for example. There's nothing wrong with that, provided the beginner grows out of it and finds his or her own voice. If Claire began by imitating somebody, she had already grown a long way out of it at eighteen. She wrote pure Claire Cooney. (Try to define that when you've finished the stories in this book.)

She is in love with literature AND the theater—yes, both at the same time. She had a double major in college and has had a double major in life. She has played Rosalind in a professional production of *As You Like It*, and I wish I could have seen it. If there was ever a girl created by God to swagger around on stage with a broadsword pushed through the knot in her sword belt, Claire is that girl. The one time I have seen her in a play, she was a South African whore; she was good in that role, too, and gave me the impression that she would be good in any role that did not require her to die coughing up blood.

What did she learn from me? Nothing, really. There is a select type of student, rare but invaluable, who will certainly succeed if not run down by a truck. You help yourself instead of helping them, putting an arm around their shoulders and making them promise to say you taught them all they know. I have had two of those, and Claire is one. I tried. I explained to her that there is no money in poetry anymore.

She continues to write poetry anytime she feels like it. It's all good, and some of it is great.

I explained that though writers learned to write by writing short stories, the money was in novels these days.

Claire insists she has a secret novel she is grinding away at; meanwhile she shows tourists through an aquarium, answers casting calls, and pens poems. Not to mention short stories starring cunning were-rats. And on rare occasions, she writes e-mails to me.

I explained the business of—well, never mind. You get the picture.

Also—this one actually took—I introduced her to science fiction conventions. To the best of my memory, her first was Readercon. (Always start at the top.) Claire, Rosemary, and I lived in greater Chicago in those dim, far-off days. Readercon, as you may know, is always held in or around Boston.

We drove.

It used to be that Rosemary would spell me at the wheel. By the time we drove to Boston, she was unable to walk more than a step or two and completely incapable of driving. So Claire spelled me, letting me for the first time ever ride in my own backseat. She would, I'm sure, have worn a chauffeur's cap, had I had wit enough to obtain one.

Doubtless you know that once upon a time, the very best cars— my father remembered them—had run by steam. The chauffeur did not drive them; he stoked the fire under the boiler. Now I was the chauffeur in the original sense, stoking our fire by encouraging Claire, praising her skill at the wheel, and so forth. Giving her confidence, too, by keeping the road atlas open on my lap and explaining that soon we would leave this federal highway and enter the other interstate. Claire held our speed between fifty and fifty-five, so that our progress resembled that of a barge on a canal. I was tempted to climb out a window and ride on the roof, ducking for low bridges like the passengers in the song, but though that might have been fun, it would almost certainly have resulted in the loss of the road atlas. I remained inside.

Claire did lots of other things, too. When I was locked in an elevator on the first floor of a large motel, and Rosemary marooned in her wheelchair on the second, Claire served as go-between, running up and down the stairs to check the condition of the elevator and report to Rosemary.

When we got to Readercon, Claire discovered a coven of witches and joined at once. ("Keep Halloween in Your Heart All Year long!") She fit right in, and before the con was over, the witches were boasting about their new member. Nobody had smartphones then, but Claire and I had brought our cell phones. Claire, I should explain, pushed Rosemary's wheelchair from time to time and was able to accompany and assist her in the ladies' room. On one occasion, Claire and I held a long conference by cell phone before I discovered that Claire was around the corner, about five short steps away.

Perhaps you feel that I have told you too much about the author in this introduction and not enough about the stories in this book. All right, let's take up a favorite of mine, "The Big Bah-Ha." Perhaps you know that you and I live in the Milky Way galaxy, an immense whorl of stars. You may also know that for years astronomers have wondered whether our own star's orbiting planets were unique. Did other stars have planets, too? A few said yes and many more no. But no one actually knew; it was all guesswork.

Science fiction (and religion) sided with the minority, the scientific world in general with the majority. Without evidence, it was foolish to assume that anything existed. To assume that things as large as planets did was the height of folly.

Now we have a little hard data, and it would appear so far that planets are the rule, not the exception.

Let's think about that. The number of stars in our galaxy is enormous, almost infinite. And yet our galaxy is only one of many. We continue to find new ones, and it may well be that their number is infinite or nearly.

Enter Claire. If there are so many galaxies, and so many stars in each of those galaxies, almost every imaginable race must also exist. What about a race similar to our clowns? A race wearing oversized shoes and rubber noses. Why, there are stranger customs right here on Earth! We know, then, what their society would be like, but what about their religion? And what if their religion were true?

God is infinite.

Life on the Sun

For Mir and Kiri

That was the day the sky went dark.

No eclipse was scheduled on the priests' calendars to spur the fervent into declaiming the last days. No dust storm had blown up from the Bellisaar Wasteland, spinning the air into needle and amber and suffering all unwary walkers the death of a thousand cuts. No warning.

Just the dark.

Outside the gates of Rok Moris, a white sun blazed. Rattlesnake basked. Sandwolf slunk to fit inside the meager shadow of a sarro cactus.

Inside the gates, blackness. Frost glistened on brick, boardwalk, dirt path, temple column. Quiet canals formed ice at the banks. Olive branches silvered and verdy bushes withered, and each bloodpink bougainvillea shed its papery petals to show the thorns.

In the hottest driest month of the year, to the hottest, driest city in the Empire of the Open Palm, a long and endless winter night had come.

Fa Izif ban Azur and his Army of Childless Men marched upon Rok Moris.

"Kantu!"

Kantu groaned and rolled. A moment for the past to catch her. Ah. There it was. Like Lady White Skull, who calls you to the canals with her song and begs a ride upon your back. And halfway across the water, her bony claws dig in, and she drowns you.

"Kantu!" The voice was nearer now, almost familiar.

Her nose was clogged. Something congealed and unpleasant. She started to touch the mess of her face, but it felt strangely spongy, with a deep throb that reached the back of her brain.

"Is it winter?" she muttered.

It was dark and cold, a darkness and a coldness that ate at you. Not a desert darkness. Not the clean, crisp, starry dark of Bellisaar's nightfall. Wizardry.

"The Fa," Kantu remembered aloud. Gooseflesh sprang to her arms. She made herself say it again. "The Fa came. And we fought."

The Bird People *had* fought—but not against the Fa. Their battle was, and had been for years, against their occupiers, the Empire of the Open Palm.

The Fa's arrival in Rok Morris had been an inadvertent blessing; his dark spell upon the city, their call to arms. No more desperate acts of midnight sabotage. No more skirmishes or staged protests. The time had come for the Bird People to rise, rise up from the middens, up from the Pimples, up from the Catacombs beneath Paupers' Grave. They rose up, armed with cudgels, torches, oil bombs. Three to a carpet they flew, bombarding the Grand Palace of Viceroy Eriphet with fire and rage, taking out the houses and offices and barracks of the Audiencia lordlings. They flew, and they fought the rulers of the city, their invaders and oppressors. At last, at long last. After so many weary guerilla years!

And the Viceroy's guards engaged them in the streets, bringing down the carpets with their nets, and the Gate Police came with their spears . . .

"Kantu!"

Kantu tried to answer, got as far as a croak. Her lips felt fat, crusted together, a pulsing purple ache.

A quick breeze rushed overhead, along with her name in an urgent whisper. Kantu groaned louder, trying to be helpful.

Rokka Luck! A matter of seconds, and the sound of a velveted landing. Footfalls. Then a soft blue light, and Mikiel was there, with a ghost of a grin on her long, bony face, helping Kantu to sit upright.

"Stupid, stupid, stupid!" hissed Mikiel. "Manuway said you jumped carpet."

"Guy with a net," Kantu murmured. "Taken us all down. You'd've done the same."

"I would have dropped a brick on his head," Mikiel answered, "not myself."

"Heat of the moment." Kantu paused. "What's that light?"

Mikiel touched the glowing blue button on her shoulder. It flickered off. At another tap, it blazed up again.

"Kipped it off a Childless Man. Once the Fa marched in, his soldiers were everywhere. I just sort of swooped down and plucked it off one of them. Figured the Fa had plenty more in his chest of wonders. Why not ward the dark with borrowed wizardry?"

Because, Kantu thought, *the wizard is a god, and all gods are vicious.*

She rubbed her bruised eyelids and tongued wincingly at the crusted coppery bits in her mouth. The weirdness of the witch light transformed Mikiel from best friend back to the alien thing she once had been. Her red hair seemed black as Kantu's own, but her skin, paler than quartz, turned almost transparent, and Kantu thought she could see to the bone.

Mikiel did not hail from Rok Moris—nor any city, village, town, or tent of the Bellisaar Desert. She had been born in the north, farther north than the fountains and flowers and silver opulence of Koss Var, the King's Capital. North, even, of Leevland where the fjords ran deep as the mountains rose high. She came, she said, from the top of the world, from a land called Skakmaht, where demons made their homes in flying castles made of ice.

Mikiel's wanderings had taken her to every land imaginable. But it was in Rok Moris she decided to stay, eight years ago, when she found the Bird People and allied herself with their suffering. Kantu knew many of Mikiel's secrets, but not this first and deepest: why Mikiel had remained. Only the Rokka Mama knew that.

The Rokka Mama had adopted Mikiel into their raggle-taggle tribe, bunking her with Kantu in a subcell of the 'Combs.

"Why?" Kantu had thundered. All the sullen rancor and blistering jealousies that characterized the age of seventeen roared in her words. "She's a stranger. She's too tall. She talks funny."

"Because, Kantu, you are of an age and very alike. Yes—very! Both of you are headstrong and preposterous. Both of you," she sighed, "still believe in justice."

"Well. She looks dead. Drowned. She's so white."

"Then she'll complement you well, my dark one. Be kind. She's come a long way."

So Kantu, grudgingly, had taught Mikiel to walk the mazepath of the Catacombs, how to weave a carpet with thread that could fly, and finally, how to take to the skies. In turn, Mikiel showed Kantu how to dance with a knife strapped to her thigh, how to use a slingshot and flirt in twelve languages. For eight years they lived and fought alongside each other. As unlike her in looks as Rok Moris from Koss Var, Kantu came to consider Mikiel her sister. Their hearts beat a twin tattoo on the Thundergod's drum.

And now, in all the chaos of the uprising, Mikiel had not forgotten her.

She found me, Kantu realized. *Even in this darkness, she found me.*

As if Mikiel caught the thought, she grinned again, and her eyes sparkled. They were a limpid, pearly blue in color, almost white. Despite the witch light, she became herself again.

"You're dreaming, Kantu," she said. "Too many blows to the head."

"Just the one. Didn't improve my nose, I'm afraid."

"That meat hook? The gods could not improve it."

"Got any salt, Mik? Want to grind it in a little?"

Mikiel made to throw her arm around Kantu's shoulders. Her movement cast a strange shadow onto the crumbling alley wall. The shadow was taller and boasted more angles than even lissome Mikiel could account for. Leaning back, Kantu glanced from the shadow to the thing casting it, and whistled through her teeth.

"Huh."

"You like? Crizion helped. She wanted to come, but it never would've carried three. So she went to scavenge food instead. Supplies are low."

"Mikiel Maris Athery, you are such a goddaft show-off!"

Her friend shrugged, the mass on her shoulders bobbling. "It's just— we're all so scattered down in the 'Combs. The Rokka Mama had no carpets to spare for finding your sorry carcass. I had to do *something*."

Her *something* had been to fashion a collapsible glider from the magic tatters and raveled rags of carpets too threadbare and patchy to carry riders. The contraption jutted up and out from Mikiel's shoulders like the Great Raptor Rok mantling her prey.

"It flies," she assured Kantu. "Sort of. You just have to talk gently to it. Lots of encouragement, that's the way."

Kantu wiped her nose with the back of her hand. Immediately regretted it. "It carries *you*, sure. Mik, a praying mantis weighs more than you. Question is, will it carry two?"

"Come on, Kantu." Mikiel neatly avoided answering by hauling Kantu to her feet. Every time she moved it was a kind of dance, even weighed down as she was. "We can't stay in the streets. Too damned dangerous."

"Wait, wait, wait a second." Kantu cupped one hand to the back of her skull, the other to her forehead, trying to keep the world in one place. "Just tell me one thing, you demonic cursespawn of the North. Did we win? Is the city ours? Where is Viceroy Eriphet?"

"Eriphet?" Mikiel laughed. "Fled or dead. Who cares? Gone. Gone with all his guards. And every lordly wormling of the Audiencia who had a camel worth riding. May they cross Bellisaar in safety."

"Safety!"

"Of course." Mikiel's smile was sour. "Let them belly-crawl back to Koss Var with cracked lips and swollen stomachs. Let Eriphet confess to High King Vorst Vadilar that he lost the Empire's southern stronghold to the desert scum he swore to crush. And then—please the Flying Gods of Thunder—let Eriphet and the Audiencia sip of the High King's mercy."

As familiar as fear was the mercy of the Empire of the Open Palm. The broken treaties, the marches, the massacres, the prison camps and slave labor, the promises that oozed poison through honey-sweet lips. This mercy had the Viceroy Eriphet shown the Bird People during the forty long and bloody years of his reign.

Kantu barked with laughter. "May Vorst Vadilar show him the same!" Heedless of her throbbing face, a wrist that was surely sprained, a broken toe, and countless contusions, she did a jolly little shuffle, puffing up dust from the gutter. "The Viceroy driven to the Waste! Rok Moris ours!"

"Kantu."

Those two syllables would have flattened a priestess's miter. Kantu stopped dancing. Every cut burned. Every bruise clenched. She collapsed, panting, against the alley wall.

"Why grim, Mik?" she gasped, though she knew. "Why, when the city is ours?"

"Well—" Mikiel gestured to the unnatural darkness. The wind moved with a black glitter, as though a billion tiny eyes traveled on it. Kantu could not smell the air, but she could taste it beneath the copper, all the way down her throat, in the acids of her stomach. The way the air tastes of glass when lightning strikes the sands.

"It's the Fa. The streets are overrun with Childless Men. They did not march into our city last night because Eriphet called for help. Nor do they seem interested in pursuing the Audiencia into the desert. But the Fa . . . When he came, he brought the night with him, and it stays. He has already taken up residence in the Viceroy's Palace. Um, the parts we didn't burn. Citizens are being rounded up for questioning. And . . ."

By the milky blue light on her shoulder, Mikiel's eyes seemed wide as windmills.

"And?"

"Kantu, a reward has been posted."

"For whom?"

"For the Rokka Mama."

Kantu's hands fell to her sides, too nerveless even to form fists.

"And for you."

They flew in slow staggering stoops across Rok Moris. Once they had to land behind a small branch library to let Kantu alight and vomit, and again after Kantu lost both her consciousness and her grip on the glider's handholds. She landed on top of a noxious midden out back of the Star and Crescent tavern.

Mikiel said, worried, "We could walk?"

"I'm fine. This is faster. And safer."

"If that trash heap hadn't been there . . ."

"I'm *fine*, Mik!"

They passed the High Temple to Ajdenia, brightly lit against the unnatural night. Its corridors and courtyards teemed with refugees harried from their homes by the invaders and the insurgents and the panicked city guards.

Kantu sent them a silent blessing. Let Ajdenia hold them, love them, calm them, keep them. Kantu had no quarrel with the Lizard Lady or Her people. But Ajdenia was not her god, and Kantu had her own people to look to.

They made a final graceless descent over the barren mounds of Paupers' Grave, at the southernmost edge of the city. After the mounds, the land ended in an abrupt cliff that sheered off into a dark crack of earth. This was the Fallgate, the boundary of Rok Moris, the end of the known world. The black aperture ran across the desert, too wide to cross. Like many a bloodstained altar, this cliff was a holy place. Viceroy Eriphet used to stage his executions there, at the very edge, proving once and for all that without their carpets, Bird People could not fly.

Beneath the mounds of Paupers' Grave, the secret burrows of long-bygone builders spiraled down and down into the cliff rock. The labyrinth, the mazepaths, the Catacombs. Where, in secret, the Bird People dwelled.

Kantu dropped from the glider with a wrenched groan, massaging the death grip out of her fists. Mikiel tumbled after but regained her balance in an instant, shifting her feet lightly until once again her sandals settled like petals on the dirt. Kantu shook her head in fond disgust, but Mikiel did not notice. She was busy shrugging the contraption off her shoulders and folding it back into her pack. She stroked the patchworks and ribbing, murmuring sweet thank-yous.

"Good old thing," she said. "Clever wings, clever threads, clever souls."

From beyond the glowing circle cast by Mikiel's blue button, Kantu spoke sourly.

"The rest of us get rugs. Rugs are good enough. They do the job. Only you would think of wings."

"And you call yourself Bird People."

"Know what kind of bird you are, Mik? A snowbird. Northern fluff flying south for winter."

"Caw," Mikiel deadpanned.

Kantu blew a sore but profoundly wet raspberry at her.

Laughing softly, Mikiel touched the blue button on her shoulder. The light winked off. For a moment, the two friends stood together, blind to each other and silent in the darkness. Something cold and fierce seized Kantu's hand. She gasped.

"It's just me."

"Mik, you're freezing."

"Nerves."

"Come here, my quivering ice maid. You and your thin Skaki blood. Put your arm about me. You can hold me up, and I'll warm you up. You'll find there's a distinct advantage to having feverish friends. Better than bonfires, really."

Mikiel twined her arm around Kantu's waist. Kantu leaned in heavily, close to collapse.

"Easy on the ribs, Mik."

"Lighten up, dead weight."

They were used to doing this part of their work in the dark, for only thus had the Bird People kept the Catacombs secret from their enemy all these years. They counted their paces across Paupers' Grave, the tombs and mounds and trenches that stretched along the entire southern border of Rok Moris, until they reached a certain burial mound. It was wider in circumference but lower to the ground than the others. The first and the oldest tomb. Their doorway underground.

As they reached it, Kantu's knees buckled. Only Mikiel's tightened grasp kept her from falling flat on her smashed face. Cursing, Kantu jerked to right herself.

Mikiel grunted in sympathy. "No rest for the recalcitrant."

Kantu laughed, said, "Ow," and sighed.

"Kantu?"

"Mmn."

"What is the Fa?"

Kantu's stomach lurched. Pretending a distraction she did not feel, she knelt before the mound, patting around for the trapdoor. Her hand caught on the round wooden dial, which, dried and splintered from centuries in the sun, scraped her fingers. Dust and sand fell away.

There, proud, the etched sign of the Thundergod, the Rok of Rok Moris, with her ragged wings shedding raindrops, and the diamond, bright upon her horned skull, shooting out lightning like a crown. The diamond needed no light to scintillate. It was older than the door, older than the tombs, the treasure of the Bird People. No thief could pry it loose from the dial, nor could even the sorriest beggar sell it for her gain. The diamond had some magic in it, deflecting attention and desire from the doorway. When the Bird People had fled to Paupers' Grave in their hour of need, the diamond and the door had responded.

Kantu closed her fingers around the dial, turned it, and started to haul.

"The Fa," she answered Mikiel on a heave, "rules Sanis Al. That's the desert at the bottom of Bellisaar, east of here, hugs the coast. Not much plant life there—not even succulents. Very duney. We call it the Red Crescent for the color of the sands."

"Yes, but . . ."

The door creaked open.

"I'll go down first," Kantu interrupted. "Since I seem to have a habit of falling on people tonight." Grasping the top rung of the hidden ladder, she swung herself into a hole she could not see, that she knew by touch and memory alone, and climbed down three short rungs. Then she dropped.

The drop was not a long one, but Kantu fell hard and forgot to roll. For a while she lay inert, breathing in short, painful gasps as her eyes tried to focus on the triple entrance to the mazepath.

The first door led, eventually, to a hole in the ground that went down a mile and had bones at the bottom. The second, to a tunnel that wound around to nowhere for as long as you had strength to walk it, then stopped. The third braided its way into the rest of the maze, and thence to the heart of the Catacombs.

In just a few minutes, Kantu promised herself, *this blackness will end. I will see my friends. I will see Manuway. And Crizion. And the Rokka Mama.*

Mikiel dropped through the darkness beside her, irritated.

"For once in your life, go slowly! Clodkin! If you haven't noticed, you're hurt."

She hauled Kantu to her feet, slung an arm about her, and propelled her toward the correct entrance.

"Thanks, Mik. I'm just about done, I think."

"I know. Kantu?"

"Yeah, Mik?"

"I know *who* the Fa is."

"I just told you."

"No, I mean—" Mikiel stopped and sucked air, as if breath were her prayer for patience.

Half of Kantu wanted to watch her friend's face. Half of her feared Mikiel once again igniting the blue light: its source, its possible sentience. Cowardice won. Kantu waited in the dark.

"I mean, Kantu," Mikiel said slowly, "I've *been* to Sanis Al. It was a year ago, on a scouting mission for the Rokka Mama. It's not nice— they're in a drought; their crops and animals are failing."

"Yeah," Kantu muttered. "The rivers dried up when the rain stopped."

Mikiel pressed on. "The Army of Childless Men exist to protect the Fa and his wives, to guard the Shiprock and drive marauders from their borders. They're peacekeepers. They have never been interested in expanding their territory. Sanis Al was ceded to them by the gods. The Fa himself holds godright to the land. It's in his blood. He never leaves it. So why is he here in Rok Moris? With all his soldiers around him? Why did he bring the wizard night? That's what I was really asking. Not who the Fa is. *What* he is. What is he here for? Why did he post rewards for you? My question is, Kantu . . . What is Fa Izif ban Azur to *you*?"

"No one." The lie sat like a live coal on Kantu's tongue. She wanted to spit it out, that it might light her way through the 'Combs. But she swallowed instead. "I've never met him. He's just a story the Rokka Mama used to tell me, when I asked what made the sun rise every dawn."

Within minutes of entering the heart of the 'Combs, Kantu left Mikiel to the tender mercy of the Carpet Keepers. The twins immediately started scolding Mikiel for running off with their ragbags.

"Miss Athery, you know better!" Vishni reproached her with a sorrowful mouth. "You, who've flown with us these eight years!"

"No carpet," Ranna spluttered, her color high, "even tatty old ragged ones that no longer fly, is to be treated lightly! They deserve respect. More than respect—reverence!"

But scolding turned to gasps of awe when they saw Mikiel's glider.

"All those pieces!" Ranna exclaimed. "Working together!"

"It flies?" Kantu heard Vishni ask.

"Sort of," Kantu murmured as she turned to go, smiling with raw lips. By the time she reached the threshold, Mikiel was flashing her stolen blue button around, chattering away about Crizion's design for the glider's construction and Mikiel's own daring rescue of Kantu.

Kantu limped down the corridor to the surgeon's cell, hoping to be scrubbed, rubbed, bandaged, and sent to bed without further ado. She had not gone far before she started tripping on the cots and bedrolls lining the halls, and wading through the wounded to get to Rahvin's cell. When she did, she found the surgeon gone, either on his rounds or for good, and his supplies scanty.

The Rokka Mama, however, was there, tending a long spear score down Manuway's chest. His back was to her, so he did not see Kantu at the doorway, and Kantu saw only the bones of his spine and the sharps of his shoulder blades, the blood that had dried his curly hair to spikes. The Rokka Mama, bending to swab out his wound, did not see Kantu, either. Her bramble of frosted black hair had been tied back in a braid and covered with a kerchief. Her round face, usually dominated by a radiant and implacable serenity, had gone haggard.

She looks, Kantu thought with a rush of shock, *old*.

The realization almost repelled her back into the hallway, back through the mazepaths, back up into the enchanted darkness and the blood-soaked city above.

"Surprise!" she croaked instead, too tired for tact.

Something in the Rokka Mama's rigid posture cracked. Her gaze flashed from Manuway's wound to fix on Kantu in the doorway, but the expression in her eyes did not change. Ghosts swam in the deep brown depths.

She thinks I'm dead, Kantu realized. *She thinks I'm a spirit sending, a terrible shadow thing, coming back one last time to tell her I am no more.*

The Rokka Mama's body shuddered and pitched forward. Manuway reached to steady her, turning slowly to look over his shoulder. His eyes widened at the sight of Kantu, and he whispered something swift and low to the Rokka Mama, who had hidden her face in her hands. At last, the Rokka Mama nodded. She raised her face and looked again at Kantu.

Kantu surged into the room, making the formal sign of the Thundergod with her fingers. Her words burst from her lips, as if she were a child.

"You're not hurt, *momi?*"

Of all the Bird People who called the Rokka Mama mother, only Kantu was hers by blood. Usually it made no difference.

Her voice ragged, the Rokka Mama replied, "Sore grieved, *pili.* But sound."

"Good. That's good."

"You're whole? Still of one piece?"

"More or less. Finish up with Manuway. I can wait."

Kantu propped herself up against a wall while the Rokka Mama finished dressing Manuway's wound. Manuway watched her, his eyes tracking Kantu's gradual slide to the floor, where she slumped, eyes slitted with exhaustion, knees crooked to her chest. He was not a man to smile often, but he smiled now.

"Last I saw you," he said, "you were hurtling through the air."

"Had to meet a man about a net."

Kantu never could manage long sentences whenever Manuway smiled.

"I saw what you did. Thank you."

"It was little enough. How many dead?"

Grim again and therefore easier to look at, he answered, "Hard to say. More than half of us are missing."

He recited the roll of absentees. Kantu felt each loss in her own skin, a thin slice of lightning.

"And Crizion jhan Eriphet," he finished.

"Crizion?" Kantu's mouth went dry.

If Mikiel was her right hand, Crizion was her left. The daughter of Viceroy Eriphet, a princess of the Audiencia, Crizion had grown up watching the Bird People fly, both on their carpets and off the cliff. She had come to the Rokka Mama in secret one morning, clothed like a beggar.

"I offer myself as blood ransom," she had said. "Cast me from the Fallgate and have your vengeance."

And the Rokka Mama had kissed her sad face, on the bridge of her nose, between big brown eyes as wide and wary as a wild antelope's. And she had said, "My vengeance is to love you. Can you bear it?"

"Crizion," Kantu repeated, swallowing. The floor moved beneath her like water, and before she could reconcile her own matter to this new consistency, she was on the table beside Manuway with the Rokka Mama's broad arms wrapped about her.

"Oh, Kantu. Drink. Drink! I don't know what you were thinking, jumping carpet."

"Noble self-sacrifice, Rokka Mama." Kantu swallowed the infusion, which tasted of mint and a mild stimulant. The latter summoned the specter of her usual swagger. "With Manuway captaining, unaware we were doomed for net meat, and Elia leaning so far off the fringe with his slingshot that a whisper would've flattened him, it was left to yours truly to act. You can't say I was wrong. Only look at Manuway. Alive. Whole. Our favorite weaver, bigger and beautifuller than ever."

Like most Bird People, Manuway was small, with a short torso, wide chest, and a large, shaggy head that sat like a stone gargoyle upon his burly shoulders. He was too thin for his frame, and his skin was laced with scars. Though his features were unsubtle, his black eyes rarely betrayed a gleam of the thought behind them. He had watched his wife Inilah step off the Fallgate while Eriphet smiled on. Her spirit, woven into thread by her widower, animated one of the swiftest, smartest, toughest carpets from which no careless rider could idly tumble.

It had taken some clever maneuvering before Kantu could jump untrammeled by that carpet's protests. It kept trying to buck her back to safety.

They had been good friends, Kantu and Inilah. Since Inilah's death, Kantu had striven not to love her widower too dearly.

Manuway stood now, squeezing the Rokka Mama's shoulders with his battered brown hands. She gave him a tired smile, scratching at her hairline beneath the kerchief. An unspoken question passed between them.

"If you can," she answered. "Don't overtax yourself."

"It is owed," he reminded her.

Sighing, the Rokka Mama stepped aside. Kantu was given no chance to concur or demur, for she did not realize his intent until Manuway had stooped close to cup her face in his palms.

It was as if she suddenly had no face at all, was nothing above the neck but a nest of downy fledglings, soft and warm and restless with too many heartbeats. She had seen him coax mice and lizards and wrens to these hands, had seen him conjure the dead to his thread so gently that the carpets wove themselves for love of him. Now, beneath his hands, Kantu's swollen tissues shrank, cuts closed, bruises vanished. With a click, her nose moved back into place, unhappily returning her sense of smell.

The stink of her body, the dried sweat, the dried blood, the gutter where she had lain, the trash she had fallen into, all rushed into her nostrils and left her feeling dizzy and shabby with rekindled memory.

When he was done, Manuway placed a thumb to the bridge of her nose and stroked down to the tip of it.

"All better," he said.

Kantu tried to swallow, found she could not. "Did you make my nose any smaller?"

"Some of us," he told her, "like it as it is."

"For myself," said the Rokka Mama in her rollingest voice, which could incite in the timid and downtrodden such acts of bravery that poets wept to write of them, "I think it is a very fine nose, a splendid organ, a queen amongst olfactory instruments. You could travel the length and breadth of Bellisaar and never stumble by accident over such magnificence."

"Unless you fall face-first into a cactus," Kantu parried. She grinned wryly at Manuway. "Thanks, friend. I owe you one."

"You saved my life, Kantu."

"My nose is larger than life."

He almost laughed then. She saw his broad, oddly bony shoulders move. "Very well. No debt."

Fearful to twitch or breathe lest his hands fall away from her flesh, Kantu continued to smile witlessly up at him, until a disturbance near the door caught her eye.

"Crizion!"

But Kantu had not slid off the table before the Rokka Mama seized her, dragging her back bodily and placing herself between Kantu and the door.

"Don't, Kantu!"

"What—?"

"She's not alone."

Then Crizion spoke. "To Tesserree, High Princess of Sanis Al, Thirteenth Wife and Favorite of Fa Izif ban Azur, God-King of the Red Crescent, I give you good and loving greetings."

The Rokka Mama's grip had not lightened, but Kantu stopped fighting it. Crizion's forehead bore a blue gem, a costlier twin to the button Mikiel had plucked from the Childless Man, though it glowed with the same eldritch light. It seemed to be embedded in her bone, for the flesh around it was raised and red, and spidery veins ran from the gem down her face and neck. Her chestnut hair was loose, but instead of lying silk-straight as it usually did, it rose around her head, licking the air like flame. When she spoke, blue fire filled her mouth.

"That's his voice," Kantu whispered, remembering.

Dreamily, drowsily, almost imperceptibly, Crizion's head turned, her attention shifting from the Rokka Mama to Kantu. Her familiar face, her lovely, dainty, friendly face, her tiny nose, keen Audiencia cheekbones, shy mouth, eyes gone whimsical and nearsighted from too much scroll-diving, her I-can-outstubborn-even-you-my-dearest-friend chin, her face—*Crizion's* face—was almost unrecognizable.

Crizion was not in possession of herself.

Kantu did not mean to move, but her head shook. And kept shaking, side to side. Tears spurted from her eyes, though nothing else in all that long, long night had made her cry.

It's like staring into the sun, she thought, *only to find it staring back.*

"To Kantu jhan Izif ban Azur," Crizion continued in a voice calm and deep as a cathedral bell, "Handprint of the Thundergod, Storm Bird, Rain Bringer, Savior and Sacrifice of Sanis Al, I extend to you my heartmost greetings. And this message: Return the life you stole from your people. The Fa your father begs you."

"No!" shouted the Rokka Mama. *"My daughter is not for you!"*

"Return," said Crizion, "or I will raze Rok Moris to the ground. Woman, man, child, all within these city walls shall perish, crushed by freezing darkness. Their dust shall be swept from the Fallgate, and night shall lay forever across this barren acreage, that no one living will rebuild upon it, and no green thing grow within it for all eternity."

Kantu did stand now, though she had to cling both to Manuway and the Rokka Mama to keep her feet. Manuway's grip was no less furious, no less tender than her mother's, and Kantu knew this meant far more than she had time to understand. The Rokka Mama was wild-eyed, her knuckles white. Her large, lined brow was sheened with sweat. She looked capable of any atrocity.

"Momi." Kantu touched a frizzled tendril of her hair, and the Rokka Mama shuddered again, like an earthquake of the bones. "We can't run any more, *momi*. We must go to him."

K antu had one strong memory of her father. The rest she had built patchwork, like Mikiel's wings, out of things the Rokka Mama had told her.

The memory was this. She was nearly five and the joy of the Shiprock. She was let to run loose wherever her dimpled limbs could carry her, and it was general knowledge that, like a cat, she followed the sun, to play in its rays or nap in its warmth at whim. When her father was at the Shiprock, she followed him, for the sun rose in his ankle and set in his eyebrow. *Momi* said so. Everyone said so.

Momi was father's thirteenth wife and his favorite. The Fa kept her bed-night sacred, shared with no other wife, and Tesserree was at his side most every day, his best friend and confidante. One night a week the Fa took a rest from his conjugal duties, and this night, too, he spent at Tesserree's side. Often Kantu joined them on the Fa's enormous bed, as they read to each other, or talked softly over palace matters.

The other Modest Women did not grudge Tesserree the Fa's partiality. Rather, they came to her for counsel, to mediate domestic squabbles before they escalated into feuds, or for comfort when they missed their families and homelands. Tesserree was Mother to all the Shiprock, it seemed, but never less than Kantu's own *momi*.

One evening, perhaps for the first time, Kantu found herself alone with the Fa her father. It was sunset, and they were standing on the roof of the Shiprock, overlooking all of Sanis Al. They saw the golden domes of her father's palace, the graceful arches and promenades and flowering towers of the city, the painted rooftops, the warm white stucco, the rainbow mosaics tiling every sidewalk and street. Best of all, running through the city and out into the distance, were the Mighty Rivers Anisaaht and Kannerak, Serpents in the Thundergod's Claws, which brought fertility and abundance to the Red Crescent.

"Do you like what you see, *pili?*"

Kantu smiled up at him. *Momi* was taller than the Fa, but he was as large as the sky. His face was painted gold like the sun, and his eyes were deep and black as night.

"It is yours. It belongs to you, as your godright. And you belong to it. Do you know why?"

Kantu nodded, bringing her right hand to her left breast. Beneath her thin cotton shift, a red handprint burned across her skin, where the god had touched her in *momi's* womb. The Fa had a mark very like it on his face, beneath all the gilding.

"You are my daughter," he said, "my beloved daughter. That mark sets you apart. Had you been born my son . . ." Here his voice frayed into sadness, and he looked away from her, across the scarlet sands.

"But you are better than a son," he said. "For if you were my son, you would be mortal, destined to bear the heavy mantle of mortality on your shoulders, the weight of living and loving and knowing that all good will sift from your fingers like sand. Had you been a boy, at the hour of your birth, I, the Fa, would have died, and passed like breath between your lips and lived again in you. She who had been your wife would become your mother, and you would have no father but yourself. From that hour to the birth of your heir, you would rule as Fa. Alone."

"But I am not a boy!" exclaimed Kantu. This she knew, and she was proud of it.

"No," he said, smiling a little, at last. "You are my beloved daughter. You are our hope, and you shall be our god. Do you understand?"

Again Kantu nodded, although she did not.

"In another month, on your birthday . . ."

Kantu held up five fingers, like the handprint on her chest.

"Yes, my love, when you turn five years old, we shall stand here, on the roof of the Shiprock, which is the tallest point of Sanis Al, and you shall fly."

The Shiprock jutted from the sands, like a stone ship with stone wings, as if it had been abandoned by colossal seafarers in the days when Sanis Al was a kingdom of merpeople and Bellisaar still an ocean. The volcanic breccia and igneous rock that composed the formation had been hollowed out and reinforced over the centuries by the mason-artisans of Sanis Al, and now the stone was home to the Fa's hundred wives, their servants, and the Army of Childless Men who guarded them. Kantu loved the Shiprock, loved her desert, loved her father, and she took his slender brown hand and kissed it.

For one warm and splendid moment, his hand rested on her head. Then he squatted down, which he had never done before, to be eye to eye with her.

"Kantu," he said, "what I am about to say is most important. On the day of your birthday, you must come to this great height willing to fly. You must say to yourself, and to me, and to all the people who will be waiting below: *This is my choice. This is my will. My life for yours. My blood for rain.* Repeat that."

Kantu did. She said it until he knew she had memorized it.

"And so," sighed the Fa, "your sacrifice saves us all."

Not long after that, *momi* came up and joined them. She kissed the Fa and smiled at him, kissed and smiled at Kantu, chatted lightly about the lustrous wheel of sunset, about the first shimmering constellations and the stories told of them, about nothing much at all.

But Kantu saw, hidden in the folds of her robes, how *momi's* fists were clenched like stones.

Every Bird Person who could still walk ascended with Kantu and the Rokka Mama to the surface of Rok Moris. Crizion went before them, the blue nimbus that crowned her lighting the way.

With the effortlessness of a shadow, Mikiel slipped in next to Kantu, saying in her deceptively mild way, "So the Fa's some kind of demonic ventriloquist, is he? Tough luck on Crizion."

But Kantu, whose fear and weariness had rubbed her nerves to screaming sensitivity, caught the shark's glint in Mikiel's eye as she gazed at Crizion's unprotected back. It reflected the razored steel in her hand.

"No, Mikiel," Kantu said quietly. "It won't hurt him, but it will kill her."

"She might thank me."

Mikiel's pitiless whisper did not carry, but Crizion turned her head. She turned it, and kept turning it, until one degree further would snap her cervical vertebrae for certain, and Crizion said nothing, but something screamed beneath the blue-eaten fires of her eyes.

The knife clattered to the ground.

The Bird People marched with Kantu and the Rokka Mama, once again driven from their sanctuary. The walking wounded bore nothing but their anguish. Others carried carpet rolls upon their backs. The carpets whispered to one another, rippling like wind things, like water things. Some Bird People carried those who could not walk but who would not be left behind. Only a few remained in the tunnels, with heartsick volunteers to tend them.

When the Rokka Mama had tried to convince everyone to stay, that the coming exchange was nothing to them, Manuway stopped her.

"We have followed you for twenty years, Rokka Mama," he said. "Do not forget—this city is ours, and you were born of it, long before you became wife to a god."

And mother of one, Kantu thought. Then—*not yet.*

Men awaited them on the mounds of Paupers' Grave. Hundreds of men, Childless Men, dressed in their vests of white bone, their red tunics that bared shoulder and knee, their sandals that laced up the legs. These were the sons of the Fa, and the sons of the Fa before him, all those who had been born without the red handprint marking him heir to the godright. These sons had been given to drink a potion at their comings-of-age which rendered them impotent, that they might never bear rogue wizard offspring in the fullness of manhood. They were at that time sent from their mothers to be trained at the barracks of the Shiprock.

They were lithe and lethal. Their faces were unlined, pure, painted silver as the Fa's was painted gold. They wore their hair unbound, beaded with glass and bone.

Kantu realized they were all blood to her. Brothers, uncles, great-uncles. Hers.

They stared back with avid interest. Some of them hated her, she could see. They blamed her for the slow death of the Red Crescent, the desiccation of Anisaaht and Kannerak, the stupefying toll of people and livestock brought down by twenty years of drought and starvation. Others watched her like the Bird People watched the Rokka Mama. As if she were all their hope. A gift from the Flying Thundergod to succor and aid them in their darkest hour.

Kantu took a deep breath, but she could not smell the Bellisaar Wasteland, the sweet, smoky green of creosquite, or the good, dry desert sands that carried the musk of night hunters upon their particles. She could smell only her father's magic and his longing, the blackness of his despair coloring the air all shades of night, calling her to his side.

"I'm here." Her voice, already rough from wear, broke.

The ranks of Childless Men parted, and the Fa her father stepped forth.

Fa Izif ban Azur was not even as tall as she remembered him. Kantu matched him height for height, and even among the Bird People she was small. His nose was like hers, a great curved hook, but with his piercing eyes and the gilded planes and hollows of his face, the prominence gave him an aspect at once regal and forbidding, like a golden eagle. He was dressed in similar garments to his sons and brothers and uncles, only without armor. A long scar ran across his throat.

And Kantu remembered what had made that scar. And she remembered that though she had thought to check Mikiel for a knife, she had forgotten the Rokka Mama.

"*Momi*—no!"

She was too late. Tesserree had broken free of Manuway's grip and was rushing on the Fa, silent but savage, her teeth bared. A deadly crescent of sharpened bronze glinted in her fist. Kantu knew the instrument, knew every image etched upon its bitter edge, and the ancient lettering laying out the strictures of sacrifice.

The Fa stood very still, watching his wife run to him.

Three Childless Men caught and held the Rokka Mama yards before she came within striking distance. Though each soldier was as sinewy as a mountain lion, not one of them handled the Rokka Mama with brutal or callous indifference. It was as if they believed they held a fanged butterfly, or a hummingbird that spat poison. Whether this was because they thought Tesserree herself dangerous, or because the Fa still loved her, Kantu could not say.

"Tess." Fa Izif ban Azur stepped close to the Rokka Mama, close enough to pull the kerchief from her hair. Dark masses fell around her face and shoulders in tired clouds, webbed in gray.

"Every night," he said, "I dream of you."

At his gentleness, the Rokka Mama collapsed. Only the grips of the Childless Men kept her more or less upright.

"I killed you," she said. "I killed you, Iz—you *cannot* be here!"

One of the soldiers handed the Fa the bronze dagger she had wielded. He stroked the edge with his thumb, his golden face absorbed.

"With this blade, you cut my throat on the eve of Kantu's fifth birthday." His voice was dark and slow, like gore welling from a wound. "And the blood ran out of me, and into the soil of Sanis Al. For a while it was enough. Even without the rain, my blood sustained the land. But without a son who bears the god's handprint, I cannot die. And as my blood returned to me, and as my wounds healed, my land grew brown and withered. Years have passed, and I have allowed them to pass, but I cannot allow it any longer. Tess. Without you, my heart is a wasteland. Without Kantu, so is Sanis Al."

"I will lay waste the world," said the Rokka Mama, "for Kantu."

"Our thoughts have always been twins," said the Fa, "running in joyous parallel. But in this, we run cross-purpose, ramming together like two boulders. It is my lifelong sorrow. But I spoke you true through my handmaiden." He gestured to Crizion, still haloed in blue. "Rok Moris falls tonight if Kantu fails to fly."

Kantu stepped between her parents, vaguely aware of Mikiel and Manuway tugging at her, of voices calling her name in protest. Her friends. These were her friends, who loved her, who had grown with her, fought beside her, laughed at her jokes, tended her scrapes, who had flown with her. Her friends, who, with Viceroy Eriphet now driven to the sands and the Fa eager to return to Sanis Al, might at last be free.

Tiredness seeped from her marrow. Kantu's sight whitened for a moment, and her body flashed on the visceral memory of falling.

She had always loved riding the carpets, ever since Manuway's older brother, now dead, taught her the way of it. The tumble, the soar, the zip, the whirl, the joy and jubilation. Especially when she was flying for flight's sake, not to escape the Gate Police or hound the Audiencia.

But not until that night, when she had thrown herself from the sky, toppling the guard with his net to save the lives of her friends, had Kantu felt completely happy. And whole. And, somehow, *right*. As if falling were her purpose. Always had been.

How awful it had been to wake up battered but alive, unfulfilled and alone.

In that moment of remembrance, Kantu understood the Fa her father. Not even Tesserree as once she had been, young and in love with her god-king husband, could fathom his secret heart and mind, but suddenly Kantu could. She bore the red handprint on her breast. And she knew beyond any last lingering doubt what she must do.

"Do I have to—" She stopped, swallowed. "Do I have to return with you? Must the ceremony take place at Sanis Al, on the Shiprock? Or can we do it here?"

"It must be from a height," said Fa Izif ban Azur, understanding her instantly. "And you must be in the desert. Here, daughter, we stand at the edge of a cliff, and this is still Bellisaar."

"All right," Kantu whispered. "All right."

Fa Izif ban Azur made a short, almost helpless gesture with his slender hands, beckoning toward the Fallgate. He wore no rings. The only gold about him was his face. Kantu slipped past him and trudged down one of the many dirt paths of Paupers' Grave, keeping her head bent until she came to the cliff's edge. She felt the Fa follow behind her, and the march of a thousand sandals on packed earth, and the bare feet of the Bird People padding along, too. When she was five feet from the edge, she stopped and asked her father, without turning around, "Will Crizion be herself again?"

"I swear it."

"And Rok Moris given back to the Bird People?"

"I swear it."

"If Vorst Vadilar's armies invade again . . ."

"You have my word," said the Fa, "that Sanis Al will fight with Rok Moris against all invaders. She has but to call."

"And the Rokka Mama?"

"Tesserree," Fa Izif ban Azur said gently, "will return to the Shiprock. For she is my wife and my chosen one. The next Fa must come of her."

How many times these last twenty years had Kantu woken to the sound of her mother's hoarse weeping? How many times had the Rokka Mama cried out her husband's name in her sleep, haunted by a love that would not die though she had done her best to murder it? For it is terrible to love a god, but more terrible to be loved by one in return—and loved best above all women.

Would the Rokka Mama, returning to Sanis Al, be whole? Or would what Kantu was about to do shatter her forever?

Turning around suddenly, Kantu cried, "I love you, *momi*," and flung her arms around her mother. The Childless Men still gripped her, but Tesserree's tears ran down Kantu's face like kisses. From there, Kantu ran to rain kisses on Mikiel's burning eyelids, and on Crizion's forehead where the blue jewel still glowered, and then she went to Manuway and pressed her lips to his, and his arms clenched around her, and his heartbeat hammered into hers. She felt, for a moment, that he would lift her and spirit her away on his carpet, saving her from death as he had not saved Inilah.

Kantu did not know where she found the strength, but something wholly inexorable filled her, and she staggered from Manuway's arms.

Then she backed up to the edge of the known world, where the Fa her father now knelt, palms upraised. His position denoted reverence and relief and grief, and Kantu understood once again with that same jagged clarity that he loved her more than his own life, and would have gladly given his life if it could possibly have made a difference.

"I want you to know," Kantu said, staring at Mikiel's fierce white eyes, her mother's streaming face, Manuway's rounded shoulders, her father's bowed head, her brothers, the Bird People. "I want you to know," she told them all, "that this is my choice. This is my will. My life for yours. My blood for rain."

Taking the bronze crescent from Fa Izif's open hands, Kantu raised it to her throat, and with one quick snicking motion, she slashed through skin, muscle, vein, and artery.

Before she could even feel the pain, she turned around and stepped off the cliff.

Night parted as she fell. Somewhere in the black depths of the canyon, a sun burst open, rose up. Belly down, Kantu fell, bleeding out. Her blood fell onto the sun and sizzled there. The dark was gone, and everything was light and song, a chorus of young girls singing.

Kantu knew them. She had almost been one of them, daughters dead at five that their land might thrive. Five times five years Kantu had outlived the Fa's long line of daughters, and now at her death was a woman grown. She had known fear and friendship and love. She had seen beyond the boundaries of Sanis Al.

At five she would have been happy to give her life for the rain. But she would not have understood all that she gave.

Kantu fell, bleeding out, and she heard the singing.

She fell into light, but even in that blind radiance, she knew her friends were with her. Three to a carpet, speeding past her freefall, keeping pace, the Bird People attended her death all the way down.

Manuway was there, and Elia. Ranna and Vishni. Mikiel, winged, and Crizion riding with her, a new scar on her forehead and her face her own again. Kantu felt them with her as she fell, but she could not see them. Everything was heat and light. She knew she should be cold by now, but her body was turning to molten gold.

And then she went to a place where even the Bird People could not follow.

Kantu fell through the center of the world, thence to the top of the skies. She crashed with a thud and opened her eyes.

There was a land here, at the end of everything.

Fiery golden roses bloomed along golden roads, and the hot wind was heavy with their sweetness. Rivers of red lava ran beside the roads, and the rivers and the roads all led to a ring of tall mountains made of glass, where crystal towers sparkled, the smallest of them taller than the Shiprock. From these towers, ten thousand girl children with diamonds on their brows and mantles of white feathers trailing from their shoulders came running, falling over themselves to greet her.

"Kantu! Kantu!" they cried.

"Beautiful Kantu!"

"Storm Bird!"

"Rain Bringer!"

"The last of us to fall!"

"The first to fly!"

Kantu wanted to beg them to explain, but her throat was slashed open, and her voice had drained out with her life's blood.

Laughing, they took her by the hands, by the hem, by the sleeve, by whatever they could touch, and like a rushing wave bore Kantu up the tallest mountainside, this one of red glass with a glaze of gold upon it. They pulled and pushed and danced around her, coaxing her along the path. They stroked the torn flesh of her throat, and the rags of her clothes, and her big, beaky, oft-broken nose, and Kantu, though she was tired, felt she had barely walked at all but they gained the peak.

The children pointed down, and Kantu looked where they gestured. From this unbelievable height, atop a mountain of the sun, Kantu could see the world. Her world. Her feeble, arid world, fragile as a child's ball—and in dire need of her attention.

"It was too big for us," the children told her. "And we were too small. But you are different. You are strong enough to last."

How? Kantu wanted to ask. *How am I different?*

For answer, the children cast her from the mountain.

She did not fall again. This time, her great white wings flared out around her, gathering the hot wind beneath them. Her bones turned hollow as flutes, and her bloody rags were changed to burning feathers. Kantu shot down from the mountaintop in a swift stoop, parting the air like a knife through silk. She swooped steeply first over that fiery country, her eyes seeing everything at once, in the most minute detail. Only when she was kissing distance from the ground did she pull up again, her massive talons snatching great clumps of flaming roses as she rose. With these clutched firmly to her feathered belly, she left that burning golden country, left all those laughing, singing, waving little girls, and returned to the world.

Such monumental winds Kantu brought back with her, gathered like nestlings under her wings. Such sheer sheets of lightning when she blinked, and dazzling white tridents of light spearing the heavens from the diamond in her brow.

In this world, the tremendous trailing roses that she gripped in her talons swelled and blackened into clouds that wept fits of rain. She seeded the sky with storm petals, and beneath her shadow, Bellisaar and Sanis Al bloomed.

By the storms, Kantu announced her presence. She also sent rain dreams, a ceaseless stream of them, to the Fa and his wives, to his sons and soldiers and to all the people of Sanis Al.

"Hear me, S'Alians, for I am your god. It is I who bring the rain, and I who put pause to it. Listen well as a new law falls upon our land. *There is to be no more sacrifice.* Sing for your thunder. Dance for your floods. Lift the first fruits of your harvest to the altars of my temples. But no more—*no more!*—will rain be bought by innocent blood. Raise your sons and daughters in the fullness of life. I am the Rok of Rok Moris. I am the Thundergod of Bellisaar. I am the Raptor of Sanis Al, and I am here to stay."

In her sleep, the Rokka Mama smiled. Lines of worry and anguish vanished from her brow, and she murmured, "That's right, *pili,*" breathing more deeply and freely than she had done for twenty-five years.

And the Fa, who had not slept since watching his daughter step off a cliff, lingered over his thirteenth wife as she dreamed. With no one to see him, his eyes wept tears that glowed as blue as wizard light. His face shone like the Red Crescent washed clean.

* * *

After weeks of good rain, the young god tired of flight. She drew the floods back into her wings and left the Red Crescent for a time, searching for something familiar. She scanned the far horizons until she landed on a low earthen hill she thought she knew, then rummaged around in herself for a form she barely half-remembered.

Her body collapsed in a heap of feathers. An ancient wooden dial scraped her palm.

Kantu did not know how long she lay there, feeling how the earth shook with her heartbeat, announcing her presence to her friends in the catacombs like a giant who first politely bangs the big brass knocker before blowing the roof of a house down. Hours passed. Or minutes. It was hard to tell these days. No one came. After a long while, she rolled to a crouch, drew her immense raptor's beak back over her head like a crown, and set it securely between her two horns that it would not fall forward at an awkward moment. Her human face emerged, everything a bit dusty. There was nothing she could do about the diamond on her brow. She wiped her prodigious nose. She stood and spat. Her tongue felt dry and rough as sandstone.

Throwing the feathers back from her body until they settled behind her shoulders like a blanket roll, she stretched, hearing all sorts of pops and crackles and creaks as her body protested this cavalier treatment. She sat down again suddenly. Her feet hurt.

"Ow," she told bare toes and overgrown nails. "You never ached as talons."

"Next time," said Mikiel from behind her, "you'll know to rest them once in a while. A solid month of rain, Kantu! We've all started to mold!"

Scrambling up and whipping around, Kantu could barely gasp before Mikiel was upon her with a rib-crushing embrace. She couldn't see Mikiel's face, but Mik's tears cut ravines into the dust upon Kantu's clavicles. Kantu laughed a little, shaking her friend, trying to get her to smile again. Something else thumped her.

Crizion had joined them, a second circle of arms. More crying and scolding:

"Kantu! You're back! You look so tired! Don't you know, even a god must rest?"

"I didn't, actually. I should've. Thanks for telling me."

They touched her face, her feathers, her new curly golden horns and the sharp maw tilting up between them, its empty mask open to the sky, the sparkle on her forehead that made the lightning, her bloody rags, the scar on her throat. Though their voices were brave, their fingers shook. They wept more than they smiled.

What—had they thought her gone for good? So transformed as to be unrecognizable? Forgetful? Did they not know they were her own, that she was theirs?

"It's all right," she tried to tell them, trying to believe it. "We're all here now."

Then Manuway was there. Kneeling there. Kneeling before *her*, head bent. And this Kantu could not bear. No one could. Not even a god.

"Oh, hell. Fjord and flame and demons of the farthest north. Manuway. Stand up. Stand up, p-please." She tugged his sleeve, his shoulder, his obdurate chin. "I'm still *me*. I am! My blood oath on it. And you know—my blood's not a thing I idly fling about. Only in dire emergencies. This is getting . . . getting dire. Up. Come. Come here, Manuway!"

When he did not stir, she lifted him with an exaggerated grunt and mashed her body to his. There was a deep thrumming in his skin that she heard like a song. And his large hands stroked Kantu's rough black hair as if trying to braid the hour before dawn. Kantu drew back to look at him. Manuway met her eyes, as even Mikiel and Crizion had not yet done, and smiled.

As ever, Kantu's tongue knotted itself into mush and monosyllables. No use coaxing speech of it—she knew *that* from long years of practice. So she kissed Manuway instead. A quick kiss that turned into a deeper kiss that might have turned into something else had not Crizion primly cleared her throat. Mikiel was bent double, whooping.

"All right, all right," Kantu said mildly. "I'm done—for now!" she added, when Manuway opened his mouth to object. "Meantime, Mik, stop cackling. Crizion, love, do you have anything to eat?"

"I have prepared a feast, Kantu," Crizion said, solemn but dimpling.

"Lead on, friends. I'm starving."

The Bone Swans
of Amandale

For the erstwhile Injustice League

Dora Rose reached her dying sister a few minutes before the Swan Hunters did. I watched it all from my snug perch in the old juniper, and I won't say I didn't enjoy the scene, what with the blood and the pathos and everything. If only I had a handful of nuts to nibble on, sugared and roasted, the kind they sell in paper packets on market day when the weather turns. They sure know how to do nuts in Amandale.

"Elinore!" Dora Rose's voice was low and urgent, with none of the fluting snootiness I remembered. "Look at me. Elinore. How did they find you? We all agreed to hide—"

Ah, the good stuff. Drama. I lived for it. I scuttled down a branch to pay closer attention.

Dora Rose had draped the limp girl over her lap, stroking back her black, black hair. White feathers everywhere, trailing from Elinore's shoulders, bloodied at the breast, muddied near the hem. Elinore must've been midway between a fleshing and a downing when that Swan Hunter's arrow got her.

"Dora Rose." Elinore's wet red hand left a death smear on her sister's face. "They smoked out the cygnets. Drove them to the lake. Nets— horrible nets. They caught Pope, Maleen, Conrad—even Dash. We tried to free them, but more hunters came, and I . . ."

Turned herself into a swan, I thought, *and flew the hellfowl off.* Smart Elinore.

She'd not see it that way, of course. Swan people fancied themselves a proud folk, elegant as lords in their haughty halls, mean as snakes in a tight corner. Me, I preferred survivors to heroes. Or heroines, however comely.

38

"I barely escaped," Elinore finished.

From the looks of that gusher in her ribs, I'd guess "escaped" was a gross overstatement. But that's swans for you. Can't speak but they hyperbolize. Every girl's a princess. Every boy's a prince. Swan Folk take their own metaphors so seriously they hold themselves lofty from the vulgar throng. Dora Rose explained it once, when we were younger and she still deigned to chat with the likes of me: "It's not that we think less of anyone, Maurice. It's just that we think better of ourselves."

"Dora Rose, you mustn't linger. They'll be tracking me . . ."

Elinore's hand slipped from Dora Rose's cheek. Her back arched. Her bare toes curled under, and her hands clawed the mossy ground. From her lips burst the most beautiful song—a cascade of notes like moonlight on a waterfall, like a wave breaking on boulders, like the first snow melt of spring. All swan girls are princesses, true, but if styling themselves as royalty ever got boring, they could always go in for the opera.

Elinore was a soprano. Her final, stretched notes pierced even me. Dora Rose used to tell me that I had such tin ears as could be melted down for a saucepan, which at least might then be flipped over and used for a drum, thus contributing in a trivial way to the musical arts.

So maybe I was a little tone-deaf. Didn't mean I couldn't enjoy a swan song when I heard one.

As she crouched anxiously over Elinore's final aria, Dora Rose seemed far remote from the incessantly clever, sporadically sweet, gloriously vain girl who used to be my friend. The silvery sheen of her skin was frosty with pallor. As the song faded, its endmost high note stuttering to a sigh that slackened the singer's white lips, Dora Rose whispered, "Elinore?"

No answer.

My nose twitched as the smell below went from dying swan girl to freshly dead carcass. Olly-olly-in-for-free. As we like to say.

Among my Folk, carrion's a feast that's first come, first served, and I was well placed to take the largest bite. I mean, I *could* wait until Dora Rose lit on outta there. Not polite to go nibbling on someone's sister while she watched, after all. Just not done. Not when that someone had been sort of a friend. (All right—unrequited crush. But that was kid stuff. I'm over it. Grown up. Moved on.)

I heard the sound before she did. Ulia Gol's ivory horn. Not good.

"Psst!" I called from my tree branch. "Psst, Dora Rose. Up here!"

Her head snapped up, twilight eyes searching the tangle of the juniper branches. This tree was the oldest and tallest in the Maze Wood, unusually colossal for its kind, even with its trunk bent double and its branches bowing like a willow's. Nevertheless, Dora Rose's sharp gaze caught my shadowy shape and raked at it like fingernails. I grinned at her, preening my whiskers. Always nice to be noticed by a Swan Princess. Puts me on my mettle.

"Who is it?" Her voice was hoarse from grief and fear. I smelled both on her. Salt and copper.

"Forget me so quickly, Ladybird?" Before she could answer, I dove nose-first down the shaggy trunk, fleshing as I went. By the time I hit ground, I was a man. Man-shaped, anyway. Maybe a little undersized. Maybe scraggly, with a beard that grew in patches, a nose that fit my face better in my other shape, and eyes only a mother would trust—and only if she'd been drunk since breakfast.

"Maurice!"

"The Incomparable," I agreed. "Your very own Maurice."

Dora Rose stood suddenly, tall and icy in her blood-soaked silver gown. I freely admit to a dropped jaw, an abrupt excess of saliva. She'd only improved with time; her hair was as pale as her sister's had been dark, her eyes as blue as Lake Serenus where she and her Folk dwelled during their winter migrations. The naked grief I'd sensed in her a few moments ago had already cooled, like her sister's corpse. Swan Folk have long memories but a short emotional attention span.

Unlike Rat Folk, whose emotions could still get the better of them after fifteen years . . .

"What are you doing in the Maze Wood?" The snootiness I'd missed was back in her voice. Fabulous.

"Is that what this is?" I peered around, scratching behind my ear. She always hated when I scratched. "I thought it was the theater. The Tragedy of the Bonny Swans. The Ballad of the Two Sisters . . ."

Her eyes narrowed. "Maurice, of all the times to crack your tasteless jokes!"

Aaaarooooo! The ivory horn again. This time Dora Rose heard it, too. Her blue eyes flashed black with fury and terror. She hesitated, frozen between flesh and feather, fight and flight. I figured I'd help her out. Just this once. For old time's sake.

"Up the tree," I suggested. "I'll give you a boost."

She cast a perturbed look at dead Elinore, grief flickering briefly across her face. Rolling my eyes, I snapped, "Up, Princess! Unless you want to end the same, here and now."

"Won't the hounds scent me there?"

Dora Rose, good girl, was already moving toward me as she asked the question. Thank the Captured God. Start arguing with a swan girl, and you'll not only find yourself staying up all night, you'll also suffer all the symptoms of a bad hangover in the morning—with none of the fun parts between.

"This old tree's wily enough to mask your scent, my plume. If you ask nicely. We're good friends, the juniper and I."

I'd seen enough Swan Folk slaughtered beneath this tree to keep me tethered to it by curiosity alone. All right, so maybe I stayed with the mildly interested and not at all pathological hope of meeting Dora Rose again, in some situation not unlike this one, perhaps to rescue her from the ignominy of such a death. But I didn't tell her that. Not while her twin sister lay dead on the ground, her blood seeping into the juniper's roots. By the time Elinore had gotten to the tree, it'd've been too late for me to attempt anything, anyway. Even had I been so inclined.

And then, Dora Rose's hand on my shoulder. Her bare heel in my palm. And it was like little silver bells ringing under my skin where she touched me.

Easy, Maurice. Easy, you sleek and savvy rat, you. Bide.

Up she went, and I after her, furring and furling myself into my more compact but no less natty shape. We were both safe and shadow-whelmed in the bent old branches by the time Mayor Ulia Gol and her Swan Hunters arrived on the scene.

If someone held a piece of cheese to my head and told me to describe Ulia Gol in one word or starve, I'd choose *magnificent*. I like cheese too much to dither.

At a guess, I'd say Ulia Gol's ancestry wasn't human. Ogre on her mama's side. Giant on her daddy's. She was taller than Dora Rose, who herself would tower over most mortal men, though Dora Rose was long-lined and lean of limb whereas Ulia Gol was a brawny woman. Her skin was gold as a glazed chicken, her head full of candy-pink curls as was the current fashion. Her breasts were like two mozzarella balls ripe for the gnawing, with hips like two smoked hams. A one-woman banquet, that Ulia Gol, and she knew it, too. The way to a mortal's heart is through its appetite, and Ulia Gol prided herself on collecting mortal hearts. It was a kind of a game with her. Her specialty. Her sorcery.

She had a laugh that reached right out and tickled your belly. They say it was her laugh that won her the last election in Amandale. It wasn't. More like a mob-wide love spell she cast on her constituents. I don't know much about magic, but I know the smell of it. Amandale stinks of Ulia Gol. Its citizens accepted her rule with wretched adoration, wondering why they often woke of a night in a cold sweat from foul dreams of their Mayor feasting on the flesh of their children.

On the surface, she was terrifyingly jovial. She liked hearty dining and a good, hard day at the hunt. Was known for her fine whiskey, exotic lovers, intricate calligraphy, and dabbling in small—totally harmless, it was said—magics, mostly in the realm of the Performing Arts. Was a little too enthusiastic about taxes, everyone thought, but mostly used them to keep Amandale in good order. Streets, bridges, schools, secret police. That sort of thing.

Mortal politics was the idlest of my hobbies, but Ulia Gol had become a right danger to the local Folk, and that directly affected me. Swans weren't the only magic creatures she'd hunted to extinction in the Maze Wood. Before this latest kick, Ulia Gol had ferreted out the Fox Folk, those that fleshed to mortal shape, with tails tucked up under their clothes. Decimated the population in this area. You might ask how I know—after all, Fox Folk don't commune with Rat Folk any more than Swan Folk do. We just don't really talk to each other.

But then, I always was extraordinary. And really nosy.

Me, I suspected Ulia Gol's little hunting parties had a quite specific purpose. I think she knew the Folk could recognize her as inhuman. Mortals, of course, had no idea what she was. What mortals might do if they discovered their Mayor manipulated magic to make the ballot box come out in her favor? Who knew? Mortals in general are content to remain divinely stupid and bovinely docile for long periods of time, but when their ire's roused, there is no creature cleverer in matters of torture and revenge.

Ulia Gol adjusted her collar of rusty fox fur. It clashed terribly with her pink-and-purple riding habit, but she pulled it off with panache. Her slanted beaver hat dripped half a dozen black-tipped tails, which bounced as she strode into the juniper tree's clearing. Two huge-jowled hounds flanked her. She caught her long train up over her arm, her free hand clasping her crossbow with loose proficiency.

"Ha!" shouted Ulia Gol over her shoulder to someone out of my sightlines. "I thought I got her." She squatted over dead Elinore, studying her. "What do you think of this one, Hans? Too delicate for the glockenspiel, I reckon. Too tiny for the tuba. The cygnets completed our wind and percussion sections. Those two cobs and yesterday's pen did for the brass. We might as well finish up the strings here."

A man emerged from a corridor in the Maze Wood. He led Ulia Gol's tall roan mare and his own gray gelding, and looked with interest on the dead swan girl.

"A pretty one," he observed. "She'll make a fine harp, Madame Mayor, unless I miss my guess."

"Outstanding! I love a good harp song. But I always found the going rates too dear; harpists are so full of themselves." Her purple grin widened. "Get the kids in here."

The rest of her Swan Hunters began trotting into the Heart Glade on their plump little ponies. Many corridors, as you'd expect in a Maze

Wood of this size, dead-ended in thorn, stone, waterfall, hedge, cliff edge. But Ulia Gol's child army must've had the key to unlocking the maze's secrets, for they came unhesitatingly into the glade and stood in the shadow of the juniper tree where we hid.

Aw, the sweetums. Pink-cheeked they were, the little killers, green-caped, and all of them wearing the famous multicolored, beaked masks of Amandale. Mortals are always fixed in their flesh, like my rat cousins who remain rats no matter what. Can't do furrings, downings, or scalings like the Folk can. So they make do with elaborate costumes, body paint, millinery, and mass exterminations of our kind. Kind of adorable, really.

Ulia Gol clapped her hands. Her pink curls bounced and jounced. The foxtails on her beaver hat swung blithely.

"Dismount!" Her Hunters did so. "Whose turn is it, my little wretches?" she bawled at them. "Has to be someone fresh! Someone who's bathed in mare's milk by moonlight since yesterday's hunt. Now— who's clean? Who's my pure and pretty chanticleer today? Come, don't make me pick one of you!"

Oh, the awkward silence of children called upon to volunteer. A few heads bowed. Other masks lifted and looked elsewhere as if that act rendered them invisible. Presently one of the number was pushed to the forefront, so vehemently it fell and scraped its dimpled knees. I couldn't help noticing that this child had been standing at the very back of the crowd, hugging itself and hoping to escape observation.

Fat chance, kiddling. I licked my lips. I knew what came next. I'd been watching this death dance from the juniper tree for weeks now.

Ulia Gol grinned horribly at the fallen child. "Tag!" she boomed. "You're it." Her heavy hand fell across the child's shoulders, scooting it closer to the dead swan girl. "Dig. Dig her a grave fit for a princess."

The child trembled in its bright green hunter's cape. Its jaunty red mask was tied askew, like a deformed cardinal's head stitched atop a rag doll. The quick desperation of its breath was audible even from the heights where we perched, me sweating and twitching, Dora Rose tense and pale, glistening faintly in the dimness of the canopy.

Dora Rose lay on her belly, arms and legs wrapped around the branch, leaning as far forward as she dared. She watched the scene with avid eyes, and I watched her. She wouldn't have known why her people had been hunted all up and down the lake this autumn. Even when the swans began disappearing a few weeks ago, the survivors hadn't moved on. Swan Folk were big on tradition; Lake Serenus was where they wintered, and that was that. To establish a new migratory pattern would've been tantamount to blasphemy. That's swans for you.

I might have gone to warn them, I guess. Except that the last time she'd seen me, Dora Rose made it pretty clear that she'd rather wear a gown of graveyard nettles and pluck out her own feathers for fletching than have to endure two minutes more in my company. Of course, we were just teenagers then.

I gave the old juniper tree a pat, muttering a soundless prayer for keepsafe and concealment. Just in case Dora Rose'd forgotten to do as much in that first furious climb. Then I saw her lips move, saw her silver fingers stroking the shaggy branch. Good. So she, too, kept up a running stream of supplication. I'd no doubt she knew all the proper formulae; Swan Folk are as religious as they are royal. Maybe because they figure they're the closest things to gods as may still be cut and bleed.

"WHY AREN'T YOU DIGGING YET?" bellowed Ulia Gol, hooking my attention downward.

A masterful woman, and so well coiffed! How fun it was to watch her make those children jump. In my present shape, I can scare grown men out of their boots, they're that afraid of plague-carriers in these parts. The Folk are immune to plague, but mortals can't tell a fixed rat from one of us to save their lives.

Amandale itself was mostly spared a few years back when things got really bad and the plague bells ringing death tolls in distant towns at last fell silent. Ulia Gol spread the rumor abroad that it was her mayoral prowess that got her town through unscathed. Another debt Amandale owed her.

How she loomed.

"Please, Madame Mayor, please!" piped the piccolo voice from behind the cardinal mask. It fair vibrated with apprehension. "I—I cannot dig. I have no shovel!"

"Is that all? Hans! A shovel for our shy red bird!"

Hans of the gray gelding trudged forward with amiable alacrity. I liked his style. Reminded me of me. He was not tall, but he had a dapper air. One of your blonds was Hans, high-colored, with a crooked but entirely proportionate nose, a gold-goateed chin, and boots up to the thigh. He dressed all in red, except for his green cape, and he wore a knife on his belt. A fine big knife, with one edge curved and outrageously serrated.

I shuddered deliciously, deciding right there and then that I would follow him home tonight and steal his things while he slept.

The shovel presented, the little one was bid a third time to dig.

The grave needed only be a shallow one for Ulia Gol's purposes. This I had apprehended in my weeks of study. The earth hardly needed a scratch in its surface. Then the Swan Princess (or Prince, or heap of stiffening cygnets, as was the case yesterday) was rolled in the turned dirt and partially covered. Then Ulia Gol, towering over her small trooper with the blistered hands, would rip the mask off its face and roar, "Weep! If you love your life weep, or I'll give you something to weep about!"

Unmasked, this afternoon's child proved to be a young boy. One of the innumerable Cobblersawl brood unless I missed my guess. Baker's children. The proverbial dozen, give or take a miscarriage. Always carried a slight smell of yeast about them.

Froggit, I think this little one's name was. The seven-year-old. After the twins but before the toddlers and the infant.

I was quite fond of the Cobblersawls. Kids are so messy, you know, strewing crumbs everywhere. Bakers' kids have the best crumbs. Their poor mother was often too harried to sweep up after the lot of them until bedtime. Well after the gleanings had been got.

Right now, dreamy little Froggit looked sick. His hands begrimed with dirt and Elinore's blood, his brown hair matted with sweat, he covered her corpse well and good. Now, on cue, he started sobbing. Truth be told, he hadn't needed Ulia Gol's shouting to do so. His tears spattered the dirt, turning spots of it to mud.

Ulia Gol raised her arms like a conductor. Her big, shapely hands swooped through the air like kestrels.

"Sing, my children! You know the ditty well enough by now, I trust! This one's female; make sure you alter the lyrics accordingly. One-two-three and—"

One in obedience, twenty young Swan Hunters lifted up their voices in wobbly chorus. The hounds bayed mournfully along. I hummed, too, under my breath.

When they'd started the Swan Hunt a few weeks ago, the kids used to join hands and gambol around the juniper tree all maypole-like at Ulia Gol's urging. But the Mayor since discovered that her transformation spell worked just as well if they all stood still. Pity. I missed the dancing. Used to give the whole scene a nice theatrical flair.

> *"Poor little swan girl*
> *Heart pierced through*
> *Buried 'neath the moss and dew*
> *Restless in your grave you'll be*
> *At the foot of the juniper tree*
> *But your bones shall sing your song*
> *Morn and noon and all night long!"*

The music cut off with an abrupt slash of Ulia Gol's hands. She nodded once in curt approval. "Go on!" she told Froggit Cobblersawl. "Dig her back up again!"

But here Froggit's courage failed him. Or perhaps found him. For he scrubbed his naked face of tears, smearing worse things there, and stared up with big brown eyes that hated only one thing worse than himself, and *that* was Ulia Gol.

"No," he said.

"Hans," said Ulia Gol, "we have another rebel on our hands."

Hans stepped forward and drew from its sheath that swell knife I'd be stealing later. Ulia Gol beamed down at Froggit, foxtails falling to frame her face.

"Master Cobblersawl." She clucked her tongue. "Last week, we put out little Miss Possum's eyes when she refused to sing up the bones. Four weeks before that, we lamed the legs of young Miss Greenpea. A cousin of yours, I think? On our first hunt, she threw that shovel right at Hans and tried to run away. But we took that shovel and we made her pay, didn't we, Master Cobblersawl? And with whom did we replace her to make my hunters twenty strong again? Why, *yourself*, Master Cobblersawl. Now what, pray, Master Cobblersawl, do you think we'll do to *you*?"

Froggit did not answer, not then. Not ever. The next sound he made was a wail, which turned into a shriek, which turned into a swoon. "No" was the last word Froggit Cobblersawl ever spoke, for Hans put his tongue to the knife.

After this, they corked up the swooning boy with moss to soak the blood, and called upon young Ocelot to dig the bones. They'd have to replace the boy later, as they'd replaced Greenpea and Possum. Ulia Gol needed twenty for her sorceries. A solid twenty. No more, no less.

Good old Ocelot. The sort of girl who, as exigency demanded, bathed in mare's milk every night there was a bit of purifying moonlight handy. Her father was Chief Gravedigger in Amandale. She, at the age of thirteen and a half, was his apprentice. Of all her fellow Swan Hunters, Ocelot had the cleanest and most callused hands. Ulia Gol's favorite.

She never flinched. Her shovel scraped once, clearing some of the carelessly spattered dirt from the corpse. The juniper tree glowed silver.

Scraped twice. The green ground roiled white as boiling milk.

Scraped thrice.

It was not a dead girl Ocelot freed from the dirt, after all. Not even a dead swan.

I glanced at Dora Rose to see how she was taking it. Her blue eyes were wide, her gaze fixed. No expression showed upon it, though. No sorrow or astonishment or rage. Nothing in her face was worth neglecting the show below us for, except the face itself. I could drink my fill of that pool and still die of thirst.

But I'd gone down that road once already. What separated us rats from other Folk was our ability to *learn*.

I returned my attention to the scene. When Ocelot stepped back to dust off her hands on her green cape, the exhumed thing that had been Elinore flashed into view.

It was, as Hans had earlier predicted, a harp.

And a large harp it was, of shining white bone, strung with black strings fine as hair, which Ulia Gol bent to breathe upon lightly. Shimmering, shuddering, the harp repeated back a refrain of Elinore's last song.

"It works," Ulia Gol announced with tolling satisfaction. "Load it up on the cart, and we'll take it back to Orchestra Hall. A few more birds in the bag and my automatized orchestra will be complete!"

B ack in our budding teens, I'd elected to miss a three-day banquet spree with my rat buddies in post-plague Doornwold, Queen's City. (A dead city now, like the Queen herself.) Why? To attend instead at Dora Rose's invitation a water ballet put on by the Swan Folk of Lake Serenus.

I know, right? The whole affair was dull as a tidy pantry, lemme tell you. When I tried to liven things up with Dora Rose a little later, just a bit of flirt and fondle on the silver docks of Lake Serenus, I got myself soundly slapped. Then the Swan Princess of my dreams told me that my attentions were not only unsolicited and unwelcome but grossly, criminally, *heinously* repellent—her very words—and sent me back to sulk in my nest in Amandale.

You should've seen me. Tail dragging. Whiskers drooping. Sniveling into my fur. Talk about heinously repellent. I couldn't've been gladder my friends had all scampered over to the new necropolis, living it up among the corpses of Doornwold. By the time they returned, I had a handle on myself. Started up a dialogue with a nice, fat rat girl. We had some good times. Her name was Moira. That day on the docks was the last I saw Dora Rose up close for fifteen years.

Until today.

Soft as I was, by the time the last of the Swan Hunters trotted clear of the Heart Glade on their ponies, I'd decided to take Dora Rose back to my nest in Amandale. I had apartments in a warren of condemned tenements by the Drukkamag River docks. Squatters' paradise. Any female should rightly have spasmed at the chance; my wainscoted walls were only nominally chewed, my furniture salvaged from the alleyways of

Merchant Prince Row, Amandale's elite. The current mode of decoration in my neighborhood was shabby chic. Distressed furniture? Mine was so distressed, it could've been a damsel in a past life.

But talking Dora Rose down from the juniper tree proved a trifle dicey. She wanted to return to Lake Serenus right away and search for survivors.

"Yeah, you and Huntsman Hans," I snorted. "He goes out every night with his nets, hoping to bag another of your Folk. Think he'll mistake you, with your silver gown and your silver skin, for a ruddy-kneed mortal milkmaid out for a skinny dip? Come on, Dora Rose! You got more brains than that, even if you *are* a bird."

I was still in my rat skin when I told her this. She turned on me savagely, grabbing me by the tail, and shook me, hissing as only swans and cobras can hiss. I'd've bitten her, but I was laughing too hard.

"Do you have a better idea, Maurice? Maybe you would be happiest if I turned myself in to Ulia Gol right now! Is that what I should do?"

I fleshed myself to man-shape right under her hands. She dropped me quickly, cheeks burning. Dora Rose did not want to see what she'd've been holding me by once I changed form. I winked at her.

"I got a lot of ideas, Dora Rose, but they all start with a snack and a nap."

Breathing dangerously, she shied back, deeper into the branches. Crossed her arms over her chest. Narrowed her lake-blue eyes. For a swan, you'd think her mama was a mule.

"Come on, Ladybird," I coaxed, scooting nearer—but not *too* near—my own dear Dora Rose. "You're traumatized. That's not so strong a word, is it, for what you've been through today?"

Her chin jutted. Her gaze shifted. Her lips were firm, not trembling. Not a trembler, that girl. I settled on a nice, thick branch, my legs dangling in the air.

"Damn it, Dora Rose, your twin sister's just been turned into a harp! Your family, your friends, your Folk—all killed and buried and dug back up again as bone instruments. And for what?" I answered myself, since she wouldn't. "So that Mayor Ulia Gol, that skinflint, can cheat Amandale's Guild of Musicians of their entertainment fees. She wants an orchestra that plays itself—so she's sacrificing swans to the juniper tree."

Her mouth winced. She was not easy to faze, my Dora Rose. But hey, she'd had a tough day, and I was riding her hard.

"You'd be surprised," I continued, "how many townspeople support Mayor Gol and her army of Swan Hunters. Everyone likes music. So what's an overextended budget to do?"

Dora Rose unbent so far as to roll her eyes. Taking this as a sign of weakening, I hopped down from the juniper tree.

"Come home with me, Ladybird," I called up. "There's a candy shop around the corner from my building. I'll steal you enough caramels to make you sick. You can glut your grief away, and then you can sleep. And in the morning, when you've decided it's undignified to treat your only ally—no matter his unsavory genus—so crabbily, we'll talk again."

A pause. A rustle. A soundless silver falling. Dora Rose landed lightly on her toe-tips. Above us, an uneasy breeze jangled the dark green needles of the juniper tree. There was a sharp smell of sap. The tree seemed to breathe. It did that, periodically. The god inside its bark did not always sleep.

Dora Rose's face was once more inscrutable, all grief and rage veiled behind her pride. "Caramels?" she asked.

Dora Rose once told me, years ago, that she liked things to taste either very sweet or very salty. Caramels, according to her, were the perfect food.

"Dark chocolate sea-salt caramels," I expounded with only minimal drooling. "Made by a witch named Fetch. These things are to maim for, Dora Rose."

"You remembered." She sounded surprised. If I'd still been thirteen (Captured God save me from ever being thirteen again), I might've burst into tears to be so doubted. Of course I remembered! Rats have exceptional memories. Besides—in my youth, I'd kept a strict diary. Mortal-style.

I was older now. I doffed my wharf boy's cap and offered my elbow. In my best Swan Prince imitation, I told her, "Princess, your every word is branded on my heart."

I didn't do it very well; my voice is too nasal, and I can't help adding overtones of innuendo. But I think Dora Rose was touched by the effort. Or at least, she let herself relax into the ritual of courtesy, something she understood in her bones. Her bones. Which Ulia Gol wanted to turn into a self-playing harpsichord to match Elinore's harp.

Over. My. Dead. Body.

Oh, all right. My slightly dented body. Up to and no further than a chunk off the tail. After that, Dora Rose would be on her own.

"Come on," I said. "Let's go."

She took my elbow. She even leaned on it a smidge, which told me how exhausted and stricken she was beneath her feigned indifference. I refrained from slavering a kiss upon her silver knuckles. Just barely.

The next morning, thanks to a midnight raid on Hans's wardrobe, I was able to greet Dora Rose at my dapper best. New hose, new shining thigh-high boots, new scarlet jerkin, green cape and linen sark.

New curved dagger with serrated edge, complete with flecks of Froggit Cobblersawl's drying tongue meat on it.

I'd drawn the line at stealing Hans's blond goatee, being at some loss as how best to attach it to my own chin. But I did not see why *he* should have one when I couldn't. I had, therefore, left it at the bottom of his chamber pot should he care to seek it there.

Did the Swan Princess gaze at me in adoration? Did she stroke my fine sleeve or fondle my blade? Not a bit of it. She sat on the faded cushion of my best window seat, playing with a tassel from the heavy draperies and chewing on a piece of caramel. Her blue stare went right through me. Not blank, precisely. Meditative. Distant. Like I wasn't important enough to merit even a fraction of her full attention.

"What I cannot decide," she said slowly, "is what course I should take. Ought I to fly at Ulia Gol in the open streets of Amandale and dash her to the ground? Ought I to forsake this town entirely, and seek shelter with some other royal bevy? If," she added with melancholy, "they would have me. This I doubt, for I would flee to them with empty hands and under a grave mantle of sorrow. Ought I to await at the lake for Hans's net and Hans's knife and join my Folk in death, letting my transformation take me at the foot of the juniper tree?"

That's swans for you. Fraught with "oughts." Stop after three choices, each bleaker and more miserably elegant than the last. Vengeance, exile, or suicide. Take your pick. I sucked my tongue against an acid reply, taking instead a cube of caramel and a deep breath. Twitched my nose. Smoothed out the wrinkles of distaste. Went to crouch on the floor by the window seat. (This was *not*, I'll have you know, the same as kneeling at her feet. For one thing, I was balancing on my heels, not my knees.)

"Seems to me, Dora Rose," I suggested around a sticky, salty mouthful, "that what you want in a case like this—"

"Like this?" she asked, and I knew she was seeing her sister's hair repurposed for harp strings. "There has never *been* a case like mine, Maurice, so do not *dare* attempt to eclipse the magnitude of my despair with your filthy comparisons!"

I loved when she hissed at me. No blank stare now. If looks could kill, I'd be skewered like a shish kebab and served up on a platter. I did my best not to grin. She'd've taken it the wrong way.

Smacking my candy, I said in my grandest theatrical style, even going so far as to roll my R's, "In a case, Dora Rose, where magic meets music, where both are abused and death lacks dignity, where the innocent suffer and a monster goes unchecked, it seems reasonable, I was going to say, to consult an expert. A magical musician, perhaps, who has suffered so much himself he cannot endure to watch the innocent undergo like torment."

Ah, rhetoric. Swans, like rats, are helpless against it. Dora Rose twisted the braid at her shoulder, and lowered her ivory lashes. Early morning light wormed through my dirty windowpane. A few gray glows managed to catch the silver of her skin and set it gleaming.

My hands itched. In this shape, what I missed most was the sensitivity of my whiskers; my palms kept trying to make up for it. I leaned against the wall and scratched each palm vigorously in their turn with my dandy nails. Even in mortal form, these were sharp and black. I was vain about my nails and kept them polished. I wanted to run them though that fine, pale Swan Princess hair.

"Maurice." Miraculously, Dora Rose was smiling. A contemptuous smile, yes, but a smile nonetheless. "You're not saying you know a magical musician? You?"

Implicit in her tone: *You wouldn't know music if a marching band dressed ranks right up your nose.*

I drew myself to my not very considerable height, and I tugged my scarlet jerkin straight, and I said to her, I said to Dora Rose, I said, "He happens to be my best friend!"

"Ah."

"I saved his life down in Doornwold five years ago. The first people to repopulate the place were thieves and brigands, you know, and he wasn't at all equipped to deal with . . . Well. That's how I met Nicolas."

She cocked an eyebrow.

"And then we met again out back of Amandale, down in the town dump. He, uh, got me out of a pickle. A pickle jar, rather. One that didn't have air holes. This was in my other shape, of course."

"Of course," she murmured, still with that trenchant silver smile.

"Nicolas is very shy," I warned her. "So don't you go making great big swan eyes at him or anything. No sudden movements. No hissing or flirting or swooning over your sweet little suicide plans. He had a rough childhood, did Nicolas. Spent the tenderest years of his youth under the Hill, and part of him never left it."

"He has lived in Faerie but is not of it?" Now both Dora Rose's eyebrows arched, winging nigh up to her hairline. "Is he mortal or not?"

I shrugged. "Not Folk, anyway—or not entirely. Maybe some blood from a ways back. Raven, I think. Or Crow. A drop or two of Fox. But he can't slip a skin to scale or down or fur. Not Faerieborn, either, though from his talk it seems he's got the run of the place. Has more than mortal longevity, that's for sure. Among his other gifts. Don't know how old he is. Suspect even *he* doesn't remember, he's been so long under the Hill. What he is, is bright to my nose, like a perfumery or a field of wildflowers. Too many scents to single out the source. But come on,

Dora Rose; nothing's more boring than describing a third party where he can't blush to hear! Meet him and sniff for yourself."

Nicolas lived in a cottage in the lee of the Hill.

I say Hill, and I mean Hill. As fairy mounds go, this was the biggest and greenest, smooth as a bullfrog and crowned at the top with a circle of red toadstools the size of sycamores that glowed in the dark.

It's not an easy Hill. You don't want to look at it directly. You don't want to stray too near, too casually, or you'll end up asleep for a hundred years, or vanished out of life for seven, or tithed to the dark things that live under the creatures living under the Hill.

But Nicolas dwelled there peaceably enough, possibly because no one who ever goes there by accident gets very far before running off in the opposite direction, shock-haired and shrieking. Those who approach on *purpose* sure as hellfowl aren't coming to bother the poor musician who lives in the Hill's shadow. They come because they want to go *under*, to seek their fortunes, to beg of the Faerie Queen some boon (poor sops), or to exchange the dirt and drudgery of their mortal lives for some otherworldly dream.

We Folk don't truck much with Faerie. We belong to earth, wind, water, and sun just as much as mortals do, and with better right. For my part, anything that stinks of that glittering, glamorous Hillstuff gives me the heebie-jeebies. With the exception of Nicolas.

I left Dora Rose (not without her vociferous protestations) hiding in some shrubbery, and approached the cottage at a jaunty swagger. I didn't bang. That would be rude, and poor Nicolas was so easily startled. Merely, I scratched at the door with my fine black nails. At the third scratch, Nicolas answered. He was dressed only in his long red underwear, his red-and-black hair standing all on end. He was sleepy-eyed and pillow-marked, but he smiled when he saw me and opened wide his door.

"Maurice, Maurice!" he cried in his voice that would strike the sirens dumb. "But I did not expect this! I do not have a pie!" and commenced bustling about his larder, assembling a variety of foods he thought might please me.

He knew me so well! The vittles consisted of a rind of old cheese, a heel of hard bread, the last of the apple preserves, and a slosh of sauerkraut. Truly a feast! Worthy of a Rat King! (If my Folk had kings. We don't. Just as all swans are royalty, we rats are every last one of us a commoner and godsdamned proud of it.) Salivating with delight, I dove for the proffered tray. There was only one chair at the table. Leaving it to me, Nicolas sank to a crouch by the hearth. I grazed with all the greed of a man-and-rat who's breakfasted solely on a single caramel. He watched with a sweet smile on his face, as if nothing had ever given him more pleasure than to feed me.

"Nicolas, my friend," I told him, "I'm in a spot of trouble."

The smile vanished in an instant, replaced by a look of intent concern. Nicolas hugged his red wool-clad knees to his chest and cocked his head, bright black eyes inquiring.

"See," I said, "a few weeks back, I noticed something weird happening in the Maze Wood just south of town? Lots of mortal children trooping in and out of the corridors, dressed fancy. Two scent hounds. A wagon. All led by Henchman Hans and no less a person than the Mayor of Amandale herself. I got concerned, right? I like to keep an eye on things."

Nicolas's own concern darkened to a frown, a sadness of thunderclouds gathering on his brow. But all he said was, "You were snooping, Maurice!"

"All right, all right, Nicolas, so what if I was? Do you have any ale?"

Nicolas pulled a red-and-black tuft of his hair. "Um, I will check! One moment, Maurice!" He sprang off the ground with the agility of an eight-year-old and scurried for a small barrel in a corner by the cellar door. He set his ear to it as if listening for the spirit within.

"It's from the Hill," he warned softly.

I smacked my lips. "Bring it on!"

Faerie ale was the belchiest. Who said I wasn't musical? Ha! Dora Rose'd never heard me burp out "The Lay of Kate and Fred" after bottoms-upping a pint of this stuff. Oh, crap. Dora Rose. She was still outside, awaiting my signal. Never keep a Swan Princess in the bushes. She'd be bound to get antsy and announce herself with trumpets. I accepted the ale and sped ahead with my tale.

"So I started camping out in that old juniper tree, right? You know the one? *The* juniper tree. In the Heart Glade."

"Oh, yes." Nicolas lowed that mournful reply, half-sung, half-wept. "The poor little ghost in the tree. He was too long trapped inside it. The tree became his shrine, and the ghost became a god. That was in the long, long ago. But I remember it all like yesterday. I go to play my pipe for him when I get too lonely. Sometimes, if the moon is right, he sings to me."

Awright! Now we were getting somewhere! Dora Rose should be hearing this, she really should. But if I brought her in now, poor Nicolas'd clam up like a corpse on a riverbank.

"Hey, Nicolas?" I gnawed into a leathery apple. "You have any idea why Ulia Gol'd be burying a bunch of murdered Swan Folk out by the juniper tree, singing a ditty over the bodies, and digging them up again? Or why they should arise thereafter as self-playing instruments?"

Nicolas shook his head, wide-eyed. "No. Not if Ulia Gol did it. She'd have no power there."

I spat out an apple seed. It flew across the room, careening off a copper pot. "Oh, right. Uh, I guess what I meant was . . . if she got a *child* to do it. A child with a shovel. First to bury the corpse, then weep over it, then dig it up again. While a chorus of twenty kiddlings sang over the grave."

Nicolas hugged himself harder, shivering. "Maurice! They are not doing this? Maurice—they would not use the poor tree so!"

I leaned in, heel of bread in one hand, rind of cheese in the other. "Nicolas. Ulia Gol's murdered most of a bevy of Swan Folk. You know, the one that winters at Lake Serenus? Cygnet, cob, and pen—twenty of them, dead as dead can be. She's making herself an orchestra of bone instruments that play themselves so she won't have to shell out for professional musicians. Or at least that's her excuse this time. But you remember last year, right? With the foxes?"

Nicolas flinched.

"And before that," I went on, "didn't she go fishing all the talking trout from every single stream and wishing well? Are you sensing a pattern? 'Cause no one else seems to be—except for yours truly, the Incomparable Maurice. Now there's only one swan girl left. One out of a whole bevy. And she's . . . she's my . . . The point is, Nicolas, we *must* do something."

Nearly fetal in his corner by the ale barrel, Nicolas hid his face, shaking his head behind his hands. Before I could press him further, a silvery voice began to sing from the doorway.

> "The nanny-goat said to the little boy
> Baa-baa, baa-baa I'm full
> I'm a bale of hay and a grassy glade
> All stuffed, all stuffed in wool
>
> I can eat no more, kind sir, kind sir
> Baa-baa, baa-baa my song
> Not a sock, not a rock, not a fiddle-fern
> I'll be full all winter long."

By the end of the first verse, Nicolas had lifted his head. By the end of the second, he'd drawn a lanyard out of the collar of his long underwear. From this lanyard hung a slender silver pipe that dazzled the eye, though no sun shone in that corner of the cottage. When Dora Rose got to the third verse, he began piping along.

"The little boy said to the nanny goat
Baa-baa, baa-baa all day
You'll want to be fat as all of that
When your coat comes off in May!"

By the time they reached the bridge of their impromptu set, I was dancing around the cottage in an ecstatic frenzy. The silver pipe's sweet trills drove my limbs to great leaps and twists. Dora Rose danced, too, gasping for breath as she twirled and sang simultaneously. Nicolas stood in the center of the cottage, tapping his feet in time. The song ended, and Nicolas applauded, laughing for joy. Dora Rose gave him a solemn curtsy, which he returned with a shy bow. But as he slipped the silver pipe back beneath his underwear, I watched him realize that underwear was all he wore. Shooting a gray and stricken look my way, pretty much making me feel like I'd betrayed him to the headsman, he jumped into his tiny cot and pulled a ratty blanket over his head. Dora Rose glanced at me.

"Uh, Nicolas?" I said. "Me and Dora Rose'll just go wait outside for a few minutes. You come on out when you got your clothes on, okay?"

"She's a *swan!*" Nicolas called from under his cover. I patted a lump that was probably his foot.

"She needs your help, Nicolas. Her sister got turned into a harp yesterday. All her family are dead now. She's next."

At that point, Dora Rose took me by the ear and yanked me out of the cottage. I cringed—but not too much lest she loosen her grip. Dora Rose rarely touched me of her own volition.

"How dare you?" she whispered, the flush on her face like a frosted flower. "*The Pied Piper?* He could dance any Folk he pleased right to the death and you *pushed* him? *Maurice!*"

"Aw, Dora Rose," I wheedled, "he's just a little sensitive is all. But he's a good friend—the best! He'd never hurt me. Or mine." She glared at me. I help up my hands. "My, you know, friends. Or whatever."

Dora Rose shook her head, muttering, "I am friendly with a magical musician, he tells me. Who's familiar with Faerie. Who knows about the Folk. He'll help us, he tells me." Her blue eyes blazed, and I quivered in the frenzy of her full attention. "You never said he was the *Pied Piper*, Maurice!"

I set my hands on my hips and leaned away. Slightly. She still had a grip on my ear, after all. "Because I knew you'd react like this! Completely unreasonable! Nicolas wouldn't hurt a fly half-drowned in a butter dish! So he's got a magic pipe, so what? The *Faerie Queen* gave it to him. Faerie Queen says, 'Here, darling, take this; I made it for you,' you don't go refusing the thing. And once you have it, you don't leave it lying around the house for someone else to pick up and play. It's his *livelihood*, Dora Rose! And it's a weapon, too. We'll use it to protect you, if you'll let us."

Her eyebrows winged up, two perfect, pale arches. Her clutch on my ear began to twist. I squeaked out, "On another note, Dora Rose, forgive the pun"—she snorted as I'd meant her to, and I assumed my most earnest expression, which on my face could appear just a trifle disingenuous—"I have to say, your idea about singing nursery rhymes to calm him down was pretty great! Poor Nicolas! All he sees whenever he looks at a woman is the Faerie Queen. Scares him outta his wits. Can't hardly speak, after. He's good with kids, though. Kid stuff. Kid songs. You were right on track with that *baa-baa* tune of yours. He's like a child himself, really . . ."

Dora Rose released my ear. More's the pity.

"Maurice!" She jabbed a sharp finger at my nose, which was sharp enough to jab back. "One of these days!"

That was when Nicolas tiptoed from the cottage, sort of slinky-bashful. He was dressed in his usual beggar's box motley, with his coat of bright rags and two mismatched boots. He had tried to flatten his tufted hair, but it stuck up defiantly all around his head. His black eyes slid to the left of where Dora Rose stood.

"Hi," he said, scuffing the ground.

"It is a fine thing to meet you, Master Nicolas," she returned with courtly serenity. "Bevies far and wide sing of your great musicianship. My own mother"—I saw a harsh movement in her pale throat as she swallowed—"watched you play once, and said she never knew such joy."

"I'm sorry about your family," Nicolas whispered. "I'm sure the juniper tree didn't want to do it. It just didn't understand." His eyes met mine briefly, pleading. I gave him an encouraging *go-ahead* nod. Some of this story I knew already, but Nicolas could tell it better. He'd been around before it was a story, before it was history. He'd been alive when it was a current event.

Nicolas straightened his shoulders and cleared his throat.

"Your Folk winters at Lake Serenus. But perhaps, keeping mostly to yourselves, you do not know the story of the Maze Wood surrounding the lake. The tree at the center of the wood is also . . . also at the center of, of your family's slaughter. . . . You see, before he was the god in the tree, he was only a small boy. His stepmother murdered him. His little stepsister buried his bones at the roots of a sapling juniper and went every day to water his grave with her tears.

"To comfort her, the boy's ghost and the juniper tree became one. The young tree was no wiser than the boy—trees understand things like rain and wind and birds. So the ghost and the tree together transformed the boy's bones into a beautiful bird, hoping this would lighten his sister's heart and fly far to sing of his murder.

"That was in the long, long ago. Later, but still long ago, the villagers of what was then a tiny village called Amandale began to worship the ghost in the tree. The ghost became a god. Those whose loved ones had been murdered would bring their bones there. The god would turn these wretched bones to instruments that sang the names of their murderers so loudly, so relentlessly, that the murderers were brought to justice just to silence the music.

"Many generations after this, these practices and even the god itself were all but forgotten. The juniper tree's so old now all it remembers are bones and birds, tears and songs. But the Mayor of Amandale must have read the story somewhere in the town archives. Learned of this old magic, the miracle. And then the Mayor, then she . . . she . . ."

A small muscle in Nicolas's jaw jumped. Suddenly I saw him in a different light, as if he, like his silver pipe, had an inner dazzle that needed no sunlight to evoke it. That dazzle had an edge on it like a broken bottle. Handle this man wrong, and he would cut you, though he wept to do it.

"The Mayor," said the Pied Piper, "is abusing the juniper tree's ancient sorrow. It is wrong. Very wrong."

This time he met Dora Rose's gaze directly, his black eyes bright and cold. "She is no better than the first little boy's killer. She has hunted your Folk to their graves. As birds and murder victims in one, they make the finest instruments. The children of Amandale helped her to do this while their parents stood by. *They are all complicit.*"

"Not all," I put in. Credit where it's due. "Three children stood against her. Punished for it, of course."

Nicolas gave me a nod. "They will be spared."

"Spared?" Dora Rose echoed. But Nicolas was already striding off toward the Maze Wood with his pace that ate horizons. Me and Dora Rose, we had to follow him at a goodly clip.

"This," I whispered to her from one corner of my grin, "is gonna be good."

The maze part of the Maze Wood is made of these long and twisty walls of thorn. It's taller than the tallest of Amandale's four watchtowers and thicker than the fortress wall, erected a few hundred years ago to protect the then-new cathedral of Amandale. But Brotquen, the jolly golden Harvest Goddess in whose honor the cathedral had been built, went out of style last century. Now Brotquen Cathedral is used to store grain—not so big a step down from worshipping it, if you ask me—and I'm quite familiar with its environs. Basically the place is a food mine for yours truly and his pack, Folk and fixed alike. And the stained glass windows are pretty, too.

Like Nicolas said, the Maze Wood's been there before Brotquen, before her cathedral, before the four towers and the fortress wall. It was sown back in the olden days when the only god in these parts was the little one in the juniper tree. I don't know if the maze was planted to honor that god or to confuse it, keep its spirit from wandering too far afield in the shape of a fiery bird, singing heartbreaking melodies of its murder. Maybe both.

Me and the Maze Wood get along all right. Sure, it's scratched off some of my fur. Sure, its owls and civets have tried making a meal of me. But nothing under these trees has got the better of me yet. I know these woods almost as well as I know the back streets of Amandale. I'm a born explorer, though at heart I'm city rat, not woodland. That's what squirrels are for. "Think of us as rats in cute suits," a squirrel friend of mine likes to say. Honestly, I don't see that squirrels are all that adorable myself.

But as well as I knew the Maze Wood, Nicolas *intuited* it.

He moved through its thorny ways like he would the "Willful Child's Reel," a song he could play backwards and blindfolded. Nicolas took shortcuts through corridors I'd never seen and seemed to have some inner needle pointing always to the Heart Glade the way some people can find true north. In no time at all, we came to the juniper tree.

Nicolas went right up to it and flung himself to the ground, wrapping his arms as far about the trunk as he could reach. There he sobbed with all the abandon of a child, like Froggit had sobbed right before they cut out his tongue.

Dora Rose hung back. She looked impassive, but I thought she was embarrassed. Swans don't cry.

After several awkward minutes of this, Nicolas sat up. He wiped his face, drew the silver pipe from his shirt, and played a short riff as if to calm himself. I jittered at the sound, and Dora Rose jumped, but neither of us danced. He didn't play for us that time but for the tree.

The juniper tree began to glow, as it had glowed yesterday when the Swan Hunters sang up Elinore's bones. The mossy ground at the roots turned white as milk. Then a tiny bird, made all of red-and-gold fire, shot out of the trunk to land on Nicolas's shoulder. Nicolas stopped piping but did not remove the silver lip from his mouth. Lifting its flickering head, the bird opened its beak and began to sing in a small, clear, plaintive voice:

"Stepmother made a simple stew
Into the pot my bones she threw

When father finished eating me
They buried my bones at the juniper tree

Day and night stepsister weeps
Her grief like blood runs red, runs deep
Kywitt! Kywitt! Kywitt! I cry
What a beautiful bird am I!"

Nicolas's expression reflected the poor bird's flames. He stroked its tiny head, bent his face, and whispered something in its ear.

"He's telling the god about your dead Folk," I said to Dora Rose with satisfaction. "Now we'll really see something!"

I should've been born a prophet, for as soon as Nicolas stopped speaking, the bird toppled from his shoulder into his outstretched palm and lay there in a swoon for a full minute before opening its beak to scream. Full-throated, human, anguished.

I covered my ears, wishing they really had been made of tin. But Dora Rose stared as if transfixed. She nodded once, slowly, as if the ghost bird's scream matched the sound she'd been swallowing all day.

The juniper tree blazed up again. The glowing white ground roiled like a tempest-turned sea. Gently, so gently, Nicolas brought his cupped hands back up to the trunk, returning the bird to its armor of shaggy bark. As the fiery bird vanished into the wood, the tree itself began to sing. The Heart Glade filled with a voice that was thunderous and marrow-deep.

"Swan bones changed to harp and fife
Sobbing music, robbed of life
String and drum and horn of bone
Leave them not to weep alone

Set them in a circle here
None for three nights interfere
From my branches let one hang
Swan in blood and bone and name

Bring the twenty whose free will
Dared to use my magic ill
Dance them, drive them into me
Pick the fruit from off this tree!"

The light disappeared. The juniper sagged and seemed to sigh. Nicolas put his pipe away and bowed his head.

Dora Rose turned to me, fierceness shining from her.

"Maurice," she said, "you heard the tree. We must bring the bones here. I must hang for three days. You must keep Ulia Gol and Hans away from the Heart Glade for that time, and bring those twenty young Swan Hunters to me. Quickly! We have no time to waste."

And here the heart-stricken and love-sore child I once was rose up from the depths of me like its very own bone instrument.

"Must I, Ladybird?"

Did I sound peevish? I hardly knew. My voice cracked like a boy soprano whose balls'd just dropped, thus escaping the castrating knife and opium bath and a life of operatic opulence. Peevish, yes. Peevish it was.

"*Must* I really? So easy, don't you think, to steal an orchestra right out from under an ogre's nose? To keep Ulia Gol from tracking it back here. To lure twenty children all into the Maze Wood without a mob of parents after us. That'll take more than wiles, Princess. That'll take *tactics*. And why should I do any of this, eh? For you, Dora Rose? For the sake of a friend? What kind of friend are *you* to *me*?"

Nicolas stared from me to Dora Rose, wide-eyed. He had placed a hand over his pipe and kneaded it nervously against his chest. Dora Rose also stared, her face draining of excitement, of grief nearly avenged, of bright rage barely contained. All I saw looking into that shining oval was cool, contemptuous royalty. That was fine. Let her close herself off to me. See if that got her my aid in this endeavor.

"I'm gonna ask you something." I drew closer, taking her slack silver hand in mine. I even pressed it between my itching palms. "If it were *me*, Dora Rose, if I'd come to Lake Serenus before your courtly bevy and said to you, 'Dear Princess, Your Highness, my best old pal! Mayor Ulia Gol's exterminating the Rat Folk of Amandale. She's trapping us and torturing us and making bracelets of our tails. Won't you help me stop her? For pity's sake? For what I once was to you, even if that was only a pest?'

"What would you have said to *me*, Dora Rose, if I had come to you so?"

Dora Rose turned her face away, but did not remove her hand. "I would have said nothing, Maurice. I would have driven you off. Do you not know me?"

"Yes, Dora Rose." I squeezed her hand, happy that it still held mine. Was it my imagination, or did she squeeze back? Yup. That was definitely a squeeze. More like a vise, truth be told. I loved a vise. Immediately I began feeling more charitable. That was probably her intention.

"Elinore now," I reflected, "*Elinore* would've intervened on my behalf." Dora Rose's head turned cobra-quick. Had she fangs enough and time, I'd be sporting several new apertures in my physiognomy. I went on anyway. "The nice sister, that Elinore. Always sweet as a Blood Haven peach—for all she loathed me tail to toe. You Swan Folk would've come to our aid on *Elinore's* say so, mark my words, Dora Rose."

"Then," said Dora Rose with freezing slowness, her grip on my hand yet sinewy and relentless, "you will help me for the sake of my dead twin, Maurice? For the help my sister Elinore would have given you had our places been reversed?"

I sighed. "Don't you know me, Ladybird? No. I wouldn't do it for Elinore. Not for gold or chocolate. Not for a dozen peachy swan girls and their noblesse oblige. I'll do it for *you*, of course. Always did like you better than Elinore."

"You," scoffed Dora Rose with a curling lip, flinging my hand from hers, "are the only one who ever did, Maurice."

I shrugged. It was true.

"As a young cygnet, I feared this was because our temperaments were too alike."

I snorted, inordinately pleased. "Yeah, well. Don't go telling my mama I act like a Swan Princess. She'll think she didn't raise me right."

From his place near the juniper tree, Nicolas cleared his throat. "Are we, are we all friends again? Please?" He smoothed one of his long brown hands over the bark. "There's so much to be done, and all of it so dark and sad. Best to do it quickly, before we drown in sorrow."

Dora Rose dropped him a curtsy and included me in it with a dip of her chin. My heart leapt in my chest. Other parts of me leapt, too, but I won't get into that.

"At your convenience, Master Piper," said she. "Maurice."

"Dark work? Sad?" I cried. "No such thing! Say, rather, a lark! The old plague days of Doornwold'll be nothing to it! My Folk scurry at the chance to run amuck. If you hadn't've happened along, Dora Rose, with your great tragedy and all, I'd've had to invent an excuse to misbehave. Of such stuff is drama made! Come on, you two. I have a plan."

We threw Nicolas's old tattercoat over Dora Rose's silver gown and urchined up her face with mud. I stuffed her pale-as-lace hair under my wharf boy's cap and didn't even mind when she turned and pinched me for pawing at her too ardently. Me in the lead, Dora Rose behind, Nicolas bringing up the rear, we marched into Amandale like three mortal-born bumpkins off for a weekend in the big city.

Dwelling by the Hill, Nicolas had lived as near neighbor to Amandale for I don't know how many years. But he was so often gone on his tours, in cities under the Hill that made even the Queen's City seem a hermit's hovel, that he wandered now through Amandale's busy gates with widening and wonder-bright eyes. His head swiveled like it sat on an owl's neck. The woebegone down-bend of his lips began a slow, gladdening, upward trend that was heartbreaking to watch. So I stole only backward glances, sidelong like.

"Maurice." He hurried to my side as we passed a haberdashery.

"Yes, Nicolas?"

"You really live here?"

"All my life."

"Does it," he stooped to speak directly in my ear, "does it ever stop *singing*?"

I grinned over at Dora Rose, who turned her face away to smile. "If by *singing* you mean *stinking*, then no. This is a typical day in Amandale, my friend. A symphony of odors!" He looked so puzzled that I took pity and explained, "According to the princess over there, I'm one who can only ever hear music through my nose."

"Ah!" Nicolas's black eyes beamed. "I see. Yes! You're a synesthete!"

Before I could reply, a fire-spinner out front of Cobblersawl's Cakes and Comfits caught his eye, and Nicolas stopped walking to burst into wild applause. The fire-spinner grinned and embarked upon a particularly intricate pattern of choreography.

No one was exempt, I realized. Not me, and not the pretty fire-spinner. Not even Dora Rose. Plainly it was impossible to keep from smiling at Nicolas when Nicolas was pleased about something. I nudged Dora Rose.

"Hear that, Ladybird? I'm a synesthete!"

"Maurice, if you ever met a synesthete, you'd probably try to eat it."

"Probably. Would it look anything like you?"

Dora Rose did not dignify this with a response but whacked the back of my head, and her tiny smile twisted into something perilously close to a grin. We ducked into the bakery, pulling Nicolas after us so he wouldn't start piping along to the fire-spinner's sequences, sending her off to an early death by flaming poi.

One of the elder Cobblersawl children—Ilse, her name was—stood at the bread counter, looking bored but dutiful. A softhearted lass, our Ilse. Good for a scrap of cheese on occasion. Not above saving a poor rodent if said rodent happened to be trapped under her big brother's boot. She'd not recognize me in this shape, of course, but she might have a friendly feeling for me if I swaggered up to her with a sparkle in my beady little eyes and greeted her with a wheedling, "Hallo, Miss . . ."

She frowned. "No handouts. Store policy."

"No, you misunderstand. We're looking for . . . for Froggit? Young Master Froggit Cobblersawl? We have business with him." Dora Rose poked me between my shoulder blades. Her nails were as sharp as mine. "If you please?" I squeaked.

Ilse's frown deepened to a scowl. "Froggit's sick."

I bet he was. I'd be sick, too, if I'd swallowed half my tongue.

"Sick of . . . politics maybe?" I waggled my eyebrows.

A smell came off the girl like vaporized cheddar. Fear. Sweaty, stinky, delicious fear.

"If you're from the Mayor," Ilse whispered, "tell her that Mama spanked Froggit for not behaving as he ought. We know we're beholden. We know we owe the fancy new shop to her. And—and our arrangement to provide daily bread to the houses on Merchant Prince Row is entirely due her benevolence. Please, Papa cried so hard when he heard how Froggit failed us. We were so proud when his name came up in the Swan Hunter lottery. Really, it's such an honor, we *know* it's an honor, to work for the Mayor on our very own orchestra, but—it's just he's so young. He didn't understand. Didn't know, didn't know better. But I'm to take his place next hunt. I will be the twentieth hunter. I will do what he couldn't. I promise." She unfisted her hands and opened both palms in supplication. "Please don't take him to prison. Don't disappear him like you did . . ."

She swallowed whatever she was about to say when Dora Rose stepped forward. Removing my cap, she shook out that uncanny hair of hers and held Ilse's gaze. Silence swamped the bakery as Ilse realized we weren't Ulia Gol's not-so-secret police.

"I want to thank him," Dora Rose said. "That is all. The last swan they killed was my sister."

"Oh," Ilse whimpered. "Oh, you shouldn't be here. You really shouldn't be here."

"Please," said Dora Rose.

Her shaking fingers glimmering by the light pouring off the swan girl's hair, Ilse pointed out a back door. We left the bakery as quickly as we could, not wanting to discomfit her further, or incite her to rouse the alarm.

The exit led into a private courtyard behind the bakery. Froggit was back by the whitewashed outhouse, idly sketching cartoons upon it with a stubby bit of charcoal. Most of these involved the Mayor and Hans in various states of decay, although in quite a few of them, the Swan Huntress Ocelot played a putrescent role. Froggit's shoulder blades scrunched when our shadows fell over him, but he did not turn around.

I opened my mouth to speak, but it was Nicolas who dropped to the ground at Froggit's side, crossing his legs like a fortune-teller and studying the outhouse wall with rapt interest.

"But this is extraordinary! It must be preserved! They will have to remove this entire apparatus to a museum. What, in the meantime, is to be done about waterproofing?" Nicolas examined the art in minute detail, his nose almost touching the graffitied boards. "What to do, what to do," he muttered.

Taking his charcoal stub, Froggit scrawled, "BURN IT!" in childish writing over his latest cartoon. Then he scowled at Nicolas, who widened his eyes at him. Nicolas began nodding, at first slowly, then with increasing vigor.

"Oh, yes! Indeed! Yes, of course! Art is best when ephemeral, don't you think? How your admirers will mourn its destruction. How they will paint their faces with the ashes of your art. And you will stand so"—Nicolas hopped up to demonstrate—"arms crossed, with your glare that is like the glare of a tiger, and they will sob and wail and beg you to draw again—*just once more, please, Master Froggit*—but you shall break your charcoal and their hearts in one snap. Yes! You will take all this beauty from them, as they have taken your tongue. I see. It is stunning. I salute you."

So saying, Nicolas drew out his pipe and began a dirge.

When he finished many minutes later, me and Dora Rose collapsed on the ground, sweating from the excruciatingly stately waltz we'd endured together. Well, *she'd* endured. I rather enjoyed it, despite never having waltzed in my life, least of all in a minor key.

Froggit himself, who much to his consternation had started waltzing with an old rake, let it fall against the outhouse wall and eyeballed the lot of us with keen curiosity and not a little apprehension. What did he see when he looked at us, this little boy without a tongue?

Nicolas sat in the mud again. This made Froggit, still standing, the taller of the two, and Nicolas gazed up at him with childlike eyes.

"Don't be afraid. It's my silver pipe. Magic, you see. Given me by Her Gracious Majesty, Empress of Faerie, Queen of the Realms Beneath the Hill. It imparts upon me power over the creatures of land, sea, air, and fire. Folk and fixed, and everything between. But when I pass into the Hill, my pipe has no power. Under the Hill it is not silver but bone that sings to the wild blood of the Faerieborn. Had I a bone pipe, I might dance them all to their deaths, those Shining Ones who cannot die. But I have no pipe of bone. Just this."

Nicolas's face took on a taut look. Almost, I thought, one of unbearable longing. His knuckles whitened on his pipe. Then he shook himself and dredged up a smile from unfathomable depths, though it was a remote, pathetic, tremulous thread of a thing.

"But here, above the Hill," he continued as if he'd never paused, "it is silver that ensorcels. Silver that enspells. I could pipe my friend the rat Maurice into the Drukkamag River and drown him. See that Swan Princess over there? Her I could pirouette right off a cliff, and not even her swanskin wings could save her. You, little boy, I could jig you up onto a rooftop and thence into the sky, whence you'd fall, fall, fall. But I will not!" Nicolas added as Froggit's round brown eyes flashed wider. "Destroy an artist such as yourself? Shame on me! How could I even think it? I have the greatest respect for you, Master Froggit!"

But Froggit, after that momentary alarm, seemed unafraid. In fact, he began to look envious. He pointed first to the silver pipe, then to his charcoal caricature of Mayor Ulia Gol, dripping gore and missing a few key limbs.

His wide mouth once more woebegone, Nicolas burst out, "Oh, but she is wicked! Wicked! She has an ogre's heart and a giant's greed. She is a monster, and we must rid this world of monsters. For what she did to the juniper tree, that alone deserves a pair of iron shoes baked oven-bright, and four and twenty blackbirds to pluck out her eyes. But for what she has done to *you* . . . and to the swans and the foxes and the trout. Oh! I would break my pipe upon her throat if I . . . But."

Drawing a shaky breath, Nicolas hid his thin face in rigid hands.

"No. I shall not be called upon for that. Not this time. Not today. No. No, Nicolas, you may stay your hand and keep to your music for now. Maurice the Incomparable has a plan. The role of Nicolas promises to be quite small this time. Just a song. Just the right little song. Or the wrong one. The wrongest song of all."

Froggit sat beside Nicolas and touched a trembling hand to his shoulder. Nicolas didn't take his hands from his face, but suddenly bright black eyes peeped between his fingers.

"Your part is bigger than mine, Master Froggit. If you'll play it. Throw in with us. You have no tongue to speak, but you have hands to help, and we'd be proud to have your help."

Froggit stared. At the huddled Piper. At proud Dora Rose standing like a silver statue in the small courtyard. At my grin that had the promise of carnage behind it. Back to Nicolas, whose hands fell away to reveal an expression so careworn and sorrowful and resolute that it terrified me, who knew what it meant. I rubbed my hands together, licking my lips. The boy took up his charcoal stub and wrote two words on the outhouse boards.

One was "Greenpea." The other "Possum."

I stepped in, before Nicolas asked if this were a recipe for the boy's favorite stew and spun off on another tangent about the virtues of Faerie spices versus mortal.

"Of course your friends are invited, Master Froggit!" I said. "Couldn't do it without 'em! You three and we three, all together now." I hooked Dora Rose's elbow and drew her nearer. She complied, but not without a light kick to my ankle. "Your job today, Master Froggit, is to take our resident Swan Princess around to meet Miss Greenpea and Miss Possum. They've sacrificed a pair of legs and eyes between them, haven't they, by refusing to help murder swans?"

Froggit nodded, his soft jaw clenching. What with the swelling of his truncated tongue, that must've meant a whopping mouthful of pain. Boy should've been born a rat!

"You're just what we need. Old enough to know the town, young enough to be ignored. Embittered, battle-scarred, ready for war. Listen up, Master Froggit. You and your friends and Dora Rose are gonna be the ones to, uh, *liberate* those pretty bone instruments from Orchestra Hall. You must do this, and you must return them to the Maze Wood tonight. It all has to be timed perfectly. Dora Rose will tell you why. Can you do this thing?"

Dora Rose put her hand on Froggit's shoulder when his panicked glance streaked to her. "Fear not, princeling," she said, as though soothing a cygnet. "Have not we wings and wits enough between us?"

Before the kid could lose his nerve, I sped on, "Me and Nicolas will be the distraction. We're gonna set Amandale hopping, starting this afternoon. No one will have time to sniff you out, I promise—no matter what shenanigans you four get up to. We'll meet you back in the Maze Wood in three nights' time, with the rest of . . . of what we need. You know where. The juniper tree."

Froggit nodded. His brown eyes filled with tears, but they did not fall. I looked at Dora Rose, who was twisting her hair back up under my wharf boy's cap and refreshing the dirt on her face.

"Help her," I told the kid, too quietly for Dora Rose to overhear. "She'll need you. Tonight most of all."

Froggit watched my face a moment more, then nodded with firm decision. His excitement smelled like ozone. He shoved his charcoal stub into his pocket and stood up, wiping his palms on his cutoff trousers. Solemnly, he offered his hand to Nicolas, who clasped it in both of his, then transferred it over to Dora Rose. She smiled down, and Froggit's gaze on her became worshipful, if worship could hold such bitter regret. I knew that look.

Stupid to be jealous of a tongueless, tousled, char-smudged bed wetter. Bah.

"Take care of each other," Nicolas admonished them.

And so, that Cobblersawl kid and my friend the Swan Princess-in-disguise made their way down a dark alley that teemed with the sort of refuse I relished. Until they disappeared from my sight.

"Shall we?" Nicolas's voice was soft and very dreadful behind me.

"Play on, Pied Piper," said I.

Nicolas set silver lip to scarlet mouth and commenced the next phase of our plan.

Have you ever seen a rat in a waste heap? The rustle of him, the nibble, the nestle, the scrabble and scrape. How he leaps, leaps straight up as if jerked by a string from the fathoms of that stinking stuff, should a clamor startle him? How swift he is. How slinking sly. Faster than a city hawk who makes her aerie in the clock towers and her dinner of diseased pigeons. A brief bolt of furry black lightning he is, with onyx for eyes and tiny red rubies for pupils.

Now imagine this natty rat, this rattiest of rats, with his broken tail, his chewed-looking fur, imagine him as he often is, with a scrap of something vile in his mouth, imagine him right in front of you, sitting on your pillow and watching you unblinkingly as you yawn yourself awake in the morning.

Imagine him.

Then multiply him.

There is a reason more than one of us is called a swarm.

Amandale, there will be no Swan Hunt for you today.

Nor will bread be baked, nor cakes be made, nor cookies, biscuits, doughnuts, nor pies. The smell arising from your ovens, Amandale, is singed fur and seared rodent meat, and all your dainty and delectable desserts bear teeth marks.

No schools remain in session. What teacher can pontificate on topics lofty and low when rats sit upon her erasers, scratch inside the stiff desks, run to and from the windowsills, and chew through whole textbooks in their hunger for equations, for history, for language and binding glue and that lovely woody wood pulp as soft and sweet as rose petals?

The blacksmith's hand is swollen from the bite he received last night as he reached for the bellows to stoke his fire. The apple seller has fled from fear of what he found in his apple barrels. The basket maker burns in his bed with fever from an infected breakfast he bolted without noticing it had been shared already by the fine fellows squatting in his larder. I'm afraid the poor chimney sweep is scarred for life. And no, I don't mean that metaphorically.

The Wheelbarrow Mollys and the Guild of Bricklayers are out in the streets with their traps and their terriers. Poor fools, the futility! They might get a few dozen of us, maybe a few hundred. They might celebrate their catch that night with ales all around. But what's a few? We are thousands. Tens of thousands. Millions. The masses. We have come from our hidey-holes and haystacks. We are out in force.

So what if the local butcher flaunts his heap of fresh sausage stuffing, product of today's rat-catching frenzy? We're not above eating our own when we taste as good as sausages! And we're not above petty vengeance, either. You, smug butcher, you won't sleep cold tonight. No, sir. You'll sleep enfolded in the living fur of my family, Folk and fixed alike, united, yellow of tooth and spry of whisker. Resolved.

In the midst of mothers bellowing at those of us sniffing bassinets and cradles, of fathers shrieking like speared boars as they step into boots that bite back, of merchants sobbing and dairymaids cursing and monks chanting prayers of exorcism, there is a softer sound, too, all around. A sound only we rats can hear.

Music.

It is the Pied Piper, and he plays for us.

He's there in a corner, one rat on his boot-top, two in his pocket. That's me right there, scurrying and jiving all up and down his arms and shoulders, like a nervous mama backstage of her darling's first ballet recital. Oh, this is first-rate. This is drama! And I am the director.

Amandale, you do not see Nicolas, the red in his black hair smoldering like live embers in a bed of coal, his black eyes downcast and dreamy, his one rat-free boot tapping time. He's keeping us busy, keeping us brave, making us hop and heave to.

Amandale, you do not see Nicolas, playing his song, doing his best to destroy you for a day.

Or even for three.

On the second Night of the Rats (as the citizens of Amandale called our little display), Mayor Ulia Gol summoned a town meeting in Orchestra Hall.

Sometime after lunch that day, I'd fleshed back into man-shape, with two big plugs of cotton batting in my ears. This made me effectively deaf, but at least I wasn't dancing. The point was to stick as close to Ulia Gol as possible without ending up in a rat catcher's burlap bag. To that end I entrenched myself in the growing mob outside the mayoral mansion and slouched there for hours till my shadow stretched like a giant from the skylands. As reward for my patience, I witnessed the moment Henchman Hans brought Ulia Gol news that the rat infestation had destroyed her bone orchestra.

"All that's left, Madame Mayor," moaned poor Hans (I'm not great at reading lips, but I got the gist), "is bits of bone and a few snarls of black hair."

Ulia Gol's florid face went as putridly pink as her wig. Her shout was so loud I heard her through the cotton batting all the way to my metatarsals. "Town meeting—tonight—eight o' clock—Orchestra Hall—OR ELSE!"

I ran back to report to Nicolas, who laughed around the lip of his pipe. Slapping my forehead, I cried, "Clever, clever! Why didn't I think of it? Manufacture false evidence; blame the rats! It'll keep thief-hunters out of the Maze Wood for sure. Did you think that up, Nicolas?"

Pink-cheeked, Nicolas shook his head and kept playing.

"Wasn't Dora Rose," I mused. "She'd view leaving fragments behind as sacrilege. One of our stalwart recruits, then. Froggit? He's great, but he's kind of young for that level of . . . Or, I suppose it could've been Possum's idea. Don't know her so well. Always thought her one of your sweet, quiet types, Possum." Readjusting my cotton batting, I mulled on the puzzle before settling on my final hypothesis.

"Greenpea. Greenpea, I'll grant you, has the brain for such a scheme. What a firecracker! Back when the Swan Hunt started, she was the most vocal opposition in town. Has a kindness for all animals, does Greenpea. Nearly took Hans's head off with the shovel when he tried to make her dig up that first murdered cob. Ulia Gol took it back from her, though. Broke both her legs so bad the surgeon had to cut 'em off at the knee. Fear of festering, you see. Least, that's what he said. But he's Ulia Gol's creature, badly gone as Hans. Yup, I'll bet the hair and bone were Greenpea's notion. Little minx. I'd like to take her paw and give it a shake. Oh, but hey, Nicolas! We'd best get a move on. You haven't eaten all day, and the sun's nearly down. Mayor Ulia Gol's called a town meeting in a few hours regarding the rat conundrum. I'll fur down and find a bench to hide under. That way I'll be ready for you."

Slipping the silver pipe under his patched tunic, Nicolas advised, "Don't get stomped."

By this time, the rats of Amandale were in such a frenzy it wouldn't much matter if he stopped playing for an hour or two. Most of the Folk rats would come to their senses and slip out of town while the getting was good. Likely they'd spend the next few weeks with wax stoppers in their ears and a great distaste for music of any kind. But they'd be back. By and by, they'd all come back.

The fixed rats, now . . . Smart beasts they may be, those inferior little cousins of mine, but their brains have only ever been the size of peas. Good thing they reproduce quickly's all I'm saying. 'Cause for the sake of drama and Dora Rose—they are going down.

The Mayor of Amandale began, "This meeting is now in—" when an angry mother shot to her feet and shouted over her words. It was the chandler, wailing toddler held high overhead like a trophy or oblation.

"Look at my Ruby! Look at her! See that bite on her face? That'll mark her the rest of her natural life."

"Won't be too long," observed a rouged bawd. "Wounds like that go bad as runoff from a graveyard."

The blacksmith added, "That's if the rats don't eat her alive first."

The noise in Orchestra Hall surged. A large, high-ceilinged chamber it was, crammed with padded benches and paneled in mahogany. Front and center on the raised stage stood Mayor Ulia Gol, eyes squinting redly as she gaveled the gathering to order.

"Friends! Friends!" Despite the red look in her eyes, her voice held that hint of laughter that made people love her. "Our situation is dire, yes. We are all distressed, yes. But I must beg you now, each and every one of you, to take a deep breath."

She demonstrated.

Enchantment in the expansion and recession of her bosom. Sorcery in her benevolent smile. Hypnosis in the red beam of her eye, pulsing like a beating heart. The crowd calmed. Began to breathe. From my place beneath the bench, I twitched my fine whiskers. Ulia Gol was by far her truer self in the Heart Glade, terrorizing the children of Amandale into murdering Swan Folk. This reassuring woman was hardly believable. A stage mirage. The perfect politician.

"There," cooed the Mayor, looking downright dotingly upon her constituents, "that's right. Tranquility in the face of disaster is our civic duty. Now, in order to formulate appropriate measures against this rodent incursion as well as set in motion plans for the recovery of our wounded"—she ticked off items on her fingers—"and award monetary restitution to the hardest-hit property owners, we must keep our heads. I am willing to work with you. *For* you. That's why you elected me!"

Cool as an ogre picking her teeth with your pinkie finger. No plan of mine could stand long against a brainstorming session spearheaded by Ulia Gol at her glamoursome best. But I had a plan. And she didn't know about it. So I was still a step ahead.

Certain human responses can trump even an ogre's fell enchantments, no matter how deftly she piles on those magical soporific agents. It was now or never. Taking a deep breath of my own, I darted up the nearest trouser leg—

And bit.

The scream was all I ever hoped a scream would be.

Benches upturned. Ladies threw their skirts over their heads. The man I'd trespassed upon kicked a wall, trying to shake me out of his pants. I slid and skittered and finally flew across the room. Something like or near or in my rib cage broke, because all of a sudden the simple act of gasping became a pain in my *everything*.

Couldn't breathe. Couldn't breathe. Couldn't . . .

There came a wash of sound. Scarlet pain turned silver. My world became a dream of feathers. I saw Dora Rose, all downed up in swanskin, swimming across Lake Serenus. Ducking her long, long neck beneath the waves. Disappearing. Emerging as a woman, silver and naked-pale, with all her long hair gleaming down. She could dance atop the waves in this form, barefoot and unsinkable, a star of the Lake Serenus Water Ballet.

I came to myself curled in the center of the Pied Piper's palm. He had the silver pipe in his other hand as if he'd just been playing it. Orchestra Hall had fallen silent.

This was Nicolas as I'd never seen him. This was Nicolas of the Realms Beneath the Hill. His motley rags seemed grander the way he wore them than Ulia Gol's black satin robes with the big pink toggles and purple flounce. His hair was like the flint-and-fire crown of some Netherworld King. Once while drunk on Faerie ale he'd told me—in strictest confidence, of course—that since childhood the Faerie Queen had called him "Beautiful Nicolas" and seated him at her right hand during her Midnight Revels. I'd snorted to hear that, replying, "Yeah, right. *Your* ugly mug?" which made him laugh and laugh. I'd been dead serious, though; I know what beautiful looks like, and its name is *Dora Rose*, not *Nicolas*. But now I could see how the Faerie Queen might just have a point. So. Yeah. Kudos to her. I suppose.

Nicolas's smile flashed from his dark face like the lamp of a lighthouse. His black eyes flickered with a fiendish inner fire.

"Ladies and Gentlemen of Amandale!" Sweeping himself into a bow, he managed to make both pipe and rat natural parts of his elegance, as if we stood proxy for the royal scepter and orb he'd misplaced.

"Having had word of your problem, I came straightway to help. We are neighbors of sorts; I live in the lee of the Hill outside your lovely town. You may have heard my name." Nicolas paused, just long enough. Impeccable timing. "I am the Pied Piper. I propose to pipe your rats away."

So saying, he set me on the floor and brought up his pipe again.

I danced—but it was damned difficult. Something sharp inside me poked other, softer parts of me. I feared the coppery wetness foaming the corners of my mouth meant nothing salubrious for my immediate future. Still, I danced. How could I help it? He played for me.

Nicolas, who at his worst was so sensitive he often achieved what seemed a kind of feverish telepathy, was eerily attuned to my pain. His song shifted, ever so slightly. Something in my rib cage clicked. He played a song not only for me but for my bones as well. And my bones danced back into place.

Burning, burning.

Silver swanfire starfall burning.

Jagged edges knitted. Bones snapped back together. Still I danced. And inside me, his music danced, too, healing up my hurts.

Nicolas took his mouth from the pipe. "I am willing, good Citizens of Amandale, to help you. As you see, rats respond to my music. I can make them do what I wish! Or what you wish, as the case may be."

On cue, released from his spell, I made a beeline for a crack in the wall. A sharp note from his pipe brought me up short, flipped me over, and sent me running back in the other direction. I can't sweat, but I did feel the blood expanding my tail as my panicked body heated up.

"For free?" called the chandler, whose wounded babe had finally stopped wailing for fascination of Nicolas's pipe.

"For neighborliness?" cackled the bawd.

Nicolas scooped me up off the floor. He made it look like another bow. "Alas, no. Behold me in my rags; I cannot afford charity. But for a token fee only, I will do this for you!"

Me he dangled by the engorged tail. *Them* he held by the balls. Oh, he had them. Well-palmed and squeezing. (Hoo-boy, did that bring back a great memory! There'd been this saucy rat girl named Melanie a few years back, and did she ever know how to do things with her paws . . .)

Mayor Ulia Gol slinked out from behind her podium. Bright-eyed and treacherous and curious as a marten in a chicken hut, she toyed with her gavel. Her countenance was welcoming, even coquettish.

"A Hero from the Hill!" She laughed her deep laughter that brought voters to the ballot box by the hordes. "Come to rescue our troubled Amandale in its time of need."

"Just a musician, Madame Mayor." Nicolas's dire and delicate voice was pitched to warm the cockles and slicken the thighs. "But better than average perhaps—at least where poor, dumb animals are concerned."

"And, of course, musicians must be paid!" Her lip curled.

"Exterminators too."

Ulia Gol had reached him. She walked right up close and personal, right to his face, and inhaled deeply. She could smell the Hill on him, I knew, and those tantalizing hints of Folk in his blood, and the long-lost echoes of the mortal he may once have been. The red glint in her eye deepened drunkenly. His scent was almost too much for her. Over there in his corner of the hall, Hans watched the whole scene, green to the gills with jealousy. It clashed with his second-best suit.

Ulia Gol's expression slid from one of euphoria to that of distaste as she remembered me. Crouched in Nicolas's open hand, I hunkered as small as I could make myself. I was not a very big rat. And she did have a gavel, you see, for all she was letting it swing from the tips of her fingers.

In a velveted boom that carried her words to the far end of the hall, she asked, "What is your price, my precious piper?"

"I take my pay in coin, Madame Mayor."

I swear they heard his whisper all across Amandale that night. Nicolas had a whisper like a kiss, a whisper that could reach out and ring the bells of Brotquen Cathedral so sweetly.

"One thousand gold canaries upon completion of the job. If you choose, you may pay me in silver nightingales, though I fear the tripled weight would prove unwieldy. For this reason I cannot accept smaller coin. No bronze wrens or copper robins; such currency is too much for me to shoulder easily."

Silence. As if his whisper had sucked the breath right from the room. The chandler's baby hiccupped.

"Paid on completion, you say." Ulia Gol pondered, stepping back from him. "And by what measurement, pray, do we assess completion? When the last rat drowns in the Drukkamag River?"

Nicolas bowed once more, more gracefully than ever before. "Whatever terms you set, Madame Mayor, I will abide by them."

Ulia Gol grinned. Oh, she had a handsome, roguish grin. I think I peed a little in Nicolas's palm. "It cost our town less to build Brotquen Cathedral—and that was three hundred years of inflation ago. Why don't you take *that* instead, my sweet-lipped swindler?"

"Alas, ma'am!" Nicolas shook his red-and-black head in sorrow. "While I am certain that yours is a fine cathedral, I make my living on my feet. I take for payment only what I can trundle away with me. As I stated, it must be gold or silver. Perhaps in a small leather chest or sack that I might lift upon my shoulder?"

He tapped the Mayor's shoulder with his silver pipe, drawing a lazy sigil there. Curse or caress, who could say? Ulia Gol shivered, euphoria once again briefly blanking out her cunning.

"One thousand bright canaries," she laughed at him, "singing in a single chest! Should not they be in a cage instead, my mercenary minstrel?"

Nicolas twinkled a wink her way. "Nay," said he, husking low his voice for her ears (and mine) alone. His next sentence fair glittered with the full formality of the Faerie court. Had I any choice when hearing it, I'd've bolted right then and there and never come out from my hole till my whiskers turned gray.

"But perhaps," he continued, "*thou* shouldst be, thou pink-plumed eyas. A cage equipped with manacles of silver and gilded bullwhips and all manner of bejeweled barbs and abuses for such a wicked lady-hawk as thee."

Pleased with the impudent promise in his eyes, and pink as her candy-colored wig, Ulia Gol spun around. The tassel on her black satin cap hopped like a cottontail in a clover patch. She addressed the hall.

"The Pied Piper has come to drive our rats away. He is charging," she threw the room a grin as extravagant as confetti, "an unconscionable fee to do so. But, my friends, our coffers will manage. What cost peace? What cost health? What cost the lives of our children? Yes, we shall have to tighten our belts this winter. What of that?" Her voice crescendoed. Her arms spread wide. "Citizens, if we do not accept his assistance now, who knows if we will even live to see the winter?"

A wall of muttering rose up against the tide of her questions. Some dissent. Some uneasy agreement. Ulia Gol took another reluctant step away from Nicolas and waded into the crowd. She worked it, touching hands, stroking baby curls, enhancing her influence as she gazed deeply into deeply worried eyes and murmured spells and assurances. Shortly, and without any overt effort, she appeared behind the podium like she'd grown there.

"Friends," she addressed them throbbingly, "already the rats are nibbling at our stores, our infants, the foundations of our houses. Recall how rats carry plague. Do you want Amandale to face the danger that leveled Doornwold fifteen years ago? We shall put it to the vote! I ask you to consider this—extreme, yes, but remember, we only need pay *if* it's effective!—solution. All in favor of the Pied Piper, say aye!"

The roar the crowd returned was deafening. The overtones were especially harsh, that particular brassy hysteria of a mob miles past the point of reasoning with. I wished I had my earplugs back. Ulia Gol did not bother to invite debate from naysayers. Their protestations were drowned out, anyway. But I could see Hans over there making note of those who shook their heads or frowned. My guess was that they'd be receiving visitors later. Probably in the dead of night.

From her place on the stage, Ulia Gol beamed upon her townspeople. But like magnet to metal, her gaze clicked back to Nicolas. She studied him with flagrant lust, and he returned her scrutiny with the scorching intensity the raven has for the hawk. He stood so still that even I, whom he held in his hand, could not feel him breathing.

"Master Piper!"

"Madame Mayor?"

"When will you begin?"

"Tomorrow at dawn." This time, Nicolas directed his diffident smile to the room at large. "I need my sleep tonight. It is quite a long song, the one that calls the rats to the waterside and makes the thought of drowning there seem so beautiful."

"Rest is all well and good, Master Piper. But first you must dine with me."

"Your pardon, Madame Mayor, but I must fast before such work as I will do tomorrow."

Her fists clenched on the edges of the podium. She leaned in. "Then a drink, perhaps. The mayoral mansion is well stocked."

Nicolas bowed. "Ma'am, I must abstain."

I wouldn't say that the look Ulia Gol gave him was a pout, exactly. More like, if Nicolas's face had been within range of her teeth, she'd have torn it off. He had toyed with her, keyed her to the pitch of his choosing, and now he would not play her like a pipe—nor let *her* play *his*. Pipe, I mean. Ahem.

His short bow and quick exit thwarted any scheme she might have improvised to keep him there. Outside in the cooling darkness, cradling me close to his chest, Nicolas turned sharply into the nearest alleyway. Stumbling on a pile of refuse, he set me down atop it, and promptly projectile-vomited all over the wall.

I'd never seen that much chunk come out of an undrunk person. Fleshing myself back to man-shape, I clasped my hands behind me and watched him. I had to curb my urge to applaud.

"Wow, Nicolas! Is that nerves, or did you eat a bad sausage for dinner?" I whistled. "I thought you couldn't talk to women, you Foxface, you! But you were downright debonair. If the Mayor'd been a rat girl, her ears would've been vibrating like a tuning fork!"

Wiping his mouth on his hand, Nicolas croaked, "She is not a woman. She is a monster. I spoke to her as I speak to other monsters I have known. It is poison to speak so, Maurice—but death to do aught else. But, oh, it hurts, Maurice. It hurts to breathe the same air she breathes. It hurts to watch her courtiers—"

"Constituents," I corrected, wondering whose face he'd seen imposed upon Ulia Gol's. If I were a betting rat, I'd say the answer rhymed with "Airy Fleen."

"So corrupted . . . Necrotic! As rotten as that poor rat-bitten babe shall be in a few days. They—these thinking people, people like you or me"—I decided not to challenge this—"they *all* agreed to the genocide. They *agreed* to make the orchestra of murdered swans, to abuse the god in the juniper tree. They traded their souls to a monster, and for what? Free music? Worse, worse—they set their children to serve her. Their babies, Maurice! Gone bad like the rest of them. Maurice, had I the tinder, I would burn Amandale to the ground!"

Nicolas was sobbing again. I sighed. Poor man. Or whatever he was.

I set my hand upon his tousled head. His hair was slick with sweat. "Aw, Nicolas. Aw, now. Don't worry. We'll get 'em. There's worse ways to punish people than setting fire to their houses. Hellfowl, we did it one way today, and by nightfall tomorrow, we'll have done another! So smile! Everything's going steamingly!"

Twin ponds of tears brimmed, spilled, blinked up at me.

"Don't you mean swimmingly?" Nicolas gasped, sighing down his sobs.

"I will soon, you don't quit your bawling. Hey, Nico, come on!" I clucked my tongue. "Dry up, will ya? You're not supposed to drown me till dawn!"

I could always make Nicolas laugh.

In a career so checkered that two old men could've played board games on it, I've come near death four times. Count 'em, four. Now if we're talking about coming within a cat-calling or even a spitting distance from death, I'd say the number's more like "gazillions of times," but I don't number 'em as "near"-death experiences till I'm counting the coronal sutures on the Reaper of Rodents's long-toothed skull.

The first time I almost died, it was my fault. It all had to do with being thirteen and drunk on despair and voluntarily wandering into a rat-baiting arena because life isn't worth living if a Swan Princess won't be your girlfriend. Embarrassing.

The second time was due to a frisky rat lass named Molly. She, uh, used a little too much teeth in the, you know, act. Bled a lot. Worth it, though.

Third? Peanut butter.

Fourth . . . one of the elder Cobblersawl boys and his brand new birthday knife.

But I have never been so near death as that day Nicolas drowned me in the Drukkamag River.

He'd begged me not to hear him. That morning, just before dawn, he'd said, "Maurice, Maurice. Will you not stop up your ears and go to the Maze Wood and wait this day out?"

"No, Nicolas," said I, affronted. "What, and give a bunch of poor fixed rats the glory of dying for Dora Rose? This is *my* end. My story. I've waited my whole life for a chance like this. My Folk will write a drama of this day, and the title of that play shall be *Maurice the Incomparable!*"

Nicolas ducked the grand sweep of my hand. "You cannot really mean to drown, Maurice. You'll never know how the end of your drama plays out. What if we need you again, and you are dead and useless? What if . . . what if *she* needs you?"

I clapped his back. "She never did before, Nicolas my friend. That's why I love the girl. Oh, and after I die today, do something for me, would you? You tell Dora Rose that she really missed out on the whole cross-species experimentation thing. You just tell her that. I want her to regret me the rest of her life. I want the last verse of her swan song to be my name. *Maurice the Incomparable!*"

Nicolas ducked again, looking dubious and promising nothing. But I knew he would try. That's what friends did, and he was the best.

You may wonder—if you're not Folk, that is—how I could so cavalierly condemn thousands of my lesser cousins, not to mention my own august person, of whom I have a high (you might even say "the highest") regard—to a watery grave. Who died and made me arbiter of a whole pestilential population's fate? How could I stand there, stroking my whiskers, and volunteer all those lives (and mine) to meet our soggy end at the Pied Piper's playing?

I could sum it up in one word.

Drama.

I speak for all rats when I speak for myself. We're alike in this. We'll do just about anything for drama. Or comedy, I guess; we're not particular. We're not above chewing the scenery for posterity. We must make our territorial mark (as it were) on the arts. The Swan Folk have their ballet. We rats, we have theatre. We pride ourselves on our productions. All the cities, high and low, that span this wide, wide world are our stage.

"No point putting it off," I told Nicolas, preparing to fur down. "Who's to say that if you don't drown me today, a huge storm won't come along and cause floods enough to drown me tomorrow? If *that* happens, I'll have died for nothing! Can any death be more boring?"

Nicolas frowned. "The weather augur under the Hill can predict the skies up to a month in exchange for one sip of your tears. She might be able to tell you if there will be rain . . ."

I cut him off. "What I'm saying is, you have to seize your death by the tail. Know it. Name it. My death," I said, "is you."

His laugh ghosted far above me as I disappeared into my other self.

"Hurricane Nicolas," he said. "The storm with no center."

Comes a song too high and sweet for dull human ears. Comes a song like the sound of a young kit tickled all to giggles. Like the sharp, lustful chirps of a doe in heat. Comes a song for rats to hear, and rats alone. A song that turns the wind to silver, a wind that brings along the tantalizing smell of cream.

Excuse me, make that "lots of cream."

A river of cream. A river that is so rich and thick and pure you could swim in it. You bet your little rat babies there's cream aplenty. Cream for you. Cream for your cousins, for your aunts and uncles, too. There's even cream for that ex-best buddy of yours who stole your first girlfriend along with the hunk of stinky cheese you'd saved up for your birthday.

Comes a song that sings of a river of cream. Cream enough for all.

Once I get there, ooh, baby, you betcha . . . I'm gonna find that saucy little doe who's chirping so shamelessly. I'm gonna find her, and then I'm gonna frisk the ever-living frolic out of her, nipping and mounting and slipping and licking the cream from her fur. Oh, yeah. Let's all go down to that river.

Now. Let's go now. I wanna swim.

Funny thing, drowning.

By the time I realized I didn't want it anymore, there was nothing I could do. I was well past the flailing stage, just tumbling along head over tail, somewhere in the sea-hungry currents of the Drukkamag. The only compass I could go by indicated one direction.

Deathward.

Rats are known swimmers. We can tread water for days, hold our breath for a quarter of an hour, dive deeply, survive in open sea. Why? Because our instinct for survival is unparalleled in the animal kingdom, that's why.

Once Nicolas's song started, I'd no *desire* to survive anymore. Until I did. I never said rats were consistent. We're entitled to an irregularity of opinion, just like mortals. Even waterlogged and tossed against Death's very cheese grater, we're allowed to change our minds.

And so, I did the only thing I had mind enough left to do. I fleshed back to man-shape.

The vigor of the transformation brought me, briefly, to the surface. I mouthed a lungful of air before the current sucked me back down into the river.

This is it, I thought. *Damn it, damn it, da—*

And then I slammed into a barrier both porous and implacable. Water rushed through it, yet I did not. I clung to it, finger and claw, and almost wept (which would have been entirely redundant at that point) when a great hook plunged at me from out of the blue, snagged me under the armpit, and hauled.

Air. Dazzle. Dry land.

I was deposited onto the stony slime of a riverbank. Someone hastily threw a blanket over my collapse. It smelled of sick dog and woodsmoke, but it was warm and dry. I think I heard my name, but I couldn't answer, sprawled and gasping, moving from blackout to dazzle and back again while voices filtered through my waterlogged ears.

Children's voices. Excited. Grim.

I considered opening my eyes. Got as far as blurred slittedness before my head started pounding.

We were under some sort of bridge. Nearby, nestled among boulders, a large fire burned. Over this there hung an enormous cauldron, redolent of boiling potatoes. A girl with a white rag tied over her eyes stirred it constantly. Miss Possum, or I missed my guess.

A bowl of her potato mash steamed near my elbow. I almost rolled over and dove face-first into it, but common sense kicked in. Didn't much fancy drowning on dry land so soon after my Drukkamag experience, so I lapped at the mash with more care, watching everything. Not far from Possum squatted Master Froggit, carefully separating a pile of dead rats from living as quickly as they came to him from the figure on the bridge. The dead he set aside on an enormous canvas. The living he consigned to blind Possum's care. She dried them and tried to feed them. There weren't many.

My slowly returning faculty for observation told me that our bold young recruits had strung a net across a narrowish neck of the Drukkamag, beneath one of the oldest footbridges of Amandale. They weighted the net with rocks. When the rats began to fetch up against it, Greenpea, seated on the edge of the bridge, leg stumps jutting out before her, fished them out again. She wielded the long pole that had hooked me out of the current.

For the first time since, oh, since I was about thirteen, I think, I started sobbing. Too much hanging out with Nicolas, I guess. Not eating properly. Overextending myself. That sort of thing. Prolonged close contact with Dora Rose had always had this effect on me.

I applied myself to my potatoes.

Once sated, making a toga of my dog blanket, I limped up to the bridge and gazed at the girl with the hooked pole.

"Mistress Greenpea."

"Hey." She glanced sidelong at me as I sat next to her. "Maurice the Incomparable, right?"

"Right-o." I warmed with pleasure. "Hand that thing over, will ya? My arms feel like noodles, but I reckon they can put in a shift for the glory of my species."

She grunted and handed her pole to me. "I don't see any more live ones. Not since you."

"Well, cheer up!" I adjured her. "We'll rise again. We're the hardiest thing since cockroaches, you know. Besides you humans, I mean. Roaches. Blech! An acquired taste, but they'll do for lean times. We used to dare each other to bite 'em in half when we were kits."

Greenpea, good girl, gagged only a bit, and didn't spew. I flopped a couple of corpses over to Froggit's canvas. "So. This whole net thing your idea, Miss Greenpea?"

She replied in a flat, unimpressed recitation, "Dora Rose said you'd try to drown yourself with the other rats. Said it would be *just like you,* and that we must save you if we could, because no way was she letting you stain her memory with your martyrdom."

I chuckled. "Said that, did she?"

"Something like that." Greenpea shrugged. Or maybe she was just rolling her stiff shoulders. "Before we . . . we hung her on that tree, I promised we'd do what we could for you. She seemed more comfortable, after." She wouldn't meet my eyes. "And then, when I saw all the other rats in the river, I tried to save them, too. Why should *you* be so special? But, then . . . So long as the Pied Piper played, even though he's still all the way back in Amandale, the rats I rescued wouldn't *stay* rescued. No sooner did we fish them out of the Drukkamag but they jumped back in again."

"Listen, kid." I returned her hard glare with a hard-eyed look of my own. "That was always the plan. You agreed to it. We all did."

The net bulged beneath us. Greenpea didn't back down, but the bridge of her nose scrunched beneath her spectacles. Behind thick lenses, those big gray eyes of hers widened in an effort not to cry. How old was she, anyway? Eleven? Twelve? One of the older girls in Ulia Gol's child army. Near Ocelot's age, I thought. Old enough at any rate to dry her tears by fury's fire. Which she did.

"It's horrible," Greenpea growled. "I hate that they had to die."

"Horrible, yeah," I agreed. "So's your legs. And Possum's eyes. And Froggit's tongue. And twenty dead swans. We're dealing with ogres here, not unicorns. Not the nicest monsters ever, ogres. Although, when you come right down to it, unicorns are nasty brutes. Total perverts. But anyway, don't fret, Miss Greenpea. We're gonna triumph, have no doubt. And even if we don't"—I started laughing, and it felt good, good, good to be alive—"even if we don't, it'll make a great tragedy, won't it? I love a play where all the characters die at the end."

* * *

The Pied Piper stood on the steps of Brotquen Cathedral, facing the Mayor of Amandale, who paraded herself a few steps above him. Hans and his handpicked horde of henchman waited nearby at the ready. Displayed at their feet was Froggit's macabre canvas of corpses. Most of the rats we'd simply let tumble free toward the sea when we cut the net, but we kept a few hundred back for a fly-flecked show-and-tell.

Nicolas's face was gray and drawn. His shoulders drooped. New lines had appeared on his forehead apparently overnight, and his mouth bowed like a willow branch. The pipe he no longer played glowed against his ragged chest like a solid piece of moonlight.

"As you see," he announced, "the rats of Amandale are drowned."

"Mmn," said Ulia Gol.

Most of the town—myself and my three comrades included—had gathered below the cathedral on Kirkja Street to gawk at the inconceivability of a thousand bright canaries stacked in a small leather chest right there in the open. The coins cast a golden glitter in that last lingering caress of sunset, and reflected onto the reverent faces of Amandale's children, who wore flowers in their hair and garlands 'round their necks. All of Amandale had been feasting and carousing since the rats began their death march at dawn that morning. Many of the older citizens now bore the flushed, aggressive sneers of the pot-valiant. In the yellow light of all that dying sun and leaping gold, they, too, looked new-minted, harder and glintier than they'd been before.

Nicolas did not notice them. His gaze never left Ulia Gol's shrewd face. She blocked his path to the gold. Hand over heart, he tried again.

"From the oldest albino to the nakedest newborn, Madame Mayor, the rats are drowned one and all. I have come for my payment."

But she did not move. "Your payment," she purred, "for what?"

Nicolas inhaled deeply. "I played my pipe, and I made them dance, and they danced themselves to drowning."

"Master Piper . . ." Ulia Gol oozed closer to him. I could see Nicolas stiffen in an effort not to back away.

I must say, the Mayor of Amandale had really gussied herself up for this occasion. Her pink wig was caught up in a sort of birdcage, all sorts of bells and beads hanging off it. The bone-paneled brocade of her crimson dress was stiff enough to stand up by itself, and I imagined it'd require three professional grave robbers with shovels to exhume her from her maquillage. She smelled overpoweringly of rotten pears and sour grapes. Did I say so before? At the risk of repeating myself, then: a magnificent woman, Ulia Gol.

"I watched you all day, Master Piper," she told Nicolas. "I strained my ears and listened closely. You put your pipe to your lips, all right, my pretty perjurer, and fabricated a haggard verisimilitude, but never a note did I hear you play."

"No," Nicolas agreed. "You would not have. I did not play for you, Ulia Gol."

"Prove it."

He pointed at the soggy canvas. "*There* is my proof."

Ulia Gol shrugged. Her stiff lace collar barely moved. "I see dead rats, certainly. But they might have come from anywhere, drowned in any number of ways. The Drukkamag River runs clean and clear, and Amandale is much as it ever was. Yes, there were rats. Now there are none." She opened her palms. "Who knows why? Perhaps they left us of their own accord."

Most of the crowd rustled in agreement. Sure, you could tell a few wanted to mutter in protest, but pressed tight their lips instead. Fresh black bruises adorned the faces of many of these. What were the odds that Ulia Gol's main detractors had been made an example of since last night's town meeting in Orchestra Hall? Not long, I'd say. Not long at all.

Ulia Gol swelled with the approval of her smitten constituents. Their adoration engorged her. Magic coursed through her. There was no mistaking what she was if you knew to look out for it. She stank like an ogre and grinned like a giant, and all that was missing was a beanstalk and a bone grinder and a basket for her bread. She loomed ever larger, swamping Nicolas in her shadow.

"Master Piper—if a Master indeed you are—you cannot prove that your alleged playing had aught to do with the rats' disappearance. Perhaps they decamped due to instinct. Migration. After all, their onset was as sudden as their egress. Perhaps you knew this. Did you really come to Amandale to aid us, or were you merely here by happentance? Seeing our dismay and our disarray, did you seek to take advantage of us, to ply your false trade, and cheat honest citizens of their hard-earned coin?"

The Mayor of Amandale was closer to the truth than she realized—ha! But that didn't worry me. Ulia Gol, after all, wasn't interested in truth. The only thing currently absorbing her was her intent to cheat the man who'd refused her bed the night before. It never occurred to her that the plague of rats was a misdirection of Amandale's attention during the theft of the bone orchestra. Okay, and part of its punishment for the murdered swans.

"Look at the color of his face," Greenpea whispered. "Is the piper all right?"

"Well . . . er." I squirmed. "It's Nicolas, right? He's never all the way all right."

But seeing his sick pallor, I wasn't sure Nicolas remembered that all this was part of a bigger plan. He looked near to swooning. Not good. We needed him for this next bit.

"Please," he whispered. "Please . . . just pay me and I'll be on my way."

"I am sorry, Master Piper." Ulia Gol laughed at him, her loud and lovely laugh. "But I cannot pay you all this gold for an enterprise you cannot prove you didn't engineer. In fact, you should consider yourself lucky if you leave Amandale in one piece."

The crowd around us tittered and growled. The children drew closer together, far less easy with the atmosphere of ballooning tension than were their parents. It was the adults whose eyes narrowed, whose flushed faces had empurpled and perspired until they looked all but smaller models of their Mayor. Nicolas took a step nearer Ulia Gol, though what it cost him, I do not know. He was a smallish man, and had to look up to her. Nicolas only sometimes *seemed* tall because of his slender build.

"Please," he begged her again. "Do not break your word. Have I not done as I promised?"

I leaned in for a closer look, brushing off Possum's anxious hand when it plucked my elbow.

"What's he doing?"

"Your guess is as good as mine, kid."

How Nicolas planned to act if Ulia Gol suddenly discovered within her scrumdiddlyumptious breast a thimble's worth of honor, compassion, or just plain sense, I do not know.

But she wouldn't. She was what she was, and behaved accordingly.

If she could but smell the furious sorrow on him, as I could . . . scent that destroying wind, the storm that had no center, the magic in his pipe that would dance us all to the grave, then perhaps even Ulia Gol might have flung herself to her knees and solicited his forgiveness. Did she think his music only worked on rats? That, because he trembled at her triumph and turned, in that uncertain twilight, an exquisite shade of green, he would not play a song Amandale would remember for a hundred years?

"Please," the Pied Piper repeated.

Something in Ulia Gol's face flickered.

I wondered if, after all, the Mayor would choose to part with her gold, and Nicolas to spare her. Never mind that it would leave Dora Rose pinioned to a juniper tree, the swans only partly avenged, and all my stylish stratagems and near-drowning in vain. Oh, he . . . naw, he . . . Surely Nicolas—even he!—wouldn't be so, so *criminally* virtuous!

Voice breaking and black eyes brimming, he appealed to her for a third and final time.

"Please."

The flickering stilled. I almost laughed in relief.

"It's gonna be fine," I told my comrades. "Watch closely. Be ready."

"Henceforth," purred the Mayor, "I banish you, Master Piper, from the town of Amandale. If ever you set foot inside my walls again, I will personally hang you from the bell tower of Brotquen Cathedral. There you will rot, until nothing but your bones and that silver pipe you play are left."

Ow. Harsh. *Fabulous.*

Nicolas nodded heavily, as if a final anvil had descended upon his brow.

Then.

To my great delight, to my pinkest tickly pleasure, his posture subtly shifted. Yes, altered and unbent, the sadness swept from him like a magician's tablecloth right from beneath the cutlery. Nicolas was totally bare now, with only the glitter of glass and knives left to him.

He sprang upright. And grinned. At the sharp gleam of that grin, even I shivered.

"Here we go," I breathed.

Beside me, Greenpea leaned forward in her wheelchair, gray eyes blazing. "Yes, yes, yes!" she whispered. "Get this over with, piper. Finish it."

Solemnly, Froggit took Possum's hand in his and squeezed. She lifted her chin, face pale behind her ragged blindfold, and asked, "Is it now, Mister Maurice?"

"Soon. Very soon," I replied, hardly able to keep from dancing. Lo, I'd had enough dancing for a lifetime, thanks. Still, I couldn't help but wriggle a bit.

"Citizens of Amandale," announced the Pied Piper, "although it causes me pangs of illimitable dolor to leave you thus, I must, as a law-abiding alien to your environs, make my exit gracefully. But to thank you for your hospitality and to delight your beautiful children, I propose to play you one last song."

"Time to put that cotton in your ears," I warned my recruits. Froggit and Possum obeyed. I don't think Greenpea even heard me; she was that focused on the motley figure poised on the steps of Brotquen Cathedral.

My caution turned out to be unnecessary. Nicolas was, indeed, a Master Piper. He could play tunes within tunes. Tunes piled on tunes, and tunes buried under them. His music came from the Hill, from Her, the Faerie Queen, and there was no song Nicolas could not play when he flung himself open to the sound.

First he played a strand of notes that froze the adults where they stood. Second, a lower, darker line strong enough to paralyze the ogre in her place. Then he played three distinct trills that sounded like names—Froggit, Possum, Greenpea—exempting them from his final spell. Greenpea licked her lips and looked almost disappointed.

Last came the spell song. The one we'd worked so hard for these three days. A song to lure twenty little Swan Hunters into the trap a Swan Princess had set. A song to bring the children back to Dora Rose.

I don't think, in my furry shape, I'd've given the tune more than passing heed. But I was full-fleshed right now, with all the parts of a man. The man I was had been a child once, sometimes still behaved like one, and the tune Nicolas played was tailor-made for children. It made the tips of my toes tingle and my heels feel spry. Well within control, thank the Captured God.

You know who couldn't control it, though?

Ocelot, the Gravedigger's daughter. Ilse Cobblersawl, her brothers Frank, Theodore and James, her sweet sister Anabel, and the nine-year-old twins Hilde and Gretel. Pearl, the chandler's eldest daughter, who let her sister Ruby slip from her arms, to join hands with Maven Chain, the goldsmith's girl. Charles the Chimneysweep. Kevin the Gooseboy. Those twelve and eight more whose names I did not know.

Heads haloed in circles of silver fire that cast a ghostly glow about them, these twenty children shoved parents, grandparents, uncles, aunts, siblings, cousins, teachers, employers, out of the way. Those too small to keep pace were swept up and carried by their fellow hunters. Still playing, Nicolas sprinted down the steps of the cathedral and sprang right into that froth of silver-lit children.

All of them danced. Then the tune changed, and they ran instead.

Light-footed, as though they wore wings on their feet, they fled down Kirkja Street and onto Maskmakers Boulevard. This, I knew, ended in a cul-de-sac abutting a town park, which sported in its farthest shrubbery a rusted gate leading into the Maze Wood.

"Step lively, soldiers," I barked to my three recruits. "Don't wanna get caught staring when the thrall fades from this mob. Gonna get ugly. Lots of snot and tears and torches. Regardless, we should hie ourselves on over to the Heart Glade. Wouldn't want to miss the climax now, would we?"

Froggit shook his head and Possum looked doubtful, but Greenpea was already muscling her chair toward the corner of Kirkja and Maskmakers. We made haste to follow.

Dora Rose, here we come.

I'd seen Dora Rose as a swan, and I'd seen her as a woman, but I'd never seen her both at once. Or so nakedly.

I confess, I averted my eyes. No, I know, I know. You think I should've taken my chance. Looked my fill. Saved up the sweet sight of her to savor all those lonely nights in my not-so-distant future. (Because, let's be honest here, my love life's gonna be next to nonexistent from this point on. Most of the nice fixed does I know are bloating gently in the Drukkamag, and any Folk doe who scampered off to save herself from the Pied Piper is not going to be speaking to me. Who could blame her, really?) But, see, it wasn't like that. It was never like that, with Dora Rose.

Sure, I *curse* by the Captured God. But Dora Rose is my religion.

It was as much as I could bear just to glance once and see her arms outstretched, elongated, mutated, jointed into demented angles that human bones are not intended for, pure white primary feathers bursting from her fingernails, tertials and secondaries fanning out from the soft torn flesh of her underarms. Her long neck was a column of white, like a feathered python, and her face, though mostly human, had become masklike, eyes and nose and mouth black as bitumen, hardening into the shining point of a beak.

That's all I saw, I swear.

After that I was kneeling on the ground and hiding my face, like Nicolas under his covers. In that darkness, I became aware of the music in the Heart Glade. Gave me a reason to look up again.

What does a full bone orchestra look like? First the woodwinds: piccolo, flute, oboe, clarinet, bassoon. Then the brass: horn, trumpet, cornet, tenor trombone, bass trombone, tuba (that last must've been Dasher—he was the biggest cob on the lake). Percussion: timpani, snare, cymbals (those cygnets, I'd bet). And the strings. Violin. Viola. Violoncello. Double bass. And the harp. One white harp, with shining black strings.

Elinore, Dora Rose's twin sister.

All of them, set in a circle around the juniper tree, glowed in the moonlight. They played softly by themselves, undisturbed, as if singing lullabies to the tree and she who hung upon it.

I'd heard the tune before. It was the same phrase of music the tiny firebird had sung, which later the tree itself repeated in its seismic voice. Beneath the full sweep of the strings and hollow drumbeats and bells of bone, I seemed to hear that tremulous boy soprano sobbing out his verse with the dreary repetition of the dead.

Only then—okay, so maybe I took another quick glance—did I see the red tracks that stained the pale down around Dora Rose's eyes. By this I knew she had been weeping all this while.

She, who never wept. Not once. Not in front of me.

I'd thought swans didn't cry. Not like rats and broken pipers and little children. Not like the rest of us. Stupid to be jealous of a bunch of bones.

That *they* merited her red, red tears, when nothing else in the world could or would. Least of all, yours truly, Maurice the Incomparable.

Me and my three comrades loitered in the darkness outside that grisly bone circle. Greenpea, confined to her wheelchair; Possum, sitting quietly near her feet; a tired Froggit sprawled beside her, his head in her lap. Possibly, he'd fallen into a restive sleep. They'd had a tough few days, those kids.

We'd come to the Heart Glade by a shortcut I knew, but it wasn't long till we heard a disturbance in one of the maze's many corridors. In the distance, Nicolas's piping caught the melody of the bone orchestra and countered it, climbing an octave higher and embroidering the somber fabric of the melody with sharp silver notes. The twenty children he'd enchanted joined in, singing:

> *"Day and night Stepsister weeps*
> *Her grief like blood runs red, runs deep*
> *Kywitt! Kywitt! Kywitt! I cry*
> *What a beautiful bird am I!"*

In a rowdiness of music making, they spilled into the Heart Glade. Ocelot was yipping, "Kywitt! Kywitt! Kywitt!" at the tops of her lungs, while Ilse and Maven flapped their arms like wings and made honking noises. A flurry of chirps and whistles and shrieks of laughter from the other children followed in cacophony. Nicolas danced into the glade after them, his pipe wreathed in silver flames. Hopping nimbly over a small bone cymbal in the moss, he faced the Heart Glade, faced the children, and his tune changed again.

And the children leapt the bones.

Once inside the circle, the twenty of them linked wrists and danced rings around the juniper tree, as they used to do in the beginning, when the first of the Swan Folk were hunted and changed. As they whirled, a fissure opened in the juniper's trunk. Red-gold fire flickered within. Like a welcoming hearth. Like a threshold to a chamber of magma.

The children, spurred by Nicolas's piping, began to jump in.

They couldn't reach the fissure fast enough. Ocelot, by dint of shoving the littler ones out of her way, was first to disappear into the bloody light. And when she screamed, the harp that had been Elinore burst into silver-and-red flame, and disappeared. The first silver bloom erupted from the branches of the juniper tree.

Dora Rose shuddered where she hung.

A second child leapt through the crack. Ilse Cobblersawl. The bone trumpet vanished. A second silver bloom appeared. Then little Pearl the Chandler's daughter shouldered her way into the tree. Her agonized wail cut off as a bone cymbal popped into nothingness. Another silver bud flowered open.

When all twenty instruments had vanished, when all twenty Swan Hunters had poured themselves into the tree, when the trunk of the tree knit its own bark back over the gaping wound of its molten heart, then twenty silver blooms opened widely on their branches. The blooms gave birth to small white bees that busied themselves in swirling pollinations. Petals fell, leaving silver fruit where the flowers had been. The branches bent to the ground under the colossal weight of that fruit and heaved Dora Rose from their tree. Into the moss she tumbled, like so much kindling, a heap of ragged feathers, shattered flesh, pale hair.

Nicolas stopped piping. He wiped his mouth as if it had gone numb. He looked over at Froggit, who'd been screaming wordlessly ever since waking to the sight of his siblings feeding themselves to the tree. Nicolas held Froggit in his dense black gaze, the enormity of his sadness and regret etching his face ancient.

For myself, I couldn't care less about any of them.

I rushed to Dora Rose and shook her. Nothing happened. No response. Reaching out, I tackled Nicolas at the knees, yanking him to the ground and pinning him down.

"Is she dead, Nicolas?" I seized the lapels of his motley coat and shook. "Nicolas, did you kill her?"

"I?" he asked, staring at me in that dreadfully gentle way of his. "Perhaps. It sounds like something I might do. This world is so dangerous and cruel, and I am what it makes me. But I think you'll find she breathes."

He was correct, although how he could see so slight a motion as her breath by that weird fruity light, I couldn't say. I, for one, couldn't see a damn thing. But when I got near enough, I could smell the life of her. Not yet reduced to so much swan meat. Not to be salted and parboiled, seasoned with ginger, larded up and baked with butter yet. Not yet.

Oh, no, my girl. Though filthy and broken, you remain my Dora Rose.

"Come on, Ladybird. Come on. Wake up. Wake up now." I jostled her. I chafed her ragged wrists. I even slapped her face. Lightly. Well, not so hard as I might've.

"Maybe she's under a spell," Possum's scratchy voice suggested. "She told us it might happen. She's a Princess, she says. She has to play her part."

"Oh, yeah?" I might have known my present agony was due to Dora Rose's inflexible adherence to tradition. Stupid swan girl. I could wring her white neck, except I loved her so. "What are we supposed to do about it, eh?"

I glanced over my shoulder in time to see the blind girl shrug. She did not move from the shadows of the Heart Glade into the juniper's feral light. Froggit at her feet sobbed like he would never stop.

Greenpea rolled her wheelchair closer to us.

"She said that Nicolas would know what to do."

I looked down again at Nicolas, who blinked at me. "Well?"

"Oh. *That*. Well." His face went like a red rose on fire. "*You* know, Maurice."

I'd had it. Time to show my teeth. "What, Nicolas?" I hissed. "Spit it out, wouldja? We're working within a three-day time frame here, okay? If today turns into tomorrow, she'll be gone. And what'll all this be for? So say it. How do we wake her?"

"True love's k-kiss," Nicolas answered, blushing more deeply and unable to meet my gaze. "It's pretty standard when one is dealing with, with . . . royalty."

"Oh." I sat back on my heels. A mean roil of jealousy and bile rose up inside me, but my next words, I'm proud to say, came out flat and even. Who said I couldn't control my basest urges? "Okay then, Nico, hop to it. But no tongue, mind, or I'll have it for my next meal."

Nicolas scooted away from me, scraping up moss in his haste. "Maurice, you cannot mean it." He ran nervous brown fingers through his hair.

"Nicolas," said I, "I've never been more serious. No tongue—or you'll be sleeping with one eye open and a sizeable club under your pillow the rest of your days."

"No, no!" He held up his hands, blocking me and Dora Rose from his view. "That's not what I meant at all. I only meant—I can't."

"You . . . what?"

"I can't k-ki . . . Do that. What you're saying." Nicolas shook his head back and forth like a child confronted with a syrupy spoonful of ipecac. His hair stood on end. His skin was sweaty and ashen. "Not on your life. Or mine. Or—or hers. Never." He paused. "Sorry."

I sprang to my feet. Wobbled. Sat down promptly. *Limbs, don't fail me now.* Grabbing him by the hem of his muddy trousers, I yanked him back toward me and pounced again, my hands much nearer his throat this time. "Nicolas, by the Captured God, if you don't kiss her right this instant, I'll . . ."

"He *can't*, Maurice," Greenpea said unexpectedly. She fisted my collar and pulled me off him, wheeling backward in her chair until she could deposit me, still flailing, at Dora Rose's side. That girl had an arm on her—even after fishing drowned rats out of the Drukkamag all day. Her parents were both smiths: she, their only child. "He can't even say the word without choking. You want someone to kiss her, you do it yourself. Leave him alone."

Nicolas turned his head and stared up at her, glowing at this unexpected reprieve. If he could have bled light onto his rescuer, I don't think Greenpea'd ever get the stains out.

"We've not been introduced, Miss . . . ? You are Master Froggit's cousin, I believe."

"Greenpea Margissett."

"Nicolas of the Hill." His mouth quirked. "Nicolas of Nowhere."

She frowned fiercely at him. She looked just like a schoolmarm I once knew, who laid a clever trail of crumbs right up to a rattrap that almost proved my undoing. She's how I ended up in that pickle jar, come to think of it. Unnerving to see that same severe expression on so young a face.

"Nicolas," she said, very sternly, "I am *not* happy about the rats."

All that wonderful light snuffed right out of his face. Nicolas groaned. "Neither am I." He slapped a hand hard against his chest, driving the pipe against his breastbone. "I am not happy." Slap. "I will never be happy again." Slap.

With that, he crumpled on the ground next to Froggit and Dora Rose and began to retch, tearing at his hair by the fistful. Me and Greenpea watched him a while. Froggit, meanwhile, crawled over to the juniper tree and hunkered down by the roots to cry more quietly. Nothing from Possum, lost behind us in the darkness.

Presently, I muttered to Greenpea, "We'll get nothing more out of him till he's cried out. It's like reasoning with a waterspout."

Greenpea studied the Pied Piper, her brow creased. "He's cracked."

"Got it in one."

"But you used him anyway?"

I bared my teeth at her, the little know-it-all. Show her I could chew through anything—metal spokes, bandaged leg stumps, leather coat, bone.

"Yeah. I used you, too, don't forget. And your friends. Oh, and about half a million rats. And all those children we murdered here tonight. I used the Mayor herself against herself and made a puppet of the puppet master. I'll tell you something else, little Rebel Greenpea—I'd do it again and worse to wake this Swan Princess now."

Resting her head on the back of her chair, Greenpea whispered, "It won't." I couldn't tell if it was smugness or sorrow that smelled so tart and sweet on her, like wild strawberries. "Only one thing can."

"But it's not—" I drew a breath. "*Seemly.*"

Greenpea's clear gray gaze ranged over the Heart Glade. She rubbed her eyes beneath her spectacles. "None of this is."

In the end, I couldn't bring myself to . . .

Not her lips, at least. That, Dora Rose'd never forgive, no matter what excuse I stammered out. No, I chose to kiss the sole of her foot. It was blackened like her mask, and webbed and beginning to curl under. If she later decided to squash me with that selfsame foot, I'd feel it was only my due. I'd let her squash me—happily. If only she'd wake.

Beneath my lips, the cold webbing warmed. The hard toes flexed, pinkened, fleshed back to mortal feet. I bowed my head to the ground and only dared to breathe again when I felt her stir. I glanced up to see Dora Rose wholly a woman again, Greenpea putting the Pied Piper's motley cloak over her nakedness and helping her sit up. Nicolas scrambled to hide behind the fortress of Greenpea's wheelchair as soon as Dora Rose was upright.

Then Dora Rose looked at me.

And I guess I'll remember that look, that burning, haughty, tender look, until my dying day.

She removed her sole from the palm of my hand and slowly stood up, never breaking eye contact.

"You're wrapped in a dog blanket, Maurice."

I leaned on my left elbow and grinned. "Hellfowl, Dora Rose, you should've seen my outfit when they fished me outta the Drukkamag. Wasn't wrapped in much but water, if I recall."

She turned a shoulder to me, and bent her glance on Greenpea. It brimmed with the sort of gratitude I'd worked my tail to the bone these last three days to earn, but for whatever reason, I didn't seem to mind Dora Rose lavishing it elsewhere. Probably still aquiver from our previous eye contact.

"You did so well, my friend." She stooped to kiss Greenpea's forehead. "You three were braver than princes. Braver than queens. When I hung on the juniper tree, I told the ghost inside it of your hurts—and of your help. It promised you a sure reward. But first . . . first I must hatch my brothers and sisters from their deaths."

Dora Rose moved through the tree's shadow in a beam of her own light. She lifted an exhausted Froggit from the ground and returned him to his cousin. He huddled in Greenpea's lap, face buried in her shoulder. Possum crept toward them with uncertain steps, feeling for the chair. Finding it, she sat down near one of its great wheels, one hand on Froggit's knee, the other grasping fast to Greenpea's fingers. She was not a big girl like Greenpea. Not much older than Froggit, really.

They all patted one another's shoulders and stroked one another's hair, ceasing to pay attention to the rest of us. There was Nicolas, huddled on the ground not far from them in his fetal curl. At least he'd stopped crying. In his exhaustion, he watched the children. Something like hunger marked his face, something like envy creased it, but also a sort of lonely satisfaction in their fellowship. He made no move to infringe, only hugged his own elbows and rested his head on the moss. His face was a tragedy even I could not bear to watch.

Where was my favorite Swan Princess? Ah.

Dora Rose had plucked the first fruit from the juniper tree. I went over to help. Heaving a particularly large one off its branch (it came to me with a sharp crack, but careful inspection revealed nothing broken), I asked, "Now what would a big silver watermelon like this taste like, I wonder?"

"It's not a watermelon, Maurice." Dora Rose set another shining thing carefully on the ground. The silver fruit made a noise like a hand sweeping harp strings. "It's an egg."

"I like eggs."

"Maurice, if you dare!"

"Aw, come on, Ladybird. As if I would." She stared pointedly at my chin until I wiped the saliva away. "Hey, it's a glandular reflex. I've not been eating as much as I should. Surprised I'm not in shock."

As Dora Rose made no attempt even at pretending to acknowledge this, I went on plucking the great glowing eggs from the juniper tree. Soon we had a nice, big clutch piled pyramid-style on the moss.

Let me tell you, the only thing more tedious than a swan ballet is a swan hatching. You see one fuzzy gray head peeping out from a hole in a shell, you've seen 'em all. It takes hours. And then there's the grooming and the feeding and the nuzzling and the nesting, and oh, the interminable domesticity. Swan chicks aren't even cute like rat kits, which are the littlest wee things you did ever see and make the funniest noises besides. Swan chicks are just sort of pipsqueaking fluff balls.

But Dora Rose's silver-shelled clutch weren't your average eggs.

For one thing, when they burst open—which they did within minutes of being harvested—they all went at once, as if lightning smote them. Up from the shards they flew, twenty swans in total, of varying aspects and sexes.

But all a bit, well, weird.

When they finally came back down to the ground, in a landing that wanted nothing in grace or symmetry, I noticed what was off about them. They had no smell. Or if they did, it wasn't a smell that matched my notion of "swan" or even of "bird." Not of any variety. Second, as the disjointed moonlight shone through the tree branches to bounce off their feathers, I saw that though the creatures were the right shape for swans, that flew like swans and waddled like swans, there was something innately frightening about them. Impenetrable. As if a god had breathed life into stone statues, and that was what they were: stone. Not creatures of flesh and feather at all.

It hit me then. These swans were not, in fact, of flesh and feather. Or even of stone. They were covered in hard white scales. Their coats weren't down at all, but interlocking bone.

Even as I thought this, they fleshed to human shape. Ivory they were, these newborn Swan Folk. Skin, hair, and eyes of that weirdly near-white hue, their pallor broken only by bitterly black mouths: lips and teeth and tongues all black together. Each wore a short gown of bone scales that clattered when they walked. Their all-ivory gazes fastened, unblinkingly, on Dora Rose.

She reached out to one of them, crying, "Elinore!"

But the swan girl who stepped curiously forward at the sound of her voice made Dora Rose gasp. True, she was like Elinore—but she was also like Ocelot, the gravedigger's daughter. She wore a silver circlet on her brow. Dora Rose averted her face and loosed a shuddering breath. But she did not weep. When she looked at the girl again, her face was calm, kindly, cold.

"Do you have a name?"

Elinore-Ocelot just stared. Tentatively, she moved closer to Dora Rose. Just as tentatively, knelt before her. Setting her head against Dora Rose's thigh, she butted lightly. Dora Rose put a hand upon the girl's ivory hair. Nineteen other swanlings rushed to their knees and pressed in, hoping for a touch of her hand.

I couldn't help myself. I collapsed, laughing.

"Maurice!" Dora Rose snapped. "Stop cackling at once!"

"Oh!" I howled. "And you a new mama twenty times over! Betcha the juniper tree didn't whisper *that* about your fate in all the time you hung. You'd've lit outta the Heart Glade so fast . . . Oh, my heart! Oh, Dora Rose! Queen Mother and all . . ."

Dora Rose's eyes burned to do horrible things to me. How I wished she would! At the moment though, a bunch of mutely ardent cygnets besieged her on all sides, and she had no time for me. Captured God knew they'd start demanding food soon, like all babies. Wiping my eyes, I advised Dora Rose to take her bevy of bony swanlets back to Lake Serenus and teach them to bob for stonewort before they mistook strands of her hair for widgeon grass.

Tee hee.

Shooting one final glare my way, Dora Rose said, "You. I'll deal with you later."

"Promise?"

"I . . ." She hesitated. Scowled. Then reached her long silver fingers to grab my nose and tweak it. Hard. Hard enough to ring bells in my ears and make tears spurt from my eyes. The honk and tug at the end were especially malevolent. I grinned all over my face, and my heart percussed with bliss. Gesture like that was good as a pinkie swear in Rat Folk parlance—and didn't she know it, my own dear Dora Rose!

Out of deference, I "made her a leg"—as a Swan Prince might say. But my version of that courtly obeisance was a crooked, shabby, insolent thing: the only kind of bow a rat could rightly make to a swan.

"So long then, Ladybird."

Dora Rose hesitated, then said, "Not so long as last time—my Incomparable Maurice."

Blushing ever so palely and frostily (I mean, it was practically an invitation, right?), she downed herself for flight. A beautiful buffeting ruckus arose from her wings as she rocketed right out of the Heart Glade. Twenty bone swans followed her, changing from human to bird more quickly than my eye could take in. White wind. Silver wings. Night sky. Moonlight fractured as they flew toward Lake Serenus.

Heaving a sigh, I looked around. Nicolas and the three children were all staring up at the tree.

"Now what? Did we forget something?"

The juniper tree's uppermost branches trembled. Something glimmered high above, in the dense green of those needles. The trembling became a great shaking, and like meteors, three streaks of silver light fell to the moss and smoked thinly on the ground. I whistled.

"Three more melons! Can't believe we missed those."

"You didn't," Nicolas replied, in that whisper of his that could break hearts. "Those are for the children. Their reward."

"I could use a nice, juicy reward about now."

He smiled distractedly at me. "You must come to my house for supper, Maurice. I have a jar of plum preserves that you may eat. And a sack of sugared almonds, although they might now be stale."

How freely does the drool run after a day like mine!

"Nicolas!" I moaned. "If you don't have food on your person, you have to stop talking about it. It's torture."

"I was only trying to be hospitable, Maurice. Here you go, Master Froggit. This one's singing your song."

I couldn't hear anything. Me, who has better hearing than anyone I know! But Nicolas went over, anyway, and handed the first of the silver eggs to Froggit. It was big enough that Froggit had to sit down to hold it in his lap. He shuddered and squirmed, but his swollen eyes, thank the Captured God, didn't fill up and spill over again.

To Possum, Nicolas handed a second egg. This one was small enough to fit in her palms. She smoothed her hands over the silver shell. Lifting it to her face, she sniffed delicately.

Into Greenpea's hands, Nicolas placed the last egg. It was curiously flat and long. She frowned down at it, perplexed and a bit fearful, but did not cast it from her. Each of the shells shivered to splinters before Nicolas could step all the way back from Greenpea's chair.

Possum was the first to speak. "I don't understand," she said, fingering her gift.

"Hey, neat!" I said, bending down for a look. "Goggles! Hey, but don't see why you need 'em, Miss Possum. Not having, you know, *eyes* anymore. Can't possibly wanna shield them from sunlight, or saltwater, or whatever. For another, even if you did, these things are opaque as a prude's lingerie. A god couldn't see through them."

"That is because they are made of bone, Maurice," Nicolas said. "Try them on, Miss Possum. You will see."

Her lips flattened at what she took to be his inadvertent slip of the tongue. But she undid the bandage covering her eyes and guided the white goggles there. She raised her head to look at me. An unaccountable dread seized me at the expression on her face.

"Oh!" Possum gasped and snatched the goggles from her head, backhanding them off her lap like they were about to grow millipede legs and scuttle up her sleeve. "I saw—I saw—!"

Greenpea grabbed her hand. "They gave you back your eyes? But isn't that . . . ?"

"I saw *him*," Possum sobbed, pointing in my direction. "I saw him *tomorrow*. And the next day. And the day he dies. His grave. It overlooks a big blue lake. I *saw* . . ."

Nicolas crouched to inspect the goggles, poking at them with a slender finger. "The juniper didn't give you the gift of sight, Miss Possum—but of foresight. How frightening for you. But very beautiful, and very rare, too. You are to be congratulated. I think."

A sharp, staccato sound tapped out an inquiry. Froggit was exploring his own gift: a small bone drum, with a shining white hide stretched over it. I wondered if the skin had come from one of his siblings.

Best not to muse about such things aloud, of course. Might upset the boy.

Froggit banged on the hide with a drumstick I was pretty sure was also made of bone.

What does the drum do? asked the banging. *Is there a trick in it?*

"Froggit!" Possum cried out, laughing a little. "You're talking!"

A short, startled tap in response. *I am?*

"Huh," I muttered. "Close enough for Folk music, anyway."

Flushed with her own dawning excitement, Greenpea brought the bone fiddle in her lap to rest under her chin. She took a bone bow strung with long black hair and set it to the silver strings.

The fiddle wailed like a slaughtered rabbit.

She looked at her legs. They didn't move. She tried the bow again.

Cats brawling. Tortured dogs. That time in the rat-baiting arena I almost died. I put my hands to my ears. "Nicolas! Please! Make her stop."

"Hush, Maurice. We all sound like that when we first start to play." Nicolas squatted before Greenpea's chair to meet her eyes. She kept on sawing doggedly at the strings, her face set with harrowing determination, until at last the Pied Piper put his hand on hers. The diabolical noise stopped.

"Miss Greenpea. Believe me, it will take months, maybe years, of practice before you'll be able to play that fiddle efficiently. Longer before you play it well. But perhaps we can start lessons tomorrow, when we're all better rested and fed."

"But," she asked, clutching it close, "what does it *do*?"

"Do?" Nicolas inquired. "In this world, nothing. It's just a fiddle."

Greenpea's stern lips trembled. She looked mad enough to break the fiddle over his head.

"Possum can see. Froggit can talk. I thought this would make me walk again. I thought . . ."

"No." He touched the neck of the bone fiddle thoughtfully. "I could pipe Maurice's broken bones together, but I cannot pipe the rats of Amandale back to life. What's gone is gone. Your legs. Froggit's tongue. Possum's eyes. They are gone."

Huge tears rolled down her face. She did not speak.

He continued, "Fiddle music, my dear Miss Greenpea, compels a body, willy-nilly, to movement. More so than the pipe, I think—and I do not say that lightly, Master Piper that I am. Your fiddle may not make *you* walk again. But once you learn to play, the two of you together will make the world dance."

"Will we?" Greenpea spat bitterly. "Why should the world dance and not I?"

Bowing his head, Nicolas dropped to one knee, and set a hand on each of her armrests. When he spoke again, his voice was low. I had to strain all my best eavesdropping capabilities to listen in.

"Listen. In the Realms Under the Hill, my silver pipe is the merest pennywhistle. It has no power of compulsion or genius. I am nothing but a tin sparrow when I play for the Faerie Queen; it amuses Her to hear me chirp and peep. Yet you saw what I did with my music today, up here in the Realms Above. Now . . ."

His breath blew out in wonder. "Now," the Pied Piper told her, "if ever you found yourself in Her court, with all the Lords and Ladies of Faerie arrayed against you, fierce in their wisdom, hideous in their beauty, and pitiless, pitiless as starlight—and you played them a tune on this bone fiddle of yours, why . . ."

Nicolas smiled. It was as feral a grin as the one he'd worn on the steps of Brotquen Cathedral, right before he enchanted the entire town of Amandale. "Why, Miss Greenpea, I reckon you could dance the Immortal Queen Herself to death, and She powerless to stop you."

"Oh," Greenpea sighed. She caressed the white fiddle, the silver strings. "Oh."

"But." Nicolas sprang up and dusted off his patched knees. "You have to learn how to play it first. I doubt a few paltry scrapes would do more than irritate Her. And then She'd break you, make no doubt. Ulia Gol at her worst is a saint standing next to Her Most Gracious Majesty."

Taking up his cloak from the spot where Dora Rose had dropped it, Nicolas swirled it over his shoulders. He stared straight ahead, his face bleak and his eyes blank, as though we were no longer standing there.

"I am very tired now," he said, "and very sad. I want to go home and sleep until I forget if I have lived these last three days or merely dreamed them. I have had stranger and more fell dreams than this. Or perhaps"— he shuddered—"perhaps I was awake *then*, and this—*this* is the dream I dreamed to escape my memories. In which case, there is no succor for me, not awake or asleep, and I can only hope for that ultimate oblivion, and to hasten it with whatever implements I have on hand. If you have no further need of me, I will bid you adieu."

Alarmed at this turn, I scrambled to tug his coattails. "Hey, Nico! Hey, Nicolas, wait a minute, twinkle toes. Nicolas, you bastard, you promised me almonds!"

"Did I?" He looked up brightly, and blasted me with his smile, and it was like a storm wrack had blown from his face. "I did, Maurice! How could I have forgotten? Come along, then, with my sincerest apologies. Allow me to feed you, Maurice. How I love to feed my friends when they are hungry!"

Greenpea wheeled her chair about to block his way. "Teach me," she demanded.

He blinked at her as if he had never seen her face before. "Your pardon?"

She held out her bone fiddle. "If what you say is true, this gift is not just about music; it's about magic, too. And unless I'm wrong, Amandale won't have much to do with either in years to come."

I snorted in agreement.

"Teach me." Greenpea pointed with bow and fiddle to her two friends. "Them too. Teach all of us. We need you."

Please, Froggit tapped out on his bone drum. *We can't go home.*

"Of course you can!" Nicolas assured him, stricken. "They'll welcome you, Master Froggit. They probably think you are dead. How beautiful they shall find it that you are not! Think—the number of Cobblersawls has been halved at least; you shall be twice as precious . . ."

Possum shook her head. "They'll see only the ones they lost."

Once more she slipped the goggles on. Whatever she foresaw as she peered through the bone lenses at Nicolas, she did not flinch. But I watched him closely, the impossible radiance that rose up in him, brighter than his silver pipe, brighter than his broken edges, and he listened to Possum's prophecy in rapturous terror, and with hope. I'd never seen the Pied Piper look anything like hopeful before, in all the years I'd known him.

"We *are* coming with you," Possum prophesied. No one gainsaid her. No one even tried. "We are going to your cottage. You *will* teach us how to play music. We will learn many songs from you, and . . . and make up even *more*! When the first snow falls, we four *shall* venture into the Hill. And under it. Deep and wide, word will spread of a band of strange musicians: Nicolas and the Oracles. Lords and Ladies and Dragons and Sirens, they will *all* invite us to their courts and caves and coves to play for them. Froggit on the drums. Greenpea on her fiddle. You on your pipe. And I?"

Greenpea began to laugh. The sound was rusty, but true. "You'll sing, of course, Possum! You have the truest voice. Ulia Gol was so mad when you wouldn't sing up the bones for her!"

"Yes," Possum whispered, "I will sing true songs in the Realm of Lies, and all who hear me *will listen*."

All right. Enough of this yammering. My guts were cramping.

"Great!" I exclaimed. "You guys'll be great. Musicians get all the girls anyway. Or, you know"—I nodded at Greenpea and Possum—"the dreamy-eyed, long-haired laddies. Or whatever. The other way around. However you want it. Always wanted to learn guitar myself. I'd look pretty striking with a guitar, don't you think? I could go to the lake and play for Dora Rose. She'd like that about as much as a slap on the . . . Anyway, it's a thought."

"Maurice." Nicolas clapped his hand to my shoulder. "You are hungry. You always babble when you are hungry. Come. Eat my food and drink my Faerie ale, and I shall spread blankets enough on the floor for all of us." He beamed around at the three children, at me, and I swear his face was like a bonfire.

"My friends," he said. "My friends. How merry we shall be."

Later that night, when they were all cuddled up and sleeping the sleep of the semi-innocent, or at least the iniquitously fatigued, I crept out of that cottage in the lee of the Hill and snuck back to the Heart Glade.

Call it a hunch. Call it ants in my antsy pants. I don't know. Something was going on, and I had to see it. So what? So I get curious sometimes.

Wouldn't you know it? I made it through the Maze Wood only to find I was right yet again! They weren't kidding when they called me

Maurice the Incomparable. (And by "they," I mean "me," of course.) Sometimes I know things. My whiskers twitch, or maybe my palms itch, and I just *know*.

What hung from the juniper tree in that gray light before full dawn wasn't nearly as pretty as a Swan Princess or as holy and mysterious as a clutch of silver watermelon eggs.

Nope. This time the ornaments swinging from the branches were much plainer and more brutal. The juniper tree itself, decked out in its new accessories, looked darker and squatter than I'd ever beheld it, and by the gratified jangling in its blackly green needles, seemed very pleased with itself.

Ever see an ogre after a mob of bereaved parents gets through with her? Didn't think so. But *I* have.

Certain human responses can trump even an ogre's fell enchantments. Watching twenty kids disappear right out from under your helpless gaze all because your mayor was a cheapskate might induce a few of them. Hanging was the least of what they did to her. The only way I knew her was by the tattered crimson of her gown.

Mortals. Mortals and their infernal ingenuity. I shook my head in admiration.

And was *that* . . . ?

Yes, it was! Indeed, it was! My old friend, Henchmen Hans himself. Loyal to the end, swinging from a rope of his own near the mayoral gallows branch. And wearing his second best suit, too, bless him. Though torn and more than a little stained, his second best was a far sight better than what I presently wore. Needed something a bit more flamboyant than a dog blanket, didn't I, if I was going to visit Lake Serenus in the morning? Bring a swan girl a fresh bag of caramels. Help her babysit. You know. Like you do.

Waste not, want not—isn't that what the wharf boys say? A Rat Folk philosophy if I ever heard one. So, yeah, I'd be stripping my good old pal Hans right down to his bare essentials, or I'm not my mother's son. And then I'd strip him of more than that.

See, I'd had to share the Pied Piper's fine repast with three starving mortal children earlier that night. It's not that they didn't deserve their victuals as much as, say, *I* (although, really, who did?), and it's not like Nicolas didn't press me to eat seconds and thirds. But I still hadn't gotten nearly as much as my ravenous little rat's heart desired.

The juniper tree whispered.

It might have said anything.

But I'm pretty sure I heard, "Help yourself, Maurice."

Martyr's Gem

For Janelle McHugh

Of the woman he was to wed on the morrow, Shursta Sarth knew little. He knew she hailed from Droon. He knew her name was Hyrryai.

". . . which means, 'the Gleaming One,'" his sister piped in, the evening before he left their village. She was crocheting by the fire and he was staring into it.

Lifting his chin from his hand, Shursta grinned at her. "Ayup? And where'd you light upon that lore, Nugget?"

Sharrar kicked him on the ankle for using the loathed nickname. "I work with the grayheads. They remember everything."

"Except how to chew their food."

"What they've lost in teeth, they've gained in wisdom," she announced with some pomposity. "Besides, that's what they have *me* for." Her smile went wry at one corner, but was no less proud for that. "I chew their food, I change their cloths, and they tell me about the old days. Some of them had parents who were alive back then."

Her voice went rich and rolling. Her crochet hook glinted on the little lace purse she was making. The driftwood flames flickered, orange with tongues of blue.

"They remember the days before the Nine Cities drowned and the Nine Islands with them. Before our people forsook us to live below the waters, and we were stranded here on the Last Isle. Before we changed our name to Glennemgarra, the Unchosen." Sharrar sighed. "In those days, names were more than mere proxy for, *Hey, you!*"

"So Hyrryai means, *Hey, you, Gleamy?*"

"You have no soul, Shursta."

100

"Nugget, when your inner poet is ascendant, you have more than enough soul for both of us. If the whitecaps of your whimsy rise any higher, we'll have a second Drowning at hand, make no mistake."

Sharrar rolled her brown-bright eyes at him and grunted something. He laughed, and the anxious knots in his stomach loosened some.

When Shursta took his leave the next morning at dawn, he lingered in the threshold. The hut had plenty of wood in the stack outside the door. He'd smoked or salted any extra catch for a week, so Sharrar would not soon go hungry. If she encountered trouble, they would take her in at the Hall of Ages where she worked, and there she'd be fed and sheltered, though she wouldn't have much privacy or respite.

He looked at his sister now. She'd dragged herself from bed to make him breakfast, even though he was perfectly capable of frying up an egg himself. Her short dark hair stuck up every which way, and her eyes were bleary. Her limp was more pronounced in the morning.

"Wish you could come with me," he offered.

"What? Me, with one game leg and a passel of grayheads to feed? No, thank you!" But her eyes looked wistful. Neither of them had ever been to Droon, capital of the Last Isle, the seat of the Astrion Council.

"Hey," he said, surprised to find his own eyes stinging.

"Hey," she said right back. "After the mesh-rite, after you've settled down a bit and met some folks, invite me up. You know I want to meet my mesh-sister. You have my gift?"

He patted his rucksack, which had the little lace purse she'd crocheted along with his own mesh-gift.

"Oohee, brother mine," said Sharrar. "By this time tomorrow you'll be a Blodestone, and no Sarth relation will be worthy to meet your eyes."

"Doubtless Hirryai Blodestone will take one look at me and sunder the contract."

"*She* requested *you*."

Shursta shrugged, sure it had been a mistake.

After that, there was one last hug, a vivid and mischievous and slightly desperate smile from Sharrar, followed by a grave look and quick wink on Shursta's part. Then he set off on the sea road that would take him to Droon.

Of the eight great remaining kinlines, the Blodestones were the wealthiest. Their mines were rich in ore and gems. Their fields were fertile and wide, concentrated in the highland interior of the Last Isle. After a Blodestone female was croned at age fifty, she would hold her place on the Astrion Council, which governed all the Glennemgarra.

Even a fisherman like Shursta Sarth (of the lesser branch of Sarths), from a poor village like Sif on the edge of Rath Sea, with no parents of note and only a single sister for kin, knew about the Blodestones.

He had no idea why Hyrryai had chosen him for mesh-mate. If it had not been an error, then it was a singular honor. For his life he knew not how he deserved it.

He was of an age to wed. Mesh-rite was his duty to the Glennemgarra and he would perform it, that the world might once again be peopled. To be childless—unless granted special dispensation by the Astrion Council—was to be reviled. Even with the dispensation, there were those who were tormented or shunned for their barrenness.

Due to a lack of girls in Sif, to his own graceless body, which, though fit for work, tended to carry extra weight, and to the slowness of his tongue in the company of strangers, Shursta had not yet been bred out. He had planned to attend this year's muster and win a mesh-mate at games (the idea of being won himself had never occurred to him), but then the Council's letter from Droon came.

The letter told him that Hyrryai Blodestone had requested him for mesh-mate. It told him that Hyrryai had not yet herself been bred. That though she was twenty-one, a full year past the age of meshing, she had been granted a reprieve when her little sister was murdered.

Shursta had read that last sentence in shock. The murder of a child was the highest crime but one, and that was the murder of a girl child. Hyrryai had been given full grieving rights.

Other than this scant information, the letter had left detailed directions to Droon, with the day and time his first assignation with Hirryai had been set, and reminded him that it was customary for a first-meshed couple to exchange gifts.

On Sharrar's advice, Shursta had taken pains. He had strung for Hyrryai a long necklace of ammonite, shark teeth, and dark pearls the color of thunderclouds. Ammonite for antiquity, teeth for ferocity, and pearls for sorrow. A fearsome gift and perhaps presumptuous, but Sharrar had approved.

"Girls like sharp things," she'd said, "so the teeth are just right. As for the pearls, they're practically a poem."

"I should have stuck with white ones," he'd said ruefully. "The regular round kind."

"Bah!" said Sharrar, her pointy face with its incongruously long, strong jaw set stubbornly. "If she doesn't see you're a prize, I'll descend upon Droon and roast her organs on the tines of my trident, just see if I don't!"

Whereupon Shursta had flicked his strand of stone, teeth, and pearl at her. She'd caught it with a giggle, wrapping it with great care in the fine lace purse she'd made.

Hyrryai Blodestone awaited him. More tide pool than beach, the small assignation spot had been used for this purpose before. Boulders had been carved into steps leading from sea road to cove, but these were ancient and crumbling into marram grass.

In this sheltered spot, a natural rock formation had been worked gently into the double curve of a lovers' bench. His intended bride sat at the far end. Any farther and she would topple off.

From the smudges beneath her eyes and the harried filaments flying out from her wing-black braid, she looked as if she had been sitting there all night. Her head turned as he approached. Perhaps it was the heaviness of his breath she heard. It labored after the ten miles he'd trudged that morning, from the steepness of the steps, at his astonishment at the color of her hair. The breezy sweetness of dawn had long since burned away. It was noon.

Probably, Shursta thought, falling back a step back as her gaze met his, she could smell him where she sat.

"Shursta Sarth," she greeted him.

"Damisel Blodestone."

Shursta had wanted to say her name. Had wanted to say it casually, as she spoke his, with a cordial nod of the head. Instead his chin jutted up and awry, as if a stray hook had caught it. Her name stopped in his throat and changed places at the last second with the formal honorific. He recalled Sharrar's nonsense about names having meaning. It no longer seemed absurd.

Hyrryai, the Gleaming One. Had she been so called for the long shining lines in her hair? The fire at the bottom of her eyes, like lava trapped in obsidian? Was it the clear, bold glow of her skin, just browner than blushing coral, just more golden than sand?

Since his tongue would not work, as it rarely did for strangers, Shursta shrugged off his rucksack. The shoulder straps were damp in his grip. He fished out the lace purse with its mesh-gift and held it out to her, stretching his arm to the limit so that he would not have to step nearer.

She glanced from his flushed face to the purse. With a short sigh, as if to brace herself, she stood abruptly, plucked the purse from his hand, and dumped the contents into her palm.

Shursta's arm dropped.

Hyrryai Blodestone examined the necklace closely. Every tooth, every pearl, every fossilized ridge of ammonite. Then, with another breath, this one quick and indrawn as the other had been exhaled, she poured the contents back and thrust the purse at him.

"Go home, man of Sif," she said. "I was mistaken. I apologize that you came all this way."

Not knowing whether he were about to protest or cozen or merely ask why, Shursta opened his mouth. Felt that click in the back of his throat where too many words welled in too narrow a funnel. Swallowed them all.

His hand closed over the purse Sharrar had made.

After all, it was no worse than he had expected. Better, for she had not laughed at him. Her face, though cold, expressed genuine sorrow. He suspected the sorrow was with her always. He would not stay to exacerbate it.

This time, he managed a creditable bow, arms crossed over his chest in a gesture of deepest respect. Again he took up his rucksack, though it seemed a hundred times heavier now. He turned away from her, letting his rough hair swing into his face.

"Wait."

Her hand was on his arm. He wondered if they had named her Hyrryai because she left streaks of light upon whatever she touched.

"Wait. Please. Come and sit. I think I must explain. If it pleases you to hear me, I will talk awhile. After that, you may tell me what you think. What you want. From this." She spread her hands.

Shursta did not remove his rucksack again, but he sat with her. Not on the bench, but on the sand, with their backs against the stone seat. He drew in the sand with a broken shell and did not look at her except indirectly, for fear he would stare. For a while, only the waves spoke.

When Hyrryai Blodestone began, her tones were polite but informal, like a lecturer of small children. Like Sharrar with her grayheads. As if she did not expect Shursta to hear her, or hearing, listen.

"The crones of the Astrion Council know the names of all the Glennemgarra youth yet unmeshed. All their stories. Who tumbled which merry widow in which sea cave. Who broke his drunken head on which barman's club. Who comes from the largest family of mesh-kin, and what her portions are. You must understand"—the tone of her voice changed, and Shursta glanced up in time to see the fleetingest quirk of a corner smile—"the secrets of the council do not stay in the council. In my home, at least, it is the salt of every feast, the gossip over tealeaves and coffee grounds, the center of our politics and our hearths. With a mother, grandmother, several aunts and great aunts and three cousins on the council, I cannot escape it. When we were young, we did not want to. We thought of little else than which dashing, handsome man we would . . ."

She stopped. Averted her face. Then she asked lightly, "Shall I tell you your story as the Blodestones know it?"

When he answered, after clearing his throat, it was in the slow, measured sentences that made most people suck their teeth and stamp the ground with impatience. Hyrryai Blodestone merely watched with her flickering eyes.

"Shursta Sarth is not yet twenty-five. He has one sibling, born lame. A fisherman by trade. Not a very successful one. Big as a whale. Stupid as a jellyfish. Known to his friends, if you can call them that, as 'Sharkbait.'"

Hyrryai was nodding, slowly. Shursta's heart sank like a severed anchor. He had hoped, of course, that the story told of Shursta Sarth in the Astrion Council might be different. That somehow they had known more of him, even, than he knew of himself. Seeing his crestfallen expression, Hyrryai took up the tale.

"Shursta Sarth is expected either to win a one-year bride at games, do his duty by her, and watch her leave the moment her contract ends, or to take under his wing a past-primer lately put aside for a younger womb. However, as his sister will likely be his dependent for life, this will deter many of the latter, who might have taken him on for the sake of holding their own household. It is judged improbable that Shursta Sarth will follow the common practice of having his sister removed to the Beggars' Quarter and thus improve his own lot."

Shursta must have made an abrupt noise or movement, for she glanced at him curiously. He realized his hands had clenched. Again, she almost smiled.

"Your sister made the purse?"

He nodded once.

"Then she is clever. And kind." She paused. The foam hissed just beyond the edges of their toes. A cormorant called.

"Did you know I had a sister?" she asked him.

Shursta nodded, more carefully this time. Her voice, like her face, was remote and cold. But at the bottom of it, buried in the ice, an inferno.

"She was clubbed to death on this beach. I found her. We had come here often to play—well, to spy on mesh-mates meeting for the first time. Sometimes we came here when the moon was full—to bathe and dance and pretend that the sea people would swim up to surface from the Nine Drowned Cities to sing songs with us. I had gone to a party that night with a group of just the sort of dashing, handsome young men we would daydream about meshing with, but she was too young yet for such things. When she was found missing from her bed the next morning, I thought perhaps she had come here and fallen asleep. I thought if I found her, I could pretend to our mother I had already scolded her—Kuista was very good at hanging her head like a puppy and looking chastised; sometimes I think she practiced in the mirror—and she might be let off a little easier. So I went here first and told nobody. But even from the cliff, when I saw her lying there, I knew she wasn't sleeping."

Shursta began to shiver. He thought of Sharrar, tangled in bladderwrack, a nimbus of bloody sand spreading out around her head.

"She was fully clothed, except for her shoes. But she often went barefoot. Said even sandals strangled her. The few coins in her pocket were still there, but her gemmaja was gone. I know she had been wearing it, because she rarely took it off. And it's not among her things."

A dark curiosity moved in him. Unable to stop himself, Shursta asked, "What is a gemmaja?"

Hyrryai untangled a thin silver chain from her hair. If she had not been so mussed, if the gemmaja had been properly secured, it would have lain across her forehead in a gentle V. A small green stone speckled with red came to rest between her eyes like a raindrop.

"The high households of the eight kinlines wear them. Ours is green chalcedony, of course. You Sarths," she added, "wear the red carnelian."

Shursta touched the small nob of polished coral he wore on a cord under his shirt. His mother had always just called it a *touchstone*. His branch of Sarths had never been able to afford carnelian.

"Later, after the pyre, I searched the sand, but I could not find Kuista's gemmaja. I was so . . ." She hesitated. "Angry."

Shursta understood the pause. Hyrryai had meant something entirely else, of course. As when calling the wall of water that destroyed your village a word so common as *wave* was not enough.

"So angry that I had not thought to check her head more closely. To see if the gemmaja had been driven into . . . into what was left her of skull. To see if a patch of her hair had been ripped out with the removal of the gemmaja—which I reason more likely. But I only thought of that later, when . . . when I could think again. Someone took the gemmaja from her, I know it." She shook her head. "But for what reason? A lover, perhaps, crazed by her refusal of him? She was young for a lover, but some men are strange. Did he beat her down and then take a piece of her for himself? Was it an enemy? For the Blodestones are powerful, Shursta Sarth, and have had enemies for as long as we have held house. Did he bring back her gemmaja to his own people, as proof of loyalty to his kinline? Was he celebrated? Was he elected leader for his bold act? I do not know. I wish I had been a year ago what I am now . . . But mark me."

She turned to him and set her strong hands about his wrists.

"Mark me when I say I shall not rest until I find Kuista's murderer. Every night she comes to me in my sleep and asks where her gemmaja is.

In my dreams she is not dead or broken, only sad, so sad that she begins to weep, asking me why it was taken from her. Her tears are not tears but blood. All I want is to avenge her. It is all I can think about. It is the only reason I am alive. *Do you understand?*"

Shursta's own big, brown, blunt-fingered hands rested quietly within the tense shackles of hers. His skin was on fire where she touched him, but his stomach felt like stone. He said slowly, "You do not wish—you never wished—to wed."

"No."

"But your grieving time is used up, and the Astrion Council—your family—is insisting."

"Yes."

"So you chose a husband who—who would be . . ." He breathed out. "Easy." She nodded once, curtly. "A stupid man, a poor man, a man who would be grateful for a place among the Blodestones. So grateful he would not question the actions of his wife. His wife who . . . who would not be a true wife."

Her hands fell from his. "You do understand."

"Yes."

She nodded again, her expression almost exultant. "I knew you would! The moment I held your mesh-gift. It was as if you knew me before we met. As if you made my sorrow and my vengeance and my blood debt to my sister into a necklace. I knew at once that you would never do. Because I need a husband who would *not* understand. Who would not care if I could not love him. Who never suspected that the thought of bringing a child into this murderous world is so repellent that to dwell on it makes me vomit, even when I have eaten nothing. I mean to find my sister's killer, Shursta Sarth. And then I mean to kill him and eat his heart by moonlight."

Shursta looked up, startled. The eating of a man's flesh was taboo—but he did not blurt the obvious aloud. Had not her sister—a child, a girl child—been murdered on this beach? Taboos meant nothing to Hyrryai Blodestone. He wondered that she had not yet filed her teeth and declared herself *windwyddiam*, a wind widow, nameless, kinless, outside the law. But then, he thought, how could she hunt amongst the high houses if she revoked her right of entry into them?

"*But.*"

He looked up at that word and knew a disgustingly naked monster shone in his eyes. But he could not help it. Shursta could not help his hope.

"But you are not a stupid man, Shursta Sarth. And you do not deserve to be sent away in disgrace, as if you were a dog that displeased me. You must tell me what you want, now that you know what I am."

Shursta sat up to shuck off his rucksack again. Again he removed the lace purse, the necklace. And though his fingers trembled, he looped the long strand around her neck, twice and then thrice, before letting the hooks catch. The teeth jutted out about her flesh, warning away chaste kisses, chance gestures of affection. Hyrryai did not move beneath his hands.

"I am everything the Astrion Council says," Shursta said, sinking back to the sand. "But if I wed you tomorrow, I will be a Blodestone, and thus be more useful to my sister. Is that not enough to keep me here? I am not so stupid as to leave when you give me the choice to stay. But I shall respect your grief. I shall not touch you. When you have found your sister's killer and have had your revenge, come to me. I will declare myself publically dissatisfied that you have not given me children. I will return to Sif. If my sister does not mesh, you will settle upon her a portion worthy of a Blodestone, that she will never be put away in the Beggars' Quarter. And we shall be quit of each other. Does this suit you, Damisel Blodestone?"

Whatever longing she heard in his voice or saw in his eyes, she did not flinch from it. She took his face between her palms and kissed him right on the forehead, right between the eyes, where her sister's gemmaja had rested, where her skull had been staved in.

"Call me Hyrryai, husband."

When she offered her hand, he set his own upon it. Hyrryai did not clasp it close. Instead, she furled open his fingers and placed her mesh-gift into his palm. It was a black shell blade, honed to a dazzle and set into a delicately scrimshawed hilt of whale ivory.

*C*herished Nugget, Shursta began his missive, *It is for charity's sake that I sit and scribble this to you on this morning of all mornings, in the sure knowledge that if I do not, your churlishness will have you feeding burnt porridge to all the grayheads under your care. To protect them, I will relate to you the tale of my meshing. Brace yourself.*

The bride wore red, as brides do—but you have never seen such a red as the cloth they make in Droon. Had she worn it near shore, sharks would have beached themselves, mistaking her for food. It was soft, too, to the touch. What was it like? Plumage. No, pelt. Like Damis Ungerline's seal pelt, except not as ratty and well-chewed. How is the old lady, anyway? Has she lost her last tooth yet? Give her my regards.

The bride's brothers, six giants whose prowess in athletics, economics, politics, and music makes them the boast of the Blodestones, converged on me the night I arrived in Droon and insisted I burn the clothes I came in and wear something worthy of my forthcoming station.

"Except," said one—forgive me; I have not bothered to learn all their names—"we have nothing ready made in his size."

"Perhaps a sailcloth?"

"Damis Valdessparrim has some very fine curtains."

And more to this effect. A droll scene. Hold it fast in your mind's eye. Me, nodding and agreeing to all their pronouncements with a fine ingratiation of manner. Couldn't speak a word, of course. Sweating, red as a boiled lobster—you know how I get—I suppose I seemed choice prey while they poked and prodded, loomed and laughed. I felt about three feet tall and four years old again.

Alas, low as they made me, I could not bring myself to let them cut the clothes from my back. I batted at their hands. However, they were quicker than I, as is most everybody. They outnumbered me, and their knives came out. My knife—newly gifted and handsomer than anything I've ever owned—was taken from me. My fate was sealed.

Then their sister came to my rescue. Think not she had been standing idly by, enjoying the welcome her brothers made me. No, as soon as we'd stepped foot under the Blodestone roof, she had been enveloped in a malapertness of matrons, and had only just emerged from their fond embraces.

She has a way of silencing even the most garrulous of men, which the Blodestone boys, I assure you, are.

When they were all thoroughly cowed and scuffling their feet, she took me by the hand and led me to the room I am currently occupying. My mesh-rite suit was laid out for me, fine ivory linens embroidered by, she informed me, her mother's own hand. They fit like I had been born to them. The Astrion Council, they say, has eyes everywhere. And measuring tapes, too, apparently.

Yes, yes, I stray from my subject, O antsiest (and onliest) sister. The meshing.

Imagine a balmy afternoon. Warm, with a wind. (You probably had the same kind of afternoon in Sif, so it shouldn't be too hard.) Meat had been roasting since the night before in vast pits. The air smelled of burnt animal flesh, by turns appetizing and nauseating.

We two stood inside the crone circle. The Blodestones stood in a wider circle around the crones. After that, a circle of secondary kin. After that, the rest of the guests.

We spoke our vows. Or rather, the bride did. Your brother, dear Nugget, I am sorry to say, was his usual laconic self and could not find his way around his own tongue. Shocking! Nevertheless, the bride crowned him in lilies, and cuffed to his ear a gemmaja of green chalcedony, set in a tangle of silver. This, to declare him a Blodestone by mesh-rite.

You see, I enclose a gemmaja of your own. You are no longer Sharrar Sarth, but Damisel Sharrar Blodestone, mesh-sister to the Gleaming One.

When you come of croning, you too, shall take your seat on the Astrion Council. Power, wealth, glory. Command of the kinlines. Fixer of fates.

There. Never say I never did anything for you.

Do me one favor, Sharrar. Do not wear your gemmaja upon your forehead, or in any place too obvious. Do not wear it where any stranger who might covet it might think to take it from you by force. Please.

A note of observation. For all they dress so fine and speak with fancy voices, I cannot say that people in Droon are much different than people in Sif. Sit back in your chair and imagine me rapturous in the arms of instant friends.

I write too hastily. Sharrar, I'm sorry. The ink comes out as gall. I know for a fact that you are scowling at the page and biting your nails. My fault.

I will slow down, as if I were speaking, and tell you something to set your heart at ease.

Other than the bride—who is what she is—I have perhaps discovered one friend. At least, he is friendlier than anyone else I have met in Droon. I even bothered remembering his name for you.

He is some kind of fifth or sixth cousin to the bride. Not a Blodestone. One of the ubiquitous Spectroxes. (Why are they ubiquitous, you ask? I am not entirely sure. I was told they are ubiquitous, so ubiquitous I paint them for you now. Miners and craftsmen, mostly, having holdings in the mountains. Poor but on the whole respectable.) This particular Spectrox is called Laric Spectrox. Let me tell you how I met him.

I was lingering near the banquet table after the brunt of the ceremony had passed from my shoulders.

Imagine me a mite famished. I had not eaten yet that day, my meshing day, and it was nearing sunset. I was afraid to serve myself even a morsel for the comments my new mesh-brothers might make. They had already made several to the end that, should I ever find myself adrift at sea, I might sustain myself solely on myself until rescue came, and still be man enough for three husbands to their sister!

I thought it safe, perhaps, to partake of some fruit. All eyes were on a sacred dance the bride was performing. This involved several lit torches swinging from the ends of chains and what I can only describe as alarming acrobatics. I had managed to eat half a strawberry when a shadow dwarfed the dying sun. A creature precisely three times the height of any of the bride's brothers—though much skinnier, and black as the sharp shell of my new blade—laughed down at me.

"Bored with the fire spinning already? Hyrryai's won contests, you know. Although she can't—ah—couldn't hold a candle to little Kuista."

I squinted up at this living beanstalk of a man, wondering if he ever toppled in a frisky wind. To my surprise, when I opened my mouth to speak, the sentence came out easily. In the order I had planned it, no less.

(I still find it strange how my throat knows when to trust someone, long before I've made up my own mind about it. It was you who first observed that, I remember. Little Sharrar, do the grayheads tell you that your name means 'Wisdom'? If they don't, they should.)

"I cannot bear to watch her," I confessed.

"Afraid she'll set someone's hair on fire?" He winked. "Can't really blame you. But she won't, you know."

"Not that. Only . . ." For a moment, my attention wandered back to the bride. Red flame. Red gown. Wheels of fire in the night. Her eyes. I looked away. "Only it would strike me blind if I gazed at her too long."

What he read in my face, I could not say (although I know you're wishing I'd just make something up), but he turned to follow her movements as she danced.

"Mmm," he grunted. "Can't say I see it, myself. She's just Hyrryai. Always has been. Once, several years back, my mother suggested I court her. I said I'd rather mesh with a giant squid. Hyrryai's all bone and sinew, you know. Never had any boobies to speak of. Anyway, even before Kuista died, she was too serious. Grew up with those Blodestone boys—learned to fight before she could talk. I wouldn't want a wife who could kill me with her pinkie, would you?"

My eyebrows went past my hairline. In fact, I have not located them since. I think they are hiding behind my ears. My new acquaintance grinned to see me at such a loss, but he grasped my forearm and gave it a hearty shake.

"What am I doing, keeping you from your grub? Eat up, man! You're that feral firemaid's husband now. I'd say you'll need all your strength for tonight."

And that, Nugget, is where I shall leave you. It is morning. As you see, I survived.

Your fond brother,
Shursta Blodestone

He was reading a book in the window seat of his room when Shursta heard the clamor in the courtyard. Wagon wheels, four barking dogs, several of the younger Blodestones who had been playing hoopball, an auntie trying to hush everyone down.

"Good morning, Chaos," a voice announced just beyond his line of sight. "My name is Sharrar Sarth. I've come to meet my mesh-kin."

Shursta slammed his book closed and ran for the door. He did not know if he was delighted or alarmed. Would they jostle her? Would they take her cane away and tease her? Would she whack them over the knuckles and earn the disapprobation of the elders? *Why had she come?*

The letter, of course. The letter. He had regretted it the moment he sent it. It had been too long, too full of things he should have kept to himself. He ought to have expected her. Would he have stayed at home, receiving a thing like that from her? Never. Now that she was here, he ought to send her away.

Sharrar stood amongst a seethe of Blodestones, chatting amiably with them. She leaned on her cane more crookedly than usual, the expression behind her smile starting to pinch.

No wonder. She'd come nearly twenty miles on the back of a rickety produce wagon. If she weren't bruised spine to sternum, he'd be surprised.

When Shursta broke through the ranks, Sharrar's smile wobbled, and she stumbled into his arms.

"I think you need a nap, Nugget," he suggested.

"You're not mad?"

"I am very happy to see you." He kissed the top of her head. "Always."

"You won't send me away on the next milknut run?"

"I might if you insist on walking up those stairs." He looked at his mesh-brothers. His mouth tightened. He'd be drowned twice and hung out to dry before asking them for help.

Hyrryai appeared at his side, meeting his eyes in brief consultation. He nodded. She slung one of Sharrar's arms about her shoulders while Shursta took the other.

"Oh, hey," said Sharrar, turning her head to study the newcomer. "You must be the Gleaming One."

"And you," said Hyrryai, "must be my sister."

"I've always wanted a sister," Sharrar said meditatively. "But my mother—may she sleep forever with the sea people—said, so help her, two children were *enough* for one woman, and that was two more than strictly necessary. She was a schoolteacher," Sharrar explained. "Awfully smart. But I don't think she understood things like sisters. She had so many herself."

For a moment, Shursta thought Hyrryai's eyes had flooded. But then she smiled, a warmer expression on her face than any Shursta had yet seen. "Perhaps you won't think so highly of them once I start borrowing your clothes without asking."

"Damisel," Sharrar pronounced, "my rags are your rags. Help yourself."

There was a feast four days later for the youngest of Hyrryai's brothers. "Dumwei," Sharrar reminded Shursta. "I don't know why you can't keep them all straight."

"I do not have your elasticity of mind," he retorted. "I haven't had to memorize all three hundred epics for the entertainment of the Hall of Ages."

"It's all about mnemonic tricks. Let's see. In order of age, there's Lochlin the Lunkhead, Arishoz the Unenlightened, Menami Meatbrain—then Hyrryai, of course, fourth in the birth order, but we all know what *her* name means, don't we, Shursta?—Orssi the Obscene, Plankin Porkhole, and Dumwei the Dimwitted. How could you mix them up?"

By this time Shursta was laughing too hard to answer. When Hyrryai joined them, he flung himself back onto the couch cushions and put a pillow over his face. Now and again, a hiccup emerged from the depths.

"I've never seen him laugh before," Hyrryai observed. "What is the joke?"

"Oh," Sharrar said blithely, "I was just mentioning how much I like your brothers. Tell me, who is coming to the feast tonight?"

Hyrryai perched at the edge of the couch. "Everybody."

"Is Laric Spectrox coming?"

"Yes. Why? Do you know him?"

"Shursta mentioned him in a letter."

Shursta removed his pillow long enough to glare, but Sharrar ignored him.

"I was curious to meet him. Also, I was wondering . . . what is the protocol to join the Sing at the end of the feast? One of my trades is storyteller—as my brother has just reminded me—and I have recently memorized a brave tale that dearest Dumwei will adore. It is all about, oh, heroic sacrifice, bloody deeds and great feats, despair, rescue, celebration. That sort of thing."

Observing the mischief dancing in Sharrar's eyes, a ready spark sprang to Hyrryai's. "I shall arrange a place of honor for you in the Sing. This is most kind of you."

Groaning, Shursta swam up from the cushions again. "Don't trust her! She is up to suh—*hic*—uhmething. She will tell some wild tale about, about—farts and—and burps and—billy goats that will—*hic*—will shame your grandmother!"

"My grandmother has no shame." Hyrryai stood up from the edge of the couch. She never relaxed around any piece of furniture. She had to be up and pacing. Shursta, following her with his eyes, wondered how, and if, she ever slept. "Sharrar is welcome to tell whatever tale she deems fit. Do not be offended if I leave early. Oron Onyssix attends the feast tonight, and I mean to shadow him home."

At that, even Sharrar looked startled. "Why?"

Hyrryai grinned. It was not a look her enemies would wish to meet by moonlight.

"Of late the rumors are running that his appetite for hedonism has begun to extend to girls too young to be mesh-fit. I go tonight to confirm or invalidate these."

"Oh," said Sharrar, "you're hunting."

"I am hunting."

Shursta bit his lip. He did not say, "Be careful." He did not say, "I will not sleep until you return." He did not say, "If the rumors are true, then bring him to justice. Let the Astrion Council sort him out, trial and judgment. Even if he proves a monster, he may not be *your* monster, and don't you see, Hyrryai, whatever happens tonight, it will not be the end? That grief like yours does not end in something so simple as a knife in the dark?"

As if she heard all that he did not speak, Hyrryai turned her grin on him. All the teeth around her throat grinned, too.

"It *is* a nice necklace," Sharrar observed. "I told Shursta it was a poem."

The edges of Hyrryai's grin softened. "Your brother has the heart of a poet. And you the voice of one. We Blodestones are wealthy in our new kin." She turned to go, paused, then added over her shoulder, "Husband, if you drink a bowl of water upside down, your hiccups may go away."

When she was gone, Sharrar nudged him. "Oohee, brother mine. I like her."

"Ayup, Nugs," he sighed. "Me, too."

It was with trepidation that Shursta introduced his sister to Laric Spectrox that night at the feast. He need not have worried. Hearing Laric's name, Sharrar laughed with delight and raised her brown eyes to his.

"Why, hey there! Domo Spectrox! You're not nearly as tall as Shursta made you out to be."

Laric straightened his shoulders. "Am I not?"

"Nope. The way he writes it, I thought to mistake you for a milknut tree. Shursta, you said skinny. It's probably all muscle, right? Wiry, right? Like me?" Sharrar flexed her free arm for him. Laric shivered a wink at Shursta and gravely admired her bicep. "Anyway, you're not too proud to bend down, are you?"

"I'm not!"

"Good! I have a secret I must tell you."

When Laric brought his face to her level, she seized him by both big ears and planted an enormous kiss on his mouth. Menami and Orssi Blodestone, who stood nearby, started whooping. Dumwei sidled close.

"Don't I get one? It's my birthday, you know."

Sharrar gave him a sleepy-eyed look that made Shursta want to hide under the table. "Just you wait till after dinner, Dumwei, my darling. I have a special surprise for you." She shooed him along and bent all her attention back to Laric.

"You," she said.

He pointed to his chest a bit nervously. "Me?"

"You, Laric Spectrox. You are going to be my friend for the rest of my life. I decided that ages ago, so I'm very glad we finally got to meet. No arguments."

Laric's shining black face broke into a radiance of dimple creases and crooked white teeth. "Do you see me arguing? I'm not arguing."

"I'm Sharrar, by the way. Sit beside me tonight and let me whisper into your ear."

When Laric glanced at Shursta, Shursta shrugged. "She's going to try and talk you into doing something you won't want to do. I don't know what. Just keep saying no and refilling her plate."

"Does that really work?"

Shursta gave him a pained glance and did not answer.

Hyrryai came late to the feast and took a silent seat beside Shursta. He filled a plate and shoved it at her as if she had been Sharrar, but when she only picked at it, he shrugged and went back to listening to Laric and Orssi arguing.

Orssi said, "The Nine Islands drowned and the Nine Cities with them. There are no other islands. There is no other land. We are alone on this world, and we must do our part to repeople it."

"No, no, see"—Laric gestured with the remnants of a lobster claw—"that lacks imagination. That lacks *gumption*. What do we know for sure? We know that something terrible happened in our great-great-grandparents' day. What was it, really? How can we know? We weren't born then. All we have are stories, stories the grayheads tell us in the Hall of Ages. I value these stories, but I will not build my life on them, as a house upon sand. We call ourselves the Glennemgarra, the Unchosen. Unchosen by what? By death? By the wave? By the magic of the gods that protected the Nine Holy Cities even as they drowned, so that they live still, at the bottom of the sea? Let there be a hundred cities beneath the waves. What do we care? *We can't go there.*"

Laric glanced around at the few people who still listened to him.

"Do you know where we *can* go, though? Everywhere else. Anywhere. There is no law binding us to Droon—or to Sif"—he nodded at Sharrar, whose face was rapt with attention—"or anywhere on this wretched oasis. We know the wind. We know the stars. We have our boats and our nets and our water casks. There is no reason not to set out in search of something better."

"Well, cousin," said Orssi, "no one could accuse *you* of lacking imagination."

"Yes, Spectrox," cried Arishoz, "and how is your big boat project coming along?"

Laric's round eyes narrowed. "It would go more quickly if I had more hands to help me."

The Blodestone brothers laughed, though not ill-naturedly. "Find a wife, cousin," Lochlin advised him. "Breed her well. People the world with tiny Spectroxes—as if the world needed more Spectroxes, eh? Convince *them* to build your boat. What else are children for?"

Laric threw up his hands. He was smiling, too, but all the creases in his forehead bespoke a sadness. "Don't you see? When my boat is finished, I will sail away from words like that and thoughts like yours. As if women were only good for wives, and children were only made for labor."

Hyrryai raised her glass to him. Shursta reached over to fill it from the pitcher and watched as she drank deeply.

"I will help you, Laric Specrox!" Sharrar declared, banging her fists on the table. "I am good with my hands. I never went to sea with the men of Sif, but I can swim like a seal—and I'd trade my good leg for an adventure. Tell me all about your big boat."

He turned to her and smiled, rue twining with gratitude and defiance. "It is the biggest boat ever built. Or it will be."

"And what will you name her?"

"*The Grimgramal.* After the wave that changed the world."

Sharrar nodded as if this were the most natural thing. Then she swung her legs off the bench, took up her cane, and pushed herself to her feet. Leaning against the table for support, she used her cane to pound the floor. When this did not noticeably diminish the noise in the hall, she set her forefinger and pinkie to her lips and whistled. Everyone, from the crones' table where the elders were wine-deep in gossip and politics, to the children's table where little cakes were being served, hushed.

Sharrar smiled at them. Shursta held his breath. But she merely invoked the Sing, bracing against a bench for support, then raising both fists above her head to indicate the audience should respond to her call.

"Grimgramal the Endless was the wave that changed the world."

Obediantly, the hall repeated, *"Grimgramal the Endless was the wave that changed the world."*

Sharrar began the litany that preceded all stories. Shursta relaxed again, smiling to himself to see Hyrryai absently chewing a piece of flatbread as she listened. His sister's tales, unlike Grimgramal, were not endless; they were mainly intended to please grayheads, who fell asleep after fifteen minutes or so. Sharrar's habit had been to practice her stories on her brother when he came in from a day out at sea and was so tired he could barely keep his eyes open. When he asked why she could not wait until morning when he could pay proper attention, she had replied that his exhaustion in the evening best simulated her average audience member in the Hall of Ages.

But Shursta had never yet fallen asleep while Sharrar told a story.

> "*The first city was Hanah and it fell beneath the sea*
> "*The second city was Lahatiel, and it fell beneath the sea*
> "*The third city was Ekesh, and it fell beneath the sea*
> "*The fourth city was Var, and it fell beneath the sea*
> "*The fifth city was Thungol, and it fell beneath the sea*
> "*The sixth city was Yassam, and it fell beneath the sea*
> "*The seventh city was Saheer, and it fell beneath the sea*
> "*The eighth city was Gelph, and it fell beneath the sea*
> "*The ninth city was Niniam, and it fell beneath the sea . . .*"

Sharrar ended the litany with a sweep of her hands, like a wave washing everything away. "But one city," she said, "did not fall beneath the sea." Again, her fists lifted. "That city was Droon!"

"*That city was Droon!*" the room agreed.

"That city was Droon, capital of the Last Isle. Now, on this island, there are many villages, though none that match the great city Droon. In one of these villages—in Sif, my own village—was born the hero of this tale. A young man, like the young men gathered here tonight. Like Dumwei whom we celebrate."

She did not need to coax a response this time. Cups and bowls and pitchers clashed.

"*Dumwei whom we celebrate!*"

"If our hero stood before you in this hall, humble as a Man of Sif might be before the Men of Droon, you would not say to your neighbor, your brother, your cousin, 'That young man is a hero.' But a hero he was born, a hero he became, a hero he'll remain, and I will tell you how, here and now."

Sharrar took her cane, moving it through the air like a paddle through water.

"The fisherfolk of Sif catch many kinds of fish. Octopus and squid, shrimp and crab. But the largest catch and tastiest, the feast to end all feasts, the catch that feeds a village—this is the bone shark."

"*The bone shark.*"

"It is the most cunning, the most frightening, the most beautiful of all the sharks. A long shark, a white shark, with a towering dorsal fin and a great jaw glistening with terrible teeth. This is the shark that concerns our hero. This is the shark that brought him fame."

"This is the shark that brought him fame."

By this time, Sharrar barely needed to twitch a finger to elicit a response. The audience leaned in. All except Shursta, whose shoulders hunched, and Hyrryai, who drew her legs up onto the bench, to wrap her arms around her knees.

"To catch a shark you must first feed it. You must bloody the waters. You must send a slick of chum as sacrifice. For five days you must do this, until the sharks come tame to your boat. Then noose and net, you must grab it. Noose and net, you must drag it to the shore where it will die upon the sand. This is how you catch a shark."

"This is how you catch a shark."

"One day, our hero was at sea. Many other men were with him, for the fishermen of Sif do not hunt alone. A man—let us call him Ghoul, for his sense of humor was necrotic—had brought along his young son for the first time. Now, Ghoul, he did not like our hero. Ghoul was a proud man. A strong man. A handsome man too, if you like that sort of man. He thought Sif had room for only one hero and that was Ghoul."

"Ghoul!"

"Ghoul said to his son, 'Son, why do we waste all this good chum to bait the bone shark? In the next boat over sits a lonesome feast. An unmeshed man whom no one will miss. Let us rock his boat a little, eh? Let us rock his boat and watch him fall in.'

"Father and son took turns rocking our hero's boat. Soon the other men of Sif joined in. Not all men are good men. Not all good men are good all the time. Not even in Droon. The waters grew choppy. The wind grew restless. The bone shark grew tired of waiting for his chum."

"The bone shark grew tired of waiting—"

"Who can say what happened then? A wave too vigorous? The blow of a careless elbow as Ghoul bent to rock our hero's boat? A nudge from the muzzle of the bone shark? An act of the gods from the depths below? Who can know? But our hero saw the child. He saw Ghoul's young son fall into the sea. Like Gelph and Saheer, he fell into the sea. Like Ekesh and Var and Niniam, he fell into the sea. Like Hanah and Lahatiel, Thungol and Yassam. Like the Nine Islands and all Nine Cities, the child fell."

"The child fell."

"The bone shark moved as only sharks can move, lightning through the water, opening its maw for the sacrifice. But then our hero was there. There in the sea. Between shark and child. Between death and the child. Our hero was there, treading water. There with his noose and his net. He had jumped from his boat. Jumped—where no man of Sif could push him, however hard they rocked his boat. Jumped to save this child. And he tangled the shark in his net. He lassoed the shark with his noose and lashed himself to that dreadful dorsal fin! Ghoul had just enough time to haul his son back into his boat. The shark began to thrash."

"The shark began to thrash."

"The shark began to swim."

"The shark began to swim."

"Our hero clung fast. Our hero held firm. Our hero herded that shark as some men herd horses. He brought that shark to land. He brought that shark onto the sand, where the shark could not breathe, and so it died. Thus our hero slew the bone shark. Thus our hero fed his village. Thus our hero rescued the child. He rescued the child."

"He rescued the child."

It was barely a whisper. Not an eye in that hall was dry.

"And that is the end of my tale."

Sharrar thumped her cane on the floor again. This time, the noise echoed in a resounding silence. But without giving even the most precipitous a chance to stir, much less erupt into the applause that itched in every sweaty palm present, Sharrar spun on her heel and glared at the table where the Blodestone brothers sat.

"It was Shursta Sarth slew the bone shark," she told them, coldly and deliberately. "Your sister wears its teeth around her neck. You are not worthy to call him brother. You are not worthy to sit at that table with him."

With that, she spat at their feet and stumped out of the room.

Shursta followed close behind, stumbling through bodies. Not daring to look up from his feet. Once free of the hall, he took a different corridor than the one Sharrar had stormed through. Had he caught her up, what would he have done to her? Thanked her? Scolded her? Shaken her? Thrown her out a window? He did not know.

However difficult or humiliating negotiating his new mesh-kin had been, Sharrar the Wise had probably just made it worse.

And yet . . .

And yet how well she had done it. The Blodestones, greatest of the eight kinlines gathered together in one hall—and Sharrar had had them slavering. They would have eaten out of her hand. And what had she done with that hand? Slapped their faces. All six brothers of his new wife.

Shursta wanted his room. A blanket over his head. He wanted darkness.

When his door clicked open several hours later, Shursta jerked fully awake. Even in his half-doze, he had expected some kind of retributive challenge from the Blodestone brothers. He wondered if they would try goading him to fight, now that they knew the truth about him. Well—Sharrar's version of the truth.

The mattress dipped near his ribs. He held his breath and did not speak. And when Hyrryai's voice came to him in the darkness, his heartbeat skidded and began to hammer in his chest.

"Are you awake, Shursta?"

"Yes."

"Good." A disconsolate exhalation. He eased up to a sitting position and propped himself against the carven headboard.

"Did your hunting go amiss, Hyrryai?"

It was the first time he'd had the courage to speak her name aloud.

The sound she made was both hiss and plosive, more resigned than angry. "Oron Onyssix was arrested tonight by the soldiers of the Astrion Council. He will be brought to trial. I don't know—the crones, I think, got wind of my intentions regarding him. I track rumors; they, it seems, track me. In this case, they made sure to act before I did." She paused. "In this case, it might have been for the best. I was mistaken."

"Is he not guilty? With what, then, is he being charged?"

"The unsanctioned mentoring of threshold youths. That's what they're calling it."

She shifted. The mattress dipped again. Beneath the sheets, Shursta brought his hand to his heart and pressed it there, willing it to hush. *Hush, Hyrryai is speaking.*

"What does that mean?"

"It means Onyssix is not the man I'm hunting for!"

"How do you know?" he asked softly.

"Because . . ."

Shursta sensed, in that lack of light, Hyrryai making a gesture that cut the darkness into neat halves.

"Well, for one, the youths he prefers are *not*, after all, girls. A few young men came forward to bear witness. All were on the brink of mesh-readiness. Exploring themselves, each other. Coming-of-age. Usually the Astrion Council will assign such youths an older mentor to usher them into adulthood. One who will make sure the young people know that their duty as adult citizens of the Glennemgarra is to mesh and make children—no matter whom they may favor for pleasure or succor or lifelong companionship. That the privilege of preference is to be earned *after* meshing. There are rites. There is," her voice lilted mockingly, "paperwork. Onyssix sidestepped all of this. He will be fined. Watched a little more closely. Nothing else—there is no evidence of abuse. The young men did not speak of him with malice or fear. To them, he was just an older man with experience they wanted. I suppose it was a thrill to sneak around without the crones' consent. There you have it. Oron Onyssix is a reckless pleasure-seeker who thinks he's above the law. But hardly a murderer."

"I am sorry," Shursta murmured. "I wish it might have ended tonight."

From the way the mattress moved, he knew she had turned to look at him. Her hand was braced against the blankets. He could feel her wrist against his thigh.

"I wished it too." Hyrryai's voice was harsh. "All week I have anticipated . . . some conclusion. The closing of this wound. I prepared myself. I was ready. I wanted to look my sister's killer in the eye and watch him confess. At banquet tonight, I wished it most—when Sharrar told her tale . . ."

"The Epic of Shursta Sharkbait? You should not believe all you hear. Especially if Sharrar's talking."

"I've heard tell of it before," she retorted. "Certainly, when the story reached the Astrion Council, it was bare of the devices Sharrar used to hold our attention. But it has not changed in its particulars. It is, in fact, one measure by which the Astrion Council assessed your reputed stupidity. Intelligent men do not go diving in shark-infested waters."

The broken knife in his throat was laughter. Shursta choked on it. "No, they don't. I told you that day we met—I am everything they say."

"You did not tell me *that* story. Strange," Hyrryai observed, "when you mentioned they called you Sharkbait, you left out the reason why."

Shursta pulled the blankets up around his chin. "You didn't mention it, either. Maybe it's not worth mentioning."

"It is why I chose you."

All at once, he could not breathe. Hyrryai had leaned over him. One fist was planted on either side of his body, pinning the blankets down. Her forehead touched his. Her breath was on his mouth, sharp and fresh, as though she had been chewing some bitter herb as she stalked Onyssix through the darkness.

"Not because they said you were stupid, or ugly, or poor. How many men in Droon are the same? No, I chose you because they said you were good to your sister. And because you rescued the child."

"I rescued the child," Shursta repeated in a voice he could barely recognize.

Of course, he wanted to say. *Of course, Hyrryai, that would move you. That would catch you like a bone hook where you bleed.*

"Had you not agreed to come to Droon, I would have attended the muster to win you at games, Shursta Sarth."

He would have shaken his head, but could do nothing of his own volition to break her contact with him. "The moment we met, you sent me away. You said—you said you were mistaken . . ."

"I was afraid."

"Of *me?*" Shursta was shivering. Not with cold or fear but something more terrifying. Something perilously close to joy. "Hyrryai, surely you know by now—surely you can see—I am the last man anyone would fear. Believe Sharrar's story if you like, but . . . but consider it an aberration. It does not define me. Did I look like a man who wrestled sharks when your brothers converged on me? When the crones questioned me? When I could not even speak my vows aloud at our meshing? That is who I am. That's all I am."

"I know what you are."

Hyrryai sat back as abruptly as she had leaned in. Stood up from the bed. Walked to the door. "When my hunt is done, we shall return to this discussion. I shall not speak of it again until then. But . . . Shursta, I did not want you to pass another night believing yourself to be a man whom . . . whom no wife could love."

The latch lifted. The door clicked shut. She was gone.

The Blodestones took their breakfast in the courtyard under a stand of milknut trees. When Shursta stepped outside, he saw Laric, Sharrar, and Hyrryai all lounging on the benches, elbows sprawled on the wooden table, heads bent together. They were laughing about something—even Hyrryai—and Shursta stopped dead in the center of the courtyard, wondering if they spoke of him. Sharrar saw him first and grinned.

"Shursta, you must hear this!"

He stepped closer. Hyrryai glanced at him. The tips of her fingers brushed the place beside her. Taking a deep breath, he came forward and sat. She slid him a plate of peeled oranges.

"Your sister," said Laric Spectrox, with his broad beaming grin, "is amazing."

"My sister," Shursta answered, "is a minx. What did you do, Nugget?"

"Nugget?" Laric repeated.

"Shursta!" Sharrar leaned over and snatched his plate away. "Just for that you don't get breakfast."

"Nugget?" Laric asked her delightedly. Sharrar took his plate as well. Hyrryai handed Shursta a roll.

"Friends," she admonished them, "we must not have dissension in the ranks. Not now that we've declared open war on my brothers."

Shursta looked at them all, alarmed. "You declared . . . *What did you do?*"

Sharrar clapped her hands and crowed, "We sewed them into their bed sheets!"

"You . . ."

"We did!" Laric assured him, rocking with laughter in his seat. "Dumwei, claiming his right as birthday boy, goaded his brothers into a drinking game. By midnight, all six of them were sprawled out and snoring like harvest hogs. So late last night—"

"This morning," Sharrar put in.

"This morning, Sharrar and Hyrryai and I—"

"*Hyrryai?*" Shursta looked at his mesh-mate. She would not lift her eyes to his, but the corners of her lips twitched as she tore her roll into bird-bite pieces.

"—snuck into their chambers and sewed them in!"

Shursta hid his face in his hands. "Oh, by all the Drowned Cities in all the seas . . ."

Sharrar limped around the table to fling her arms about him. "Don't worry. No one will blame you. I made sure they'd know it was my idea."

He groaned again. "I'm afraid to ask."

"She signed their faces!" Laric threaded long fingers through his springy black hair. "I've not played pranks like this since I was a toddlekin. Or," he amended, "since my first-year wife left me for a man with more goats than brains."

Sharrar slid down beside him. "Laric, my friend, just *wait* till you hear my plans for the hoopball field!"

"Oh, the weeping gods . . ." Shursta covered his face again.

A knee nudged his knee. Hyrryai's flesh was warm beneath her linen trousers. He glanced at her between his fingers, and she smiled.

"Courage, husband," she told him. "The best defense is offense. You never had brothers before, or you would know this. My brothers have been getting too sure of themselves. Three meshed already, their seeds gone for harvest, and they think they rule the world. Three of them recently come of age—brash, bold, considered prize studs of the market. Their heads are inflated like bladder balls."

Sharrar brandished her eating blade. "All it takes is a pinprick, my sweet ones!"

"Hush," Laric hissed. "Here come Plankin and Orssi."

The brothers had grim mouths, tousled hair, and murder in their bloodshot eyes. Perhaps they had been too bleary to look properly at each other or in the mirror, for Sharrar's signature stood out bright and blue across their foreheads. Once they charged the breakfast table, however, they seemed uncertain upon whom they should fix their wrath. Sharrar had resumed her seat and was eating an innocent breakfast off three different plates. Laric kept trying to steal one of them back. Hyrryai's attention was wholly on the roll she decimated. Orssi glared at Shursta.

"Was it you, Sharkbait?" he demanded.

Shursta could still feel Hyrryai's knee pressed hard to his. His face flushed. His throat opened. He grinned at them both.

"Me, Shortsheets?" he asked. "Why, no. Of course not. I have minions to do that sort of thing for me."

He launched his breakfast roll into the air. It plonked Plankin right between the eyes. Unexpectedly, Plankin threw back his head, roaring out a laugh.

"Oh, hey," he said. "Breakfast! Thanks, brother."

Orssi, looking sly, made a martial leap and snatched the roll from Plankin's fingers. Yodeling victory, he took off running. With an indignant yelp, Plankin pelted after him. Hyrryai rolled her eyes. She reached across the table, took back the plate of oranges from Sharrar and popped a piece into Shursta's mouth before he could say another word. Her fingers brushed his lips, sticky with juice.

It did not surprise Shursta when, not one week later, Laric begged to have a word with him. "Privately," he said, "away from all these Blodestones. Come on, I'll take you to my favorite tavern. Very disreputable. No one of any note or name goes there. We won't be plagued."

Shursta agreed readily. He had not explored much of Droon beyond the family's holdings. Large as they were, they were starting to close in on him. Hyrryai's mother Dymorri had recently asked him whether a position as overseer of mines or of fields would better suit his taste. He had answered honestly that he knew nothing about either—and did the Blodestones have a fishing boat he might take out from time to time, to supply food for the family?

"Blodestones do not work the sea," she had replied, looking faintly amused.

Dymorri had high cheekbones, smooth rosy-bronze skin, and thick black eyebrows. Her hair was nearly white but for the single streak of black that started just off center of her hairline, and swept to the tip of a spiraling braid. Shursta would have been afraid of her, except that her eyes held the same sorrow permeating her daughter. He wondered if Kuista, the youngest Blodestone, had taken after her. Hyrryai had more the look of her grandmother, being taller and rangier, with a broader nose and wider mouth, black eyes instead of brown.

"Fishing's all I know," he'd told her.

"Hyrryai will teach you," she had said. "Think about it. There is no hurry. You have not been meshed a month."

True to his word, Laric propelled him around Droon, pointing out landmarks and places of interest. Shops, temples, old bits of wall, parks, famous houses, the seat of the Astrion Council. It was shaped like an eight-sided star, built of sparkling white quartz. Three hundred steps led up to the entrance, each step mosaicked in rainbow spirals of shell.

"Those shells came from the other Nine Islands," Laric told him. "When there were nine other islands."

"And you think there might be more?"

Laric cocked his head, listening, Shursta suspected, for the derision that usually must flavor such questions. "I think," he answered slowly, "that there is more to this world than islands."

"Even if there isn't," Shursta sighed, "I wouldn't mind leaving this one. Even for a little while. Even if it meant nothing but stars and sea and a wooden boat forever."

"Exactly!" Laric clapped him on the back. "Ah, here we are. The Thirsty Seagull."

Laric Spectrox had not lied about the tavern. It was so old it had hunkered into the ground. The air was rank with fermentation and tobacco smoke. All the beams were blackened, all the tables scored with the graffiti of raffish nobodies whose names would never be sung, whose deeds would never be known, yet who had carved proof of their existence into the wood as if to say, "Here, at least, I shall be recognized." Shursta fingered a stained, indelicate knife mark, feeling like his heart would break.

Taking a deep, appreciative breath, Laric pronounced, "Like coming home. Sit, sit. Let me buy you a drink. Beer?"

"All right," Shursta agreed, and sat, and waited. When Laric brought back the drinks, he sipped, and watched, and waited. The bulge in Laric's narrow throat bobbled. There was a sheen of sweat upon his brow. Shursta lowered his eyes, thinking Laric might find his task easier if he were not being watched. It seemed to help.

"Your sister," Laric began, "is . . ."

Shursta took a longer drink.

"Wonderful."

"Yes," Shursta agreed. He chanced to glance up. Laric was looking anywhere but at him, gesturing with his long hands.

"How is it that she wasn't snatched up by some clever fellow as soon as she came of age?"

"Well," Shursta pointed out, "she only recently did."

"I know, but . . . but in villages like Sif—small villages, I mean, well, even in Droon—surely some sparky critter had an eye on her these many years. Someone who grew up with her. Someone who thought, 'Soon as that Sarth girl casts her lure, I'll make damn sure I'm the fish for that hook! Take bait and line and pole and girl and dash for the far horizon . . .'"

Shursta cleared his throat. "Hard to dash with a game leg."

Laric plunked down from the high altitude of his visions. "Pardon?"

"Hard to run off with a girl who can't walk without a cane." Shursta studied Laric, watching Laric return his look with full somber intent, as if seeking to read the careful deadpan of his face. "And then, what if her children are born crooked? You'd be polluting your line. Surely the Spectroxes are taunted enough without introducing little lame Sharrar Sarth into the mix. Aren't you afraid what your family will say?"

"*Damisel* Sharrar Sarth," Laric corrected him stiffly, emphasizing the honorific. He tried to govern his voice. "And—and any Spectrox who does not want to claim wit and brilliance and derring-do and that glorious bosom for kin can eat my . . ."

Shursta clinked his mug to Laric's. "Relax. Sharrar has already told me she is going to elope with you on your big wooden boat. Two days after she met you. She said she'd been prepared to befriend you, but had not thought to be brought low by your—how did she put it—incredible height, provocative fingers and . . . adorable teeth." He coughed. "She went on about your teeth at some length. Forgive me if I don't repeat all of it. I'm sure she's composed a poem about them by now. If you find a proposal drummed up in couplets and shoved under your door tonight, you'll have had time to prepare your soul."

The look on Laric's face was beyond the price of gemmajas. He reached his long arms across the table and pumped Shursta's hand with both of his, and Shursta could not help laughing.

"Now, my friend," he said. "Let *me* buy *you* a drink."

It was at the bar Shursta noticed the bleak man in the corner. He looked as if he'd been sitting there so long that dust had settled over him, that lichen had grown over him, that spiders had woven cobwebs over his weary face. The difference between his despair and Laric's elation struck Shursta with the force of a blow, and he asked, when he returned to Laric's side, who the man might be.

"Ah." Laric shook his head. "That's Myrar Yaspir, poor bastard."

"Poor bastard?" Shursta raised his eyebrows, inviting more. It was this same dark curiosity, he recognized, that had made him press Hyrryai for details about Kuista's death the first day they met. He was unused to considering himself a gossip. But then, he thought, he'd had no friends to gossip with in Sif.

"Well." Laric knocked back a mouthful. His gaze wandered up and to the right. Sharrar once told Shursta that you could always tell when someone was reaching for a memory, for they always looked up and to the right. He'd seen the expression on her face often as she memorized a story.

"All right. I guess it began when he meshed with Adularia Yaspir three years ago. Second mesh-rite for both. No children on either side. He courted her for nearly a year. You could see by his face on their meshing day that there was a man who had pursued the dream of a lifetime. That for him, this was not about the Yaspir name or industry or holdings, but about a great, burning love that would have consumed him had he not won it for his own. Adularia—well, I think she wanted children. She liked him enough. You could see the pink in her cheeks, the glow in her eyes on her meshing day. And you thought—if any couple's in it past the one year mesh-mark, this is that couple. It's usually that way for second meshings. You know."

Shursta nodded.

"So the first year passes. No children. The second year passes. No children. Myrar starts coming here more often. Drinking hard. Talk around Droon was that Adularia wanted to leave him. He was arrested once for brawling. A second time, on more serious charges, for theft."

"Really?" Shursta watched from the corner of his eye, the man who sat so still flies landed on him.

"Not just any theft. Gems from the Blodestone mines."

Shursta loosed a low whistle. "Diamonds?"

"Not even!" Laric leaned in. "Semi-precious stones, uncut, unpolished. Not even cleaned yet. Just a handful of green chalcedonies, like the one you're wearing."

The breath left Shursta's body. He touched the stone hanging from his ear. He remembered suddenly how Kuista Blodestone's gemmaja had come up missing on her person, how that one small detail had so disturbed him that he had admonished his sister to hide her own upon her person, as if the red-speckled stone were some amulet of death. He opened his mouth. His throat clicked a few times before it started working.

"Why—why would he take such a thing?"

Shrugging, Laric said, "Don't know. They made him return them all, of course. He spent some time in the stocks. Had to beg his wife to take him back. Promised her the moon, I heard. Stopped drinking. But she said that if she was not pregnant by winter, she'd leave him, and that was that."

"What happened?"

"A few months later, she was pregnant. There was great rejoicing." Laric finished his drink. "Of course, none of us were paying much attention to the Yaspirs at that time, because we were all still grieving for Kuista."

"Kuista. Kuista Blodestone?"

Laric looked at Shursta, perturbed, as if to ask, *Who else but Kuista Blodestone?*

"Yes. We burned her pyre not a month before Adularia announced her pregnancy. Hyrryai was still bedridden. She didn't leave the darkness of her room for six months."

"And the child?" Shursta's mouth tasted like dehydrated fish scales.

"Stillborn. Delivered dead at nine months." Laric sighed. "Adularia has gone back to live with her sister. Sometimes Myrar shows up for work at the chandlery, sometimes not. Owner's his kin, so he's not been fired yet. But I think that the blood is thinning to water on one end, if you know what I mean."

"Yes," said Shursta, who was no longer listening. "I . . . Laric, please . . . please excuse me."

Shursta had no memory of leaving the Thirsty Seagull, or of walking clear across Droon and leaving the city by the sea road gates. He saw nothing, heard nothing, the thoughts boiling in his head like a cauldron full of viscera. He felt sick. Gray. Late afternoon, evening, and the early hours of night he passed in that lonely cove where Kuista died. Where he had met Hyrryai. Long past the hour most people had retired, he trudged wearily back to the Blodestone house. Sharrar awaited him in the courtyard, sitting atop the breakfast table, bundled warmly in a shawl.

"You're back!"

When his sister made as if to go to him, Shursta noticed she was stiff from sitting. He waved her down, joined her on the tabletop. She clasped his cold hand, squeezing.

"Shursta, it's too dark to see your face. Thunder struck my chest when Laric told me how you left him. Are you all right? What died in you today?"

"Kuista Blodestone," he whispered.

Sharrar was silent. She was, he realized, waiting for him to explain. But he could not.

"Sharrar," he said wildly, "wise Sharrar, if stones could speak, what would they say?"

"Nothing quickly," she quipped, her voice strained. Shursta knew her ears were pricked to pick up any clue he might let fall. Almost, he saw a glow about her skull as her riddle-raveling brain stoked itself to triple intensity. However he tried, he could not force his tongue to speak in anything clearer than questions.

"What does a stone possess other than . . . its stoneness? If not for wealth . . . or rarity . . . or beauty—why would someone covet . . . a hunk of rock?"

"Oh!" Sharrar's laughter was too giddy, almost fevered, with relief. She knew this answer. "For its magic, of course!"

"Magic."

It was not a common word. Not taboo—like incest or infanticide or cannibalism—but not common. Magic had drowned, it was said, along with the Nine Cities.

"Ayup." Sharrar talked quickly, her hand clamped to his, as if words could staunch whatever she thought to be his running wound. "See, in the olden days before the wave that changed the world, there was magic everywhere. Magic fish. Magic birds. Magic rivers. Magic . . . magicians. Certain gems, saith the grayheads, were also magic. A rich household would name itself for a powerful gem, so as to endow its kinline with the gem's essence. So, for instance, of the lost lines, there is Adamassis, whose gem was diamond, said to call the lightning. A stormy household, as you can imagine—quite impetuous—weather workers. The Anabarrs had amber, the gem of health, the gem that holds the sun, said to wake even the dead. Dozens more like this. Much of the lore was lost to us when the Nine Islands drowned. Of the remaining kinlines, let me think . . . The Sarths have sard—like the red carnelian—that can reverse the effects of poison. Onyssix wears onyx, to ward off demons. The jasper of the Yaspirs averts the eyes of an enemy—"

"And the Blodestones?" Shursta withdrew his hand from her stranglehold only to grip the soft flesh of her upper arm. "The Blodestones wear green chalcedony . . . Why? What is this stone?"

"Fertility," Sharrar gasped. Shursta did not know if she were frightened or in pain. "The green chalcedony—the bloodstone—will bring life to a barren womb. If a man crushes it to powder and drinks it, he will stand to his lover for all hours of the night. He will flood her with the seed of springtime. Shursta... Why are you asking me this, Shursta? Shursta, please..."

He had already sprinted from the courtyard. Faintly and far behind him, he heard the cry, "Let me come with you!"

He did not stop.

The Thirsty Seagull was seedier by night than by day. Gadabouts and muckrakes, sailors, soldiers, fisherfolk, washing women, street sweepers, lamplighters, and red lamplighters of all varieties patronized the tavern. There were no tables free, so Shursta made his way to the last barstool.

Shursta did not have to pretend to stumble or slur. His head ached, and he saw only through a distortion, as if peering through a sheet of water. But words poured freely from his mouth. None of them true, or mostly not true. Lies like Sharrar could tell. Dark lies, coming from depths within him he had never yet till this night sounded.

"*Women!*" he announced in a bleared roar. "Pluck you, pluck you right up from your comfy home. Job you like. Job you know. People you know. Pluck you up and say, it's meshing time. Little mesh-mesh. Come to bed, dear. No, you stink of fish, Shursta. Wash your hands, Shursta. Oh, your breath is like a dead squid, Shursta. Don't do it open-mouthed, Shursta. Shursta, you snore, go sleep in the next room. I mean, who are these people? These *Blodestones*? Who do they think they are? In Sif—in Sif, at least the women know how to use their hands. I mean, they *know* how to use their hands, you know? And all this talk, talk, talk, all this whining and complaining, all this saying I'm not good enough. What does she expect, a miracle? How can a man function, how can he *function* in these circumstances? How can he rise to the occasion, eh? Eh?"

Shursta nudged the nearest patron, who gave him a curled lip and turned her back on him. Sneering at her shoulder blades, Shursta muttered, "You're probably a Blodestone, eh? *All women are kin.* Think that's what a man's about, eh? Think that's all he is? A damned baby maker? Soon's you have your precious daughters, your bouncing boys, you forget all about us. Man's no good to you till he gets you pissful of those shrieking, wailing, mewling, shitting little shit machines? Eh? Well, what if he can't? What if he cannot—is he not still a man? *Is he not still a man?*"

By now the barkeep of the Thirsty Seagull was scowling black daggers at him. Someone shoved Shursta from behind. He spun around with fists balled up. Nobody was there.

"Eh," he spat. "Probably a Blodestone."

When he turned back to the bar, a hand slid a drink over to him. Shursta drank before looking to see who had placed it there.

Myrar Yaspir stared at him with avid eyes.

"Don't know you," Shursta mumbled. "Thanks for the nog. Raise my cup. Up. To you. Oh—it's empty." He slammed it down. "Barkeep, top her up. Spill her over. Fill her full. Come on, man. Don't be a Blodestone."

Amber liquid splashed over the glass's rim.

"You're the new Blodestone man," Myrar Yaspir whispered. "You're Damisel Hyrryai's new husband."

Shursta snarled. "Won't be her husband once my year's up. She'll be glad to see the back of me. Wretch. Horror. Harpy. Who needs her? Who wants her?" He began to blubber behind shaking hands. "Oh, but by all the gods below! How she gleams. How she catches the light. How will I live without her?"

A coin clinked down. Bottle touched tumbler. Myrar's whisper was like a naked palm brushing the sandpaper side of a shark.

"Are you having trouble, Blodestone man? Trouble in the meshing bed?"

"Ayup, trouble," Shursta agreed, not raising his snot-streaked face. "Trouble like an empty sausage casing. Trouble like—"

"Yes, trouble," Myrar cut him off. "Yet you sit here. You sit here drunk and stupid—you. You of all men. You, whose right as husband gives you access to that household. Don't you see, you stupid Blodestone man?" His hand shot out to grab Shursta's ear. The cartilage gave a twinge of protest, but Shursta set his teeth. When Myrar's hand came back, he cradled Shursta's gemmaja in his palm.

"Do you know what this is?"

Shursta burped. "Ayup. Green rock. Wife gave me. Wanna see my coral?" He fished for the cord beneath his shirt. "True Sarths wear carnelian, she says. Carnelian's the stone for Sarths. You ask me, coral's just as good. Hoity-toity rich folk."

"Not rock. This—is—not—*rock*," Myrar hissed. His fingers clenched and unclenched around the green chalcedony. By the dim light of the wall sconces, Shursta could barely make out the red speckles in the stone, like tiny drops of blood.

"This is your *child*. This is the love of your wife. This is life. *Life*, Blodestone man. Do you understand?" Myrar Yaspir scooted his stool closer. His breath was cold, like the inside of a tomb. "I was you once. Low. A cur who knew it was beaten. Beaten by life. By work. By women. By those haughty, high-nosed Blodestone bastards who own more than half this island and mean to marry into the other half, until there is nothing left for the rest of us. But last thing before he died, my granddad sat me down. Said he knew I was unhappy. Knew my . . . my Adularia wept at night for want of a child. He had a thing to tell me. A thing about stones."

Dull-eyed, Shursta blinked back at him.

"Stones," he repeated.

"Yes. Stones. Magic stones. So." Myrar Yaspir set the green chalcedony tenderly, even jealously, into Shursta's palm. "Take your little rock home with you, Blodestone man. Put it in a mortar—not a wooden one. A fine one, of marble. Take the best pestle to it. Grind it down. Grind it to powder. Drink it in a glass of wine—the Blodestone's finest. They have fine wine in that house. Drink it. Go to your wife. Don't listen to her voice. Her voice doesn't matter. When she sees how you come to her, her thighs will sing. Her legs will open to you. Make her eat her words. Pound her words back into her. Get her with that child. Who knows?" Myrar Yaspir sank back down, his eyes losing that feral light. "Who knows? It may gain you another year. What more can a man ask, whose wife no longer loves him? Just one more year. It's worth it."

All down his gullet, the amber drink burned. In another minute, Shursta knew, he would lose it again, vomiting all over himself. He swallowed hard. Then he bent his head to the man beside him, who had become bleak and still and silent once more, and asked, very softly:

"Was it worth the life of Kuista Blodestone? Myrar Yaspir, was it worth the death of a child?"

If cold rock could turn its head, if rock could turn the fissures of its eyes upon a living man, this rock was Myrar Yaspir.

"What did you say?"

"My wife is hunting for you."

Myrar Yaspir became flesh. Flinched. Began to shudder. Shursta did not loose him from his gaze.

"I give you three days, Domo Yaspir. Turn yourself in to the Astrion Council. Confess to the murder of Kuista Blodestone. If you do not speak by the third day, I will tell my wife what I know. And she will find you. Though you flee from coast to bay and back again, she will find you. And she will eat your heart by moonlight."

Glass shattered. A stool toppled. Myrar Yaspir fled the Thirsty Seagull, fast as his legs could carry him.

Shursta closed his eyes.

The next three days were the happiest days of Shursta's life, and he drank them in. It was as if he, alone of all men, had been given to know the exact hour of his death. He filled the hours between himself and death with sunlight.

For the first day, Sharrar watched him as the sister of a dying man watches her brother. But his smiles and his teasing—"Leave off, Nugget, or I'll teach Laric where you're ticklish!"—and the deep brilliance of peace in his eyes must have eased her, for on the second day, her spirits soared, and she was back to playing tricks on her mesh-brothers, and kissing Laric Spectrox around every corner and under every tree, and reciting stories, and singing songs to the children of the house.

Hyrryai, who still prowled Droon every night, spent her days close to home. She invited Shursta to walk with her, along paths she knew blindfolded. He asked her to teach him about spinning fire, and she said, "Let's start with juggling, maybe," and taught him patterns with handfuls of fallen fruit.

Suppers with the Blodestones were loud and raucous. Every night turned into a competition. Some Shursta won (ring-tossing out in the courtyard), and some he lost (matching drinks with Lochlin, now known to all, thanks to Sharrar, as Lunkhead), but he laughed more than he ever had in his life, and when he laughed, he felt Hyrryai watching him, and knew she smiled.

On the evening of the third day, he evaded his brothers' invitation to play hoopball. Sharrar immediately volunteered, so long as she and Laric could count as one player. She would piggyback upon his shoulders, and he would be her legs. Plankin, Orssi, and Dumwei were still vehemently arguing against this when Shursta approached his mesh-mate and set a purple hyacinth into her hands.

"Will you walk with me, wife?"

Her rich, rare skin flushed with the heat of roses. She took the hand he offered.

"I will, husband."

They strolled out into the scented night, oblivious to the hoots and calls of their kin. Their sandals made soft noises on the pavement. For many minutes, neither spoke. Hyrryai tucked the hyacinth into her hair.

An aimless by and by had passed when they came to a small park. Just a patch of grass, a bench, a fountain. As they had when they met, they sat on the ground with their backs to the bench. Hyrryai, for once, slumped silkily, neglecting to jolt upright every few minutes. When Shursta sank down to rest his head in her lap, her hand went to his hair. She stroked it from his face, traced designs on his forehead. He did not care that he forgot to breathe. He might never breathe again and die a happy man.

The moon was high, waxing gibbous. To Shursta's eyes, Hyrryai seemed chased in silver. He reached to catch the fingers tangled in his hair. He kissed her fingertips. Sat up to face her. Her smile was silver when she looked at him.

"The name of your sister's murderer is Myrar Yaspir," he said in a low voice. "I met him in a tavern at the edge of Droon. He had three days' grace to confess his crime to the Astrion Council. 'Let them have him,' I thought, 'they who made him.' But when I spoke to your grandmother before dinner, she said no one had yet come forward. I believe he decided to run. I am sorry."

The pulse in her throat beat an inaudible but profound tattoo through the night air.

To an unconcerned eye, nothing of Hyrryai would have seemed changed. Still she was silver in the moonlight. Still the purple flower glimmered against her wing-black hair. Only her breath was transformed. Inhalation and exhalation exactly matched. Perfect and total control. The pale light playing on her mouth did not curve gently upward. Her eyes stared straight ahead, unblinking sinkholes. The gleam in them was not of moonlight.

"You have known this for three days."

Shursta did not respond.

"You talked to him. You warned him."

Again, he said nothing. She answered anyway.

"He cannot run far enough."

"Hyrryai."

"You—do—not—speak—to—me."

"Hyrryai—"

"No!"

Her hand flashed out, much as Myrar Yaspir's had. She took nothing from him but flesh. Fingernails raked his face. Shursta did not, at first, suffer any sting. What he did feel, way down at the bottom of his chest, was a deep snap as she broke the strand of pearl and teeth and stone she wore around her throat. Pieces of moonlight scattered. Fleet and silver as they, Hyrryai Blodestone bounded into the radiant darkness.

One by one—by glint, by ridge, by razor edge—Shursta picked up pieces from the tufted grass. What he could salvage, he placed in the pouch he had prepared. His rucksack he retrieved from the hollow of a tree where he had hidden it the night before. The night was young, but the road to Sif was long.

Despite having begged her in his goodbye letter to go on and live her life in joy, with Laric Spectrox and his dream of a distant horizon, far from a brother who could only bring her shame and sorrow, Sharrar came home to Sif. And when she did, she did not come alone.

She brought her new husband. She brought a ragged band of orphans, grayheads, widows, widowers. Joining her too were past-primers like Adularia Yaspir, face lined and eyes haunted. Even Oron Onyssix had joined them, itching for spaces ungoverned by crones, a place where he might breathe freely.

Sharrar also brought a boat.

It was a very large boat. Or rather, the frame of one. It was the biggest boat skeleton Shursta had ever seen. They wheeled it on slats all the way along the sea road from the outskirts of Droon where Laric had been building it. Shursta, who had thought he might never do so again, laughed.

"What is this, Nugget? Who are all these people?"

But he thought he knew.

"These," she told him, "are all our new kin. And this"—with a grand gesture to the unfinished monstrosity listing on its makeshift wagon—"is *The Grimgramal*—the ship that sails the world!"

Shursta scrutinized it and said at last, "It doesn't look like much, your ship that sails the world."

Sharrar stuck her tongue out at him. "We have to *finish* it first, brother mine!"

"Ah."

"Everyone's helping. You'll help, too."

Shursta stared at all the people milling about his property, pitching tents, lining up for the outhouse, exploring the dock, testing the sturdiness of his small fishing boat. "Will I?" he asked. "How?"

Laric came over to clap him on the shoulder. "However you can, my mesh-brother. Mend nets. Hem sails. Boil tar. Old man Alexo Alban is carving us a masthead. He says it's a gift from all the Halls of Ages on the Last Isle to Sharrar." Taking his mesh-mate's hand, he indicated the dispersed crowd. "She's the one who called them. She's been speaking the name *Grimgramal* to anyone who'll stand still to listen. And you know Sharrar—when she talks, no one can help but listen. Some sympathizers—a very few, like Alexo Alban, started demanding passage in exchange for labor. Though"—his left shoulder lifted in a gesture eloquent of resignation—"most of the grayheads say they'll safe stay on dry land to see us off. Someone, they claim, must be left behind to tell the tale. And see?"

Laric dipped into his pocket, spilling out a palmful of frozen rainbows. Shursta reached to catch a falling star before it buried itself in the sand. A large, almost bluish, diamond winked between his fingers. Hastily, he returned it.

"Over the last few weeks, the grayheads have been coming to Sharrar. Some from far villages. Even a few crones of the Astrion Council— including Dymmori Blodestone. Each gave her a gem, and told her the lore behind it. Whatever is known, whatever has been surmised. Alexo Alban will embed them in the masthead like a crown. Nine Cities magic to protect us on our journey."

Shursta whistled through his teeth. "We're really going, then?"

"Oh, yes," Sharrar said softly. "All of us. Before summer's end."

It was not to Rath Sea that Shursta looked then, but to the empty road that led away from Sif.

"*All* of us," Sharrar repeated. "You'll see."

Dumwei Blodestone arrived one afternoon, drenched from a late summer storm, beady-eyed with irritation and chilled to the bone.

"Is Sif the last village of the world? What a stupid place. At the end of the stupidest road. Mudholes the size of small islands. Swallow a horse, much less a man. Sharkbait, why do you let your roof leak? How can you expect to cross an ocean in a wooden boat when you can't even be bothered to fix a leaky roof? We'll all be drowned by the end of the week."

"We?" Sharrar asked brightly, slamming a bowl of chowder in front of him. "Are you planning on going somewhere, Dimwit?"

"Of course!" He glanced at her, astonished, and brandished a spoon in her face. "You don't really think I'm going to let you mutants have all the fun, do you? Orssi wanted to come, too, but now he's got a girl. Mesh-mad, the pair of 'em."

His gaze flickered to the corner where Oron Onyssix sat carving fishhooks from antler and bone. Onyssix raised his high-arched eyebrows. Dumwei looked away.

With a great laugh, Laric broke a fresh loaf of bread in two and handed the larger portion to Dumwei.

"Poor Orssi. You'll just have to have enough adventure for the two of you."

Dumwei's chest expanded. "I intend to, Laric Spectrox!"

"Laric Sarth," Laric corrected.

"Oh, yes, that's right. Forgot. *Maybe* because you didn't *invite* me to your *meshing.*"

"Sorry," the couple said in unison, sounding anything but.

"And speaking of impossible mesh-mates . . ." Dumwei turned to Shursta, who knelt on the floor, feeding the fire pit. "My sister wants to see you, Shursta."

For a moment, none of the dozen or so people crammed in the room breathed. Dumwei did not notice. Or if he noticed, he did not care.

"Mumsa won't talk about her, you know. Well, she talks, but only to say things like, if her last living daughter wants to run off like a wild dog and file her teeth and declare herself *windwyddiam*, that's Hyrryai's decision. Maybe no one will care then, she says, when she declares herself a mother with six sons and no daughters. And then she cries. And Granmumsa and Auntie Elbanni and Auntie Ralorra all cluck their tongues and huddle close, and it's all hugs and tears and clacking, and a man can't hear himself think."

Shursta, who had not risen from his knees, comprehended little of this. If he'd held a flaming brand just then instead of ordinary wood, he might not have heeded it.

Sharrar asked, carefully, "Have you seen Hyrryai then, Dumwei?"

"Oh, ayup, all the time. She ran off to live in a little sea cave, in the . . . *That* cove." Dumwei seemed to swallow the wrong way, though he had not started eating. Quickly, he ducked his head, inspecting his chowder as if for contaminates. When he raised his face again, his eyes were overbright. "You know . . . you know, Kuista was just two years younger than I. Hyrryai was like her second mumsa, maybe, but I was her best friend. Anyway. I hope Hyrryai does eat that killer's heart!"

In the corner of the room, Adularia Yaspir turned her face to the wall and closed her eyes.

Dumwei shrugged. "I hope she eats it and spits it out again for chum. A heart like Myrar Yaspir's wouldn't make anyone much of meal. As she's cast herself out of the kinline, Hyrryai has no roof or bed or board of her own. And you can only eat so much fish. So I bring her food. It's not like they don't know back home. Granmumsa slips me other things, too, that Hyrryai might need. Last time I saw her . . . Yesterday? Day before?" He nodded at Shursta. "She asked for you."

Shursta sprang to his feet. "I'll go right now."

But Sharrar and Laric both grabbed fistfuls of Shursta's shirt and forced him down again.

"You'll wait till after the storm," said Laric.

"And you'll eat first," Sharrar put in.

"And perhaps," suggested Oron Onyssix from the corner, "you might wash your face. Dress in a clean change of clothes. Shave. What are they teaching young husbands these days?"

Dumwei snorted. "Think you can write that manual, Onyssix?"

"In my sleep," he replied, with the ghost of his reckless grin. Dumwei flushed past his ears, but he took his bowl of chowder and went to sit nearer him.

Obedient to his sister's narrowed eyes, Shursta went through the motions of eating. But as soon as her back was turned, he slipped out the front door.

It was full dark when Shursta finally squelched into the sea cave. He stood there a moment, dripping, startled at the glowing suddenness of shelter after three relentlessly rainy hours on the sea road. There was a hurricane lamp at the back of the cave, tucked into a small natural stone alcove. Its glass chimney was sooty, its wick on the spluttering end of low. What Shursta wanted most was to collapse. But a swift glance around the flickering hollow made it clear that amongst the neatly stacked storage crates, the bedroll, the tiny folding camp table, the clay oven with its chimney near the cave mouth, the stockpile of weapons leaning in one corner, Hyrryai was not there.

He closed his eyes briefly. Wiping a wet sleeve over his wet face, Shursta contemplated stripping everything, wrapping himself in one of her blankets, and waiting for her while he dried out. She hadn't meant to be gone long, he reasoned; she left the lamp burning. And there was a plate of food, half-eaten. Something had disturbed her. A strange sound, cutting through the wind and rain and surf. Or perhaps a face. Someone who, like he had done, glimpsed the light from her cave and sought shelter of a fellow wayfarer.

Already trembling from the cold, Shursta's shivers grew violent, as if a hole had been bored into the bottom of his skull and now his spine was slowly filling with ice water. Who might be ranging abroad on such a night? The sick or deranged, the elderly or the very young. The desperate, like himself. The outcasts, like Hyrrai. And the outlaws: lean, hungry, hunted. But why should they choose *this* cove, of all the crannies and caverns of the Last Isle? Why this so particular haunted place, on such a howling night? Other than Hyrryai herself, Shursta could think of just one who'd have cause to come here. Who would be drawn here, inexorably, by ghosts or guilt or gloating.

His stomach turned to stone, his knees to mud. He put his hand on the damp wall to steady himself.

And what would Hyrryai have done, glancing up from her sad little supper to meet the shadowed, harrowed eyes of her sister's killer?

She would not have thought to grab her weapons. Or even her coat. Look, there it was, a well-oiled sealskin, draped over the camp stool. Her fork was on the floor there by the bedroll, but her dinner knife was missing.

Shursta bolted from the cave, into the rain.

The wind tore strips from the shroud of the sky. Moonlight splintered through, fanged like an anglerfish and as cold. Shursta slipped and slid around the first wall of boulders and began to clamber back up the stone steps to the sea road. He clutched at clumps of marram grass, which slicked through his fingers like seaweed. Wet sand and crumbled rock shifted beneath his feet. Gasping and drenched as he was, he clung to his claw-holds, knowing that if he fell, he'd have to do it all over again. He'd almost attained the headland, had slapped first his left hand onto the blessedly flat surface, was following it by his right, meaning to beach himself from the cliff face onto the road in one great heave and lie there awhile, catching his breath, when a hand grasped his and hauled him up the rest of the way.

"Domo Blodestone!" gasped Myrar Yaspir. "You must help me. Your wife is hunting me."

The first time Shursta had seen Yaspir, he had looked like a man turned to stone and forgotten. The second time, his eyes had been livid as enraged wounds. Now he seemed scoured, nervous and alive, wet as Shursta. He wore an enormous rucksack and carried a walking stick that Shursta eyed speculatively. It had a smooth blunt end, well polished from age and handling.

"Is that how you killed Kuista Blodestone?" he blurted.

Myrar Yaspir followed his gaze. "This?" he asked, blankly. "No, it was a stone. I threw it into the sea, after." He grasped Shursta's collar and hefted. Myrar Yaspir was a ropy, long-limbed man whose bones seemed to poke right through his skin, but rather than attenuated, he seemed vigorously condensed, and his strength was enormous, almost electrical. Hauled to his feet, Shursta felt as though a piece of mortal-shaped lightning had smote down upon the Last Isle just to manhandle him. "Come," he commanded Shursta. "We must keep moving. She is circling us like a bone shark, closer, ever closer. Come, Domo Blodestone," he said again, blinking back rain from his burning eyes. "You must help me."

Shursta disengaged himself, though he felt little shocks go through him when his wrists knocked Myrar Yaspir's fists aside. "I already helped you, child-killer. I gave you three days to turn yourself in to the Astrion Council. I am done with you."

Myrar Yaspir glanced at him, then shook his head. "You are not listening to me," he said with exasperated patience. "Your wife is hunting me. I will be safe nowhere on this island. Not here and not in Droon cowering in some straw cage built by those doddering bitches of the council." He bent his head close to Shursta's and whispered, "No, you must take me to Sif where you live. Word is you are sailing from this cursed place on a boat the size of a city. I will work for my passage. I work hard. I have worked all my life." He opened his hands as if to show the calluses there; as if, even empty, they had always been enough.

Shursta felt his voice go gentle, and could not prevent it, although he knew Myrar Yaspir would think him weakening.

"*The Grimgramal* is the size, maybe, of a large house, and we who will sail on it are family. You, Domo Yaspir, are no one's family."

"*My wife is on that boat!*" Myrar flashed, his fist grasping the sodden cloth at Shursta's throat. His expression flickered from whetted volatility to bleak cobweb-clung despair, and after that, it seemed, he could express nothing because he no longer had a face. His was merely a sandblasted and sun-bleached skull, dripping dark rain. The skull whispered, "My Adularia."

Shursta was afraid. He had only been so afraid once in his entire life, and that was last year, out on the open ocean, in that breathless half-second before he jumped in after Gulak's young son, realizing even as he leapt that he would rather by far spool out the remainder of his days taunted and disliked and respected by none than dive into that particular death, where the boy floundered and the shark danced.

Now the words came with no stutter or click. "You have no wife."

The skull opened its mouth and screamed. It shrieked, raw and wordless, right into Shursta's face. Its fists closed again on the collar of Shursta's coat, twisted in a chokehold and jerked, lifting him off his feet as though he had been a small child. Shursta's legs dangled, and his vision blackened, and he struck out with his fists, but it was like pummeling a waterspout. Myrar was still screaming, but the sound soon floated off to a faraway keening. Shursta, weightless between sky and sea, began to believe that Myrar had always been screaming, since the first time Shursta had beheld him sitting in the tavern, or maybe even before. Maybe he had been screaming since killing Kuista, the child he could not give his wife, and who, though a child, had all the esteem, joy of status, wealth, and hope for the future that Myrar Yaspir, a man in his prime and a citizen of proud Droon, lacked.

Is it any wonder he screamed? Shursta thought. This was followed by another thought, further away: *I am dying.*

The moment he could breathe again was the moment his breath was knocked out of him. Myrar had released his chokehold on Shursta, but Shursta, barely conscious, had no time to find his feet before the ground leapt up to grapple him. He tried to groan, but all sound was sucked from the pit of his stomach into the sky. Rain splattered on his face. The wind ripped over everything but did not move back into his lungs.

By and by, he remembered how to breathe, and soon could do so without volunteering the effort. His mouth tasted coppery. His tongue was sore. Something had been bitten that probably should not have been. Shursta's hands closed over stones, trying to find one jagged enough to fend off further advances from a screaming, skull-faced murderer. Where was his mesh-gift, the black knife Hyrryai had given him? Back in Sif, of course, in a box with his gemmaja, and the pressed petals of a purple hyacinth that had fallen from her hair that night she left him. All his fingers found now were pebbles and blades of grass, and he could not seem to properly grip any of them. Shursta sat up.

Sometime between his falling and landing the awful scream had stopped. There was only sobbing now: convulsive, curt, wretched, interrupted by bitter gasps for breath and short, saw-toothed cries of rage. Muffled, moist thumps punctuated each cry. Shursta had barely registered that it could not be Myrar Yaspir who wept—his tears had turned to dust long ago—when the thumps and sobs stopped. For a few minutes it was just rain and wind. Shursta blinked his eyes back into focus and took in the moon-battered, rain-silvered scene before him. His heart crashed in his chest like a fog-bell.

Hyrryai Blodestone crouched over the crumpled body of Myrar Yaspir. She grasped a large stone in her dominant hand. Myrar's bloody hair was tangled in her other. Her dinner knife was clamped between her teeth. As he watched, she let the head fall—another pulpy thump—

tossed the dripping stone to one side, and spat her knife into her hand. Her movements ragged and impatient, she sliced Myrar's shirt down the middle and laid her hand against his chest. She seemed startled by what she felt there—the last echoes of a heartbeat or the fact there was none, Shursta did not know.

"It's not worth," he said through chattering teeth, "the effort it would take to chew."

Hyrryai glanced at him, her face a shocky blank, eyes and nose and mouth streaming. She looked away again, then spat out a mouthful of excess saliva. The next second, she had keeled over and was vomiting over the side of the cliff. Shursta hurried to her side, tearing a strip from his sleeve as he did so, to gather her hair from her face and tie it back. His pockets were full of useless things. A coil of fishing line, a smooth white pebble, a pencil stub—ah! Bless Sharrar and her clever hands. A handkerchief. He pulled it out and wiped Hyrryai's face, taking care at the corners of her mouth.

Her lips were bloodied, as though she had already eaten Myrar Yaspir's heart. He realized this was because she had been careless of her teeth, newly filed into the needle points of the *windwyddiam*. Even a nervous gnawing of the lip might pierce the tender flesh there.

Blotting cautiously, he asked, "Did that hurt?"

The face Hyrryai lifted to Shursta was no longer hard and blank but so wide open that he feared for her, that whatever spirits of the night were prowling might seek to use her as a door. He moved his body more firmly between hers and Myrar Yaspir's. He wondered if this look of woeful wonder would ever be wiped from her eyes.

"Nothing hurts," she mumbled, turning away again. "I feel nothing."

"Then why are you crying?"

She shrugged, picking at the grass near her feet. Her agitated fingers brushed again a dark and jagged stone. It was as if she had accidently touched a rotten corpse. She jerked against Shursta, who flailed out his foot out to kick the stone over the cliff's edge. He wished he could kick Myrar Yaspir over and gone as well.

"Hyrryai—"

"D-Dumwei f-found you?" she asked at the same time.

"As you see."

"I c-called you to w-witness."

"Yes."

"I was going to make you, make you w-watch while I—" Hyrryai shook her head, baring her teeth as if to still the chattering. More slowly, she said, "It was going to be your punishment. Instead I came upon him as he was, as he was k-killing you."

And though his soul was sick, Shursta laughed. "Two at one blow, eh, Hyrryai?"

"Never," she growled at him, and took his face between her hands. "Never, never, *never*, Shursta Sarth, do you hear me? No one touches you. I will murder anyone who tries. I will eat their eyes, I will——"

He turned his face to kiss her blood-slicked hands. First one, then the other.

"Shh," he said. "Shh, Hyrryai. You saved my life. You saved me. It's over. It's over."

She slumped suddenly, pressing her face against his neck. Wrenched back, gasping. A small cut on her face bled a single thread of red. When next she spoke, her voice was wry.

"Your neck grew fangs, Shursta Sarth."

"Yes. Well. So."

Hyrryai fingered the strand of tooth and stone and pearl at his throat. Shursta held his breath as her black eyes flickered up to meet his, holding them for a luminous moment.

"Thief," she breathed. "That's mine."

"Sorry." Shursta ducked his head, unclasped the necklace, and wound it down into her palm. Her fist snapped shut over it. "Destroy it again for all of me, Hyrryai."

Hyrryai leaned in to lay her forehead against his. Even with his eyes shut, Shursta felt her smile move against his mouth, very deliberately, very carefully.

"Never," she repeated. "I'd sooner destroy Droon."

They left Myrar Yaspir's body where it lay, for the plovers and the pipers and the gulls. From the sea cave they gathered what of Hyrryai's belongings she wanted with her when she sailed with *The Grimgramal* into the unknown sky, and they knelt and kissed the place where Kuista Blodestone had fallen. These last things done, in silent exhaustion Shursta and Hyrryai climbed back up to the sea road.

Setting their faces for Sif, they turned their backs on Droon.

How the Milkmaid Struck a Bargain with the Crooked One

For Francesca Forrest

There's that old saying:
"Truth is costly, dearly bought
Want it free? Ask a sot."

Don't you believe it. There's no wisdom in wine, just as there's no brevity in beer. And while I don't accuse Da of malice aforethought, I wouldn't have minded some—any!—aforethought in this case, being as times are harrowed enough without you add magic in our midst.

In a fit of drunkenness, Da had slobbered out the sort of rumor our own local pubbies wouldn't half heed, chin-drowned in gin as they were. But the Archabbot's Pricksters from Winterbane, having hungry ears for this sort of thing, ate the rumor right up and followed him home. To me.

"And just who are these nice folks, Da?" I asked as he stumbled through my new-swept kitchen. The Pricksters who had trooped in after stood in a half circle. They blocked the door, thumbs in their belts, staring.

"My friends, Gordie!" he belched. "Best friends a man could have."

If these were friends, I'd sooner have climbed out the back window than face his enemies. Poor drunk bastard. By this time of night, the whole world was his friend.

I curtsied with scant grace, and they smiled with scant lips, and Da fell to his cot. His beatific snores started midway between air and pillow. I looked again at the Pricksters. No question they were strangers to Feisty Wold, but anyone awake to the world would recognize them. They each wore a row of needles on their bandoliers, a set of shackles on their belts right hip and left, and there were silver bells and scarlet flowers broidered on their boots to protect them from Gentry mischief.

143

"Miss," they said.

"Misters and Mistresses," said I. "Care for a drink? We have milk straight from the udder, or the finest well water in Feisty Wold."

I did not let Da keep spirits under Mam's roof—not if he wanted his clothes mended and his meals regular. Truth be told, he'd do near anything in her name. It was not her dying that had driven him to drink. It'd been her living that had kept him from it.

The head Prickster waved away my offer with a gauntleted hand. Her hair was scraped back under the bright red hat of captaincy, leaving large, handsome ears and a strong neck exposed. She was a good-looking-enough woman, but even under other circumstances, I'd've disliked her on sight, for the pinch at her nose and cold glint in her squinted eyes.

She said, "Your honored father has been boasting of his only daughter."

I never had that trick of arching just one eyebrow. Both shot up before my frown mastered them.

"Nothing much to boast of, as you see," said I.

"Your unrivaled beauty?" suggested the Prickster woman.

"Pah," was my reply, and several of the other Pricksters nodded in agreement. Not a lot of beauty here, just your average pretty, and only that by candlelight and a kindness of the eye.

"How about your, shall we say, quiet success with your cattle?"

"Annat's the grandest milk cow in the Wold," I retorted, bristling. "Wise and mild, as fertile as she's fair. And Manu's worth three of any other bull I've met. A sweetheart still, for all he's kept his balls. Bought those cattle both myself from a farm at Quartz-Across-the-Water, with some money my mam left me."

"Yes," grunted the Prickster woman, "so we've heard. And just what *was* your mother, pray?"

"My mam?" I asked. "She . . ."

Had sung a thousand songs while washing dishes. Had woken me at night to watch stars falling. Had made us hot chocolate for sipping while the thunder gods drummed. Couldn't sew a seam for damn, but could untangle any knot given her. Walked long hours on the shore, or under the leafy Valwode, which is now forbidden. Had sickened during the First Invasion and slowly faded through the Second. Said her last words in a whisper. Left her man a wreck and me in charge. Missed her every morning first thing as I woke.

"Was your mother Gentry?" the Prickster woman pressed.

"My mam?" I asked again, stupidly.

"Did she pass along her Gentry ways to the daughter of her blood?"

"She's wasn't a—"

"Where did you get the money for those cattle?"

"I told you, from—"

"Yes, your mother. And what a wealth she must have left you. Does her immortal Gentry magic flow through your veins?"

"What?"

"Your uncanny talent's hidden in your surname. Faircloth."

"That's Da's name, for *his* da was a tailor. Himself," I indicated the treacherous snore-quaker on the cot, "was defty with a needle before the shakes got to his hands. Mam was an Oakhewn before she married him."

The Prickster woman smiled, and my little kitchen grew chill and dim. I'd've laid another log on the hearth if I dared.

"Ah, yes. Now we come to it, Miss Faircloth. Your honored father. This evening in Firshaw's Pub, he boasted to one and all that as he loves his soul, his only daughter, comely as a summer cloud, clever as a cone spider, has fingers so lively she can spin straw into gold. What say you to that, unnatural girl?"

"I can't spin to save my life," I blustered. "Not nettle-flax nor cotton thread nor silk!"

"You're lying," said the Prickster woman, and drew a needle from her bandolier.

I knew what it was for. Three drops of blood, no more no less, to be kept in a small glass vial. Later tested by the Archabbot's wizards. If they found my blood tasted of honey, if it sparkled in the dark, if it cured the sick or lame, if it caused a maid to fly when the moon was full, or bewitched a man into loving only me, I'd be doomed and dead and damned.

Of course, I knew my blood would do none of these things, but I fought the needle anyway. My blood was mine, and it belonged to me, and I belonged here, and if they took me away to Winterbane, who would care for my cows?

"Bind and blind you!" I shouted. "I'm no Gentry-babe, no changeling! I was born in Feisty Wold! Right here in this kitchen—right there on that hearth! Ask the neighbors! Ask the midwife, who is the old midwife's daughter. Me, I don't know a spindle from a spearhead! Let me go! Hex your hearts, you blackguards!"

I think I bit one of them. I hope it was the woman. I tried to wake Da with screaming, but he snored on, bubbles popping at the crease of his lips. In the end, I called to my cows, "Annat! Manu! To the woods! To the wild! Let no mortal milk you, nor yoke you, nor lead you to the ax! To the woods! Be you Gentry beasts, to graze forever in the Valwode—so long as you be safe!"

In retrospect, I realize that this was the wrong thing to have shouted. I shouldn't have shouted at all, in fact. I ought to have been docile and indulgent. I ought to've exposed Da as the only sot in town who could light a fire with his farts alone. I ought to've paid them off, or batted my eyelashes or begged, or something.

But I didn't.

So it was that the Pricksters of Avillius III, Archabbot of all monasteries in Leressa, our Kingdom Without a King, collared me, caged me, and carted me off in chains to the Holy See at Winterbane.

Don't think I'm the only victim in Feisty Wold. The Archabbot's Pricksters are everywhere, in number and urgency ever increasing since the Gentry Invasions began twenty years ago. You can meet them any time, smaller teams combing our island villages, or strolling in force around the greater towns and cities across the water on Leressa proper.

They'll haul an old gray gramamma all the way to the Holy See just for sitting in a rocker and singing while she knits. It might be a spell, after all: a Gentry grass-trap that will open a hole in the ground for the unwary to fall through, or mayhap a Wispy luring like the one that bogged King Lorez on the swamp roads and drowned him dead. (Not that many grumbled over that. "Old Ironshod," we called him, on account he liked to stomp on people's throats.) You can guess how long Gramamma survives in His Grace the Archabbot's forgetting hole, down in the darkness without food or warmth.

Not long ago, the Pricksters bagged a young schoolteacher at Seafall just because he kept both a cat and a dog as pets (this being unnatural). He tested mortal on all counts. Cold iron didn't scorch him. His blood dried brown. Starved just like a real man when fed on naught but nectar. Did that prove anything? No. The Pricksters just got all muttery about changelings having better mortal glamours than their pureblood forebears; therefore harsher methods must be applied!

Out came the dunking stool, and there drowned a nice man. His poor dog and cat were driven off the cliff at Seafall and into the tides below.

I know we're supposed to hate the Gentry for killing our king, for putting his daughter into a poisoned sleep for (they say) one hundred years, and enchanting his son to look like a bear. For the many thefts and murders that made up the First Gentry Invasion, we should despise them, ring our iron bells at dawn and at dusk to drive them out of range, never leave the house in summer but we primp ourselves in daisy chains, or wreaths of mistletoe in winter. For the horrors of the Second Invasion we should take right vengeance—for the wives and daughters and sisters who bore Gentry-babes as a result of passing through a fall of light, a strong wind, a field of wildflowers. For the appropriation of our wombs and the corruption of our children.

But some of us ask questions.

Why did the Gentry invade at all, when our people have always coexisted in a sort of scrap-now, make-up-later, meet-you-again-at-market-maybe, rival siblings' harmony, occasionally intermarrying, mostly ignoring each other? All easy enough to do, what with that Veil between our worlds, the Gentry keeping mostly to the wild Valwode, us mortals to our mills and tilled earth and stone cities. Why did they invade, why so viciously, and why in our retaliation did we turn against ourselves?

Some of us ask these questions. I'm not saying I'm one of them. I'm no troublemaker, but I always listened, especially to Mam as she washed dishes, and later when she did nothing but stare out the window and whisper to herself.

The closer my cage on wheels came to Winterbane, the more these questions weighed on me.

Let them be as locks upon my lips. Let me say nothing that will bring me further harm. Let Da at home awake with the world's worst headache but with memory enough to milk Annat and let Manu to pasture. Gods or ghosts or Gentry. Anyone who will listen. Hear my plea.

Avillius III had rosy cheeks and lively light blue eyes. His white hair had all but receded, but the baldness suited him, made him seem sleek and streamlined, like a finch about to take flight. He was slight, his skin only faintly lined. His robes were modest blue wool with no gold crusting, and he played with his miter as though it were a toy. A young lady in the undyed cotton shift of the Novitiate sat on a stool near his knee. Her hair drew my eye, a russet thorn bush just barely beaten into submission, curling like a tail over her shoulder.

She looked at me, and I could see the fox in her eyes.

Changeling, I thought. *Gentry-babe. Foxface. Skinslipper.*

She looked at me with yellow eyes slitted with horizontal pupils. They saw everything, even those things I'd hoped to keep hidden: the opal on my finger, the locket at my throat, the cow hair on my skirt. All the songs my mam had ever sung me fisted in my throat.

She smiled at me, and I could not help but smile back, though the Prickster guard at my elbow jostled me into a bow.

"Your Grace," he said, "we picked this one up at Feisty Wold. Her own father claimed, out loud and in the public house, that she spins straw into gold. As you know, such gifts are a trait of Gentry royalty. Her mother was a woodcutter's daughter, so she claims. But the Veil Queen sometimes glamours herself as common raff and lives a spell in the mortal world. Could be this girl is her get."

I snorted, very quietly. Surely any Veil Queen worth her antler crown would've chosen better for herself than *Da*. Even when young and sober and ruby-lipped with charm, he couldn't have been much of a prize.

I felt the foxgirl look at me again, but did not dare meet her yellow eyes.

"Good afternoon, young lady," said the Archabbot in a kindly way. He leaned forward on his great, curvy chair, hands on knees. I swear his nostrils flared.

"Morning, Your Grace."

I looked at his face and read nothing but concern. Was this the face of the monster who drowned a man for keeping a dog and a cat under the same roof? Was this the highest authority of the red-capped woman who had insulted my mother and dragged me in chains from Feisty Wold?

I reminded myself to take care, to beware—no matter how syrupy and convincing the Archabbot's voice when he asked:

"Are you Gentry then, child? Do not fear confession; it is not your fault if you are. Are we to be blamed for the indiscretions of our parents? If indeed you have a talent for ore-making, why, you are still half-mortal, little spinner, and may use it for the good of mortal kind."

"Your Grace." My voice echoed in that vast glass-paned hall. "I have no gift but for calming the cow Annat so she'll stand for milking. Or for leading the bull Manu 'round a shadow on the ground he mistook for a snake. I'm a milkmaid, not a spinner, and my mam was a woodcutter's daughter. She could whittle a face from a twig, but I did never see her vanish into the heart of a tree. We're just plain folk. And Da's a drunk fool, which is why he was tongue-wagging at Firshaw's in the first place!"

The Archabbot nodded and sat back, idly stroking the foxgirl's russet tail of hair. His eyes were lidded now, all that avid interest shuttered. Still with that curling smile, he asked the foxgirl, "Is she telling the truth, Candia?"

"*That* wench ain't Gentry-born." Her voice was rough and low, like a barmaid's after decades of pipe smoke and gin. Her years could not have numbered more than twelve. Her voice was well at odds with her irregular, gawky features, her translucent skin. "There is something about her, though." Her gaze flickered quickly to my ring, my locket, my narrowing eyes. With a shrug of her pointed shoulders, she finished, "She does look sly, don't she? Shifty-eyed. Tricks up her sleeve. Up to just about anything. Your Grace, I've no doubt she could somehow manage to turn straw to gold *if* she wished!"

"I don't wish it!" I flashed, angry at the lie. "Who would?"

The foxgirl, with a quick, sharp grin, seemed about to reply when the Archabbot tweaked her tail. The motion was short but vehement. Tears stood out in her eyes from the sting.

"Enough, Candia."

The Archabbot's hands bore no jewel but a thick, colorless seal. Cold iron. I was not close enough to make out the mold, but I felt the violence in it, as if the ring had smashed across a hundred faces, as if the memory of shattered bones and broken teeth hovered all about it. I wondered if the foxgirl felt the threat of iron every time he touched her. Doubtless.

"I am satisfied that this woman is not Gentry-born," the Archabbot announced. "Have I not had it on authority of the Abbacy's own house-trained Gentry-babe?" This, while stroking the head of the novice. "Therefore, I deem that Miss . . ."

"Gordie," I said.

"*Gordenne* Faircloth—" continued the Archabbot.

"Gordie Oakhewn." But I only muttered it.

"—shall be retained at Winterbane as a . . . a *guest* until the confusion surrounding her alleged talent is resolved. After all, it is obvious she has a splendid power, one that princes will covet and alchemists envy. And if her power is *not* a curse of the Gentry, it may prove to be a gift of the gods. Candia, will you show her to her . . ."

But the words fell unfinished from his mouth. The Archabbot bounded to his feet, looking at something past my shoulder. The roses on his cheeks spread until even the crest of his skull glowed. No longer did he seem kind and concerned. Angry as a salamander in a snowstorm, more like. I shrank back. There was no cover for me, no escape.

"Good afternoon, Your Grace," said a voice behind me. I shrank from that, too, for the sound sent sick ripples up and down my spine. I had no place left to go but inside myself and very still.

The Archabbot spat, "The Holy See does not recognize the petitions of pretenders!"

"I did not come to petition, Your Grace. I came to attain your little ore-maker here. My army has need of her services."

I spun around then, hoping that the speaker—whoever he was—did not mean who I thought he meant. The tallest man I'd ever seen stared right down into my face. Me. He'd meant me.

"My dear," said the tall man. "My fairest Gordenne Faircloth! I am your obedient servant. Allow me to make my bow!" He did, and the very jauntiness of the gesture mocked me. "Rumor has it you spin straw into gold."

Whatever sauce I'd served to the Prickster woman had dried with my spit on the long ride to Winterbane. I could only shake my head, mute.

The man's hair was like sunlight striking dew, his eyes so cold and bright and gray that they speared me where I stood. He laughed to see my look, casually swinging his red cloak off his shoulder to hand to his page.

The youth untangled the rich cloth and folded it over his arm. His movements were graceful, though he was a gangly thing. His face tugged at me, familiar and strange. Red hair. Slitted eyes. A face too triangular to be completely human.

It all came clear.

The tall man and his cruel mouth faded from the forefront of my mind. Even the Archabbot's fury slipped away. My ears filled with silence, a roar, a twinned heartbeat. All I saw were two Gentry-babes staring at each other with whole other worlds widening their yellow eyes. If I could imagine words to fit what flared between them, they would go like this:

"Brother!"

"Sister!"

"You are unhurt?"

"Yes, unhurt. You? Unhappy?"

"Not unhappy. But unwhole."

"How you have changed!"

"How I have missed you!"

"Say nothing."

"Be still."

"Look away."

The lightning of their gazes sparked once, went dark. As if such shuttings off had been polished by practice. The foxgirl gave me a furtive look from under the bloody fringe of her lashes. I had only a dizzy countenance to show her. No time, however, to unmuzzle this mystery, for the tall man grabbed my right elbow, and the Archabbot darted down his dais to grab my left.

"General," said Avillius III, "our interrogations here have not yet reached a satisfactory conclusion. We must retain Miss Faircloth for further questioning, perhaps rehabilitation."

The tall man smiled. "I myself heard your little vulpona bitch pronounce this maiden mortalborn. As she does not traffic with the dark spirits of the Valwode, Winterbane has no jurisdiction over her."

"If Winterbane has none, Jadio has less so!"

"No, no jurisdiction," laughed the tall man, "but an army at my back. Come, Miss Faircloth; my palace awaits you. Your Grace, I am your most humble . . ." He laughed again.

It was then I knew what I stood between. On my left, Avillius III, who, with his Pricksters and his parish priests, wanted total control over Leressa, secular as well as spiritual. On my right, the one man who stood in his way: the great General Jadio, Commander of the Kingless Armies, and Leressa's unofficial liege lord.

My nose had swelled shut, my eyes burned, and my throat was parched. Had I been crying, sobbing, begging General Jadio on bended knee for my freedom?

No. Wouldn't have done any good, anyway. Jadio was a right monster, no mistake, and if you could prove that blood ran through his veins instead of bitter winter waters, I'd eat my own dairy stool.

What I *had* done was been shut up in a silo with enough straw to stuff a legion of scarecrows. From the itching in my arms and the tickle in my nose, I apprehended a heretofore unknown but deeply personal reaction to straw. In sufficient quantities, and given enough time, the straw might actually murder me.

Time was one thing I didn't have.

If I didn't spin *all* of this sneeze-making, hive-inducing stuff to gold by dawn—so declared my gold-haired, laughing captor—I'd be hung toe-first from an iron tree, pocked by stones and pecked by crows until I had no flesh left to pock or peck, and by which time, I'd heed neither foul wind nor fair, for, and I quote, "The dead feel no discomfort."

Huddled in a hollow between mounds of the wretched straw, I stewed.

How are you supposed to spend your last hours? Praying? Cursing?

The first option was out. I was too mad to pray. Who did the gods think they were, anyway, sticking people like Jadio and Avillius in charge, who were good for nothing but drowning dogs and mangling men and was that any good at all? It was the gods that killed my mam with a long, low fever that had sapped even her smile, the gods that drew the Pricksters to Feisty Wold, snatching me up and leaving my cows in the care of drunken folk like Da. A pox of itches on the gods. I'd rather be a heathen and worship the beauty of the Valwode, like the Gentry.

Curses it was.

So I bundled up a fistful of straw into two tight bunches perpendicular to each other and bound them tightly with thread torn from the hem of my skirt. I used another ravel of thread to differentiate the head from its cross-shaped body. Holding the poppet high with my left hand, I glared at it and growled:

"General Jadio, Commander of the Kingless Armies, I curse thee, that all thy wars will be unwon and all thy wenches as well. Oh, *and*,"

I hastened to add, forgetting formality, "that, being as they are unwon, you lose all taste for war and wenching until you sicken and turn flaccid. And when you die, I hope it's a querulous and undignified death. You jackass."

I punched the little bundle with short, vicious jabs until the threads loosened and the whole thing burst apart. The straw fell. I gathered up a fresh fistful and fashioned another faceless poppet.

"Avillius III, Archabbot of Winterbane, I curse thee, that your shackled pet will bring thy order to ruin. That she will escape you, to rouse mortals and immortals alike under the banner of the Red Fox and win Leressa back for all free people. I curse thee to rot forgotten in thine own forgetting hole, and that after thy death, the word *Archabbot* is used only in stories to frighten uppity children."

I kicked the poppet so hard it flew up over my head and was lost somewhere behind me. Wiped my nose. Went on. There was nothing else I could do.

I'd have spun gold from that straw if I could, spun until my fingers were raw, I was that scared. The creeping, cold fear numbed even my screaming red skin. But Annat the cow might as soon have used that spinning wheel as I. I bent to work on another straw doll. Shook it and squeezed it until I felt the muscles standing out in my neck. Rage choked me, thickening my words.

"Prickster woman who dared blood me, who mocked my mother and took the word of a known sot as law, I curse thee to get lost in the Valwode without thy rowan-berry-broidered boots or silver bells, and to suffer what befalls thee there! That thou wilt be dragged before the Veil Queen herself for judgment and be shown such mercy as thou hast shown me."

I spat on the poppet, wrenched off its head, and crushed it under my heel.

One more bundle. Just one more. Then I'd stop. I was tired, though outside the silo I was certain it was not yet dusk. Besides, if I kept on, I'd fray my only skirt past the decency required for burial. Not that Jadio had any plans to bury me, I'd been assured. Burn my remains, maybe. After they'd been displayed a goodly time.

"Da," I said. I stopped. My eyes filled up. Blight this straw. If only I could sneeze, I'd feel better.

"What's the point, Da? She died and left us, didn't she? Any punishment after that would only pale. Poor bastard. When your pickled innards finally burst to bloody spew, I hope you die with a smile on your face. That's all."

I laid the little effigy gently on the ground and covered it.

"Does it help?" asked a voice from the corner, near to where the spinning wheel stood.

My head snapped up too quickly, and that's when the sneezes started. One—two—three—four—five—six—seven! So violent they knocked me backward into a pile of, that's right, straw, which jostled another, bigger pile into toppling all over me. Dust and critters and dry bits filled my nose and mouth until I flailed with panic. But a pair of hands locked around my wrists and pulled. I was heaved out from under the avalanche. Exhumed. Brushed off. Set down upon a stool. And smiled at.

Which is how I found myself face-to-face with the ugliest man I'd ever seen.

Now, I got nothing against ugliness. As I've said, I'm no Harvest Bride myself, to be tarted up in fruits and vines and paraded about the village on a pumpkin-piled wagon. General Jadio was pretty much the prettiest man I'd seen to date, and right then I was in the mood to cheerfully set fire to his chiseled chin.

This man was an inch or two shorter than I and so thin as to be knobbly. His crooked shoulders were surmounted by a painful-looking hump, and his wrists stuck out from ragged sleeves. A mass of hair swirled around his head in unruly black tangles, framing a face irregular with scars. His mouth, well . . . was smiling. In sympathy. And though some of his teeth were crooked, some too sharp and some completely missing, those he had kept seemed to glow in the dark.

Besides the teeth, it was his eyes gave him away, set at a slant so long and sly. The starry black of his stare left no room for white.

"You're Gentry!" I stammered.

"Me? *You* just hexed four folks in effigy," he said.

Red and sweaty and covered in rash as I was, maybe he wouldn't notice that I blushed.

"Mam always told me hexes only work if you've a bit of the hexies with you," I explained. "To put in the poppet, like? Fingernails or hair or a bit of their . . . You know. Fluids. Plus, you must be magic to begin with. And I'm not."

"Mortal to the bone," he agreed, smiling. His smile sort of made his face disappear, the way certain smiles do. He had a good voice, too. Not as smoky as the foxgirl's, but greener and freer, like it had matured by sunlight. And if I was mortal to my bone, that was where his voice echoed, and I trembled there.

He plucked a poppet from his sleeve and dangled it. 'Twas either Da or the Archabbot; I couldn't tell, nor how he'd managed to unearth the thing without my noticing.

"What did your hexies do to deserve such censure?"

"Cads," I snorted, "one and all. They took me from my cows and slandered me with lies and forgot to feed and water me. In a very few hours, one of them will kill me for not being the miracle maid he says I am. And that's after he does whatever comes *before* the killing."

"What does he say you are, miracle maid?"

"Spinner," I told him, "ore-maker. Sent by the gods to the armies of Jadio to change all their straw to gold." I spread my arms, all pompous and public-oratorish like our village alderman. The stranger's crooked smile went wider, crookeder. "Thus will the soldiers of the Kingless Army, richly clad and well-armed, march against the Gentry demons and purge Leressa of their foulness. Pah!" I spat, though I had nothing left to spit with. "Had I a hammer, a piece of flint, and some steel, I'd break that spinning wheel to splinters and use it for kindling. This place would go up in a poof and me with it. I wasn't born to hang."

The little dark man laughed. A green flame erupted in the palm of his hand, shooting sparks so high I flinched. He blew lightly on the flames until they spiraled up to flirt with his fingertips.

"Say the word, lady. If truly thou wouldst have this death, it is in my power to give it thee."

I, despite my morose grandiloquence, said nothing.

Laughing again, he urged the green flames to chase up his arm, his neck, his face, the crown of his head, where they raced in gleeful circles. By their weird light, the silo seemed a vast undersea trove, the mounds of straw gone verdigris as waterweeds, softly breathing.

"You do not desire the burning? All right, then. What do you wish?"

"To go home. To my cows."

"The soldiers of Jadio will find you there and bring you back. Perhaps first they will slaughter your cows and make you feast upon their flesh, that you taste your own defiance. What do you *really* wish?"

"I don't know!" I threw up my arms. "To make this go away?"

I meant everything that had occurred since Da's ill-advised boast in Firshaw's Pub, up to and including this current assignation, enchanting as it was. The little dark man picked up a single piece of straw and tickled my nose with it.

"Where to? There will always be another cell, another spinning wheel . . ."

I batted the straw away. "Ah-choo!"

"Blessings befall."

"Thank you."

His turn to flinch.

"Oh!" I yelped. "Sorry. Mam taught me better! I know I'm not supposed to thank the Gentry. She said saying those words out loud was like a slap in the face to them—to you, I mean, your people—but she didn't say why, and anyway, I forgot! Are you—are you all right?"

He waved his hand. "It's naught. Briefer than a sting. Like a Prickster's needle, I'd wager."

I pressed the pad of my thumb where three weeks ago in my own chilled kitchen, my blood had welled to the needle's prodding. It was still a bit sore. I wondered suddenly what the Archabbot's wizards might do with that tiny vial now that they knew I was no Gentry-babe. Destroy it? Drink it? Put it in a straw poppet and influence me from afar?

I shivered.

"What do you wish?" the little dark man asked for the third time. His voice was barely a whisper.

I stomped my foot.

"Ack! Very well! I wish to change this mess into something that doesn't make me sneeze."

"Such as gold?"

"Such as gold."

"I can do this thing."

"Can you?" I eyed him, remembering what the Prickster had told the Archabbot about Gentry ore-makers. How only Gentry royalty had the golden touch. How my own mam must've been the Veil Queen herself, to have borne a child with such gifts as mine. And though I was not that child, might *he* be?

"Whyever would you want to?" I asked.

He shrugged. Shrugging could not have been a simple or painless gesture with those shoulders. It cost him something.

"Word reached me," he said, "through regular but reliably suspicious channels, that you had something on your person I would find of value."

I felt his gaze fall on my hand before I thought to cover it. As though kindled by his verdant flames, the opal on my ring began to burn green.

"This ring belonged to my mother!" I protested.

"It belonged to my mother before that," he retorted.

"It—*what?*"

"What use does a milkmaid have for such a bauble?"

"For keeping's sake. For memory."

"Do you know what the jewel is called?"

"Yes—the Eye of . . . The Queen's Eye."

"Did your mother tell you whence she had it?"

"She said it was a gift. From a friend."

"Your mother was my mother's friend. Mortalborn, ignorant and common as she was, she was kind when my mother needed kindness. Not once, but twice. Give me that jewel, and I will turn this straw to gold."

"For friendship's sake?"

He shrugged again. How he punished himself, this little crooked man, for no reason I could tell. He was a stranger to me. But if he missed his mother half as much as I missed mine, we were kin.

"Right." I tugged my ring a bit to loosen it, breathing deeply. "Well. Mam didn't hold much with worldly goods anyhow. Never owned a pair of shoes but she gave them away to the first beggar she crossed."

"I know," said the little crooked man. "And so my mother went shod one winter's night, when the cold had nearly killed her."

Hearing this, I tugged harder. The ring would not come free. I'd never tried to take it off before. Fact is, until the day I'd stood before Avillius III and his clever foxgirl, I'd mostly forgotten it was there. As with Mam's locket, which I also wore, the ring had always seemed able to hide itself. I couldn't remember it once getting in the way of chores like dishes or milking or scrubbing floors.

Now it burned. But it wouldn't budge.

I almost wept with frustration, but the little crooked man took hold of my hand and I quieted right down. *Just like Annat*, I thought, *when she is upset and I scratch behind her ears . . .*

And then he bent his head and kissed the fiery opal. Kissed that part of my hand when fingers met knuckle. Kissed me a third time on my palm where I was most astonishingly sensitive. His tongue flicked out and loosened everything. Before I knew it, the ring was in his hand.

"You are bold. But you are innocent." He looked at me. Had Mam bequeathed me jewels enough to deck all my fingers and toes, I'd have handed them over that instant.

He slipped the silver ring onto his thumb.

"What comes next, you may not see. Dream sweet, Miss Oakhewn," said the little crooked man, and rubbed the opal once, as if for luck.

The stone responded with a sound like a thunderclap. A flash there came like a star falling, followed by a green-drenched darkness.

I know what that *is*, I had time to think, *that's the sound of a Gentry grass-trap.*

He's opened one up to swallow me down, and will I sleep now a hundred years the way they do in stories when mortals fall through grass-traps into the Valwode, and will a ring of mushrooms sprout up all around me, followed by a ring of fire, and will he be there to pull me out when at last I wake . . .

"*Tar his limbs and boil his skin*
  Carve his skull for dipping in
Acid piss and stony stool
Wrack his eyeballs, rot his rule

All hail Jadio! Let him hang!
Long his rope and brief his reign!"

My rhymes were improving. With no one to talk to in this vast, dusty room but myself, all standard imprecations swiftly palled.

I stomped around Jadio's warehouse. Slogged, more like. Not an inch of floor to be seen under all that straw, and I was knee-deep in it, not to mention hampered by satin skirts. I'd lost one pearl-studded slipper already while pretending one of those straw heaps was a recumbent Jadio (sleeping peacefully and off his guard), and subsequently kicking him to death. I did not mind the slipper's loss, but I think I pulled a muscle in my enthusiasm.

It had been an eventful month. The Kingless Armies finally had their king. With the golden skeins he had found piled high in the silo the morning after he'd set me to spinning, General Jadio had bought himself Leressa's crown and the Archabbot's blessing with it. (Or the appearance of a blessing. Remembering the Archabbot's sweating red pate, his furious grip on my elbow, I was not convinced.)

King Jadio decided not to take up residence where old King Lorez's palace lay in ruins. Lirhu is a city of ghosts, a drowned city. They say one of the Deep Lords of the ocean destroyed it with a great wave after the First Invasion, when the Crown Prince was enchanted into bear-shape and his sister sent into a hundred-year sleep, and King Lorez lured by a Will-o'-Wispy off his road, bogged in a marsh, and drowned dead.

Whether the Deep Lord had sent the wave out of solidarity with his landed Gentry-kin or out of pique because Lorez, being dead, did not tithe to the tides at the usual time and place, no one knew.

No, Jadio was too canny to repeat Old Ironshod's mistakes. He had built his grand house inland, in a very settled city, far from any wilderness, where even the river ran tame. There he brought me, across the wide waters and away from the island where I had been born, under full guard and in chains, but dressed up in such gowns and choked with such jewels that I was the envy of all who looked on me. Plenty did. Jadio liked a good parade.

I'd glared back at every crowd he set me against. My face froze into an expression of bitter unfriendliness. Before the Pricksters had invaded my cottage, I was perhaps a bit brusque by temperament, but I'd harbored goodwill to my neighbors, and smiled, and sang, proud of being Mam's daughter and wishing to do well by her name.

Now *my* name might have been Stonehewn, my heart was that cold. I wished that instead of eyes, I looked with mounted cannons on the world, to blast all gawping bystanders to the other side of the Veil.

But I wasn't quite alone. They say beggars can't be choosy, and as Jadio's slave, I was less than a beggar. But even they (whoever *they* are) would've blinked at my choice for a friend. Indeed, he was the only friend I had at Jadio House—if a milkmaid might call a fox "friend" and keep her throat untorn.

Jadio's young page Sebastian, twin to the Archabbot's novice, sometimes came to my cell to slip me news of the outside. If he felt generous, he'd bring a bit of fruit, or bread and cheese, along with his gossip. Jadio insisted I sup on the rarest steaks and richest wines, but I had no stomach for these victuals.

"His Majesty'll soon have you spin again," Sebastian had told me at his last visit.

I'd been startled. "By rights last batch should've lasted him three lifetimes!"

Sebastian enjoyed riling me, friend or not. He grinned, sharp-toothed. He tapped out a tattoo with his strangely jointed fingers on the bars of my door. "I've met some ignorant peasants in my life, but you sure do take the dunce cap, my milksop maid. Don't you know anything? His Majesty's been selling off yon goldie skeins like he's afeared they'll fall to ash."

My eyebrows sprang high. "If the Gentry ore were going to go bad, would it not have done so overnight? I thought those were the rules."

Sebastian shrugged. He had bony elbows and skin so clear it was like looking into a pail of skimmed milk. His rusty hair smudged his forehead like a fringe of embers.

"Depends on your enchanter. Some Gentry tricks don't last an hour. Some last a year. Some last the life of the enchanter. Hard to say." His forehead scrunched. In so many ways he was still a child, but creased up like that, his expression went deep and devious.

"What's that look for?" I asked. "Is there something else?"

He nodded. "Gossip goes you *must* be Gentry, no matter how loudly the Archabbot proclaims you gods-gifted. Folks want you quartered in the square and all your witchy bits exposed on the Four Tors. I never did see a dead witch in pieces. Promise I can watch while they kill you?"

"Bloody-brained child!" said I, approaching the bars and prying his tapping fingers free. "You've lived among soldiers too long. Even your sister Candia insists I'm mortal."

He tweaked a lock of my ash-brown hair, but I pulled away before he could kip a strand.

When young Sebastian grinned, the fox flashed out in his face. Oh, in a couple of years, give this page boy a velvet suit and silver swordstick and let him loose upon the town. Won't be a maid within miles not pining for those sharp white teeth to bite the plumpness of her thigh.

"What Candy says and Candy thinks are as different as cat's purr from catamount's hunting cough. She lies all the time, for spite or jest, and 'specially when the Archabbot tugs her hair. She hates that, always has. Might even have lied for the sheer wanton pleasure of it. Never can tell. Not even me."

"Do you lie as well as your sister, Sebastian?"

"His Majesty does not let me lie." The foxboy showed me a thin ring of iron welded about his left wrist. I had one like it, but of gold. A braid of the gold thread I had ostensibly spun for him, to remind me of my place.

"Nor may I change my shape, nor pierce the Veil between worlds with my Gentry sight. He'll have his cub to heel, he says."

Sebastian's yellow eyes with their thin, vertical pupils warned me not to put my trust in him. That though he may like and pity me, he was treacherous by nature. And had been a prisoner longer.

"What do *you* think I am?" I asked him.

"I know what you are," the foxboy answered with a gods-may-care shrug. "Fair warning, Gordie. You'll be put to spinning soon."

He'd been right. Not three days after that conversation, here I was. A warehouse stuffed with straw and my ears stuffed with dire death threats if I didn't do something about it. Gold was wanted. Mounds of gold. Pounds of gold. Gold to rival a field of daffodils on a sunny day.

My lot hadn't notably improved since the last time I'd been locked up with enough straw to make a giant's mattress tick, though I was perhaps cleaner as I paced and sneezed, lavished with lavender soap as I was, my hair braided with ropes of pearls, half a pair of useless slippers on my feet. This time, the spinning wheel squatting in the middle of the warehouse was made of solid silver. None of it helped me. I was still going to die at dawn.

All I could do was invent couplets to curse my captor with.

"All hail Jadio: let him hang
Long his rope and brief his reign
Yank his innards, chop his head . . ."

A voice I had not heard in a whole month finished: *"Grind his bones to make your bread!"*

Unthinking, I laughed, spinning on my heel all the way around. Haste lost me my battle for balance. From a heap of satin and straw, I sat up again and craned for the voice—*there* he was! My hunch-backed goblin wreathed in smiles, straddling the spinning wheel's stool, with his arms draped over the machine and his head resting on crossed wrists.

He, too, looked less raggedy than last time. Perhaps he had combed his hair once or twice in the days since I met him. My opal still flickered on his finger.

"You! How did you find me? I was afraid, when they took me from the island you wouldn't—I mean, did you traipse all this way? The roads are so dangerous for Gentry . . ."

A torque of his crooked shoulders. I winced, but he did not.

"I did not take the roads. I took the Ways. Time is different in the Veil. It did not seem a month to me."

I humphed. No better reply came to mind than, *I hope it felt a full year then, you flame-crowned bugaboo, for that's how it did to me,* which would not have been at all prudent to speak aloud.

He spun the silver wheel with a lazy finger.

"So," he observed, "another room."

"Yes."

"Mmn. Bigger."

"Much."

"Still sneezing?"

"Aye. Enough to cause typhoons in Leech. Also, I have new rashes."

"Rashes even?"

"Rashes in places no rash e'er ventured yet."

"My condolences."

"Ah, stick 'em where they'll do most good."

We lapsed. He spun the empty wheel. I drew my knees up, wrapped my arms about them, and thought of all the questions I did not dare ask. What were the Ways like? Did he walk them alone? Had he many friends in the Veil? Did he drink nectar with them in Gentry pubs, dance barefoot when the sweetness went to his head? Did *any* raucous movement jar his crooked back—or did his body only hurt him in the mortal realm? What had his life been like all this while I'd never known him, and what would it be like when I was dead and gone?

He seemed to have been thinking along some of these same lines. Or at least the part about my corpse.

"What will happen to you tomorrow, milkmaid, if this straw is not spun to gold?"

I related Sebastian's jolly vision of my witchy bits exposed on the Four Tors.

"Not," I added, "that I have any witchy bits. Not real ones, anyway."

"Not a one," he concurred, looking deeply at all of me with his thorn-black eyes. "Though what bits you have are better clad than last I saw them."

"Yes," said I, "a pretty shroud to wrap my pieces in."

"Pearls do not suit you."

"No—I prefer opals."

"A healthy milkmaid needs no adornment."

"Doesn't mean we won't prize a trinket if it comes our way."

"What good are trinkets to you, lady? You'll die tomorrow."

"Maybe so, mister," I huffed, "but it's rightly rude to mention it out loud like that."

He scratched his nose. It was not so blade-thin as the foxboy's, but it was harder, more imposing, with a definite downward hook like a gyrfalcon's beak. Such a nose would look fine with a ring through the septum, like my good bull Manu had. A silver ring, I thought, to match the one on his finger, and when I wanted him to follow me—*wherever*—I'd need only slip my pinkie through it and tug a little.

My blush incinerated that train of thought when his eyes, which seemed to read words I did not speak aloud as written scrip upon my face, widened with surprise. The instant he laughed, green flames danced up from his hair and swirled about his skull.

"Come, milkmaid!" he cried, standing up not-quite-straight from his stool. "Do not be so melancholy, pray! Am I not here, merchant and laborer? Is this warehouse not our private marketplace? Your life is not yet forfeit. What have you to trade?"

I laughed at his ribbing but shook my head. "Not a thing that is my own, sir!"

"I have it from my usual source—"

" —'Regular if reliably suspicious'?"

"Yes, of course—that you wear a fine ivory locket on a black ribbon 'round your neck."

The locket was hidden now beneath layers of silk. I clutched it through the cloth and shook my head.

"Mister, you can have any pearl that pleases you. You can have my braided hair with it! Take my gown, my slippers, see? Gifts from a king! But do not take my locket . . ."

"It belonged to your mother?" His voice was gentle.

"Aye." I scowled at him. "And I suppose it belonged to your mother before her?"

"Aye," he mocked me, glare for glare. You quite forgot he was an ugly creature while his shining eyes dissected you. "Your mam, may I remind you, never cared for worldly treasures."

"Unlike yours?" I asked.

"My mother is made of treasure, though decidedly unworldly. Opal and ivory, silver and gold. If you ever meet her, you will understand."

"If I die tomorrow, I'll never meet her," I growled.

"Just so." His smile became a coax. Almost a wheedle. "Give over, milkmaid, and you'll live another day in hope."

"Who says I want to meet your mother?"

"Is the friend of your mam not your friend, too? Have you so many friends in this world?"

There he had a point. Back at Feisty Wold, our neighbors had liked Mam well enough, but during the Invasions, as illness queered her and fever weakened her, they dropped out of her life. Sometimes one would leave a basket of jams or new baked bread at our doorstep, but not a one wished speech with a sick woman who only ever whispered, and never of safe or comfortable topics. The memory stung my eyes. My hands flew up to unknot the ribbon. That little ivory locket hung around my neck with the weight of a dead heart. I could almost feel it bleeding into my lap.

"I can't!" I cried. "It's stuck!"

Then he stood before me, his nearness calming my struggles. My hands fell to my sides. He seized my wrists, squeezed once, then inched his grasp upward, my arms the purchase his arms needed to attain any height above that of his chest. The crease of pain between his eyes deepened to agony. The hump on his back shuddered. The gesture I took for granted while combing hair or brushing teeth cost him ease of breath, grace, comfort of movement.

By the time his hands had gained my shoulders, he was gasping. His head bent heavily before me, and his whole body sagged, but his grip on me only tightened. I placed my hands lightly on either side of his rib cage, hoping to support him if he should collapse. His flames were utterly damped by the sweaty dark tangle of his hair, which smelled of sweetgrass and salt sea. A few strands of shining green twined with the black. I pressed a brief kiss to the crown of his head.

"Mister," I told him, "take the locket quickly. You look pale and weary."

He wheezed a laugh and loosed the knotted ribbon at my neck with a touch. The ivory locket fell into his palm. He pressed it hard against his heart.

"Let me," I whispered. "Let me."

He did not relinquish it, but allowed me the ribbon's slack. I tied it around his neck, smoothing his wild hair down over the knot. He shivered.

"Are you very hurt?"

"No." His voice was almost as gruff as the foxgirl's. "Where did you learn to be kind?"

I shook my head and turned away. "You saved my life. Twice if we include tonight."

"You paid that debt. Twice if we include tonight. You did not, do not have to—to . . ."

I wished he would not speak so, not in those tones, not brokenly. My heart was on the verge, if not of explosion than of collapse, hurtling to an inward oblivion, sucking down with it the very ground I stood on. For a moment I believed my bones were Gentry bones, hollow as a bird's. I was that light. I missed the locket's weight around my neck. I missed my mother.

Without turning back to him, I confessed, "There is no one here who cares for me. For me to care for. I feel like I'm dying. The parts of me that matter. If you save my life a thousand times it won't mean anything unless I—unless I can still . . . *feel something*. Tenderness."

"Yes," he whispered. "That is it exactly."

I covered my face with both hands, unwilling to sob in front of him.

"Put me out!" I begged. "Now! Please. Like you did before. I am so tired."

This time his grass-trap was less like a thunder tunnel, all green flash and brash spectacle, and more like a hammock of spider silk and flower petal rocking, rocking, rocking me to slumber on a dozy summer evening. I swear I heard him singing lullabies all the way down.

Another month went by, much like the last: too much satin, too little hope, and only intermittent visits from my friend the foxboy to alleviate the tedium of despair.

It was early morning—not Sebastian's usual hour for visiting—when I woke to footsteps outside my door. The king strode into my cell, his gold-braided crown bright upon his pale hair, his long red cloak sweeping the tiles of turquoise and lapis lazuli. He leaned one hip against my pillow, stroked a single fingernail down my face, and when I flinched fully awake, smiled.

"How do you feel, Miss Faircloth?"

Should I sit up? Cover myself with the blanket? Dare answer? It seemed safest to bob my chin. The dagger on his belt was very near my cheek. He was not looking at me, but at what the blanket did not cover. My shift was thin, of silk. His cold eyes roved.

"My page boy is in regular contact with his twin at Winterbane. She apprises him of the Archabbot's movements. Did you know?"

I shook my head. I hadn't known, but I had guessed.

His hand, as if by accident, drifted from my face to my collarbone. Had I anything of value left, I'd've wagered it that he felt my pounding heart even in that lightest graze.

"Just this morning," said the king, "Sebastian passed me the latest of his sister's news. Avillius is conscripting an army of his own. He thinks to march on Jadio House, to wreck all I have assembled, and from the rubble rebuild a temple to his gods." He leaned closer to me, studying my face intently. "But I am favored by the gods. They have turned their faces from him. They have sent me you."

"Me?" This was no time for sudden movement. His palm pressed me hard into the mattress, very hot and very dry.

"You, Gordenne Faircloth. The Archabbot's coffers are fat, but they are no match for the treasure troves of heaven. He cannot feed and clothe his army with prayer—especially when by his actions today he proves himself a heretic. His toy soldiers are of tin while mine are of gold."

They are not toys, I wanted to scream. *They are people! Not gold or tin but flesh. And if this war is let to rage, we shall all be crushed to dust between the inexorable convictions of crown and miter. You shall be king of a graveyard realm. The temples will stand empty with no one to worship in them, and the Archabbot will have only himself to pray to.*

But I said nothing.

First of all, and obviously, Jadio was bent on this war. Lusted for it. Had done his damnedest to incite it, for all I could see. Secondly, I knew very well (for her brother had told me, not that he could be trusted to keep tail or tale straight) that half of what Candia gabbled were lies so wild only a consummate actor could hear them with a somber face. Thirdly, if Avillius were building an army, it wouldn't be an army of tin weaklings as Jadio seemed to expect. Pricksters a-plenty did Avillius have already, and zealots. He would hire mercenaries, too, and not hesitate to use those Gentry or Gentry-babes who had fallen under his power, whether from greed or grief or some dark hold he had over them to swell his ranks. He was not the kindly man he appeared, no more than Jadio was as good as he was beautiful.

The king hauled me out of my thoughts and onto his lap, where he proceeded to crush me breathless.

"Therefore, Miss Faircloth. Gordenne."

"Your Majesty?" I braced both hands against his chest, hoping to keep some distance, but he took it as an invitation for further intimacies. After swiping my mouth soundly with his tongue, mauling my ears, and sucking at my neck, he pulled back and grasped my shoulders, shaking me. His fingernails drew blood.

"Therefore, my darling," he said brusquely, "today you'll get to spinning. I have filled the ballroom at Jadio House with all the straw in Leressa. You are not to leave the room until your alchemy is performed. You are not to eat or drink or see a soul until that gold is mine. And when it is, Miss Faircloth"—he crushed me to him again, harder, letting me feel the power of his body and the weakness of my own—"when you give me that gold, I will give you my name, my throne, and my seed. You shall be Queen of Leressa. The mother of my heir. The saint of our people. My wife."

I opened my mouth to explain how I could not do what he asked, had never been able to do it, how I'd started out a nothing, and now was even less than that. But he dug his nails into the gouge wounds he had made and shook me by the shoulders all over again.

"If you do not!" he whispered. *"If you do not!"*

I waited in the shadow of the spinning wheel. Dusk came, and midnight, and dawn again. My friend did not come. By the king's orders I'd nothing to eat or drink, no blankets to cover me, no visitor to comfort me. Dusk, then midnight, dawn again. I cleared a small space on the floor and pressed my face to the cool tile, and slept. High morning. High noon. Late afternoon. Twilight. Night.

Perhaps a hundred years passed.

He held a flask of water to my lips. Quicksilver, crystal, icicle, liquid diamond. Just water. Followed by a blackberry. A raspberry. An almond. The tip of his finger dipped in honey. I sucked it eagerly.

"Milkmaid," he said.

"Go away." I pressed the hand that pressed my face, keeping him near. "I have nothing left to give you. And anyway, why should Jadio win? Keep your gold. Go back to the Ways. There's a war coming. No one's safe . . ."

"Hush." He slipped a purple grape into my mouth. A green grape. A sliver of apple. His scars were livid against his frowning face.

"Milkmaid." He sighed. "I can do nothing without a bargain. Even if I—but do you see? It doesn't work without a bargain."

I felt stronger now. I could sit up. Uncoil from the fetal curl. My legs screamed as I stretched them straight.

He'd been kneeling over me. Now he kept one knee bent beneath him and drew up the other to rest his chin on. This position seemed an easy one. The frown between his brows was not of pain but inquiry.

"I heard how you were . . . I could not come sooner. I was too deep within the Veil." He smiled. His teeth glowed. "With the Deep Lords, even—in the Fathom Realms beneath the sea. Do I smell like fish?"

I sniffed. Green and sweet and sunlight. Maybe a little kelp as an afterthought. Nothing unpleasant. On an impulse, I leaned my nose against his neck and inhaled again. He moved his cheek against mine, and whispered with some shortness of breath:

"Milkmaid, have you nothing to offer me?"

I shook my head slightly so as not to disconnect from him.

"You are *not* to take my cows in trade! Gods know what you Gentry would do to them."

It was he who drew away, laughing, and I almost whimpered at the loss. "Much good they'll do you where you're going."

"Eh," I shrugged, pretending a coldness I did not feel. "Da has probably already sold them off for mead."

"Perhaps he did," my friend agreed. "Perhaps he sold them to a hunchbacked beggar whose worth seemed less than a beating, but who offered him, in exchange for the fair Annat and the dulcet Manu, a wineskin that would never empty."

For that alone I would've whapped him, had he not tucked a wedge of cheese into my mouth. The finest cheese from the finest cow that ever lived. It was like being right there with her, in that homely barn, where I sang Mam's songs for hours and Annat watched me with trustful eyes.

"You have my cows already."

"Aye."

"So I can't trade 'em. Even if I wanted to. Which I don't."

"Nay."

I smoothed my silk dress. Three days' worth of wrinkles smirked back at me.

"Time moves differently, you said, in the Veil?"

He nodded carefully, smiling with the very corners of his mouth.

"It does indeed." He sounded almost hopeful.

"Well. That being so, would you take in trade a piece of my future? See," I rushed to explain, "if he gets that gold, Jadio means me to wear his crown. Or a halo, I can't tell. When that happens, you may have both with my blessing, and all the choirs of angels and sycophants with 'em."

"*I do not want his crown,*" the little crooked man growled. For all he had such a tortuous mangle to work with, he leapt to his feet far faster than I could on a spry day.

"You're to wed him, then?" he demanded, glaring down.

Oh.

This needed correcting—and quickly.

"*He's* to wed *me*, mister, provided he deems this night's dowry suitably vulgar. Oh, do get on going!" I begged him. "Let us speak no more of trade. Leave me with this tinderbox and caper on your merry way. For surely as straw makes me sneeze, I can withstand Jadio's torments long enough to die of them, and then it will all be over. But if he marries me, I might live another three score, and *that* would be beyond bearing."

He snorted. A single green flame leapt to his finger, dancing on the opal there. The light lengthened his face, estranged the angles from the hollows, smoothed his twists, twisted his mouth.

"I've a trade for your future." His voice was very soft. "I'll spin you a king's ransom of gold tonight—in exchange for your firstborn child."

"Jadio's spawn?" I laughed balefully, remembering that hot, dry hand on my neck. "Take him! And take his father, too, if you've a large enough sack."

"You barter the flesh of your flesh too complacently."

"No one cares about my flesh. It's not mine anymore. I'm not even *me* anymore."

"Milkmaid." He stared at me. It was strange to have to look up at him. How tall he seemed suddenly, with that green flame burning now upon his brow. "Some of my dearest friends are consummate deceivers, born to lie as glibly as they slip their skins for a fox's fur. I was sure they were lying when they told me you were sillier than you seemed, soft in the head and witless as a babe. Now, I must believe them. To my sorrow."

"What are you talking about?" I asked.

"Your flesh," he murmured, rolling his eyes to the ceiling. "How can you say no one cares for it, when I would risk the wrath of two realms to spare it from harm?"

My heart too full to speak, my eyes too full to see, I lifted both my hands to him. When he grasped them by the wrists, I tugged gently, urging him back to the floor, and to me.

He fingered the ribbon of my bodice. Triple-knotted as it was, it fell apart at his touch. The sleeve of my shift sagged down my shoulder. Our eyes locked. There was a pearl button at his collar. A black pearl. I unhooked it. For the first time I noticed the richness of the black velvet suit he wore, its fantastic embroidery in ivory and silver, the braids and beads in his hair.

"Were you courting a Deep Lord's daughter?" I asked. "Is that why you were in the Fathom Realms? Did the distant sound of my sneezes interrupt you mid-woo?"

The sound he made was maybe a "no," more of a sigh, slightly a groan. Then I was kissing him, or he me, and we were both too busy happily undressing each other to do much talking, although when we did, it all came out sounding like poetry, even if I don't remember a word of what we said.

Of my wedding three days later I will say nothing. That brutal night of consummation, and all nights following until Jadio marched east with his armies to meet the Archabbot at the drowned city of Lirhu, I will consign to dust and neglect.

Though I would not have wished Jadio near me again but we had an impregnable wall spined in spikes between us, I did regret the loss of the page boy Sebastian. Upon taking his leave, he told me with his usual feral insouciance, "I'll probably not return, Gordie. You know that?"

I knew the look in his yellow eye—that of a fox in a trap, just before he chews off his paw to escape. Not long was that rusty iron bracelet for Sebastian's wrist. Nor would too many months pass, I guessed, before King Jadio learned this cub would never again come to heel.

"Luck." I clasped his arm. "Cunning. Speed. Whatever you need, may it await you at the crossroads."

"Same to you, Your Majesty," he said with a cheeky grin. (He had no other kind.) "If I can't stick around to see you hacked apart and flung about, you may as well live a few years yet."

I flicked the back of his russet head. "So young and yet so vile."

"You'll miss me."

"More than I can say."

"Gordie?"

"Aye?"

"When he comes to claim his own, ask yourself, 'the One-Eyed Witch lives where'?" I blinked. That was the name of an old children's skip-rope rhyme. But Sebastian did not let me catch up with my thoughts. "Go to her. She'll have a notion how you're to go on."

Gentry pronouncements are often cryptic, indefinite, misleading, and vacuous—which makes them, amongst all oracular intimations, the most irritating. But just try to interrogate a fox when everything but his tail is already out the door.

In my neatest printing, I wrote, "The One-Eyed Witch Lives Where?" on a thin strip of parchment. When this was done, I whittled a locket out of ash, the way Mam had taught me, shut Sebastian's advice up safe inside it, strung the locket with a ribbon, and wore it near my heart. It had not the heft of ivory, but it comforted me nonetheless.

After Jadio's departure came nine months of gestation, the worst of which I endured alone.

I was facedown in a chamber pot one morning when a messenger brought me news of the Archabbot's victory at the Cliffs of Lir outside the drowned city. Heavy losses to both sides, after which Jadio's soldiers retreated, regrouped, and launched several skirmishes that further decimated the Archabbot's armies.

Some weeks later, another messenger came to shake me from my afternoon nap. The Archabbot had found the lost heir of Lirhu wandering the ruins of the city. The prince, dead King Lorez's only son, was still enchanted in the form of a great black bear and a wore a golden crown to prove it. The Archabbot had goaded the bear-prince into challenging Jadio to hand-to-hand combat on the field for the right to rule Leressa.

Jadio had defeated, beheaded, and skinned him, then drove the Archabbot's armies out of Lirhu and into the Wayward Swamps.

In the turmoil of their retreat, the Holy Soldiers abandoned a most singular object: a glass coffin bearing the sleeping Princess of Leressa, whom no spell could wake. This, too, they had discovered in the ruins of the drowned city. Jadio claimed the princess as a prize of war but did not destroy her as he had her brother. He would have sent the coffin back with the bearskin (it was explained) but he feared some harm might befall it on the road.

The bearskin made me sick every time I saw it, so I avoided the great hall and took my meals in my rooms.

When at last the hour of the birth came upon me (and an early hour it was, sometime between midnight and the dusk before dawn), I bolted the door to my room and paced the carpet like a she-wolf.

I wanted no one. No chirurgerar with his bone saws and skully grin. No Prickster midwife with tainted needles and an iron key for me to suck that I might lock up the pain. I'd do this alone or die of it. Mam survived my bursting into this world, after all, screaming blood and glory. Mam survived fourteen years of me before she up and snipped her mortal coil from the shuttle of life.

"Mam!" I pressed my back hard against the bedpost. "Please. Let Jadio's spawn be stillborn. Let him be grotesque. Let him be soup, so long as I don't look on him and love him. I don't want to love this child, Mam. Don't let me love this child."

After that I screamed a great deal. And once I fainted. I seem to remember waking to a voice telling me that this was not the sort of thing one could really sleep through, and for the sake of my cows, my house, my hope of the ever-after, would I please push?

If he hadn't've called me Milkmaid in all that begging, I might've chosen to ignore him utterly. But he did, so I didn't.

Some hours later the babe was born.

"Give her over, mister!"

"That your rancor may cast her forth into yon hearth fire?"

"I did not know she would be yours! Come on! Give. She'll need to feed."

"Had I tits, Milkmaid, I'd never let her go."

I smirked sweatily, winning the spat. His cradling arms slipped her into my lap, where he had arranged clean sheets and blankets, a soft pillow for her to rest upon. She was a white little thing. White lashes, white lips, white eyes. Silent when she looked at me. No mistaking her for a mortal child. A Gentry-babe through and through.

"What's your name?" I asked my daughter. She blinked up from her nursing, caught my eye, grinned. Gentry-babes are born with all their teeth.

The little crooked man laughed. "She'll never tell."

"Not even her mother?"

He laid hands on my belly, and the bleeding stopped. Aches, throbs, stabbing pains, deep bruises—all vanished. Warmth spread through my body. He stroked my hair once before walking quickly to the hearth, turning his hunched back to me. I stared after him. Best, perhaps, he could not see the look on my face.

"That you are her mother does not matter," he muttered. "There is war between our people. The Gentry have learned never to speak our names out loud. Not to anyone. Too much is at stake. Our lives. Our souls."

"You have those, then?"

No answer. He crouched near the hearth, poking at the blinding green flames there. In my lap the baby choked.

"What's wrong?" I yelped. I lifted her, tried to burp her. "Did I—I didn't curse her, did I? When I was giving birth? And all those times before. Little one, my sweetest girl, I didn't mean you! I meant Jadio's son. Never you."

My friend came to my side. "It isn't that. It's the milk. The more magic flowing through a Gentry-babe's veins, the less able we are to suckle at a mortal's breast."

"She'll starve!"

"Nay, sweet," said he, "for do I not have the prize cow of cream-makers in my very barn?"

The panic clenching my heart eased. "She can drink cow milk?"

"She'll suck it like nectar from Annat's udder. It's what we like best."

"But—" I stared at my baby's still white face, the bead of milk trembling on her lip. I wiped it off quickly, for a rash of color spread from it across her skin, along with a feverish heat.

He touched one finger to her mouth. The rash vanished. "She must eat. She will die if she remains, Milkmaid. You owe me her life."

"What?"

"Our bargain."

"You said Jadio's—"

"I said your firstborn."

"You didn't say ours."

"Nay, but it mightn't have been."

"You!" I picked up the nearest pillow and threw it at his head. Another and again—until the bed was in disarray. "You swindler! You cheat! You seducer of innocent maidens!"

My arm was weak, but he did not duck my missiles. Pillows bounced from his fine black clothes. He stood very still.

"Take me with you!"

"I cannot."

"Why?"

"You are wed to another."

"As if Gentry cared for such mortal nonsense!"

He shrugged. By this I knew he cared.

"I was sent," he said softly, "to fetch three things from the mortal realm. My quest is done. When I return to the Veil, the Ways will close behind me, and I will breathe this cursed air no more. You cannot follow."

"Why not?" I demanded. "You came to me. To help me. *You* took the Ways. *I'll* take the roads. I'd chase you to the Valwode itself, mister, no matter that it's forbidden. Into the Fathom Realms, even! Do you think I fear the drowning?"

He shook his head again, more slowly this time, as if it wearied him. Then he approached the bed and lifted up our daughter from my arms. She sighed deeply, whether content or dismayed no one but she could say. My tears fell onto his sleeve. When they touched him, they turned to diamonds. None of my doing, I'm sure.

As he made to leave, I grabbed the tail of his velvet jacket, fisted it hard as I could and yanked. I knew it could shred to smoke the instant he desired it. Velvet it remained.

Desperately I cried, "A bargain! I'll bargain for the chance to win you. Both of you. It doesn't work without a bargain, you said. Let me . . ."

Before I'd blinked, he'd turned back 'round again, his free hand flush against my cheek. His fingers were cool except for the silver ring, which burned.

"Gordie Oakhewn," he said, "you have seven days to guess my true name. If on the seventh day you call it out loud, the Veil shall part for you, and I will pull you through into my household, where you might stay forever with the child, with me—as, as my—in whatever capacity you wish. This is our bargain. Do not break it."

I pressed a frantic kiss to his palm. "Call you by name? But you said Gentry never—"

Smoke.

The Gentry leave semblances of the children they steal. My semblance was a red-faced boy-brat who squalled like a typhoon and slurped my breasts dry. For two days he kept me awake all hours and scratched me with his hot red hands. On the third day he sickened and turned black. We buried him in the garden of Jadio House. A peach tree shaded his grave. I wondered if any lingering levin of Gentry magic would affect the taste of its fruit.

The chirurgerar assured me that sudden deaths were not uncommon among firstborns, that Jadio's was a virile enough appetite to populate a dozen nurseries, that it was none of my fault. It was kind of him. His grin seemed less skully than sad. He left me with a soothing draught that I did not drink. I had packing to do. Maps to consult. Lists to make. Lists of every name I ever knew or could invent.

That night I recited to myself:

"There's Aiken and Aimon and Anwar and Abe
Corbett and Conan and Gilbert and Gabe
There's Berton and Birley and Harbin and Hal
Keegan and Keelan and Jamie and Sal
There's Herrick and Hewett or whom you might please
So long as you love me, your name might be . . ."

"Sneeze?" asked the three-legged fox who had climbed through my casement window. "*He's* not the one allergic to straw, Gordie. Remember?"

"Sebastian!" I scrambled up from my escritoire. "How do you do?—you've learned to skinslip!—no more iron bracelet?—what a handsome fox!—your poor hand!"

Next a vixen slid through the aperture, shuddering off her russet fur as she leapt to the floor to stand bright in her own bare skin. Her hair flamed loose about her shoulders. The only thing she wore was a heavy gray signet ring on her index finger. I'd seen it once before on the Archabbot's own hand. There was a smear of rust upon it that I knew to be blood. Had she taken it off his dead body? Had she bitten it off his living one? Either thought made me grin.

"Candia!"

She made a warding gesture. "Candy, Candy, call me Candy! Sweet as syrup, twice as randy. Hallo, Gordie. We've come to warn you."

"Warn me? Of what?" Even before they began to answer, I folded my maps, buckled my boots, and fetched my quilted jacket with the deep red hood.

"Jadio is but a day's march behind us," Sebastian said. "But he's sent a deathly rumor running before him. Claims you were a Gentry witch all along, who'd fuddled the Archabbot into thinking you were holy and glammed his own gray eyes the same. That you tricksied him into wedding and bedding you."

"An honor I'd have sold my left ear to live without," I growled.

Candy had strolled across the room to examine the empty cradle. She said over her shoulder, "Jadio claims you killed the babe you bore him, and mean to replace it with a changeling that will bring ruin to Leressa."

"Really?" I looked from one twin to the other. "Wouldn't that be a shame?"

Grins all around.

"Jadio claims," Sebastian finished, "that he will see you hang ere the week's out. That he will wed Princess Lissa of Lirhu by the light of your funeral pyre."

This stayed my hands where they'd been strapping on my pack.

"Old Ironshod's daughter?" I asked. "But she sleeps, doesn't she? A hundred-year sleep. Poisoned by Gentry magic, same as what changed her brother to a bear. How did he manage to wake her?"

"He did not," Candy said. Her blade-thin nose serrated at the bridge, as though she had smelled something foul. Her yellow eyes glowed in the dark. "But an heir of her blood will strengthen his claim to the crown."

"Who will wake her?" I asked wildly. "We can't let him— We *must* wake her!"

"Not you!" laughed Sebastian. "That's for other folk to do, milksop, in some other tale. Don't you know anything? As if you didn't have the hardest part of your own ahead of you." He paused and looked at me, yellow-eyed and mischievous. "Do you remember what I told you before I left?"

I clutched the ashwood locket at my chest and rattled off through a suddenly dry throat, "'The One-Eyed Witch lives where?'"

"That's it. You ain't milky as all that, if I say so my own self, Your Majesty."

"Am too!" I ruffled his hair before he jerked away, baring his teeth not so much out of displeasure as habit.

Sebastian waved his one good arm like a conjurer. It had been the right hand, I'd noticed, that he'd managed to chew off, or chop off, or what. The left was still skinny as a branch, wiry as whipcord. He let me admire the brutal unevenness before explaining.

"Candy did it for me. With an ax. Good and clean. Licked it once to seal it. Then we escaped." So proud he sounded, so nonchalant.

"Brave children. How many died chasing you?"

"Oh, one or two," said Sebastian.

"Dozen!" coughed his twin.

"You should not be here," I scolded. "Jadio will surely punish you if he finds you."

"We're fast, Your Majesty, and double sly," returned Sebastian. "It is you who should escape, who have no real witchy ways to save you."

Candy looked up from my escritoire, at my lists of names in long columns labeled: COMMON, DIMINUTIVE, PET, FAMOUS MORTAL, INFAMOUS GENTRY. She started snickering at something she saw written there.

I hesitated before asking, "I don't suppose *you* know his name?"

"Whose?" both said at once, wary.

"Are you not his friends? Born liars, his two young foxfaces, his 'regular but reliably suspicious informants.' You have spied for him and lied for him and led him to my many cells. Will you not help me find him now?"

"We'll never tell," the twins said together. They puddled down in copper fur and clicking claws, black muzzles, twining tails, and rubbed against my legs, barking:

> *"It's Ragnar! It's Reynard!*
> *It's Stockley! It's Sterne!*
> *It's Milford! It's Misha!*
> *It's horny old Herne!"*

They leapt out the window. I stopped just long enough to add those names to my list, then left Jadio House myself, under cover of night.

The old skip-rope chant called *The One-Eyed Witch Lives Where?* goes like this:

> *"Where does she live?*
> *"In her cottage of bone.*
> *Where are the bones?*
> *In a city of stone.*
> *Where is the city?*
> *At the edge of the sea.*
> *Where the Deep Lord drownded*
> *You and me."*

In other words, *if* I were interpreting the riddle aright, and *if* Sebastian hadn't been flaunting his tail and canting my path astray, I had four days to get to the drowned city of Lirhu, find a one-eyed witch, and make her tell me the crooked man's name.

The road was long. I was not as bold as I once had been.

Had not the squalling semblance left to replace my daughter dried my milk and the little crooked man stopped my bleeding after the birth, I'd never have lasted the first day. As it was, the worst I felt were twinges. And a nagging clench that nine months meant nothing if I failed now.

If mortal roads were not safe for Gentry in these dark days of civil strife, they were no more safe for a youngish woman on her own, be she ever so plainly dressed. On the first day I encountered soldiers. Jadio's men—possibly sent ahead to the House to prepare it.

"Ain't she a pearl?" one asked.

"Cute hood," said another, flipping it off my hair.

"Where's your basket of goodies for Gramamma?"

A year ago, I'd've clouted them with a dishrag, or sniffed and stuck my nose in the air, or showed them the sharp side of my tongue. A year ago, this kind of behavior had got me clapped in chains and dragged to the Holy See at Winterbane. Instead I made my eyes wide and mild, slightly popped, with the whites showing all around. All gentleness, all complacency, all bovine. With the mightiest will in the world, I pretended I was my cow Annat.

"Moo?"

The first soldier laughed. "Is that your name? Little Miss Moo?" and tried to tickle me. I backed away and pawed the dirt of the road with the scuff of my toe, and then galloped forward and rammed his stomach with the hardest part of my head. He went down with an *oof* and an oath. All his comrades laughed.

I reeled back, nostrils flaring—like my bull Manu on a cranky day when the flies are at full sting.

"Moo!" I bellowed, and bent my head again.

"Easy there, Bessie!" cried a square-faced man, catching the hem of my skirt to pull me off-balance. I staggered, spun 'round, and glared, huffing. The soldier had blunted hands and a beaten face, but his squinting eyes were kindly. Though he'd not been among those teasing me before, he seemed fully in charge now, and he took my measure at a glance. His chin jerked in a slightest nod.

"She's Gentry-touched," he told the others. "Best not brush up too near her, or the enchantment's like to run off and addle you. How'd you like to show up to Jadio House chewing cud and sucking at each other's teats? His Majesty'll have us butchered for his wedding feast. Come on. Move along, men."

The soldiers marched back the way I'd come. They gave wide berth to the one who'd tickled me and been rammed, as if waiting for him to grow horns and a tail and start a stampede at the first loud noise. The square-faced man sauntered after them, after giving me a shy salute and a wink.

As soon as they were out of sight, I ran.

On the second day, I hitched a ride with a vegetable seller as far as Seafall, where I scrounged for an unoccupied bit of mossy embankment beneath a bridge and slept there like a troll, shivering. From Seafall to the Cliffs of Lir was thirty miles, and I started at dawn on the third day, following the sea road south.

No one traveled to Lirhu regularly anymore since it was wave-wrecked by the Deep Lord. The road was in disrepair. There were signs that Jadio's army and the Holy Soldiers had been through. Graves like raw wounds in the chalk. On the fourth day of my journey and the seventh day of my quest, I came to Lirhu by twilight.

This near the sea, a frantic, long-smothered homesickness burst upon me. The drumming of the breakers, that tang on my tongue, the whip of the wind. So long as I had time enough to drown myself before they took me back, I'd never live inland again.

Dry-mouthed and with cracking lips, I chanted my litany of names as I walked, punctuating the rhymes with every blood-blistered footstep.

"Jack Yap or Jessamee. Pudding or Poll. Gorefist the Goblin. Tonker the Troll. Dimlight the Dwarf King. The Faerie Fin-Shu. Azlin the Angel. The Wizard Samu."

The ruins of Lirhu rose before me, white stone streaked with veins of rose quartz. Ragged battlements, perilous parapets, watchtowers and clock towers—all crumbling to rubble. Each blind, weed-wracked, ivy-grown window seemed a doorway into some lightless, airless, awful hole in reality. Wind howled through a shattered labyrinth of arches and pillars.

I glared about the city to fend off my fear of ghosts.

"What a racket! So the Deep Lord drowned you, stones and bones and all. The earth might have quaked and done the same. There are droughts and forest fires and plagues, too, and all manner of horrid things in the world—without you adding the Gentry into it. Do you hear the rest of us whinging?"

"I quite like the wind," said the woman beside me. "I find the sound of futility soothing."

She had materialized so naturally out of the twilight I could no more question her appearance than that of the first evening star. Her one eye, white, with no hint of iris or pupil, washed now and again with a pulse of gold, like the tide. Her skin glowed like antique ivory. Her hair was silver-gilt and fell about her like a mantle. The plainness of her robe, the long scars running down her face and her chest, these made her no less beautiful.

The Witch gestured for me to sit with her on a stone that may have once been a pedestal.

"I would invite you in for tea, but you might find the architecture of my cottage upsetting to your digestion."

I sank with a grateful groan, letting my pack tumble to the ground. "No argument here, lady. I've had enough of walls for a lifetime."

The Witch sat very near me, palms on knees, straight-backed and still as the lost statue she replaced might have been. We watched the fireflies blink about for a while. Then she sighed.

"You've come a long way, Gordie Oakhewn. Tell me what you've learned."

So I recited the five hundred seven names I'd clobbered together on the journey, mortal and Gentry, royal, ridiculous, just plain bad. The Witch listened patiently while the ghosts of Drowned Lirhu did their best to shout me down.

When at last I gasped to a halt, the Witch shook her head. I'd known already I had failed. Had I guessed his name aright, he would have appeared himself, in rags or velvet or verdant flames, to part the Veil with one hand and draw me through with the other. Where I might see our daughter, and hear her laugh, and learn her name.

I bowed my head. Nine months for nothing, and a whole empty life ahead. For what? Maybe someone would hire me as a goose girl or shepherdess. How far would I have to run to flee the shadow of Jadio's gallows?

"Your mother was fond of stories," said the Witch, breaking into my thoughts. "Are you?"

Elbows on knees, head hanging, I nodded. "Mam told the best."

"She had the best from me."

I snorted. Had Mam known every single Gentry exile stuck this side of the Veil? Sure would've explained her distress at the Invasions, being friendly with our sworn enemies and the killers of our king. Though not why I never'd seen even a one before that day at Winterbane.

"Long, long ago," the Witch began, and my thoughts fell away with her words, "one full score and a year more, the Veil Queen set down her antler crown and ventured forth from the Valwode. No Gentry sovereign may evade this fate. It is laid on them to bear their heirs to mortal lovers, renewing the bonds between our people. Thus, she arrayed herself nobly and presented herself to Leressa's king. Lorez the Ironshod was a widower with two children of his own: Prince Torvald, a boy of nine. Princess Lissa, two years younger. They mourned their mother's passing and did not take well to their father's new mistress.

"Truth be told, the Veil Queen did not overmuch concern herself with wooing the children. Lorez it was she wanted. Handsome, with a sharp black beard and teeth like a tiger's. She gave herself to him and took pleasure in it. By and by she bore a child of that union.

"At first Lorez seemed pleased with both of them, but his people whispered, and his children complained, and soon he waxed wroth. One night he visited his mistress's chambers, drunken and angry, a sprig of rowan on his tunic to protect him from enchantment. He rang a silver bell that froze the Veil Queen where she stood (had he not surprised her, such a tawdry spell would hardly have been effectual), then bound her with that iron against which she could do nothing.

"'No bastard son,' he declared, 'would threaten Torvald's crown.'

"While the Veil Queen looked on, Lorez snatched her baby from his cradle and dashed him to the floor. This would have killed a mortal babe, for it broke his back and cracked his skull and snapped his neck. But this boy was a Gentry prince, heir to the antler crown, and possessed of great magic. Nearer to a god you cannot come while breathing. He did not die. Lorez left both child and mother bleeding. Greatly weakened, for the Veil Queen could not remove her iron shackles on her own, she managed to flee with her broken child in a small coracle across the sea. She took shelter on an island, in the village of Feisty Wold.

"The village tailor's young wife helped her. She struck the shackles from her wrists. Cleaned and bound the baby's wounds as best she could. He had already begun to heal, too rapidly, before his bones could be reset. In gratitude for this good woman's kindness, the Veil Queen removed one of her eyes and set it in a ring.

"'Should any of my people see this ring,' she said, 'they will know the wearer to be under my protection and do what they can to aid you.'

"This debt of gratitude repaid, the Veil Queen returned to her people.

"Her curse was on Lorez. She called the Folk from their hollows and hidey-holes, from tree and bog and bedrock. The Will-o'-Wispies, the hobs and hobgoblins, the wolfmen, the crowgirls, the Women Who Wail. She called to her brother the Deep Lord in the Fathom Realms of the sea. Together they roused the Veil against Leressa. They drowned Lorez and demolished Lirhu. They trapped Torvald in the body of a beast—and rightly, for it fit the shape of his soul, and consigned Lissa to the long dark of dreaming, to match the darkness of her scheming. They sent warriors to grapple back mortal-worked lands for the wild, to seed Gentry children in the wombs of mortal women.

"Fiercely did the Gentry fight for their queen, but in one thing they would not yield. They would not put a monster on their throne. A hunchback boy to wear the antler crown? A scarred and crooked thing to be their king? Never. Yet while he lived, no one but he could ascend the throne. A few of the Queen's bravest and brazenest subjects set upon the child—who was now just three years old. They tortured him almost unto death.

"Again the Veil Queen took her child and fled. She returned to Feisty Wold, hoping to find succor and friendship again. The tailor's wife, Mava Oakhewn, welcomed her to her house. She whittled wooden toys for the boy in his convalescence. She set him to sleep in the same cradle as her own tiny daughter Gordie. Mava entreated the Veil Queen to stop the battle between their people. The Veil Queen refused.

"'Your heart is hardened,' Mava told her in despair.

"'Then will I give it over to thy keeping,' did the Veil Queen reply. 'I have no use for it now.'

"So saying, she cut out her heart and strung it on a ribbon, disguised it as a bauble under Mava Oakhewn's stewardship. For a third time she took her son and disappeared, to a place where neither Gentry nor mortal could find her. She raised her son in the ruins of that city which had ruined him."

In the silence that followed, the wind shrieked.

She was his mother. I sat not a hand's span from his mother. My own mam's friend. Queen of all the Valwode and cause of the war. Just cause, if her story was to be trusted.

Did I trust anyone anymore?

Yes. One. And *she* was his *mother.*

"Now," said the Witch, "this broken boy is full grown and of an age to rule. He is both wise and good, as puissant with power as ever his mother was. Still the Gentry cannot bear that he must wear their antler crown. The war rages between Gentry and mortalkind; the Valwode withers without its sovereign. But the Folk are stubborn.

"One year ago today did the Gentry Prince come before the queen. He knelt before her—he, to whom all worlds should bow!—and begged to give his life for his people, to make way for another heir. This the Veil Queen could not stomach. She bargained with him instead.

"'Go you questing to the mortal realm,' said the Veil Queen. 'Return only when you have my eye, my heart, and a child of our blood to sit upon the throne.'"

The Witch subsided. My whole face was numb with revelation, but when she said, "The rest you know," I leapt off our sitting stone.

"No!" I cried. "The rest I don't! For I don't know his name. Without his name, there's no end for me. And no beginning, neither! It's all just another ghost story."

The Witch rolled her one eye up to me. The long white oval pulsed with gold. When she spoke again, the subject was so changed I nearly kicked up a foot and popped her in the knee.

"Were children never cruel in your village, Gordie Oakhewn?"

"Aye," I snapped. "All children can be cruel."

"Did they never sing songs while clapping hands or jumping rope?"

I jerked my chin and began to pace. "Of course." I did *not* say, *That's how I found you, isn't it?*

"Did you never join in their games?"

Turning to scowl at her, I said, "Me? Mam would've clouted my backside with her dishrag, she heard me singing some of those naughty rhymes. Which you'd know if you'd really met her, Your Majesty."

"But you listened," the Witch continued. "You watched from your window. You stopped at the side of the road to hear their songs."

"Sometimes!"

"What did they sing?"

"What did they sing?"

"What. Did. They. Sing."

With a rub of my face and a shrug, I rattled off a few of the old chants. "'Shark in the Cellar.' 'How the Fox Ate the Moon.' 'Come and Cut the Cute Cat's Head.' 'The One-Eyed Witch Lives Where?'" I gestured about extravagantly. "Here, apparently. Oh, and the companion song, about the Witch's—" I stopped.

That gold eye glared.

"About the Witch's Crooked Son." My gorge rose too fast. That terrible song. In her last days of life, Mam had lain beside her open window whispering it, frail and sobbing, and I could do nothing to comfort her.

"Sing it."

"I won't!"

"Sing it."

"Never! How could you ask it of me? His own mother?"

The Witch grasped my chin in her hand. I had never felt fingers so strong and fell. I, who had been wife to boorish Jadio. Cold as the claws of the White One, they were, who rides your neck until you run off a cliff to escape her.

"You are not your mother's daughter. You are craven. You do not deserve him."

"Listen, you!" I bellowed, knocking her hand aside. "Twenty years the tots of Leressa have been singing that song. Cutting his soul into snippets and wounding him with every unwitting word. How could you—the Queen of the Valwode—you who *know* better—let his name be wrecked like that? Gentry never tell, he said—not even their own mothers. Is this why? Who let his secret name out? Who gave it like a golden ball into the hands of heedless children, until years of low games so dirtied and dented it you can hardly see the glistening? Twenty years of mockery. It must have been like a knife in his back every time some kiddie jumped rope."

The Witch's white shoulders seemed almost as hunched as her son's. She whispered, "In the early days I trusted Lorez too dearly. I underestimated his knowledge of the Gentry. Too well did he understand our ways. The night he betrayed us, he called Torvald and Lissa into our room. 'Witness the Witch's imprisonment,' he said. 'The ruins of your baby brother on the floor. Do you see what your father does for you?'

"Perhaps they were repulsed at the sight. Perhaps they were delighted. The faces they showed their father were pitiless as his own. Then Torvald made up that rhyme to sing while Lissa danced around the baby's body. He had been silent until then. Stunned. That was when he began to scream. How they made him dance, rhyming him back his own name."

The night air was wet and cool, but my skin baked so with anger that it might have been high summer. Shrugging off my quilted coat, I rummaged in my pack for the length of gold-braided rope I'd planned to sell off in pieces for food if my quest failed, or hang myself with if Jadio's soldiers captured me.

My hands shook. Nevertheless, I stood, turned my back on the Witch, and began to skip.

Swoop, slap, thud. Swoop, slap, thud. The old rhythms entered me. My breath came faster. My heart began to drum.

> *"Rickedy-din, the Wicked One*
> *Quick—let's kill the Witch's Son*
> *Roast his hump until it's done*
> *How meet's the meat of Ricadon!"*

Tears slicked my face. My nose began to run. My throat tightened till I could do no more than squeak. A few skips more, and the rope tangled my legs. I stopped to extricate myself, puffing for breath.

It came to me then, doubled over, that I'd been a rhymer for nearly as long as I'd been a prisoner. True, my couplets had all been curses like the one Torvald and Lissa had lain upon the Witch's Son. I'd never tried to compose a countercurse to coax a shy thing from the Veil. Point was, rhymes meant something to the Gentry, where a song was life or death depending on which you followed through the bog. Rhymes could make a broken baby dance with pain, or a twisted mouth flash out with laughter in the dark. My golden rope glittered in the moonlight as I got my breath back. I began skipping again.

> *"Rickedy-din, the Kindly One*
> *How I love the Witch's Son*
> *Woo him well until he's won*
> *My vows I'll make to Ricadon."*

The ruins of Lirhu vanished. The Witch with one eye vanished (but a second before she did, I saw her smile). So did the night disappear, and the chill, and my weariness. I could not breathe. My innards turned to soup and streamed out of holes in the soles of my feet. Then the world steadied. My body unjellied. I stood in a sunlit cow pasture—near enough the sea to smell it, though I did not know in which direction it lay.

My cow Annat grazed not far from me, her brown-dappled hide agleam. My heart jumped for joy in my chest.

"Annat, my love! You're looking fat and happy!"

In a distant corner of the pasture, my good red bull Manu trotted back and forth, a tiny white figure clinging to his corded neck and giggling.

Now, I knew time moved differently in the Veil, that Gentry children did not develop as mortals did, but oh! I feared for her! She was so small, both her worlds so unsafe. I thought of my fox twins, and others like them. The war was not over—not by many a long mile and a longer year. King, Archabbot, Prickster, peasant, Gentry warrior, mortal soldier: our battles would rage ever bloodier before we knew an end. Such a tangle. Such a terror. If only the children were let to reach a reasonable age, perhaps together they might build a more reasonable world. But they had to survive it first!

"Be careful!" I shouted, "Manu, not so fast!" and set off at a run. Not two steps I'd taken before someone had caught the back of my skirt. People were always stopping me this way. I should start wearing trousers.

"Peace, Milkmaid! She won't fall. We've taken to calling her the White Raven. If we don't tie a thread to her ankle and tether her to something solid—like Manu—she'll fly right up into the air and only come down again when she's hungry."

My body strained forward, not quite caught up to my ears.

"But—she's—just—"

"A child. Our child. Seven days old and stubborn as the sea." He released my skirt abruptly. I splattered into the dirt as was my wont—charmingly, just shy of a cowpat. This was so reminiscent of the moment we'd first met, I laughed.

His long black eyes danced as he gazed down. His hair was wild as a thundercloud. Clad like a farmer but for the opal on his finger, the ivory at his throat, the green flame on his brow, he looked . . . healthy. His shoulders still hunched, his torso still torqued, but his brow was unfurrowed, free of pain. No farmer or fisherman, prince or soldier had ever been so fine and fey, so gladdening to my eyes. Wiping my face briefly with the hem of my skirt, I took my first true breath in what seemed like a lifetime.

"If our Raven can fly, Ricadon, she gets it from your side of the family. Me, I'm mortal to the bone—remember?"

"Not anymore, Gordie Oakhewn," said my friend and lifted me from the ground.

 # The Big Bah-Ha

For Bea LaMonica and Gillian Hastings

Beatrice did not wake up in Heaven.

She lay flat on her back. The surface beneath her was hard as concrete, maybe bouncier, like those playgrounds made from recycled tires. Bitter crazy cold out, but she could not see her breath.

"Dead, then," said Beatrice.

Not panic. Not exactly. A pang, maybe. Best not to pay attention to that. Might begin to gnaw holes in a girl when a girl most needs to be whole.

So Beatrice sat up and patted her head. Pigtails still held, thank the Good Goddess Durga, as Dad used to say . . . although Dad hadn't believed in any pantheon predating Darwin, had gone gravy to the slaprash an atheist and a scientist and taking in vain the names of all fiend-eating ladygods sharing cross references in the 'cyclopedia.

'Spossible, she thought with an inward sparkle of enthusiasm, *I meet up Dad in this place. We'll discuss gods, or death, or breathing without breath, or whatever, like we used to do in the olden days, except . . .*

Except this place seemed to stretch out forever like an elastic elephant skin. Empty. Or—not empty? There. A gleam of red and white, listing not too far from where she sat. A striped barber's pole. A fat white glove at its pinnacle wriggling HELLO. The arrow of its index finger urged her down a path.

The path, Beatrice saw, was the same gray as ground and horizon, easy to miss. Just a thin groove to be picked across like the wirewalkers used to do under the big tops. Or a girl might elect to stroll with more dignity along its side. If a girl followed it at all.

But standing still invited the biting chill, and Beatrice shivered. The pointing glove reminded her of the Flabberghast's hands, which were just as white, but much slimmer. Slim and graceful, nearly transparent, the fingers too long and the wrists too bony. He was the last thing she remembered: his long painted face peering at her through the bushes, his eyes shining black as beetles.

"He killed me!" Beatrice said aloud, startled. "Him and his diamond teeth."

Well, she didn't remember that part, not ezzactly. Not the getting gobbled part, only the part where he smiled.

But she was here, wasn't she? And here could be anywhere, but it could also be in the Flabberghast's stomach. And even if here were really elsewhere, she'd bet she'd left her bones behind to undergo eternal digestion. Danged Flabberghast! Old carrion eater. Old clown.

But how'd he get close enough? Beatrice had lived by the same command she'd drummed into her little Barka Gang. If she'd told Tex, Diodiance, Granny Two-Shoes, and Sheepdog Sal once, she'd told them a kajillion times: "Beware the Flabberghast."

And when they asked her why, she'd said, "Well, because he's a Tall One. Because he appeared in the gravy yard with the other eight after the world ended. Because he's here to eat the bones, and he'll eat yours when you go."

"So?" Diodiance always asked. Diodiance liked the Flabberghast, liked his cardboard hut, his yellow shoes, his little way of bowing low. "We ain't dead yet, so he can't rightly eat us. Till our slaprashes show, Queen B, mayn't he come over to play?"

Quick as a slung-shot rock, Beatrice always parried, "What if Ol' Flabby don't feel like waiting till your slaprash shows? What if he picks up a crushing stone with his weird white hand and caves in your skull, strips your flesh to stretch upon a great moony drum, and sucks your bones good and fresh? The Flabberghast's not *contained* like the other Tall Ones. The gravy yard gates don't hold him. Lives outside the arch in his cardboard hut, don't he, while his friends slaver and babble and gobble up crypt-crunch behind the black iron bars, those white lights on their shoulders a-shinin'. And don't he smile to be so free, aiming his big, bright teeth at any kiddo strayin' bold from her gang."

Tex, taking her pause for breath as permission, would jump in to plead with Diodiance: "Di, don't stray." Those two were just each other's age, just shy of nine. His ashy, stiff hair stood on end at the thought of losing her.

"Oh. Awright." Diodiance never did sound convinced.

And Beatrice, more quietly, made sure to repeat what they'd all heard before. "Don't stray." She gazed at her Barkas with the solemnity of her age. Twelve now, or thereabouts, and they all knew the slaprash would get her soon. Watching them remember this, she'd soften her fierceness to a smile.

"Barka dears, this is world's end. You've only got a few years left to your names. You gotta live 'em, not go playin' flirt to Death's own maggotman—no matter how he smiles and bows. Don't go near the gravy yard. Don't stray. And beware the Flabberghast."

Or not.

Sighing for her lost Barkas, Beatrice pushed herself up from the squishy hard ground. Her gait felt off. She glanced down.

"Appears," she observed aloud, "I'm missing my shoe."

Not only that, but the white cotton lace edging her left sock had gone all rusty. Looked old. Looked like it'd been dragged oh, many a long mile. Or like something had bled all over it. Someone.

Beatrice bit her lip, and even that felt like nothing, and she covered her eyes with her hands, but there was only the same gray inside as everywhere else. The thought of limping listlessly along that thin gray groove with only one shoe and a rusty sock was the three-ton straw set atop a brittle-boned and spindly-kneed camel, and it was enough, it was *outside enough*!

Beatrice crumpled and began to cry.

"Please!" she sobbed, her tears all dried to dust. "Oh, please! Oh, Durga! Oh, Dad! Daddy!"

Above her, pouring from a rip in the empty sky, something like ravens circled.

Tex crept back to the Catchpenny Shop-'n'-Save where the other members of the Barka Gang awaited.

"Beatrice is gone."

His face, gussied up for recon, was ghoulish under the black paint. The whites of his eyes were very white, but his teeth looked yellow. Tex never did learn to brush regular, though Diodiance nightly whupped him upside his rattlebox for forgetting.

"Gone?" Diodiance asked. "Like, to the gravy yard?"

Tex shook his head. Fleas flew. "Nope. But I found a ribbon from her hair right there by the black iron gates. So I axed the Tall Ones through the bars if they'd seen her, and they smacked their lips and said, *Nothing fresh has come in oh so long,* and won't I stand a little closer please, and what nice fat hands I have. I'm thinking, Di, you can't go into the gravy yard 'less you pass the Flabberghast. And I'm thinking, Di, it's the Flabberghast what's got Queen B for sure."

Diodiance shook her head. "Ate her up, poor dead Beatrice!" She wrapped her arms hard around herself and tried to think how Beatrice would sound in their situation. Cool. Assured. At least four years older than anyone present.

"No more than we should've 'spected," she said at last. "Queen B told us her own dang self that the slaprash was bounded to boom her pretty soonish. And when it did, her body is bargained to the gravy yard. That's the deal; our slaprash shows, we go and die where the Tall Ones can see us and eat us after. We do this, they stay behind the gates till the last of us is gonnered. They leave us alone."

Tex did not look comforted. He squatted on the floor near the shoe racks. They were used shoes, lightly scuffed. You could still smell the feet of people who'd donated them to the Catchpenny way back in the olden days. A dead-people-feet smell. He turned to the third member of their gang.

"Whaddya think, Granny Two-Shoes? 'Bout Beatrice? Is she not just gone but dead?"

Granny Two-Shoes looked up from the red-and-yellow race cars she'd found in the toy aisle. She had contemplated a race between the cars and the bullet casings she'd gleaned from the gutters, but decided that, while bullets indeed moved faster than cars, even a toy car bests a spent bullet. No race, really. No glory. It would be much more interesting to stack as many of them on top of each other as could balance unwobbled, then push them down for the smash! The lap of her white nightgown sagged under the weight of her treasures.

Granny Two-Shoes didn't have regular language. Didn't want it. She was half past three and thought she got on pretty well with Sheepdog Sal as interpreter. Tex buckled under her eloquent gaze and redirected his question to the dog.

"Okay, Granny. Tell Sal what you think, then. Have her bark once for dead, twice for gone, three for she'll be home in time to feed us Cheerios."

Bending her head to Sheepdog Sal's flopsy ear, Granny Two-Shoes imparted her opinion in a way Sal would understand.

Sheepdog Sal barked once.

Tex and Diodiance stared at each other in despair. Sighing, Granny Two-Shoes went back to her pile of race cars and casings. She was rarely wrong, but that didn't make being right any easier.

Tex knuckled the inner corners of his welling eyes. Diodiance never could bear his crying. Made her bawl like a swoll-bellied baby herself, not the pragmatic nearly nine-year-old she was. If the two of 'em turned this into a big ol' snotfest, it might upset Granny Two-Shoes into becoming ever more stoic. And Beatrice always said, "Let Granny be as much a child as she can bear. She's the youngest girl in the whole wide world, and we owe her that."

Diodiance got her squeezing heart under control. Opened her dark eyes wide. Squared her shoulders. Flung back her matted cornrows. Bared her teeth. She'd once fought off a wild Doberman with nothing but a yardstick and the Barka war cry. She could do what needed doing. Just watch.

"Tex. Granny. Sal. Way I'm seein' it, we gotta do us some death rite. Queen B showed us how. Pick out a place she loved. Dec'rate it. Tinfoil balloons and Silly String, that picture of her dad she loved. Put what's left of her there in a crow box. But keep of hers what's useful," she added mindfully, "like her slingshot."

Tex sucked on his overbite. "To do the thing proper, we'd need her . . . leftovers."

"Yup," answered Diodiance, too quickly. "Which means . . . the Flabberghast."

Tex groaned.

Diodiance sped ahead even faster. "We can win her stuff from him with games. Flabby likes games, and we Barkas are the best. No grown-up games, we'll say. No chess or checkers or Scrabble-like stuff with words and counting. Maybe tag?"

Granny Two-Shoes cleared her throat. She contemplated the peeking tips of her pink, patent leather Mary Janes, and wondered how best to alert the others to the dangers she perceived. Sheepdog Sal was an angel of understanding, but there were nuances even she could not manage. Quickly, Granny laid out four race cars. She pointed to the first, then jabbed her finger at Tex. Likewise, she associated herself, Diodiance, and Sheepdog Sal with corresponding vehicles.

At last she showed them all a slim bullet casing, held in her pinched thumb and forefinger. With her free hand, she made a gesture in precise mimicry of the Flabberghast's formal bow, with which he unfailingly greeted his visitors. The bullet casing, then, was the Flabberghast.

At Tex and Diodiance's nods of comprehension, Granny Two-Shoes moved her playing pieces around the dirty tile floor in a game of tag. As the cars separated from one another and scattered in all directions, the deadly bullet casing sought each of them out separately and pounced, dragging them back to base. Checkmate.

Tex gulped.

"Granny's right," he said. "We gotta stick together. No tag, or even Hide-and-Seek, or Flabby'll pick us off for sure."

"Red Rover?" Diodiance suggested pragmatically.

Tex scratched his freckles. "Dunno. Ol' Flabby's pretty big. One of the tallest Tall Ones. He might break through, and then he'd win the game and bargaining rights. That won't win us back B's bones. "

Diodiance slowly lifted one leg behind her the way she'd learned in ballet, in the olden days, back before the slaprash. Easier to focus when balance was at stake. She stretched out an arm to finger the sleeve of a secondhand coat that hung on the fifty-percent-off rack.

Maybe she remembered, or maybe she had dreamed, shopping with her momma at the Catchpenny. Eight-dollar winter coats. Made of real wool. Red wool. From red sheep, Momma used to say. All the way from London. That was all acrost the sea, which was bigger than the big lake to the East, and even the lake was like something out of Queen B's bedtime stories, for Diodiance had never seen it, and never would. She settled into a plié.

"Here's what, Barkas. Come noon-up, we'll parley with the Flabberghast. We owe Queen B her death rite. Remember when she faced off Aunt Oolalune with fisticuffs? Remember when she led the march on the Rubberbaby Gang, and won Granny Two-Shoes back for the Barkas? Not for her, Granny'd be slave bait still to those dirty snotbums."

Tex shifted. Not quite a shrug. Not quite an agreement. Diodiance had never understood his problem with the Flabberghast. With her it was never, "Isn't the Flabberghast scary as thunder?" but always, "Isn't the Flabberghast fancy and strange?" and, "Isn't the Flabberghast's voice so sweet?" and, "Don't the Flabberghast smell like pineapples and toothpaste and broken perfume bottles and the moonlight on pine trees?"

Her obsession was, in his opinion, unfortunate. But she was correct; Beatrice deserved this much from them upon her death. She had taken care of them far back as he could remember. He could not remember the olden days. Sometimes he didn't think he believed in them.

Oh, if only they could deal with any other Tall One but the Flabberghast. At least the rest of them dwelled *behind* the gravy yard wall. You could keep the gate between you and the white lights on their shoulders. You could offer them old bones through the bars in exchange for stuff that came from the graves they exhumed for their banquets. Diamond rings, or pictures in fancy frames, or bouquets of flowers tied up in someone's braided hair. Best were their queer shiversome stories about life under the hills, with the folks they only ever referred to as "those underground."

But to creep close to the gray stone arch, where the Flabberghast lived in his cardboard house? Where he lived *outside* the black iron gates, with nothing keeping him in?

That was like cutting off your finger in shark water.

WELCOME TO CHUCKLE CITY*!!! IT'S A LAUGH A MINUTE!!!*
Beatrice stood before a high wall. The stones of the watchtower were as shiny a pink as a piece of watermelon bubblegum all blown up.

The billboard that announced the city was lettered in bold yellow, with six orange exclamation points like floating construction cones.

Balloons everywhere.

Balloons tangled in the portcullis. Balloons tied to the barbed wire lining the heights of the walls. Balloons flying like pennants from the watchtower's parapet, lurid against the uniform sky.

From beyond the balloon-obscured grid of the portcullis came a thin strain of cheerful music. It sounded as if a very small person in a very large coffee can played it, just for laughs.

If she ever felt less like laughing, Beatrice couldn't remember. Her mouth pulled down at the edges as if weights hung from her lips. She could feel the hard pinch of her brows drawn tightly together. Dad had always called that look "Nana Larsson's Evil Eye," and said he knew what side of the family Beatrice favored that day, and for Durga's sake, might he be spared?

Today, Beatrice didn't feel like sparing anyone her Evil Eye. Not the billboard, not the city, not the gray groove, or the gray sky, or the large gray ravens circling above.

She just wanted Dad. That was all. And Dad was not here, though she had been walking forever.

A silky, silly breeze danced over her brow. It was not sunshine, but it was the closest thing to it Beatrice had known since her arrival in these deadlands. The breeze seemed to chime, seemed to tickle and tingle and ring. Beatrice almost smiled. But before she could make up her mind, the breeze went away again, and so did her inclination.

About that time, a jolly shout echoed down from the pink watchtower:

"Ho there, girlington! Are you new to the Big Bah-Ha?"

"Is that where I am?" Beatrice asked, looking up but not raising her voice.

"Why, of course you are here! Where did you think you were?"

Beatrice shrugged. "Been walkin' alone since I got here. Except for the—the critterbirds."

"The which?"

Beatrice pointed at the sky, toward the gray ravens. From a window in the watchtower, out popped a small, round face with round, pink-painted cheeks, glittering tinsel-green eyelashes, and a head of hair as blue as radioactive violets. Owl-like, the head twisted nearly full circle to stare up into the sky. Seeing the gray ravens for herself, she gasped.

"Gacy Boys!" squeaked the little clown. "And you still all in one piece! Bless my soul!"

"I threw my shoe at one when it got too close," Beatrice said. Her socks she had stripped a while back, tossing them over her shoulder like salt to ward off ghosts. After a lot of walking and squinting at the sky, she couldn't help but notice that the ravens only looked like ravens when you expected them to be ravens. But if you stared through your lashes and a little sideways-like, weren't they something else again?

Something with heads that might be human, hooded like hangmen.

But Beatrice did not tell the little clown any of that. She already seemed upset enough. Even her pink paint seemed to blanch. She whimpered what sounded like, "Oh, the poor tidbit! The poor cutlet!"

"I'm Beatrice," said Beatrice.

"Oh! How rude I am!" The little clown's body followed her face right out of the tower window. She crawled in all her crinoline and sequins down the pink stones, face first and feet clinging to the plastic ivy. Her frills fell over her shoulders, revealing big polka-dot bloomers and spangled green tights. She did a neat flip near the bottom of the tower, and landed on her tiptoes on the ground.

Diodiance would die, Beatrice thought, almost grinning.

But the idea of Diodiance dying and waking up here made her feel oh, so very sick, so she frowned all the more blackly. The little clown, who looked as if she'd wanted to do a "Ta-da!" decided against it.

"I'm Rosie Rightly," she blatted instead. "Hello! Hi! Hello! Oh, Beatrice, it's so good to see you! Welcome to Chuckle City! It's a laugh a minute! All laughs, all the time! Come in! Come in!"

"How?" asked Beatrice. "Gate's closed."

"Oh. Um." Rosie Rightly stared at the portcullis as if she'd never seen one before. Then she shrugged and banged a fist on the balloon-festooned grid. The grate creaked up slowly. Several balloons popped with the sound of bullets, reminding Beatrice of home, of the end of the olden days, back when the grown-ups had tried to contain the slaprash to one area. It hadn't worked. The slaprash took all the grown-ups first. Even the ones with masks and guns.

"Easy-peasy," said Rosie Rightly, trying to usher Beatrice through the gate. Beatrice dug her feet in a little. "Only, you forget it's there sometimes. Silly to have a gate here anyway. There's only one city in all the whole Big Bah-Ha, and nothing beyond it. Nothing. Nothing. So why keep anyone out? Everyone wants in, don't they? Why shouldn't they?"

When Beatrice glanced uneasily at the sky, Rosie Rightly patted her hand. "They're okay. The Gacy Boys live here. They belong to the Gray Harlequin. But sometime he lets them out to eat."

"What do they eat? If there's nothin' outside Chuckle City."

Rosie Rightly's pink mouth formed a great big O. Then she stretched her lips over a toothy grimace and said, "Haven't had one like you in a while. You're one of those sparky-smarts, ain't you?! That's great! Only maybe it'd be better if you wasn't. Not that you can help it. But come on!"

She slipped her little hand, gloved in pink net, her fingernails painted with sparkly green glitter, through Beatrice's arm and tugged her through the open gate. Beatrice almost backed out again as the first wave of heat licked her face.

What she saw stopped her deader in her tracks.

Every building in Chuckle City was on fire.

Diodiance combat-crawled through the weeds for a better look. Seemed all clear, so she signaled the A-Okay to Tex, who slouched into a squat in the overgrown hydrangea behind her. Further down the road, Granny Two-Shoes lay in the gutter with Sheepdog Sal sitting "guard" nearby. Granny had her binoculars, so she saw what was about to happen, but it was too late to warn them, and besides—wasn't it what they all wanted? So she watched, but did not set Sal to barking.

Diodiance strained her senses and took stock of the scene. Cardboard house—empty. Blue lawn chair—vacant. Emissary at the eastern gates— defected.

A worm of a scant of an inch closer. Adjust the thornstick sheathed in her belt loop. Squint. Sniff. Wipe nose on sleeve. Glance again.

The Flabberghast's hut was an old refrigerator box with a green- and-gold silk sari thrown over it. Icicle lights all the colors of a crayon box dripped from its edges, the unplugged prongs dangling in the wind. Come dusk they'd light up. No one knew why.

Sometimes a frayed edge of the sari flapped aside, showing a palatial foyer just beyond the front flap. Marble halls. Portraits. Tapestries. Vases. The Tall Ones lived in two worlds at once, Beatrice used to say. Or more.

Pounding fist to dirt, Diodiance whispered, "It's a wash." Then, louder, so Tex could tell the others, "Ain't even a left-handed shadow to wave us hello! Granny? Sal? Tex, come on out here. No need to sneak. Flabby ain't home."

Tex emerged from his blind, brushing leaves from his hair. Granny rode up on Sal's back, clutching her fur like a mane. She dismounted beneath the arched entrance of the gravy yard, with its creakily swinging sign that said, WELCOME TO HILLSIDE in cut out letters.

Having seen what was to come from way back in her gutter, Little Granny Two-Shoes was the only Barka who did not jump when a great voice shattered the silence.

"Good afternoon, children!"

That voice was like a Slinky toy going downhill, like shouting into a well after someone fell in, like a piece of expensive caramel melting in a slant of afternoon sunlight. It was a voice that made Diodiance pirouette, and set a rigid scowl upon Tex's brow. Sheepdog Sal began to bark. Little Granny Two-Shoes scratched her just beneath the jaw.

"By all the skulls of Arlington National Cemetery!" cried the Flabberghast. "If it isn't the Barka Gang!"

They all turned to look. Banana-yellow shoes rocked about his feet like dinghies. Up. Legs as long as stilts and thin as straight pins in their loose white silk trousers. Up. Past a coat of sweeping peacock feathers, a vest of red brocade, a fine lawn cravat. Up, and up, and up to his white-painted face, his long black mouth, his long black eyes, those curls of flaming orange hair peeking out from beneath a sequined derby hat.

"And how may I help you?" asked the Flabberghast politely.

"Beatrice is dead," Tex blurted before Diodiance said something happy and solicitous.

"Ah."

"We need her stuff for a death rite. We're pretty sure you have it."

"I see. Yes. That might prove . . . problematic."

Tex stepped forward with fists up, to show the Flabberghast the meaning of *problematic*, but Diodiance shoved him to the side before he got too close. He fell against Sheepdog Sal's flank, and Sal turned to lick his wrist. Granny Two-Shoes took his hand in hers, and this more than anything stopped Tex from launching himself at the Flabberghast.

The Flabberghast gave no sign of noticing this altercation. His gaze had meandered beyond the Barka Gang. Beyond the black iron gates, a few of the Tall Ones left off their endless feasting and began to drift curiously toward them. The white lights on their shoulders flickered and burned.

The Flabberghast put a long white hand on top of Diodiance's head. Blissfully, she leaned in.

"Allow me to offer armistice and hospitality. Come with me into my hut. As per the edicts stipulated in the original bargain between vestigial Homo sapiens and the Tall Ones, I shall not harm a single split hair on any one of your heads till the day you are marked to die. We must speak further of your Beatrice, but the situation is far too complex for casual graveside chatter. While I do not doubt my colleagues would find our forthcoming conversation stimulating, as civilized people, we may exercise the right to exclude whom we will from our private affairs. Do not you agree?"

"Ain't goin' in your stinky old house," Tex muttered.

"Fine," Diodiance snapped at him. "Stay outside, you cowardbaby. That'll get Queen B her death rite quick enough."

"Aw, Di!"

Granny Two-Shoes, who still held his hand, now squeezed with intent. Tex allowed her to tug him into the cardboard hut after Diodiance, with Sheepdog Sal trotting behind, and the Flabberghast following last.

The first thing they saw, after the marble-floored foyer itself, was her skin.

It hung from one blank wall, stretched out and tacked there with silver nails. They knew the skin belonged to Beatrice because her hair was red. Not orange-red like the Flabberghast's. Red like when a fire dies.

"Beatrice!" Diodiance screamed. This time Tex did punch the Flabberghast. Right in the knee.

The Flabberghast stumbled against a small table that held, among other things, a flensing tool and a familiar brown loafer (a scuffed size six, women's) all under the coating of gray dust that comes from crunching bones. He hit the table's edge and his peacock coat snarled him. Searching for purchase, his hands closed on air. This close up, he was not graceful. Not like he'd always seemed, sitting out in his blue lawn chair with his legs stretched before him like unfurled fire hoses.

Diodiance flinched against the wall, shielding Granny Two-Shoes with her body, Tex at her side, Beatrice's skin at her back. Granny Two-Shoes saw something on the floor and bent to pick it up. Beatrice's slingshot.

This put the Flabberghast between them and the door. He stood very still now, arms hanging loosely at his sides.

"You killed her!" Diodiance said. It wasn't a sob, and it wasn't a growl, but it was something like both.

"I do not eat the living," said the Flabberghast.

"You killed her and stripped her flesh and ate her bones."

The Flabberghast splayed one hand over his stomach. His diamond teeth gleamed and glinted, as if a spotlight in his belly shone up and out his throat, through his lips, casting rainbows all around him.

"She died at my feet," he said. "She was in the final stages when I found her. The slaprash marked her face, all down one side. Nothing to save. She was just that age." He shrugged, as if to say, "The rest you know. I am what I am."

Tex gnawed his lip to keep back a wail.

"I wish your Beatrice had come to me earlier," reflected the Flabberghast. "Those underground have informed us here of a matter in the deadlands that needs our immediate attention. Not being bound by the black iron gates, I am the only Tall One at liberty to perform the task. However. To do so, I shall need the help of a living child. *Willing* help, I should say. Otherwise, the door to the deadlands opens only one way, and I have no particular desire to be stuck on the far side of it. Had your Beatrice trusted me more, or perhaps loved you less, she would have done splendidly. She was so strong. Not fearless, but not one to fear foolishly. This journey would have prepared her for the one she now must undergo. Alas, she died too soon. I liked her. I might have used her to better purpose than as a lunchbox." He paused. "I don't suppose any of you might volunteer to be of assis—"

"Never!" spat Diodiance through her tears. "Never, until the end of the end of the world! I'd sooner slap myself right now and bleed out bawlin' murder!"

Hearing the quaver in her voice, Tex slung an arm around her, and stated, "Me, neither!"

His free hand grasped a stone in his pocket. He was already gauging distance, velocity, angle, wondering if Tall Ones felt pain like humans, if they had brains to concuss, if the great holes that were their eyes could be put out . . .

The Flabberghast turned those black-dark eyes on him. Tex's hand went numb.

"A pity." The Flabberghast's long fingers drummed the silver buttons on his red brocade vest. "For, in return for your ready collaboration, I would offer my brave adventurer a chance to see Beatrice again. I need to travel to a certain level of the deadlands, to the place she now resides. Only a child may bring me there. And only a living child may bring me out again."

A bark, and Tex and Diodiance sprang apart. Granny Two-Shoes, once again mounted like a maharani atop Sheepdog Sal, came forward. Her thin blond hair had not been combed in two days. There was chocolate on her face from the icing she'd eaten for breakfast, a cut on her knee where she'd fallen that morning. But her eyes were steady, blue as the Flabberghast's were black, and she held out her hand. He stared down at her.

"Even in an epoch that deplores such conventions," said he, "and though you are by far the most superior three-year-old representative of your species I have ever come across, I cannot help but feel that you are not quite of an age to consent." His long black mouth twisted a little as if he wanted to say something more. Instead he flipped his palm like a playing card. When Granny laid her own hand there, he bowed over it.

"You are very brave. And I thank you for the offer, but—"

Tex barged forward, breaking their link of flesh. "Think you can stop her, Flabby? You? Stop Granny Two-Shoes?" And he laughed a laugh like wet tissue paper tearing. "You can't keep Granny from her Beatrice, and you can't keep us from Granny. If she's a-goin', I'm a-goin'."

"I'll go, too," Diodiance announced, stepping away from the wall. "We'll do Queen B's death rite to her face. We'll say goodbye." She didn't look over her shoulder at that horrible skin.

"My stars!" cried the Flabberghast. "What enterprising children you are! What pioneering spirits! What gumption. You don't faint at the sight of blood, do you?"

They all glared at him, wearing, between them, more scab than rags, and he grinned, and the marble foyer of the cardboard hut danced with the rainbows cast by his diamond teeth.

"Of course not," he murmured. "How silly of me."

The Flabberghast held up his left hand, folding thumb and fingers into palm, all except for his pinkie. This he held erect like a spindle, and the Barka Gang saw that his long nail was sparkling clear as his teeth.

"I'll just need a drop of your blood," he explained. "Your canine companion's, too, if you wish her to accompany us."

One by one, at the Flabberghast's direction, they pricked the soft spot at the center of their wrists, and the tip of Sal's panting tongue, too, and filed over to the stretched skin on the wall. They pressed their blood upon it. Diodiance signed her name. Tex made a big "T." Granny drew something that could have been a flower or a bone or a bullet. Sheepdog Sal licked the place where Beatrice's big toe had been.

The Flabberghast himself scored open his own palm. The hut filled with a smell that drowned the copper trickle of mortal blood in citrus-wine-wildflower-campfire-tidewater-leaf, and what leaked out of his skin was black like his eyes, and like his eyes full of tiny, whirling lights.

The blackness spread over Beatrice's stretched skin, overwhelming the tiny dots of blood like raindrops converging on a windowpane. The drop becomes a stream, the stream a puddle, the puddle a lake. The blackness spread. And Beatrice's skin became a door.

Granny Two-Shoes was the first one to step through.

Every building in Chuckle City was on fire. The buildings were tenements, and from their high, flaming windows rained a constant bombardment of grotesque little clowns. They smashed on the cobblestones below. Sometimes they jumped right up from the stones and dragged themselves back into the burning buildings to do the thing all over again. More often they just lay there and writhed on the cracked stones, ragged clothes smoking, the white greasepaint on their faces gray with soot, red noses charred. They twitched.

In the middle of Main Street, a skinny girl in a monkey mask, or perhaps a skinny monkey in a girl suit, cranked out "Ode to Joy" on her hurdy-gurdy. Beatrice shivered. The whole city smelled like ash.

"Isn't it FUNNY?" asked Rosie Rightly. "Isn't it a RIOT?"

Beatrice looked at her with solemn eyes. "You think that's funny?"

But Rosie Rightly was undaunted, or seemed to be. "It's always funny when things fall out a window."

Another bright upchuck of screaming bodies hit the pavement. A tiny clown near Beatrice's feet made a burbling sound that might have been laughter. Beatrice really did not think it was.

"Look at them bounce!" screamed Rosie Rightly. "Ga-DOING! Ga-DOING!"

When Beatrice did not respond, Rosie Rightly patted her on the shoulder. "Don't worry your warts, Bee-Bee-licious. You can't kill the dead. They're fine. They're all fine." She pushed a lock of blue hair from her forehead. "So just relax. Have a laugh, would you?" Her lips trembled. "Please?"

Beatrice studied the bodies on the ground. Heaps of little clowns. Smoldering.

Just like this two years ago, she remembered, when the slaprash first came to town. For a while the grown-ups tried to put up some kind of . . . quartermain? Or, calamine . . . She forgot what Dad had called it. Roadblocks at all entrances and exits. To keep the slaprash in. To prevent panicked folks from getting out.

At first they tried burying their dead in big pits, then they were just burning them, but soon there weren't enough grown-ups left to do any of that. Fires got out of control. Whole neighborhoods burned down. That was when the soldiers came. They didn't last long, either. None of the grown-ups lasted. The slaprash took them all and left the children behind. With a lot of bullet casings and bones.

"First comes the handprint
Then comes the flush
Then come the shaky-shakes
All—in—a—rush!
Breath starts to rattle
Like dice in a cup
And the slaprash'll getcha
When—you're—all—growed—up!"

Beatrice slammed her hands over her ears and shook off the nasty din of jump ropes. Worst thing in a long list of bad that the Rubberbaby Gang ever did, inventing that jump rope rhyme and spreading it 'round. Their leader Aunt Oolalune, nearly Beatrice's age, remembered all the rhymes from the olden days, Seuss and Silverstein, Gorey and Lear. The kiddy gangs loved her for her rhymes, but especially that one. It was their own, the only gravestone they'd get. Forget "Ring Around the Rosie" and "Susie Has a Steamboat." "The Slaprash Rhyme," like its namesake, went viral, went everywhere. What Dad would've called ubittinus. No, that wasn't the word.

Beatrice watched the little clowns scrape themselves off the ground and trudge into the burning buildings. Flames swallowed them. Bodies plummeted from high windows. The gleeful (or not) screaming began again.

Beatrice turned to Rosie Rightly, who grinned her manic grin. "Whaddya think, Bee-Bee?"

"Is this it, Rosie? This all there is?"

"We-ell." Rosie Rightly squirmed like she had to pee. "I could show you something else, sure! There's lots of great things here. It's Chuckle City! It's a laugh a minute. Like, like, look at these guys! The rustics! I love me some rustics!" She pointed at an approaching ambulance. "These guys are FUNNY. Wait and see!"

The tiny ambulance whizzed past them. Three rustics hung from its windows. They wore straw hats and overalls, glasses without lenses, fake tufts of white hair glued to their chins. Their faces were contorted in identical expressions of constipation. The ambulance itself was locomotioned by no engine but the hustle of their bare feet. When the feet stopped moving, the ambulance dropped, neatly squashing one of the supine victims of the tenement fires.

From beneath the steel frame came a soft moan. A splatter of bodies later and the moan was lost to the tautophony of the scene. The rustics climbed out of their ambulance, cursing one another's clumsiness.

"If ya'll'd dropped it over there, Mr. Wick, we could've smushed two!"

"Weren't two bodies lying close enough together for that, Mr. Jones."

"Could've waited, Mr. Gibbs. More come down every second, like bird poop!"

They clustered around the smushed clown like farmers at a town hall meeting, discussing blight.

"Broked, Mr. Wick!" said one.

"Backbone clean severed, Mr. Gibbs!" said another.

"What to do, Mr. Jones?" asked a third.

"I know!" answered the first. "Let's make balloon aminals!"

"Balloon aminals! Oh, yay!" squealed Rosie Rightly, dancing around Beatrice, who tried not to feel sick. "BULLY! Oh, they're great, Bee-Bee! You're going to love them!"

From pockets, hats, folds of cuffs, rolls of socks, the rustics drew out flaccid balloon skins and began inflating them with such gust and vigor that behind fake beards and empty glasses frames, their smooth young faces turned purple and puce and orange. Soon the balloons humped up, took on vivid, twisted shapes, the shapes of things best left under beds and in the dark of closets, and they grew large and larger, aerial sculptures that vied for the greatest ghoulishness. Only when they became truly huge and horrible did the rustics at last tie them off, whipping out black Sharpies from their bibs to scribble in teeth, eyes, scales, claws. Soon the balloons were not balloons at all, but buoyant beasts that turned on their makers and began chomping at them. The rustics tried to fight them off, but were snapped up, shaken apart, eaten, spat out again.

Rosie Rightly no longer danced. She stared at the balloons with an expression of abject misery. But she did not move.

Beatrice stumbled back from the bright melee, dragging Rosie Rightly by her pink chiffon princess sleeve.

"Let's go, Rosie. Show me the way out of Chuckle City. You can come, too. I'll take care of you, I—"

"Too late." Rosie Rightly's tinsel-lashed eyes were bright with tears she could no longer cry, but her never-ending smile showed a full crescent of teeth. "It's the Big Bah-Ha for me and for you, lambikin, unless—"

A balloon aminal loomed too close, leering. Beatrice batted at it with a fist and pulled Rosie Rightly out of range behind a charred building. Rosie Rightly began to slump against the wall, but Beatrice took her blue head between her hands and pressed their foreheads together.

"Focus. We have to stay in the Big Bah-Ha, you said, unless . . .?"

Rosie Rightly fiddled with her gloves. They had torn in the scuffle. Beatrice saw her wrists through the pink net, where two large wounds glowed as red as coals. Seeing her look, Rosie Rightly clasped her hands behind her.

"Unless," she stammered, "the—the Gray Harlequin releases you. There's a place beyond the mirror, but—but it's so hard. Hard to get there. Too hard."

They stared at each other, clown and girl. Beatrice tried to interpret Rosie Rightly's expression. The shine of her very-nearly-tears had already vanished. Her smile was fixed. She tore her puffy pink sleeve from Beatrice's grip and fluffed it up again.

"Poor Bee-Bee," she giggled. "So serious all the time! If you want, I'll take you to the Gray Harlequin. He's probably by the mirror. Always looking into it, and no wonder, for he's the prettiest clown of all. He wears the August Crown. I think he's been here forever. Or at least," she added, "since I arrived. Same thing."

* * *

"This is where dead kids have to go? The Big Bah-Ha?" Diodiance scanned the lay of the land, her round brown eyes skeptical. "Maybe I'll just become a Tall One instead. Wear a white light on my shoulder. Eat some bones. I tell ya, Tex, our good ol' gravy yard is lookin' like a big bucketful of screamin' monkey-fun from where I'm standin'."

Tex scratched under his left arm. "Look there." He pointed to a sunken gray groove where an empty sock ringed in rusty lace lay. Picking it up, he put it in his pocket.

"Very astute," breathed the Flabberghast. "What keen eyes you have, Young Texas! Like the Prince of Peregrines, you watch the world below."

"Shut up, Flabby," said Tex.

The Flabberghast crossed his arms, portraying nonchalance not very well at all. The corner of his mouth got up a tic. His peacock coat swung with the force of his shrug. All the Tall Ones wore white lights upon their shoulders, but the top of the Flabberghast's coat sleeve carried only a scorch mark. The Barka Gang used to spend whole nights speculating where that light had gone.

"Children," he observed in a hurt voice, "too often take the aggressive myth of the Napoleon complex to an unbecoming extreme."

Granny Two-Shoes cleared her throat. It made a sound in the dead gray air like a wooden spoon banged with no particular rhythm against a plastic bucket. She put her hand over her heart. Had it missed a beat? Was this dying? Was she dead?

The Flabberghast's painted-on creases softened when he gazed at her. "No. Not yet, Miss Granny. But our time here must perforce be limited, for these are the deadlands, and you must not lavish them too long with the extravagance of your living youth. Perhaps in the past, you might have stayed a trifle longer, but the very equivalence of air here seems sucked dry. This land," he sighed, "is too much changed from what it was."

Granny Two-Shoes paused to nuzzle her face against Sheepdog Sal's brown fur. In return for this she received a reassuring lick. It cleared her head.

In these deadlands, thought Granny Two-Shoes, *might merely being alive mean being too* alive? *Are we flaunting our liveliness to these dead gray skies? Are we attracting the attention of the dead? Can the dead harm the living? What does harm mean* here, *where hurt doesn't necessarily stop with the cessation of a heartbeat? Where there is no hope of healing?*

The Flabberghast caught her eye and held a finger to his lips. *Hush* was implied, but all he said aloud was, "Check your cuts, children," in a voice that even Tex obeyed.

Diodiance dabbed at her wrist, at the place she had torn it against the Flabberghast's fingernail. "Still bleedin'."

"Good," said the Flabberghast. "We can stay here until your scab forms and closes. Keep a lively eye upon it. And another on the sky."

Tex's eyes narrowed in suspicion. "What're we lookin' for?"

For answer, Granny Two-Shoes threw out her arms and flapped so vigorously she almost fell off of Sheepdog Sal. Sal turned around in circles, trying to keep her rider astride.

"Bad birds?" Diodiance guessed.

"Sad birds," Tex corrected.

"Not birds at all," said the Flabberghast. "But"—he bowed to Granny Two-Shoes—"I am impressed."

Nothing more was said on the subject. The Flabberghast unfurled his hands in a herding gesture, and once more they all started moving along the gray groove. Tex and Diodiance marched at the vanguard, taking inventory of their pockets, swapping out what they didn't want with each other. PayDay candy bars for watermelon-flavored Jolly Ranchers, bullet casings for smooth pebbles, bones for crayons. A happy breeze riffled their hair like a mother's fingers, conveying sunshine and safety and the promise of joyful rest. Gone too soon.

The Flabberghast, taking up the rear, sniffed for traces of that breeze when it departed. He frowned at what lingered.

Equidistant between them, Granny Two-Shoes rode Sheepdog Sal at a pleasant trot. She didn't bother listening in on Tex's and Diodiance's conversation, which she generally considered comfortable white noise to stimulate her own ruminations. She didn't look over her shoulder to see what shenanigans the Flabberghast got up to; he had his own agenda, and it was not hers. But she did check the twin holsters she wore beneath her nightgown. One for her switchblade. One for Beatrice's slingshot. She was ready for anything.

Rosie Rightly led Beatrice away from the burning buildings. They passed a dusty little market square with tattered awnings over abandoned booths that read, TENDER LEONARD'S JOKES AND GAGS! and SOLOMON SOT'S SOCIETY OF CAREFREE KIDDIES! and FRABJOUS THE FOOL'S POPULAR PUPPETS!

"Where is everyone?"

Rosie Rightly shrugged. "Those're the clowns that did their job. Made the kids laugh, helped 'em move on. When the kids moved on, so did they. That's why the Big Bah-Ha's here—'cause it's never funny when a kid dies. We have to learn to laugh again, before we can go through . . . to whatever's next."

"That's what all the clowns are for?" asked Beatrice.

Rosie Rightly nodded. "That's what they *were* for, way back before I got here. I think the Big Bah-Ha was different then. But that's done with. The Gray Harlequin says we're all clowns now."

Beatrice tugged one of her braids. One of her ribbons was missing, and another had gone all loosey-goosey. The thought of losing another ribbon gave her a sick jolt of panic. She tightened it fiercely. The panic receded.

"Were you always a clown, Rosie?"

"No," Rosie Rightly sighed. "I just . . . never learned to laugh." She touched her painted face.

"Oh."

Rosie Rightly started skipping. Her flounces flounced. Her sequins flashed. Everything about her was gleeful with cheer, except her round blue eyes. She pointed at the dusty market with glittering fingernails.

"I know it looks all sad and dusty and stuff. But really it's GREAT! It means that if we do our jobs, then some day, we can go back to the mirror. Take a look at ourselves again. Tell ourselves, we brought joy to the joyless. We deserve the next world, too. And this time, this time, we'll be able to meet our own eyes without flinching. We'll know we're worthy. Like Solly Sot, and Frabjoojooface, and Lenny, and Sudsy Aimee, and Snotty Sue. They did it. They learned to see themselves as something other than dead. They got through. I will too. Someday."

Beatrice nodded, frowning. "Is that hard? Seein' yourself?"

"It's the hardest. You look in the mirror the first time, and all you see . . ." Rosie Rightly gulped. "But the Gray Harlequin says . . ." Here she stopped, shook herself. Poked Beatrice in the ribs. "Hey. Bee-Bee. You think I'm funny? You do, right? You think I'm the funniest?"

Beatrice patted her gloved hand, avoiding the luminous wound on her wrist. "Keep tryin', Rosie."

Rosie Rightly hunched her shoulders. They were just coming upon a section of Chuckle City where a colossal tent loomed larger than any three of the burning tenements put together. The tent's canvas was striped red and white like the barber's pole Beatrice had seen in her first moments of the Big Bah-Ha. Red and white. Blood and bone. Near the curtained-off entrance, a twinkling Ferris wheel turned and turned into eternity.

"That's the Big Top," Rosie Rightly whispered. Her expression said she wanted to scurry by, but her feet dragged to a standstill. "The tramps live there. They ride tigers and swing from wires." A shiver wracked her. Beatrice could see the raised bumps beneath her painted flesh.

"When you're inside the Big Top and you look up, all you see are spiderwebs. The Eleven Lovely Emilies spin them, web on web. The Emilies all have beautiful red hair, like yours." Rosie Rightly's eyes lingered on Beatrice's hair. "And they have red eyes like hourglasses, and four arms and four legs apiece. They spin nets to catch the tramps should they chance to tumble from their wires. Whenever a tramp falls, the Eleven Lovely Emilies can eat. Their red tongues go all the way down to here!" Rosie Rightly touched her tummy.

Like Dad's dark ladygods, Beatrice thought, *with their many limbs, and scarlet mouths, and the way they could eat whole armies.*

Beatrice did not want to see the Emilies. Not without Dad at her side to explain them. Sure, in legends the ladygods could be brought to compassion, to show a mercy as miraculously ardent as their appetites. But no mercy remained here in the Big Bah-Ha, she thought, else Chuckle City would long since have been razed to dust.

"Do you want to see them?" Rosie asked, as if afraid of the answer.

Whatever Dad's old 'cyclopedia used to say, these Eleven Lovely Emilies could only be hideous. If Beatrice saw them, she knew her heart would break. She tightened her ribbon again.

"I want to see the Gray Harlequin," she said.

Rosie Rightly began to bounce on the balls of her feet. "We could do that, or . . . Or! Or! Or!"

"Or?"

"Instead of seeing the G-gray Harlequin, we could go to the petting zoo!"

Beatrice vaguely remembered petting zoos from the olden days. Sad sheep and decrepit llamas, dirty chickens running underfoot, rabbits in cages, bristly pigs setting the stable a-snore, and the whole place smelling earthy and unsavory. But the animals were pretty neat-o. They ate from the palm of your hand.

"Sometimes," Rosie Rightly nattered on, "the Gacy Boys go big game hunting out beyond Chuckle City. They bag prizes to bring back—and *that's* the petting zoo."

Beatrice did not remind Rosie Rightly of her first assertion—that nothing lived in the Big Bah-Ha outside Chuckle City. No place but here. But if the Gacy Boys could fly beyond these walls, she wondered if she might scale them. Was there a back door? If she ran free, would the Gacy Boys bag her next, and bring her back to put in their petting zoo, and feed her to the beasts trapped there?

"At night, in the arena under the Big Top, the Gray Harlequin will pit one of the petting zoo against his prize tigers. Or sometimes against one of us! It's stu-stupendous! Action-packed! Irresistible. Wanna see?"

"No," said Beatrice, very firmly. "I don't like fights."

"You don't like anything!"

Back with her Barka Gang, Beatrice had fought several battles against the Rubberbaby Gang and Aunt Oolalune. The skirmishes were usually quick and dirty. The weapons were grab-what-you-can. Sticks, stones, switchblades, slingshots. Rules were generally, *"First blood ends the fight / Whoever's not bleeding wins."* But of course, first blood had a tendency to enrage and incite. Often it was followed by second blood, and third blood, until there was blood everywhere, and the Tall Ones were slavering at the gravy yard gates in the hopes that their next meal succumbed to death sooner than the slaprash scything them down.

How could any such rule as "first flood" apply here, where nothing bled? You could be burned, smushed, and ripped apart, but you'd still go on and on. Like the fires, and the balloon aminals, and Rosie Rightly's grin. Horrors without end.

"I wanna see the Gray Harlequin," said Beatrice grimly.

"All riii-iiight." Rosie Rightly drooped. "If you're sure."

"Sure as spit means a promise."

"It's just . . ."

"What?"

"You're gonna have to look in the mirror before he'll meet you, and I just don't think you're ready, I really don't." Rosie Rightly's grin bent upsy-daisy of itself. "You don't want to—to—get stuck here, Bee-Bee. Like me. And the rest. You still have time. You might learn how to laugh again before you go and look." She canted her pink-gloved hands helplessly. "Maybe I could try a cartwheel? I usually fall. Bam! Right on my face. Maybe you'll think that's funny?"

Beatrice shook her head. "I'm sorry, Rosie. I know this ain't my territory. I know I'm new and don't have all the rules down straight. But I guess I'm used to dealin' with leaders. You say the Gray Harlequin runs things? He's the one I gotta see. 'Cause I ain't puttin' on no red nose and sweatin' blood for laughs. There *has* to be another way outta here." She shrugged. "I'll find it. I'm good at that."

"Maybe you were before," Rosie Rightly whispered.

Beatrice nudged her, even tried a wink. "Hey," she said. "I brought myself along with me when I died, didn't I? That's the sum of somethin'."

But Rosie Rightly would not be comforted.

Tex sniffed the air as they slipped beneath the portcullis. "Smells like bad eggs."

"Sulfur," the Flabberghast said absently. "And brimstone. So picturesque."

Diodiance stood en pointe in her tennis shoes. Widened her nostrils. Nodded agreement. "Reminds me of our Rotten Egg War. Who won that one again?"

"Aunt Oolalune. But we got her back the next week at the Battle of the Baseball Diamond. Sent her howlin' back to her side of town. Remember—"

Diodiance shushed him. Pointed. "What're those?"

Granny Two-Shoes petted Sheepdog Sal. *Balloons*, she thought through her stroking hands. *Bad balloons.*

Seven sharp barks, staccato, conveyed the message to their comrades. "Balloons?" was all Tex got out before the first one dove upon them.

"Flee!" cried the Flabberghast. "I will hold them off!"

Springing at the yawning purple maw that snapped with black piranha teeth, the Flabberghast raked its bulbous sides with his thin white hands. The balloon whipped around and pounced at his back, squeaking like a tricycle left too long out in the rain. Two more balloons joined it: one tiger-striped with the long neck of an ostrich, one with the face of a bear and the body of a snake.

Then—*POP!*

Tex had turned out his pockets of rocks and pointy bullet casings and began to bang that artillery—*pop-pop-whap!*—right into the polychromatic fray. Beatrice used to say how she bet Tex'd been a Junior League pitcher back in the olden days. He couldn't rightly know either way, but ever since the world ended, his aim had just improved.

Diodiance unstrapped the thornstick from the loop on her belt, and—*BLAM! WHAP! POP!*—laid about her. Even Granny Two-Shoes jumped perch, snatching the switchblade from its sheath to thrust it up into the air. *WHAP! POP! KERBLOOEY!* Sheepdog Sal rose to her hind legs, lunging and gnashing with far greater gusto than any measly thin-skinned balloon beast. *Pop! Pop! Wheeeeeeeze!* went the whistling things as they rocketed away, deflating as they died.

Suddenly the air was still again. Gray and still. The cobblestones of Chuckle City were littered with rainbow skins. Diodiance whooped out the Barka Gang's war cry and chanted, "Tex! Tex! Our boy's the best! Fastest arm in the whole Midwest!"

Leaping up and down Main Street in those great gazelle arcs she'd learned in ballet, Diodiance hollered, "Jeté! Jeté! Tour jeté!" and landed back in front of them with a mighty ululation. Tex received her clap on the back with a sweaty grin, picking up his stones and bullet casings and pocketing them again. He caught Granny's eye, who returned his gaze with blazing blue solemnity, and said, "Thanks for the warning, Granny Two-Shoes."

Granny tugged at his camo cutoffs, shrugged, smiled. Her baby teeth were white as Diodiance's tyranny and fluoride toothpaste could make them, except for the iron gray one in the middle. Dead at the root, Beatrice had said. The Rubberbabies did that, that time they took her for their slave.

"Hey!" Diodiance stopped dancing. "Where's the Flabberghast anyway?"

"Who cares?" Tex muttered.

Granny Two-Shoes pointed down a street, where the Flabberghast crouched near a tiny ambulance. Balloon skins hung all about his person, making motley of his peacock coat. He appeared to be prodding something with his long fingers, which the Barka Gang, joining him, saw to be the painted head of a small clown. The rest of its body was crushed to death under the ambulance.

"Are you hopin' the head'll pop off?" Tex stiffened to kick him. "Gettin' hungry, are you?"

"This is not a body. Not really. And I do not eat souls. It is forbidden."

The Tall One almost sounded regretful. He tugged off his lawn cravat and used it to scrub the dead clown's small face. Off came the ash. Off came the paint. Off came the singed red nose, the curly wig. The child was pale and bald, with sunken eyes the same gray as the sky. As everything.

"Leukemia," the Flabberghast said. "From long before the slaprash. Here, you see? The ravages of her treatment? She's been in the Big Bah-Ha awhile. It must have been a harsh death to keep her here so long, and then when the Gray Harlequin came, she found herself fixed. Like the rest of them. Insects on his corkboard. Poor little butterfly."

His voice had dropped like he was talking to himself, but the Barkas leaned in, paying close attention. "Those underground said the situation here was dire, but the others did not heed their voices. They mocked me when I paced before the gates and worried. They called my frowns the best jest yet. But I was right to come when I did—no matter how questionable my methods."

Granny Two-Shoes knelt beside him and closed the clown's gray eyes. The Flabberghast smiled at her softly, teeth sparkling.

"You are a good girl, Granny Two-Shoes," he said. "Would that you were a Tall One, and I could stay your friend forever."

"Seems to me," Tex grunted, "the dead shouldn't have to die twice. Not like this—no death rite, no shrine, no gang to go and sing her final lullaby. It just seems wrong."

Diodiance scowled. "Queen B'd call this whole darn place ice cream."

Granny looked up sharply. Sheepdog Sal barked twice. Diodiance corrected herself. "Sorry. I mean obscene."

"Beatrice would be perfectly correct."

The Flabberghast stood up. The Tall One had never seemed so tall. The Barkas each thought, but did not say aloud, that the sky of the Big Bah-Ha might crack if he jumped.

"What happens when a child dies?" he asked them.

"Well, Flabby, you go and eat 'em."

Diodiance jabbed Tex in the ribs. "Tex, that's rude. He's tryin' to help us."

"*We're* here to help *him*, you mean!"

The Flabberghast calmed her with a wave of his white hand. "Peace, Miss Diodiance. That is indeed what we do. We eat the bones. But what manner of being, one might ask, eats what's left when the bones are gone? What kind of carrion monster eats the *haeccitas*? The thisness of being? The soul?" He paused, and into his pause came the rushing of a hundred wings. Behind his slender shoulders a shadow moved across the sky, too fast and too low for a cloud.

"Gacy Boys," he noted. Then, "How are your scabs, children?"

"Still runny," said Diodiance. "Startin' to scratch some at the edges. Queen B says that means healin's a-comin' close up, makin' you itch."

The Flabberghast nodded. "There is still time. But not much." He pointed to the dead clown on the ground. "The Gacy Boys will try to take this little soul away and bring it where it will be devoured and lost to all memory. Will you let this happen?"

"No!" cried Tex and Diodiance as one. Sheepdog Sal growled. Granny Two-Shoes unsheathed her switchblade again.

"Then stand," urged the Flabberghast as gray wings beat around them. "Let us drive these boybirds back to the sky and pursue where they flee. This is the beginning of the end."

In a field at the edge of Chuckle City, two massive elephants danced. Rampant, they stood on the great columns of their hind legs, their forelegs rearing to create the crest of an archway. Two opposite pairs of flat feet pressed together, without a seam in the stone to show where one elephant ended and the other began. Ears flared like frozen wings. Tails neither hung straight down nor jerked erect, but seemed caught in a jaunty swish. Their long trunks met, entwining skyward like a single great tree. The inner curves of their hulking bodies supported a mirror.

Had it lain flat, Beatrice might have mistaken the mirror for a lake. Warped and rippled, smoky with age and fissures, the vast glass reflected nothing that stood at any distance from it.

"Where is the Gray Harlequin?" asked Beatrice. "Where are the Gacy Boys?"

Rosie Rightly clung to her elbow. "I don't know, Bee-Bee. He's always near here. He lives just outside the arch."

Involuntarily, Beatrice remembered someone else who lived just outside a great stone arch. She would have shuddered, but the dread inside her could not make her flesh creep or her hair stand on end. *I'm not really flesh anymore*, she thought. *My hair is just the memory of my hair.*

"I never liked it here," Rosie said, teeth chattering.

Beatrice wanted to tell Rosie that she was not really cold; she would never be cold again, but she held her tongue. *My* memory *of a tongue*, she corrected herself.

"I can't—I can't go with you. I don't want to use up my last chance. I'm not ready! I'm not happy yet."

"Hush, it's all right." Beatrice spoke in the voice she'd used whenever Granny Two-Shoes woke her up with a midnight crying jag. Granny did not wake often, but when she did, it was bad. She cried like she was the last little girl left alive in the whole wide world. "It's all right. I can go by myself."

Leaving Rosie Rightly hunched on the low hill, hands clasped over the radiant wounds on her wrists, painted head bowed, Beatrice descended.

The incline had quickened her pace, or perhaps it was her body that seemed to grow lighter. The stone elephants were the first beautiful things Beatrice had seen in the Big Bah-Ha. Regal and welcoming, they seemed to smile. They made her stand straighter and remember one of Dad's favorite words. *Dignity*. Right up to the mirror she walked, patting a huge hoof nail on her way, and stared into it.

At first she saw only a crack. It was small, a golden ribbon against the gray. Dancing light reached out from the crack and tickled her face like a breeze. It gladdened her eyes, made her skin feel a flush of true warmth. She wanted to put her mouth to the crack and suck the joy all the way into her. Put her ear to it and hear Dad's voice again. Because he would be there, where the gold was. She knew he would.

But Beatrice thought, *No. I must focus. I must look at myself.* So she took a half-step back.

And cried out at the dead thing she saw.

She was really, truly dead. Cold, small, lightless, breathless, heartless, quenched. Indistinguishable from anything else that had ever lived and died. There was nothing luminous about her except the ugly red handprint mantling her gray face like some hellish lobster. Beatrice scratched it. She scraped and clawed, but the handprint would not come off, and Beatrice fell to her knees and covered her eyes so that she would not have to bear herself, her dead self, her never-to-be-anything-else-ever-again self, one second longer.

A gentle hand touched her shoulder. *It's Dad*, she thought, and flung herself into his arms. She pressed her face into his silver scales, sobbing without tears.

"Oh," she said a moment later, edging away. "Sorry."

"Do not be ashamed," the creature answered. "I am here to succor you."

"You're the Gray Harlequin."

"Yes."

Slim and supple as the Flabberghast, not quite as tall perhaps, but tall enough. Skin that glittered as if a million silver sequins overlapped him. A black velvet ribbon wrapped the upper part of his face like a bandit mask—only it had no slits for eyes.

Beatrice wasn't sure he had eyes, although she felt certain he was watching her. A cloth of diaphanous saffron silk wound his body like a toga, clasped at his left shoulder by a glass bird that glowed from the white light inside it, and knotted into a saffron rose at his right hip. The rest billowed to his feet.

The crown upon his brow was part thorn, part berry, part leaf-bell-branch-bird's-nest, part flower, part pale pink seashell. Wings grew from it, and antlers, and the soft ears of some small brown creature. This must be, then, what Rosie Rightly had called the August Crown. It proclaimed the Gray Harlequin Lord of the Big Bah-Ha. King of Clowns.

To see that crown was to feel its weight. Beatrice fell to her knees, thinking even as they scraped down, *I never kneel. Not in defeat. Not to anyone. I pummeled Aunt Oolalune when she tried to make me. Why now?*

"Do you come to ask a boon, little one?" The Gray Harlequin's voice was warm as maple-flavored corn syrup on a cold December morning.

"I want to leave." Beatrice spoke to the ground, hating herself for muttering. "I want to see my dad. I don't want to stay here anymore."

The Gray Harlequin made a sound between a cluck and a tsk. She risked a look up at him. He shook his glittering head to and fro.

"I am afraid," said he, "that rules are rules. You looked into your own face, but you did not laugh. The best I can offer you now is a place here in Chuckle City. You might join the tramps under the Big Top. Ride the tigers. Learn to walk the wires." He chuckled. A splatter of hot syrup. Bodies falling from a burning building.

"Or perhaps the Eleven Lovely Emilies will take you up, up, up into their webs and teach you how to spin. How to measure time by a red hourglass. How to eat what falls into your snares." He stooped to cup her chin before she could jerk away. "Or you can blow balloons with the rustics, or immolate yourself with the grotesques. Although, from the look of you, I'd say you've seen enough burning."

He laid his hand over the handprint on her face. She could feel the fit, how his fingers conformed to the slaprash's shape exactly. This time, Beatrice did flinch, but he grasped her by the jaw and did not let her go.

"But you cannot leave my city, little Beatrice," said the Gray Harlequin. Beatrice closed her eyes when he smiled. "And you cannot move forward through the mirror. Unless you want to take another look? Go on. Of all the children who have passed through the Big Bah-Ha, surely you are neither the most wretched, nor the saddest. Go on." His ruby lips curled like vipers. "Look. And smile at what you see."

It was a dare and a command. Releasing her jaw, he flung her forward. Beatrice dragged herself to her feet, pressed both fists to the glass, leaned in, looked. Her reflection sprang at her like a monster. She flung herself back, once again tearing at the slaprash on her face, trying to dig it from her flesh.

"Make it go away!"

"That," smiled the Gray Harlequin, "I can do."

So he pressed her once more to her knees, and she went, docile now. And he smeared white paint on her dull gray face, and painted a single blue tear beneath her right eye to represent all the tears she could no longer cry. From his saffron robes he drew a round red sponge attached to two white strings, and he placed the sponge over her nose and knotted the strings behind her head. He told her to look into the mirror a third time, now that he had made all things well.

Beatrice obeyed. Her reflection had grown bearable, although in wearing the red nose, she could no longer smell the warm gold wind pouring through the mirror's cracked surface. She reached up to unknot the strings that held the nose affixed. The Gray Harlequin slapped her hand.

"Now, Beatrice. That's no way for a clown to behave!"

Once more he began securing the strings behind her head, but before he had quite finished, the Gray Harlequin gave a loud shout and jumped back. The red nose tumbled from her face. Beatrice made only a half-hearted attempt to catch it, ashamed for being so relieved at its absence.

Above her, the Gray Harlequin hissed, shaking out his hand like it had been stung.

A sharpened shell casing bounced off Beatrice's foot. She began to smile. Then the sky opened.

Overhead, thirty-three ravens exploded into being. Dropping to the ground around the Gray Harlequin so quickly they drew from the air a thunderclap, they threw back their gray feathers and became young men. Hangman's hoods were thrust back, revealing ivory eyes and ebony teeth and coxcombs that writhed like Medusa's snakes. Instead of clothes, their bodies were wrapped like mummies in gaffer's tape. One wore half of a pair of handcuffs like a bracelet. Another, a length of heavy chain for a belt. Their throats were as radiant a red as a clown's face, red as the wounds on Rosie Rightly's wrists.

"Well?" asked the Gray Harlequin. "Where is my meat and drink? In all of Chuckle City, did not one of my little subjects relinquish their last hope?"

The Gacy Boys spoke in a ragged chorus of whispers and whistles. Their voices ran together. Beatrice could only pick out fragments.

"A nice, fresh one, sire—a grotesque from the tenements, but…"

"Intruders—"

"Driven off—"

"Three heartbeats, with weapons. Rocks. Knives. Sticks—"

"One, tarted like a clown, but far too tall—"

"A dog, sire, with terrible teeth—"

"A dog?" Beatrice pushed past the line of Gacy Boys, would have marched right to Chuckle City to see for herself, but the Gray Harlequin shoved her to the ground.

"Stay where you are!" he growled.

"Sire," said a Gacy Boy, "they were right behind us."

Beatrice, choking on a mouthful of dust, tried to raise her head. But the Gray Harlequin had stepped upon it. She could only turn it to one side. Beyond the forest of Gacy Boy legs, several familiar pairs of feet moved toward her.

First: white tennies, worn with more grace than a pair of satin ballet slippers. Second: scuffed and scarred combat boots, boys' size eight. Third: a pair of pink patent leather Mary Janes smaller than a Snickers bar. Fourth: four brown paws, dusty and dear. Fifth and last: two banana-yellow boats.

"It's my Barkas," Beatrice whispered. "But how did . . .?"

"Oh, hallo, Harlequin!" cried the Flabberghast. "So good to behold your blindfold again! A few of us wondered where you'd gone when the hills opened up and the world was ours. How is your hand? Necessity demanded the damage; we hope you will forgive. By the way, Young Texas, you have a most excellent arm!"

"Thanks, Flabby. You in there somewhere, Queen B?"

Beatrice spat dust to bellow, "Down here! Tex! Di! Granny! Sal!"

The Gray Harlequin's velvet-shod foot pressed hard upon her skull. Her mouth filled. The dust of the Big Bah-Ha tasted like ash.

"Had I known, my friend," said the Gray Harlequin, "that you intended to visit, I would have prepared a welcoming party. Ceremonies, parades, cannonades . . ." His rancor ground Beatrice beneath his heel.

Snorting, the Flabberghast noted, "Nothing in this blasted heath remembers how to throw a party, Harlequin, least of all you. You brought the Big Bah-Ha to the brink of ruin. Cannons could only improve the place."

The Gray Harlequin grinned most redly. "Perhaps. But who is left to care? Only the dead come here, and those are all mere children. They don't know any better. They barely know their own names. The wretched brats needed a keeper. Who better to wear the August Crown than myself?"

The Flabberghast rocked in his yellow shoes. "Let us set aside for the nonce a debate regarding the befitting resettlement of souls, the governance of the deadlands, and the corruption of the August Crown. Let us instead, dear Harlequin, turn to the more important question of aesthetics. The plain truth is, Harlequin, you have made the Big Bah-Ha far too ugly. And I cannot abide ugliness."

"You live in a cardboard box," sighed the Gray Harlequin. The tension in his toes did not ease. Beatrice thought that if he pressed any harder, her skull would explode.

"It only looks like a cardboard box," the Flabberghast retorted. "Anyone who enters knows it for a palace. But this place?" He shook his head. "Last I visited the Big Bah-Ha, the skies were endless and sapphirine. Where now only thin grooves mark the dust, there once flowed seven mighty rivers. Manticores, glatisants, silver-bearded unicorns abounded, offering songs, riddles, rides to the young newcomers, who looked upon them with awe and wonder. Green was the grass, sweet were the flowers, and everything smelled of something even better blooming in the distance. Such wild, clear music rang from dryad lips and satyr horns. Such dancing gadabouts were held, such glad feasts. Chuckle City, your degraded city, was a city of silken tents, not tenements, each flowing canopy woven of silver silk spun anew every morning by the Eleven Lovely Emilies. And how lovely they were, the Keepers of the Hourglass, the Guardians of the Gate. How lovely they were, but see what they have become!"

The ring of Gacy Boys hooted and cooed uneasily. Perhaps they remembered such a time, remembered too how they had forgotten it. But the Gray Harlequin only sneered.

"They are all still here, Flabberghast—the monsters of whom you so fondly reminisce. Glatisants, manticores, centaurs, tra-la, tra-la, et cetera, they are all to be found in my petting zoos. As for your Eleven Emilies—it is a stretch, is it not, to call them lovely?—they work for me now. In exchange for food. I do not think there is a prettier sight than an Emily feeding on what falls from the wires to her web."

"What is the food?" asked the Flabberghast. Beatrice thought she heard a thread of nervousness and longing running through his words. "This is the Big Bah-Ha. It is the last and lowest of the deadlands. There is nothing to eat here but the souls of those who died too young."

"Exactly so," hissed the Gray Harlequin. "Can't you smell them, Flabberghast? So sweet, so rare, so plump with potential. So much finer than the coarse stuff of carbon."

"Souls!" That one word was almost a wail. Beatrice squirmed beneath the Gray Harlequin's crushing shoe. "What need have you of souls, when all the bones of a dead world are ours for the digging?"

The Gray Harlequin's laughter was like a cougar sharpening its claws on a hollow tree. "Digging in the dirt like worms, like maggots, like old blind moles under Hillside Cemetery, where we voluntarily entered a debasing confinement until the last human falls. The whole world is *not* ours for the eating, not for years yet, my Flabberghast, not unless you've sped along the deaths of all those little ones running wild in their packs. Have you, Flabberghast? You alone among us had the freedom to do so. You alone of the Tall Ones were allowed passage beyond the gates. Our great ambassador to those little human meat lumps. You, who were once our jester! Our fool!"

"No one objected at the time." The Flabberghast had smoothed his voice again. If the Gray Harlequin was syrup, the Flabberghast was a rich, tasty grease of butter, and Beatrice, squashed flat between their voices, was beginning to feel like the pancake.

Then she heard Tex shout, "Hey, Flabby, is that snotbum another of all y'all Tall Ones? Thought you said only kids were allowed in here."

Diodiance asked, "How'd he even get in?"

At Granny's behest, Sheepdog Sal barked, and at the sound, the others of the Barka gang hushed, remembering how *they'd* gotten in. They fingered the half-healed holes in their wrists. Somehow they couldn't see the Gray Harlequin asking a living child politely for his blood. He'd just take it and paint his red doorway on any old skin. He wouldn't even have bothered bringing a living child in with him, for he'd never planned on coming back out. The Flabberghast spoke into their awful silence.

"Our prison term, if that is what you wish to call it, Harlequin, is only a matter of a few short years. The slaprash lingers. When the last human remnant comes of age . . ."

Here he stopped, but Beatrice knew how the sentence would end. They all did, back home.

"Breath starts to rattle
Like dice in a cup
And the slaprash'll getcha
When—you're—all—growed—up!"

Even for the youngest among them, even for Granny Two-Shoes, it was only a matter of time. Till they grew up and died dead, slapped red. Beatrice closed her eyes against the pain of it, the futility, the hopelessness of such a future. What was the point?

And, as if summoned, Granny's face appeared between one of the Gacy Boys' sticklike legs. She waved at Beatrice and smiled. Her one gray tooth was like a keyhole amid the bright glare of the whiter ones.

"Hey, Granny!"

Granny Two-Shoes slid something across the ashy ground. Beatrice crept one arm out from her side, slowly, so slowly, hoping she could snatch the slingshot without the Gray Harlequin noticing. But he was entirely caught up in his indignation, she saw. Just like Aunt Oolalune back in the land of the living. So marvelously self-absorbed and easy to distract.

That's what the Flabberghast is, Beatrice realized. *A distraction. One I'm meant to use.*

Still the Gray Harlequin argued. "A few years, you say? A decade, perhaps, if we're lucky. A decade of gnawing flavorless femurs and sucking stale marrow in some moldy old Midwestern cemetery." He laughed bitterly. "Do you think I—I, who witnessed the Black Death and the birth of Pantalone—wish to spend my hard-won perpetuity scrabbling for sustenance and listening to your infernal jokes, Flabberghast, all day and all night, until the stars burn out, when here, here in this place where there are no stars, I can be God and King together, presiding over an eternal feast?"

He reached a long arm to stroke the feral head of a Gacy Boy. "Here, among my little friends?" he asked, more softly. "Who require my guidance, welcome my tutelage? I gave them wings to fly. They deliver my messages. They capture monsters for my entertainment. They hunt the deadlands for the souls that are my meat and drink. They are very useful, and so very *grateful* to be of use. To have a little power, where before they had none."

The Flabberghast hesitated before replying, but Beatrice watched the rocking of his yellow shoes come to a standstill.

Be ready, she thought. *Be wary. Be watchful. Take your best chance.*

"You guide them nowhere but over their own dusty traces time and again. You offer them a little glamour, and they mistake it for power.

You have turned the children's only door, their rightful door, into a distorted mirror where they must see themselves marked with murder, disease, accident, neglect, lack, with no hope of anything better. You lock them in perpetual despair until their souls wither, and then you devour their souls. No God or King, you, Harlequin. Jailer. Tormenter. Executioner."

The air filled with whistles and whispers as the Gacy Boys turned to the Gray Harlequin.

"You said it was a magic mirror."

"You said there was no way out."

"You said we must look at ourselves."

"At our own dead faces."

"Into our own dead eyes."

"Acknowledge what was done to us."

"And laugh."

"You said," keened the smallest Gacy Boy, whose cap and bells sat a bit awry, "if I could laugh, I would see my mother. But I couldn't look—I couldn't look at that again! I've done everything you said . . ." He bent his head and sobbed. His ivory eyes spurted tears like crude oil.

The others broke formation to comfort him, handcuffs dangling, chains clinking. They drifted off together in desolate clumps, leaving the Gray Harlequin exposed. He turned in sudden fury to the Flabberghast, his foot slipping from Beatrice's skull.

"You've upset them!"

The Flabberghast shrugged.

"Tell me," said the Gray Harlequin, "you who've traveled all this way. Did you even wait until she died to peel off her skin and nail it to your wall?"

Beatrice breathed without breath. She remembered the flensing tool. How the Flabberghast had started with her foot. Her left foot. Just as the last blood oozed from her pores and the last of her convulsions ceased.

Enough.

She gripped the slingshot Granny Two-Shoes had slid her. Swiped from the dirt the bullet casing that had spared her the red nose. Wriggled onto her back. Slid out of range of that crushing foot. And took her shot.

BING!

She couldn't throw like Tex, but she was still the best shot in Hillside.

Knocked askew by the flying missile, the August Crown went hurtling from the Gray Harlequin's head. It spun, it glistened, the wings that grew from it seemed to flap and fly. Bald as a vulture, the Gray Harlequin dove for it, but the Flabberghast caught him by the folds of his saffron robe and ripped him away from his goal.

In thew and sinew, the Gray Harlequin was stronger than the Flabberghast, who, though taller, was thinner, too, almost frail. Perhaps old bones were not as nourishing as young souls. When the Gray Harlequin fisted the lapels of the Flabberghast's red brocade vest, he lifted him out of his shoes. His ruby mouth yawned open. Black gums studded with diamond fangs shone with saliva. A black tongue flicked out, split like a snake's.

"How passing sweet will a living Tall One taste, after all these years of eating death? Do you remember the old days, Flabberghast, when we had only each other to devour under the hills? How thin we grew then. But *we* always had enough, you and I."

The Flabberghast said a word that Beatrice did not know. She thought it was not a human word.

In answer, the Gray Harlequin slammed him into the mirror. Not once, not twice, not thrice, but over and over again, and each time the Flabberghast's body against the glass made a sound like lightning striking cathedral bells.

Beatrice turned to the other members of her Barka Gang, who watched the scene with wide, frightened eyes. Could the Flabberghast fall? Fail? Would he be ate up, and they in their turn? Beatrice snapped her fingers. Their focus shifted. Their faces cleared.

"We got this, Barkas," she whispered with a cheerful grin. "Won't cost us more sweat than can make a salt lick. Remember the Battle of the Baseball Diamond? How we brung Big Johnny low?"

"Like yesterday, Queen B!" Diodiance said happily.

"Go on, then!"

Diodiance and Tex dashed forward to grasp hands. Granny Two-Shoes slung herself from Sal's back into the stirrup they made of their fingers. They heaved her into the air, and she flew like a Gacy Boy, high and higher, until she landed on the Gray Harlequin's saffron-swathed shoulders. Her switchblade was ready. A snick. A plunge. A sideswipe. Black blood gushed from his throat in geysers, spraying the Flabberghast and the silver mirror behind him.

As it had before, upon Beatrice's flayed skin, the black bloodstain with its tiny white lights began to spread in all directions. There came a mighty crack. And the Flabberghast, against a rain of stained shards, laughed as the Gray Harlequin crumpled to the ground. Before he hit, Granny Two-Shoes jumped clear of him. Beatrice embraced the little girl out of the air, and spun her three times, and cradled her close like she used to do every night, when she and Granny were the only Barkas left awake.

"You're the world's last wonder, Granny Two-Shoes!" Beatrice murmured into her ear. "I wish you'd live forever."

Granny Two-Shoes buried her head in Beatrice's shoulder and let her switchblade fall.

Diodiance and Tex, still holding hands, leapt about, whooping the Barka victory song. The Flabberghast shook the last of the glass splinters from the cuffs of his sleeves. He crouched over the bald corpse of the Gray Harlequin and said in a low voice, "You were a bad clown. You couldn't make a jackal laugh."

With that, he stripped the black velvet ribbon from the Gray Harlequin's face, dug one long finger deep into the single central socket there, lifted out a round white thing like a great, blind eyeball, and popped it into his mouth. A shudder shook him, as though the pleasure of it were more than he could bear.

Twelve of the Gacy Boys left the Big Bah-Ha forever that day. The smallest went first, the golden wind from the newly opened Elephant Gate burning away the chains and gaffer's tape, the cap and bells, the hangman's hood, until he was simply dressed in playclothes, his face clean and calm and unafraid. He cried out, "Oh! I see her! I see her!" and ran ahead of the rest, laughing.

The other boys looked past the gate with longing, but some dread gripped them still. They turned their backs on the great elephants, and trudged away into the low hills of the Big Bah-Ha.

"Don't they want outta here?" asked Diodiance.

"Not ready yet," said Beatrice. "Maybe they still see a mirror. Or think they don't deserve to laugh. I dunno. But give 'em time. They got all the time in forever."

When one way or another the Gacy Boys were gone, a few children crept down the hill from Chuckle City. Rosie Rightly led three rustics, four grotesques, and a tramp riding an old white tiger from the Big Top. Pacing them, a contingent of eleven beautiful women, whose four arms and four legs apiece were clear like crystal and flute-thin. Their red hair blew around them like the flames of Chuckle City. The red hourglasses of their eyes shone.

"Those're the Emilies," Beatrice explained to the Barka Gang. "They guard the Elephant Gate."

Granny Two-Shoes, still hanging tightly onto Beatrice's neck, strained to see. Beatrice swung her onto her shoulders for a better view. Rosie Rightly came bounding up to them.

"Hi, Bee-Bee! Bee-Bee! Hi! Hello! Is it true? The Gray Harlequin is dead?"

"Done to death by Granny here." Beatrice patted Granny Two-Shoes's knee. Rosie Rightly took one of Granny's pink Mary Janes and kissed the toe of it.

"Thank you, girlington!" she breathed. "Oh, thanks ever so. He made me bring him here, you see. Back at the end of days. No one came home that night. The other houses in my neighborhood were all on fire, and the Tall Ones marched through town toward Hillside Cemetery, wearing white lights on their shoulders. My house was dark, and I was hiding, but the Gray Harlequin knocked on my front door anyway. He saw me through the screen and came right in. He tore my wrists on his teeth and painted me with my own blood. Then he bit his mouth and bled on me from the wound, and walked right through my skin to the deadlands, taking my soul along with him."

She showed her glowing wounds. Before Beatrice could say anything—and what could she say but "I'm sorry?" Too paltry and lacking by half—a wind from the Elephant Gate rushed upon them, bathing Rosie Rightly in light, turning her wounds to gold.

"Oh!" Rosie Rightly clapped delighted hands to her mouth and bounced. "Look! Look! Look! Big brother, and little brother, and baby brother, too! And Papa, and Mama, and puppy, and kitty, and Grandma, and Cousin Albert, and . . ." Her laughter pealed out. She bounced right past the huge stone elephants and into somewhere else.

There, too, went the rustics, the grotesques, the tramp and the tiger. But the Eleven Lovely Emilies stayed. They settled near the gate and set to spinning. Something silver and flowing. Something fine, of silk.

Beatrice looked toward Chuckle City, frowning. "There should be more. There were hundreds of clowns—kids—back there."

"It never happens all at once," the Flabberghast told her. All this time, he had been sitting on the ground quietly chewing bits of the Gray Harlequin until the corpse was riddled. For the first time since dying, Beatrice was glad she didn't have a stomach.

"Oh," he exclaimed. "Look at this! I had all but forgotten!"

Bending at the waist, he reached out and swiped a glinting object from the gray dust. It was the August Crown. In his hands it twinkled and fluttered, shimmered and rang as if asking him a question.

The Flabberghast laughed in answer and told the chiming crown, "Me? Oh, no. You are quite mistaken if you think that." He shook his curly orange head and popped another of the Gray Harlequin's fingers into his mouth. He glanced up at Beatrice with his strange black eyes, but aimed his chatter at the crown.

"Despite present evidence to the contrary," he said around his mouthful, "I really do prefer bones. I like my cardboard hut out front of the gravy yard. I even find it enjoyable to keep up with the kiddy gangs, and learn their rhymes, and bear witness to their final wars. And—no offense"—Beatrice wondered who he thought would take offense; the

August Crown wasn't the world's liveliest conversationalist—"I just hate babysitting. Really, this entire venture stretched even my illustrious ambassadorial tolerance to its absolute limit, and this with the Barka Gang being doubtless the least vexing specimens of their species. I chalk that up to the benefits of strong leadership, you know. Nothing like discipline, and cleverness, and kindness in a leader to create harmonious cohesion in the underlings."

He eyed Beatrice. He twirled the August Crown in his long white hands.

Startled, she took a step backward. "I don't think . . ."

But the Flabberghast spun up from the ground like a motley tornado, a bone sticking out of his mouth like a cigarette, his long, oddly jointed hands extended, and plopped the August Crown upon her head. Granny Two-Shoes patted it and laughed. The sound was rare and small. Barely a breath.

"There!" cried the Flabberghast. "Three cheers for Beatrice, Queen of the Big Bah-Ha!"

No one cheered, but Diodiance did stretch to her tiptoes to ding one of the August Crown's bells.

"Ha! Look atcha, Queen B! Ain't you just like one of those ladygods your Dad used to whopper on about? Not Durga. One of the others. Those deadland queens. Remember all those stories you told us, B? 'Bout Hel and Ereshkigoogle and Pursopoly?"

"Persephone," Beatrice murmured. Then, with longing, "Dad."

She could feel him right behind her, so near, just beyond the stone elephants and the warm golden splash of light. She wanted to go to him, go right now, tell him how she'd lived, how she'd died, everything that had happened since, ask him what came next, and if they'd ever have to part ways again.

Beatrice sighed, and turned away from the Elephant Gate. "All right. I'll wear your August Crown."

The Flabberghast's voice was gentle. "It is not mine, Beatrice. It is yours—very simply, because it needs you. And it is only for a little while, after all."

"I know." Beatrice laughed a little. "Ten years, right? Give or take."

Granny Two-Shoes climbed down from her shoulders and into her arms again, and Beatrice clasped her close and looked over at Tex and Diodiance. "What do you think, Barkas dear? Figure I can sort out this here Big Bah-Ha in ten years or so?"

Tex blew a raspberry. "B, you'll have it spick-and-span by the time I get slapped up. That's what? Four years? Three if my growth spurt comes young. Whaddya think, Di?"

Diodiance shrugged. "Two years tops, she's whupped this place to shape. After that, you 'n' me, Tex, we'll get here in no time flat. But I'm thinking, Queen B, we'd best not pass the Elephant Gate ourselves till Granny Two-Shoes joins us. No fair tryin' to make us laugh for joy before then. We all go in together or not at all."

"I will wait," Beatrice promised. "We will all wait."

The Flabberghast took Granny Two-Shoes's hand in his, and squinted to inspect her wrist. "Hark, friends. Our time draws to an end. Your scabs are almost completely formed."

Granny Two-Shoes tugged her hand free and pressed it to her heart. Yes, she noticed. It was squeezing. Had been feeling strained for some time. Her ears made a noise like being born.

She remembered. Granny Two-Shoes remembered everything.

Beatrice helped her up onto Sheepdog Sal's back and tousled her tangled hair. "See you later, kiddo. In every pinch, just ask yourself, 'what would Durga do?' Keep that knife sharp. Serve those Rubberbabies ding-danged tarnation in a soup tureen whenever you can."

Granny Two-Shoes nodded. Looked down. Blinked and blinked at Sal's flopsy ears so as not to cry. It was not yet night. She only cried at night.

Beatrice tossed her slingshot to Tex. "Yours, my man."

"Thanks, Beatrice," he mumbled. His tears fell into the gray dust, hot and living. The water welled up, sparkled, began to form a stream.

The first of seven rivers, Beatrice thought.

She unwound a blue ribbon from her hair and dropped it into Diodiance's outstretched palm. Diodiance wrapped it twice around her arm and tied it off with her teeth. Her lips trembled.

Drip. Drip. Splash.

Another river.

"Quickly now, children," said the Flabberghast. "Not through the arch, but through the elephant's legs. The *left* elephant, mind. The one on the right takes you to a far different place." He winked a long black eye and lifted his slender wrist. "Ah, speaking of which, before you go . . . Might you spare me those last precious dewdrops of your wet blood? That I may myself get back through, you understand. The doors to the deadlands are tricky and likely to lock behind one."

Tex hesitated, but Diodiance whacked him on the arm. Granny Two-Shoes acquiesced before either of them, anointing him with the sticky remnant of her wound. Tex and Diodiance followed suit, then slung their arms around each other and disappeared between the stone legs. Sheepdog Sal licked Beatrice's hand and bounded away with Granny Two-Shoes clinging tightly to her fur. Lastly, the Flabberghast shouldered what was left of the Gray Harlequin like a sack of presents. He turned his stagger into a bow for Beatrice.

"I apologize," he said, "for flensing your skin before you were quite dead all the way through, then stretching it upon my wall. But I needed a doorway. And your skin was so very, very clear."

Bent low like that, he came face-to-face with her. In the blackness of his eyes, stars.

Beatrice asked softly, "We'll never know, will we? Whatever it is you are."

"I," he answered, laughing, "am the Flabberghast!"

Then off he danced with that weight on his back, awkward as tumbleweed. Only Beatrice noticed he did not leave through the left set of stone legs. He'd taken the ones on the right. Went elsewhere. Where the Tall Ones go.

Resolutely, Beatrice turned her back again on the Elephant Gate. A golden wind warmed her neck. A rent in the gray sky showed a gleam of blue.

Eleven Lovely Emilies smiled down at her.

Acknowledgments

I should begin, as this book begins, with Gene Wolfe. As he mentioned, my father introduced us when I was eighteen. Quite unrelated to this life-changing event, I had just read my first Gene Wolfe novel, *The Shadow of the Torturer*. Kismet? You bet. In Gene I found a mentor and correspondent, a kindred spirit who brought me to my first convention (it was actually World Horror in Chicago, where he and Neil Gaiman were the Guests of Honor; Readercon and the ostensible witch coven came a bit later), gave me my first graphic novel (*Sandman: Fables and Reflections*), and critiqued my first short stories. He's the one who told me to write short stories in the first place. He said that's how writers begin. Then they work their way up to novels after they had some credits to their byline. He taught me how to write a cover letter, and the proper format for a manuscript. He taught me everything I know. One of the brightest moments of our friendship for me came when he introduced me to the waitress at his favorite restaurant as "my honorary granddaughter." If ever an apprentice earned her journeyman papers through the kindness and acuity of a true master, I am that apprentice, and my undisputed master is Gene Wolfe.

I have dedicated this collection to John O'Neill and Tina Jens. From the earliest years of my would-be career, these two have been my champions and friends. They are tireless advocates for any new writers they meet, canny editors, and brilliant writers in their own right. Some of my first publication-worthy short stories wouldn't have been without them. Through Tina Jens and *Twilight Tales*, I met a bevy of Chicago horror writers. Through John O'Neill and *Black Gate*, the rich world of sword and sorcery, along with its finest swashbuckling scriveners, like

James Enge, Martha Wells, and Howard Andrew Jones, opened its ruby-crusted dungeon doors to me. It was John O'Neill who published "Life on the Sun" in *Black Gate*, as a sequel to my novella "Godmother Lizard," also set in the Bellisaar Wasteland, and my first *Black Gate* sale.

For "The Bone Swans of Amandale," I must thank (or perhaps blame) the erstwhile Injustice League: Delia Sherman, Ellen Kushner, Cat Valente, Lev Grossman, Kat Howard, and particularly Doctor Theodora Goss. It is to them I owe my brief taste of a for-real-and-true New York City writing group. In Ellen's and Delia's living room, between clothing swaps and writing critiques, I happened to be flipping through Mercer Mayer's *The Pied Piper* and grew particularly enamored of his little illustrated rats. Sometime in an idle moment, Theodora Goss mentioned that she'd love to have a rose named after her. The name "Dora Rose" sprang to mind, along with the image of a swan princess. I defy you to spend any amount of time around Theodora Goss and *not* start hallucinating about swan princesses. That, and my innate obsession with the Grimms' tale of "The Juniper Tree" was what got me to my own Pied Piper retelling.

The genesis of "Martyr's Gem" came from a dream, but the daytime writing was aided by so many: Ann Leckie, who first published it in *GigaNotoSaurus*, and whose keen editorial eye only improved it. My beautiful mother Sita, who has listened to every draft. Amal El-Mohtar and her parents Leila and Oussama, at whose house I took up the story thread after neglecting it for many months. With Amal, I must also mention our Caitlyn Paxson; as the Banjo Apocalypse Crinoline Troubadours, we three have performed the storytelling scene from "Martyr's Gem" at several conventions and concert venues, which is always thrilling. Janelle McHugh, who strung me a necklace like the one Shursta made for Hyrryai. Erik Amundsen, Magill Foote, and Grant Jeffery, together with drummer Will Sergiy IV and several actors of Flock Theatre, who helped me put together an animated short of that same scene. Rich Horton for selecting it for his *Year's Best* anthology. Geoff Leatham, Ben Leatham, and my friend Eric Michaelian, who gave me a rare and beautiful few minutes of hearing three readers discuss my story unabashedly right in front of me, as I grinned and glowed at them and occasionally spun pirouettes for pure joy.

Many a discussion I've had with my friend and fellow writer "Dread" Patty Templeton about the ubiquitous presence of beautiful people in all our storytelling media. The heroes and heroines of "Martyr's Gem" and "Milkmaid" came out of our ardent assertion that those of us who are plain or just plain ugly are as capable of passionate, witty, romantic, terrifying adventures as pretty people. As Leonard Cohen wrote, "Well, never mind it / We are ugly, but we have the music." I think of Patty

Templeton when I think of my Milkmaid and her Gentry Prince. I also think of my best friend Kiri-Marie O'Mahony, who once sat there and described the entire story of "Milkmaid" to me and then asked, "So, have you ever read it?" And looked so very astonished when I reminded her, amid whoops of laughter, that I had *written* it.

For "The Big Bah-Ha," I thank JoSelle Vanderhooft, who originally acquired it for Drollerie Press. I thank Jeremy Cooney for creating two marvelous trailers for it. I thank Rebecca Huston (always and forever), whose collaboration and artwork awake fires in me. I thank Gillian Hastings again for being my roommate at the time it was written, and a luminous one at that.

I cannot leave off without mentioning the names of these my beloved community of writers, readers, musicians, and artists (and not even as many of them as I'd like): Samu Rahn, Miriam Mikiel Grill, Ysabeau Wilce, Tiffany Trent, Sharon Shinn, Katie Redding, Jeanine Vaughn, Shveta Thakrar, Julia Rios, Karen Meisner, Dominik Parisien, Nicole Kornher-Stace, Jack Hanlon, Francesca Forrest, Jennifer Crow, Jessica Wick, and S. J. Tucker.

For the support of my family, who always told me to "follow my bliss"—in those words and in so many others—I can but be wholly indebted. Particularly I wish to mention again Sita Aluna, Rory Cooney, Terry Donohoo, Louise Riedel, Rose DeFer, and my brothers Joel, Aidan, Jeremy, Declan, and Desmond.

Last but not least (in fact, the opposite), thank you, Mike and Anita Allen. Without you, (ha! Literally) this book would not have been possible.

About the Author

C. S. E. Cooney is a Rhode Island writer who lives across the street from a Victorian strolling park. She is the author of *The Breaker Queen* and *The Two Paupers* (Books One and Two of the Dark Breakers trilogy), *The Witch in the Almond Tree*, *How To Flirt in Faerieland and Other Wild Rhymes*, and *Jack o' the Hills*. She won the 2011 Rhysling Award for her story-poem "The Sea King's Second Bride."

Other examples of her work can be found in Rich Horton's *Years Best Science Fiction and Fantasy* (2011, 2012, 2014), *The Nebula Awards Showcase* (2013), *The Mammoth Book of Steampunk Adventures* (2014), *The Moment of Change*, *Black Gate*, *Uncanny*, *Strange Horizons*, *Apex*, *GigaNotoSaurus*, *Subterranean*, *Ideomancer*, *Clockwork Phoenix*, *Steam-Powered II: More Lesbian Steampunk Stories*, *The Book of Dead Things*, *Cabinet des Fées*, *Stone Telling*, *Goblin Fruit*, and *Mythic Delirium*.

Her website is http://csecooney.com/.

COURTESY OF PATTY TEMPLETON

WITHDRAWN

Made in the USA
Middletown, DE
20 September 2015